Manx on her mother's ~~~~~ Dyson was born and brought up on Merseyside. She spent many happy childhood holidays on the Isle of Man, and later lived there. After studying modern languages at university she trained as a translator and secretary, going on to win the 'Secretary of the Year' award. She is an experienced author of self-help books, including *Bluff Your Way as a Top Secretary*, *Coping Successfully with Migraine* and *The Migraine Diet Book*. Her first novel, ACROSS THE WATER, is also available from Headline.

Sue Dyson now lives in Gloucestershire and makes frequent visits to the Isle of Man.

Also by Sue Dyson

Across the Water

A Far Tomorrow

Sue Dyson

HEADLINE

First published in 1996
by HEADLINE BOOK PUBLISHING

First published in paperback in 1996
by HEADLINE BOOK PUBLISHING

10 9 8 7 6 5 4 3 2 1

ISBN 0 7472 4953 9

Typeset by CBS, Felixstowe, Suffolk

Printed and bound in Great Britain by
Cox & Wyman Ltd, Reading, Berks

HEADLINE BOOK PUBLISHING
A division of Hodder Headline PLC
338 Euston Road
London NW1 3BH

A Far
Tomorrow

Prologue

March 1940

'After all, dear, it's not as if you've got anything much to give up.'

Mad March winds blew a gale across Port Erin bay, ruffling the water into foam-crested peaks. In the drawing room of the *Bradda Vista* guesthouse, the storm had only just begun.

Cora Quine glared at her sister-in-law.

'What exactly is that supposed to mean?'

Grace treated Cora to her sweetest smile.

'Oh, I know you like your little job in the shop, but if you took on the *Bradda Vista* you'd have something *useful* to do.'

William Quine, sensing the anger rising in his sister's throat, stepped in to avert disaster.

'Look, Cora . . . sis . . . it would only be for a little while, until this war's over . . .'

'Or until we get shot of this place,' cut in Grace. She glanced around her and sniffed. 'Can't imagine why anyone would want to buy it, mind.'

'This place used to be my home,' seethed Cora. 'I grew up here.'

'Then you won't mind coming back for a bit, will you?'

Cora could have cheerfully smacked Grace across her smug little face. She wondered what William had ever seen in her. Spoiled, spiteful and perpetually bored, Grace Quine was hardly the perfect seaside landlady. And it was a wonder

1

she dared show her face in Port Erin, after what had happened to her baby son.

Cora forced herself to be calm.

'Sit down,' she said. 'We have to talk about this. Properly,' she added, motioning to her brother who showed signs of wanting to leave the women to argue it out between them.

Grace plonked herself down on the sofa, taking the time to cross her ankles neatly so as to show off her new red shoes. *More* new shoes, thought Cora; no wonder this place isn't making any money.

Cora sat down on a hard-backed chair and folded her arms. At twenty-nine, she was three years younger than William, and only seven years older than Grace, but she felt like a scolding headmistress. She shook out her neat golden-brown curls.

'Now. Let's discuss this like sensible adults.'

'I don't see what there is to discuss,' replied Grace. 'William and I are going to Banbury so you'll take care of this place for us while we're away. Stands to reason, doesn't it?'

'It would be a great help if you would,' said William, mouthing at Grace to be quiet. 'Look, sis, I feel I have to enlist. Somebody's got to stop Hitler getting what he wants, haven't they? And it would be a relief to know the *Bradda Vista* was in safe hands . . .'

Cora let out a gasp of exasperation. She always found arguments upsetting, but she couldn't just let Grace and William walk all over her like this.

'Fair enough, William, there's a war on and you're enlisting in the Catering Corps. But what's to stop you staying here, Grace?' Cora fixed Grace with a triumphant stare. Grace didn't even squirm.

'Yes, well, with me away, Grace doesn't really feel she could cope on her own,' ventured William weakly. Grace interrupted him.

'Don't be stupid, of course I could cope. I'm going back to Banbury so I can be near William.'

2

'Very convenient that your parents only live a couple of miles from the training camp,' commented Cora. 'Almost as if you planned it this way.'

'Look, Cora,' said William, any guilt he might have felt rapidly submerged by desperation. Grace had him in a corner. She was flatly refusing to stay here one moment longer, and he had to get the old place sorted out before he left for the camp. 'You will help us out, won't you? It would mean a lot.'

'My job means a lot to me,' replied Cora. 'Why should I give it up?'

'It wouldn't be difficult running the hotel. The Government say they're going to send over evacuees from Liverpool – it'll be easy money.'

'Oh? And what makes you think I know the first thing about running a guesthouse?'

'You used to help Mum and Dad when we were kids.'

'That was years ago!'

'You do the books at the shop.'

'It's hardly the same.'

'And you'd have Grandad to help you . . . and Uncle Harry.'

'Grandad!' Cora thought of Grandad Quine, who knew more about vegetables than he knew about hotels; and Harry Kerruish, who spent weeks at a time away on his fishing boat.

'And there's Bessie Teare,' pointed out Grace. 'She's always giving *me* advice, whether I want it or not.'

'Look, sis,' said William softly. He took Cora's hand. 'The old place is important to me, but I want to go and do my bit.'

'Do your bit? Teaching NAAFI girls how to fry sausages?'

'Please, sis, listen. If I don't find someone to take care of the guesthouse, I'll have to sell it. And you know how much it meant to Mum and Dad.'

Cora looked from Grace to William, and back again. William's selfishness she could understand; but Grace . . . Grace defied belief.

'You know what you are, Grace Quine?' she declared.

'You're nothing but a spoilt, self-centred bitch.' Grace's jaw fell open.

'Well, I'll . . .'

'Shut up, Grace,' said Cora, 'and listen.' She took a deep breath. 'All right, I'll do it.'

Grace's expression changed instantly from a thunderous scowl to a delighted smirk.

'Not for you, Grace, and not for William. For the family. This place was my home, and I couldn't bear to see it go to a stranger.'

'Thanks, Cora, you're one in a million.'

'No, William, I'm a sentimental fool,' replied Cora. 'And you owe me. I just hope you realise how much.'

Chapter 1

14 May 1940. Somewhere off the coast of Holland

It was night. Deepest, blackest night. The deck of the lifeboat heaved on an oily swell beneath a heavy, cloud-laden sky.

'How long, Reuben? How long?'

Reuben Kotkin slipped his arm around his pregnant wife and drew her closer to him, willing all the strength in him to transmit itself to her and sustain her through this new and frightening ordeal.

'Not too much longer, Rachel, I swear.'

The moon emerged fleetingly from behind a cloud and he saw her upturned face, ghost-white in the pale luminescence. He kissed her and tasted the salt on her lips.

'Are we safe now? Far enough away from Holland?'

Reuben was silent for a moment. They had always shared everything – the hopes, the fears, the despair. Such things they had seen. There was no room for sentimentality or lies.

'Perhaps,' he told her, stroking the damp hair away from her cheek and lips. She was so young, only nineteen, far too young for all this. And yet, even at twenty-eight, he felt as angry and frightened and frustrated as a child. 'But soon, if all goes well, we will be safe.'

Rachel crouched closer under the slight shelter of Reuben's raincoat, which he had spread like a tarpaulin over their heads. Like the fifty or so others crammed into the lifeboat, they had managed to bring nothing with them beyond their identity papers and the clothes they stood up in. And now the clothes were half-soaked, and the identity papers little more than useless. What good was an old German passport to a stateless Jew?

The situation was grave, but even so Rachel and Reuben were silently counting their blessings. They had stayed on in Berlin as long as they possibly could – perhaps too long. And then, in 1938, they had lost everything when Reuben's tailoring business was burned to the ground in the carnage of Kristalnacht. They would be safe in Holland, or so they had fondly imagined. It had taken a few months, but Reuben had managed – with the help of friends – to establish himself in a small way as a tailor's cutter.

And then, only days ago, Hitler's armies had marched into the low countries. How could Holland resist the might of Blitzkrieg?

Rachel and Reuben had fled towards the coast, not really knowing what they would do when they got there. By an amazing stroke of good fortune, they had reached Scheveningen on the very day of the Dutch surrender, just as the lifeboat of South Holland was preparing to set sail for England. The crew were mere boys, students from the technical high school in Delft – but they knew enough to sail a boat.

And so it was that Rachel and Reuben Kotkin found themselves huddled on the deck of the lifeboat, praying that they might make it to Britain before the Nazis caught up with them.

'Will it be better . . . in Britain?' Rachel snuggled close, drinking in the warm strength of Reuben's embrace.

'Of course it will. They are fighting Hitler, they are his enemies, just as we are.'

'And we will be together,' whispered Rachel, taking Reuben's hand and placing it on her swelling stomach, 'when the child is born?'

'Together.' Reuben hugged her and they did the only thing they could: they waited.

It was eerily quiet on the boat, thought Rachel. So many

people making hardly a sound. Even the children were quiet, the habit of fear stilling their fidgeting and their cries. They had learned early in their short lives that to be quiet and unobtrusive was safer. Perhaps across the Channel, they would learn to trust again.

A shout cut through the low, gentle hum of the engines.

'I see something. Ahead of us.'

Reuben strained his eyes. There was something there, something huge and dark. His breath escaped in a shudder, half of hope and half of fear.

'A ship.'

He felt Rachel's hand tighten about his. She was trying not to tremble, but he could feel the tremors vibrating through her. He knew what she was thinking, the question that was on everyone's lips.

Somewhere close by, he heard a single, very quiet sob. And then he heard the soft sounds of many voices whispering together. They were praying. Praying that their lives would be spared.

The dark shape loomed up out of the darkness, and suddenly Reuben felt like weeping and singing, all at once. He took Rachel's hand to his lips and kissed it.

'It is British,' he told her, his voice cracking with emotion. 'A British warship. We're safe, *bubeleh*. Everything is going to be all right.'

'A slice of Trench Cake, Bessie?'

'Well . . .'

'Oh, go on, do. I made it specially, from Mum's old recipe. You'd never know there were no eggs in it.'

Cora Quine held out the willow-patterned plate and Bessie slid a slice of the dark-brown fruitcake off the doily.

'I shouldn't really,' she smiled. 'Not with my gall bladder.' She bit into the cake. 'Mmm, lovely and moist. Where's the pleasure in life if you can't enjoy a slice of cake?'

Where indeed, thought Cora as she sat back on her chair,

7

sipping tea from a pretty china cup. Mind you, it would take more than cake to make up for what William had gone and done.

As she drank her tea the afternoon sunlight glinted off her neatly rolled, golden-brown hair and the small marcasite brooch on the collar of her lilac crepe dress. She wore no make-up save a dusting of rouge, but her fine, unblemished complexion had little need of make-up. She looked young for her twenty-nine years.

'How are you settling in, dear?' enquired Bessie, dabbing her mouth with her napkin. At fifty-one, Bessie Teare was almost twice Cora's age, but they had always got on well together. 'Are you enjoying being a seaside landlady?'

'Oh, you know.' Cora shrugged as she set her teacup down on the table. She glanced over her shoulder and out of the large bay window. From the front of the *Bradda Vista* guesthouse you could see to the end of the street, then right across the bay, over the wet ribbed sands and the choppy grey waters to the high cliffs of Bradda Head. She wished she was up there right now, walking the anger out of her system. 'I'll get used to it.'

'I'm sure you will. And the other landladies will rally round.' Bessie had run her guesthouse, the *Ben-my-Chree*, for almost thirty years – but she could still remember how daunting it had all been in the beginning.

'Thanks, Bessie.' Cora wiped her forehead with the back of her hand. It was damp, slightly clammy. 'Do you think there will be any summer visitors on the Island this year?'

Bessie picked up her cup.

'I shouldn't think so for a moment, dear. Who'd want to go on holiday with Hitler just across the water? I suppose the Government might still send us some evacuees . . .'

'I suppose so.' Cora picked up a sugar lump, thought twice about it and dropped it back into the bowl. 'The thing is, Bessie . . .'

'Hmm?'

8

'Didn't you see the *Examiner*? They're starting to round up all the Germans on the mainland and intern them, like they did in the last war. Everybody's saying they're going to come here.'

Standing up, Bessie folded her napkin and laid it on the tray.

'I'm sure it's all talk.'

'But they've already approached boarding house owners in Ramsey and Douglas. What if . . .?'

'Oh, I'm sure they'd never think of sending any Germans to Port Erin,' smiled Bessie. 'No, no, Cora, you can be sure it won't come to that.'

After a beautiful, flawless day came the sort of night when James McArthur wished he'd taken his father's advice and become a dentist. A couple of hours ago he'd been sitting down to a fancy club dinner in Douglas. And now . . .

Lightning ripped across the sky as he parked the Austin Seven and lifted his medical bag off the back seat. Glancing up, he felt the first fat drops of rain splash on his nose and cheeks, and he turned up the collar of his mackintosh. Ah well, at least it was warm rain – not like that lashing wind and sleet he'd faced when he'd last come up to Farmer Gawne's croft, for a difficult lambing. Good job he'd thought to sling his wellingtons into the car – even if they didn't look very elegant with his dinner suit.

Slamming the car door shut he switched on his pocket torch. It wasn't much help, since blackout regulations stipulated that the bulb had to be masked with paper, leaving only a tiny pin-head of light to guide him through the dark.

'Ow!' He cursed as his walking stick slipped and he stumbled on the iron-hard, rutted track, his foot twisting as it went down a hole. Damn. He swore soundlessly as he rubbed the pain away. Trust it to be his bad leg, injured a few months ago in a farm accident he could have avoided if he'd treated that bull with more respect. Damn everything.

9

'*Misther* McArthur, is it?' wheezed a familiar voice somewhere up ahead. James raised the beam of his torch and just made out two lumbering shapes: the tall, thin, dessicated form of Farmer Alfie Gawne, and the short, square bulk of his brother, Morris. Morris Gawne might be a bit simple in the head, but he was as strong as an ox and very useful in an emergency.

'Evenin', vet'nary,' mumbled Morris.

'Evening, Morris. What's the trouble, Alfie?' called out James, finding a surer footing on the flagged yard behind Alfie's whitewashed cottage. 'The phone line was so bad, I could hardly make out what you were saying.'

'It's old Rumpus,' said Farmer Gawne. 'He's gaun an' took a fall in the ditch.'

'Rumpus? What's he doing here?'

Alfie kept a handful of ewes, but James knew that old Rumpus – a prizewinning Laoghtan ram – lived at a farm on the other side of Cregneash.

'Aw, it's that Evan Christian – you know, sheep man over Gansey way. He's only up an' enlisted, an' like a fool I said I'd take Rumpus till they find him somewhere else.'

'I see.' James was mentally assessing the consequences if Rumpus had hurt himself badly. He was a valuable animal, and Alfie Gawne wasn't a rich man. 'Where is he then?'

'Ower in the west field. Will you take a sight on him now?'

'You'd better lead the way with that lantern. This torch is worse than useless.'

Alfie led the way, holding up an oil lamp shaded with an ancient wide-brimmed hat. They set off across the yard and through the gate, James almost grateful for the odd flash of forked lightning which lit up the scene in a brief but vivid snapshot. The rain was coming harder now, dripping off the brim of his hat and down to the end of his nose.

'You've still got the stick then, vet'nary,' commented Morris. 'That leg still botherin' you, is it?'

James gripped his walking stick resentfully. He hated to be

reminded of the injury which had laid him low.

'It's better than it was. It'll mend.'

'Painful, is it?'

'Like I said, it'll mend.'

'Aye, sure enough. But 'twill be time in the mendin', I don't doubt.'

James had to fight down the tide of irritation. Any minute now, Alfie Gawne would start on about his son in the Merchant Navy, and his other son in the Manx Territorials. The old man's pride was hard for a man like James McArthur to take. More than his leg had been injured in the accident – his belief in himself had taken a knock, too. He should be overseas, fighting for his King and Country, not pulling rams out of ditches.

'Soon as I'm fit, I'll join up,' he declared. 'Now, where's this ram of yours?'

As Alfie Gawne held up the lantern and James slid painfully down the bank to help Morris attach a stout rope round the ram's middle, he felt for the young vet. That leg fracture had been a bad one, right enough. It would be time enough in the mending. And who could say how long it might take to mend a young man's wounded pride?

The uniforms were unfamiliar, the surroundings far from comfortable, but the faces at least were friendly. For the first time in months, Reuben and Rachel Kotkin allowed themselves a few faint glimmerings of hope.

By some amazing stroke of good fortune they had been picked up by a British destroyer, and were now huddled below decks with the other refugees, their chilled bodies slowly recovering warmth.

'What are they saying, Reuben?' asked Rachel. 'They speak so quickly . . .'

'They are saying that they are going to take us to England.' Reuben could scarcely suppress the wild wave of optimism breaking in his heart. In England, there would be hope.

11

'What will we do when we get there? They won't make us go back to Holland . . .?'

'*Nu*, Rachel, calm yourself. They won't do that to us. They will find work for us to do, useful things. We have skills – we can use them to live somehow . . .'

And they must live – somehow, anyhow; because already so many had died. Reuben cast his mind back to the little tailor's shop on the outskirts of Berlin. His father had owned it before him, built it up from nothing after fleeing from the pogroms in Russia at the turn of the century. It had been a good business, solid and respectable; easy enough for a hard-working man to support his young family.

But that was before the Nazis had come to power and changed everything. First the taxes, then the loss of civil rights, even of citizenship. When Hitler had ordered the compulsory aryanisation of all businesses, forbidding Jews to carry on any kind of trade, Reuben had known they could stay in Berlin no longer. But even in the aftermath of Kristalnacht old Efraim Kotkin had refused to go to Holland with his son and daughter-in-law. Only last month they had heard of his arrest: rounded up by the SS and taken to the East for 'resettlement'.

Others were in hiding – cousins hidden in a Rotterdam cellar by a businessman and his wife. A sister's child, blonde and beautiful, taken in by a sympathetic Dutch family and brought up as their own. She would be raised a Christian, but at least she would live, God willing. And then there was Rachel's cousin Isaac, a teacher dismissed from his job, starved out of his home, left behind in Holland. What had happened to him?

He felt Rachel's head grow heavy on his shoulder, and saw that she had drifted off into sleep. Pulling the dark naval-issue blanket around her shoulders he cradled her like a child, and prayed silently to the rhythm of her breathing.

It was night when the ship docked at Dover. A naval officer, very smart in navy blue and gold, addressed them in precise, schoolboy German. Rachel wanted to like him because he was British, but in recent years she had grown to dread men in uniform.

'You will please be calm. When you are instructed to do so, you will leave the ship in an orderly manner.'

Questions ricocheted around him from all sides.

'*Wo sind wir?*'

'Yes, yes, where are we? Tell us.'

'You are in England. That is all you need to know.'

'Please . . . tell us. What will be done with us?'

'When you disembark there will be people waiting to take charge of you.'

'There, you see.' Reuben reassured his wife with a smile. 'There will be people to care for us. Good people.'

Rachel squeezed his hand.

'You are a good man, Reuben Kotkin.'

He laughed, the first time in many days. It sounded peculiar.

'That is not what your mother used to say about me, do you remember? She was so sure I was no good for you.'

She smiled her remembrance.

'I was her little baby, my *mamale* could not bear to see me go, that is all.'

'She called me a good-for-nothing *shlemiel*! She had her heart set on you marrying that fine doctor.'

Rachel stood on tiptoe and planted a kiss on the end of Reuben's nose.

'I could never have found a better husband than you.'

There was no time to talk any more. They were being ushered up the companionway and onto the deck. It was very dark, the port blacked out with only a few dim lights, masked and shielded against enemy bombers.

'Hurry, please,' barked a harsh English voice, somewhere below on the quayside.

They began walking down the gangplank; a long, bedraggled

13

procession of lost humanity, some with the odd battered suitcase or parcel, most with nothing but the damp and tattered clothes they wore. As they stepped down onto the quayside, Rachel felt her heart skip a beat. She clutched at Reuben's sleeve.

'Soldiers, Reuben. Soldiers with guns.'

A rifle barrel glinted in the starlight, then another and another. There were perhaps a dozen, soldiers and military police, and a couple of English policemen waiting for them. One of the policemen was counting them as they stepped onto the quay.

'It's all right, Rachel. They won't hurt us.'

'Names?' The policeman stopped them from going any further.

'Kotkin,' replied Reuben. 'Reuben and Rachel Kotkin.'

'Nationality?'

'We have no nationality. We are stateless.'

The policeman scratched his ear.

'Any papers?'

Reuben nodded to Rachel and she took the two old, battered passports from her pocket, handing them to the policeman. He regarded them with interest.

'German,' he commented.

'No, no.' Reuben shook his head. 'We are not German, our citizenship was taken away. We are Jews. You see, there is a letter "J" marked by the names . . .'

'Jews,' nodded Rachel. '*Juden*. Refugees.'

'German,' repeated the policeman, and pushed them gently but firmly to the side. 'Next . . .'

'Please . . .' But no one was listening.

'Women to the left, men to the right,' announced a soldier, gesturing with his rifle.

'No, no, you can't separate us,' protested Reuben. 'My wife . . . she's pregnant . . .'

'Your wife will be looked after, sir. Now if you would just step over here . . .'

Reuben turned back but Rachel seemed suddenly very far away from him, her face a white oval of shocked silence. They were being separated, no, this wasn't happening. Always they had been together. He had sworn only one thing to her, and that was that he would never desert her . . .

'Where are you taking us?' demanded another man.

'You'll find out soon enough.'

'Reuben! Don't leave me. Don't take my husband away from me . . .'

'You can't do this . . .'

'Sir,' said the policeman with quiet exasperation. 'You are Germans. You are enemy aliens, you must be interned for our and your own safety.'

'Interned?' asked Rachel, uncomprehending.

'Imprisoned,' cut in one of the other women. 'We're going to be put in prison!'

'No!' shouted Reuben. 'We are not your enemies, we are Hitler's enemies!'

'Then I am sure you will have a chance to prove that, sir. Now if you would just go quietly, it will be all the better for everyone.'

'Let me go. Please . . . you have to let us go!'

He was still shouting as the doors of the Black Maria closed behind him.

Rachel wanted to cry, but the tears would not come. It was all like a horrible nightmare. Why had they even bothered to escape from Holland? England was to have been their place of welcome and safety, but instead they had been welcomed with guns.

She felt numb. As they climbed into the prison van, a dark-haired, thin-faced woman put her arm round her shoulders.

'It'll be all right, Rachel. It'll be all right.'

Would it? It scarcely seemed possible. Alone and pregnant in a foreign land, how could anything ever be all right again?

Chapter 2

Cora opened the front door of the *Bradda Vista*.

'Oh, James, I'm so glad you could come. Archie's quite poorly.'

James McArthur took off his hat and stepped into the entrance hall, carefully wiping his feet on the 'welcome' mat. A small black Scottie dog with a red tartan collar came bouncing and barking down the corridor towards him.

'Bonzo – come here at once, behave!' exclaimed Cora, amusement masking indignation as James bent to stroke the dog and it nipped playfully at the dangling end of his tweedy tie.

'It's my pleasure,' James replied, his face crinkling into a smile. 'I was just on my way home when you telephoned, so I'd be passing your front door anyway.'

James scratched Bonzo behind the ear and he rolled onto his back, his long pink tongue lolling in ecstasy.

'This one seems right as rain, anyway. But what's this about old Archie?'

'He's still not eating. And he'll hardly let me near him.' She held out her hand. 'Shall I take your coat?'

James slipped off his raincoat and handed it to Cora, who hung it on a hook by the door, carefully smoothing the folds so that it hung perfectly straight. There was something about Cora's careful neatness which James found enchanting. That, and the way her cheeks dimpled like a child's when she laughed. He was glad their mutual fondness for animals had given them a chance to get to know each other.

'Aye, well, sounds like I'd best take a look at him straight away.'

'He's in the kitchen, by the stove. Best watch your ankles, though, he's in a mood.'

Cora pushed open the kitchen door and James followed her in. An immense ginger cat was curled up tightly by the side of the big gas range. To all outward appearances he was asleep, but his ears swivelled at the sound of the door opening and James knew Archie was on the alert.

Cora had inherited Archie along with the *Bradda Vista*. He had been her parents' cat, and when they died William had taken him on. Grace, however, hated cats – and just about everything else, mused Cora grimly.

James took a step towards the cat and it opened one large, yellow eye, drew back its lips and hissed.

'Now, boy, there's no need for that,' murmured James soothingly. Propping up his stick against the kitchen table, he crouched down stiffly beside the cat.

'Would you like me to pick him up for you . . .?' Cora wished she hadn't spoken even before the words were out of her mouth.

'No.' James spat out the word, then immediately regretted his short fuse. He knew he was too touchy about his leg, but frustration just kept on eating away at him – wasn't it all his own fault that he was like this? His own fault that he wasn't in uniform like his senior and junior partners? 'No thanks, Cora, I can manage.'

Archie took a swipe at James's outstretched fingers, but he succeeded in seizing the cat by the scruff of its neck. With some difficulty, he hoisted the wriggling bundle onto a newspaper on the kitchen table. His leg throbbed, but he bit his lip. He hated showing weakness, especially to Cora. 'Well, there's plenty of fight in him!'

He spent some moments just calming down the cat, scratching its head, stroking it along the long arch of its back.

'How're you managing now?' he asked. Cora was busying

18

herself with a kettleful of water and cups and saucers. He thought he saw her back stiffen at the question.

'Well enough, I suppose. So far. But I can't pretend it's what I wanted.'

'You're a good organiser, anyhow,' pointed out James, still stroking the ginger tom-cat. It looked back at him with wary, indignant eyes, as though defying him to coax a purr out of it. 'You've had all that experience at the shop . . .'

'Yes, but helping to run a haberdasher's is hardly the same, is it?'

'Still you've a fine business head. If anyone can sort this place out, you can.'

And someone needs to, he thought to himself as he glanced around the faded decor. It was obvious that ever since Grace had married William Quine and moved into the *Bradda Vista*, it had been going downhill. What would happen to it now that it was going to house internees?

'How is he?' Cora looked back over her shoulder at James. A little shiver of appreciation ran through her as she reminded herself how good-looking he was. His tall, muscular frame was at once strong and athletic, his hair dark and crinkly, with the faintest auburn sheen when the sun was on it, his features rugged yet sensitive.

'I can't feel any swelling, so that's good – there's no diarrhoea?'

'No, no, nothing like that. But he's hardly eating a thing. He just sort of dribbles all the time, and scratches at his face.'

'Could you hold him still? I need to take a look in his mouth.'

Cora wiped her hands on her apron and came over.

'Hold him by the scruff, that's it.'

James took her hand and placed it on the cat's back. His fingers felt warm and strong, thought Cora, and she found it hard to ignore the exhilaration she felt when they were together. As yet they were friends – good friends, it was true, but still only friends. She wished she could see inside James's head, and know for sure what he felt for her. She had no intention of making a fool of herself over a man. Even a man as attractive as James McArthur.

'Aha! So that's what's going on in there . . .'

'You can see what's wrong?'

'Hold on. Don't let him go.' James dived into his medical bag and took out a pair of tweezers. 'Right, Archie, just you behave yourself . . .'

'There!' He held up the tweezers. 'That's what's been causing him all this trouble.'

'What is it?' Cora peered at the small, hard thing. It was about an inch long, no more.

'It's a bit of shattered chicken bone. Poor old feller.' He rubbed the top of Archie's head. 'It must have hurt him pretty badly, that's why he kept on scratching at his face.'

'But I don't feed him chicken . . .'

'Then I expect Archie has been stealing out of people's dustbins.' He stroked the cat under its chin. 'Anyhow, he should be all right if he doesn't go doing it again.'

Cora picked up the cat and it flopped across her shoulder, immediately rumbling into life like a miniature earthquake. Awkward old bugger, thought James as he repacked his bag.

'Thanks, James. What do I owe you?'

'One cup of tea and a homemade biscuit.'

Cora laughed.

'Be serious!'

'All right, two biscuits. But there's no need to pay me. Like I said, you were on my way home. And I owe you for having to leave you in the middle of that club dinner.'

'It's all right.' She smiled. 'I forgive you. Sit down, the kettle's just boiled.'

Cora watched James ease himself onto one of the kitchen chairs. She admired his courage, the bloody-minded determination which had got him back on his feet and back to work within months of that terrible farm accident. But she hated the way he martyred himself, refusing all help as if he wanted to punish himself for getting hurt.

She placed a plate of biscuits in front of him.

'You could stay for dinner if you wanted.'

'I wouldn't want to put you to any trouble . . .'

'Don't be silly. And I'd like to thank you for making Archie well again.'

'Well . . .'

'I'll let you pay next time we go to the pictures.'

'All right, but only if you let me take you to the theatre. There's a new show on at the Gaiety next week . . .'

The chatter subsided abruptly as the kitchen door opened and old Thomas Quine came in, with Bonzo trotting in his wake.

'You here again then, Mr McArthur?' Grandad Quine shuffled in and took a seat at the table. He rubbed his hands together. 'By gough, but it's chilly. Got a bite to eat?'

'There's biscuits and scones in the tin. James just called in to see Archie.'

'Oh aye?'

Old man Quine nodded slowly. He didn't need Cora to tell him what was going on. He knew courting when he saw it. He didn't exactly disapprove, although the middle of a war wasn't the best place to be doing it.

'That a fresh pot of tea I can see there, Cora?'

'Fresh-made, just how you like it.' Some sixth sense had guided an extra spoonful of tea from the caddy to the pot. 'James . . . Mr McArthur . . . is staying for dinner tonight, Grandad.'

'That so?' Thomas rummaged in his pocket for a handkerchief and blew his nose with a sound like the *King Orry* docking at Pier Head. 'You heard, have you?'

'Heard about what, Mr Quine?'

Thomas tut-tutted his impatience.

'About the internee women.'

'Er . . . yes.' It would have been hard not to, thought James – it was the talk of the Island. Besides, he too lived within the

21

area designated for the new Rushen Internment Camp, and had mixed feelings about being wired in with a load of detainees. 'So when exactly are they arriving? Soon, I'd heard.'

'The next few days, apparently.' Cora sat down at the table and poured the tea. Her hand was steady, but he could see the tension in her. 'It's going to be strange – having all these Germans and Austrians and what have you living here.'

'Strange!' Thomas snorted into his teacup. 'It's madness. If you take my advice, James boy, you'll lock your door at night.'

'Bessie was in tears yesterday,' commented Cora. 'She was so certain it wouldn't happen, and we'd be sent evacuees. And then the Government said it would be internees instead . . .'

'What about you? How do you feel about it?'

James watched Cora's face.

'It's not as if we have much choice. And maybe they won't be as bad as all that. I read somewhere that some of them are refugees, not Nazis at all.'

'You don't want to believe everything you read, gel,' muttered Thomas, but Cora preferred to ignore him.

'The worst thing will be living behind barbed wire,' she reflected. 'Bessie's sure it'll be just like being in jail.'

'Oh, I don't expect it'll be that bad. We'll be able to get in and out with a pass. How many women will be coming to the *Bradda Vista?*'

Cora took a sip from her cup.

'Everybody's being very vague. Maybe twelve, no more than sixteen.'

'Sixteen!'

'They'll have to share rooms – beds too, if they're doubles. The money will help though, what with all this to keep up.' She gazed around the kitchen. It needed new lino, new cupboards – in fact the whole hotel could do with a coat of paint.

''Tisn't enough, though, is it?' reflected Thomas, helping

22

himself to a second cup of tea. 'Three bob a day for each woman? That's hardly enough to keep a sparrow in bird seed.'

'No, Grandad. But there's no point in getting worked up about this, is there? At least they haven't thrown us out of our homes, like the landlords in Douglas and Ramsey.'

She picked up a biscuit and bit into it. Why not indulge yourself while you could? Tomorrow might be too late.

It was a fine May morning, but as far as Rachel Kotkin was concerned, it might just as well have been the middle of the night.

She couldn't remember exactly how long she had been here – nine days, maybe ten. After a night spent at the Fulham Institute, the refugee women had been brought by coach to Holloway Prison: to horrible, dingy single cells that smelt of disinfectant and grime. At least if they had shared cells Rachel would have had someone to talk to. Alone, she felt so isolated and afraid. She knew that Reuben would want her to be brave, but being brave was a lot easier when you had somebody to be brave with.

Where was Reuben? No one would tell her anything – not a single word about where he had been taken or what had been done to him. Her English was not too bad, and she had listened carefully to what she had been told by the doctor and the wardresses: that everything would be all right, that she would be cared for and that nothing bad was going to happen to her.

But how could she believe what they were telling her, when even the sign on the outside of her cell door was a lie? She saw it every time they escorted her to the washroom: it said 'ENEMY ALIEN'.

Enemy? How could that be? Reuben had told her that they would be welcomed here, that the British were as much the enemies of the Nazis as the Jews were. But instead she had been thrown into prison like some common criminal. It wasn't that she had been treated cruelly – not in the way the Germans treated Jews – but even the chaplain's kind words had enraged and upset her.

She had run away to be free – and instead they had put her in a cage.

She sat on the side of the hard wooden bed and laid her hand on the rounded bulge of her stomach. At least she had her baby. And Reuben had promised that they would be together when the baby was born. He would find a way.

Just as she was about to lie down she heard a small sound. Where was it coming from? It wasn't the click-clack of the wardresses' flat-heeled shoes on the tiled landing, nor was it the grate and squeak of the book trolley.

Her eyes followed the sound to a tiny hole in the cracked tiling of the wall, just a couple of inches above floor-level. Something – something small and white – was pushing its way through the hole and into her cell.

Rachel got off the bed and walked across the cell. Kneeling down, she took the little white thing from the hole. It was a small piece of paper, rolled up. Her heart pounding, she flattened it out. It was a message from the woman in the next cell – a Jewess she had met for the first time on the lifeboat. It read:

'Have courage, Rachel. We will be strong together. Sarah.'

'Good morning, madam. It is a beautiful day.'

The old lady in the bed blinked and shielded her eyes as Elsa Nadel drew back the heavy brocade curtains on the full bay window. Elsa walked back to the bed and helped the Duchess to pull herself up into a sitting position.

'All days are beautiful when you are as old as I am,' replied the old lady.

'I have brought the morning post. Shall I read it to you now?'

The Grand Duchess Marie-Louise of Meerschloss nodded and folded her hands neatly in her lap. The morning routine

24

was the same every day. She was woken at seven-thirty by her companion, who brought her the morning mail. At eight o'clock precisely she would breakfast on strong black coffee and fresh rolls baked by her faithful old cook, Martha. It had always been so, and the Duchess was far too old to think of changing now, war or no war.

'There is another letter from the bank,' began Elsa, slitting it open with the silver paper-knife, one of the many beautiful things the Grand Duchess had brought with her from Germany.

The Duchess waved it away with a dismissive gesture.

'I cannot concern myself with such distasteful matters. You may give it to Mr Whateley-Smythe to deal with.'

'Yes, madam.' Elsa knew it was no use trying to get through to the Duchess. This grand old lady was much too aristocratic and otherworldly to comprehend her pressing financial problems. Why, Elsa had not been paid for two months, and Whateley-Smythe – the family solicitor – continued to work for the Duchess purely out of personal regard for her.

Elsa turned to the next envelope and opened it.

'It is from your nephew, madam. In Bavaria.'

'Ah, my dear little Hermann. How is he?'

'He tells you that he is well, and has been called up for military service with a tank regiment.'

The Grand Duchess shook her head.

'Such a brave boy is my dear Hermann. But this war is such foolishness. England and Germany should have no quarrel, they should be punishing Russia for what it did to my poor mother's cousin . . .'

'Yes, madam.' Elsa knew it was not good policy to express her own opinions. It was expressing socialist convictions that had forced her and her brother to leave Germany in such a hurry, back in 1935.

'I will read Hermann's letter after Martha has brought me my breakfast.' The Grand Duchess opened her eyes and looked at Elsa with a flicker of interest. 'You have a twin brother, do you not?'

'Yes, madam. His name is Max.' She had told the Duchess many times, but the old lady lived in the past, her memory of recent events paling beside cherished recollections of the days when she was young, rich and beautiful.

'Ah yes, Max. What did you say he did?'

'He is an artist.' Elsa felt anxiety tugging at her belly as her thoughts returned to her twin brother – her irresponsible, talented firebrand of a brother, who was always getting himself into trouble. Was that what had happened this time, too?

'And where is he?'

I wish I knew, thought Elsa.

'In Scotland, I think. In his last letter he said he had found wealthy patrons. But that was ages ago . . .' It was 27 May now, and she hadn't heard from him in months. Still, she told herself, Max was like that. He could vanish off the face of the earth for weeks or months, and then turn up as if nothing had happened. Responsibility had never sat easily on Max Nadel's shoulders.

'Scotland. Such a beautiful place. Did I ever tell you about the Christmas I spent at Balmoral? Perhaps this summer, if I am feeling stronger . . .'

The Duchess's face relaxed into a faraway smile as she drifted away into another waking dream of pleasures gone by. Pleasures which she relived endlessly in the bright world of her mind.

A distant jangling announced a visitor at the front door.

'Madam, the door, I must leave you for a moment.'

'What?'

'The door. We have a visitor.'

'Before noon? How unmannerly. If it is a tradesman, you must send him away and tell him to use the back entrance in future. If it is one of our acquaintances, you will take a calling card.'

'Yes, madam.' Elsa stood up. 'I shall come straight back.'

Quite unexpectedly, the Duchess reached out and patted her hand.

'You are a good girl, Elsa. A very good girl.'

'Thank you, madam.' The bell jangled again, more urgently this time. 'I must go now.'

Elsa hurried down to the front door, her short brown hair bobbing up and down as she took the stairs two at a time. She was an athletic woman in her thirties, gawky in her youth but now matured into a tall, striking figure.

Back in her days as a pharmacology student, she had never imagined in her wildest dreams that she would end up as companion to a frail old Prussian aristocrat. But necessity could make you do strange and unexpected things, and against all the odds she had grown fond of the Grand Duchess. Besides, apart from Martha the old lady was practically alone in the world.

She checked her hair in the mirror before opening the front door. Through the stained-glass panes, criss-crossed with anti-blast paper, she could see the outlines of two figures standing on the doorstep. Curious, she opened the door.

'Miss Elsa Constanze Nadel?'

Elsa gazed in surprise at the police constable, his helmet tucked under his arm and his notebook flipped open in his right hand. As a Registered Alien, she vaguely recognised him from her occasional obligatory visits to Streatham South police station. Beside him stood a middle-aged woman in green WVS uniform.

'Yes. Can I help you?'

'May we come inside?' asked the woman. She seemed motherly and quite nice. Perhaps she was here to arrange more help for the Duchess. But why the policeman?

'Of course.' Elsa stood back to allow the woman and her companion into the entrance hall. The constable pushed the door shut behind him. 'I hope there isn't a problem with my work permit?'

'Not exactly.' The constable seemed ill at ease. 'I'm afraid we've come to collect you and take you to the police station. We have to intern you.'

'Intern me!' Elsa's face went white. The WVS woman put out her hand to steady her, but the touch felt threatening rather than comforting. Out of the corner of her eye, Elsa saw Martha standing in the doorway to the kitchen. Standing. Staring. 'But why?'

'My Chief Constable has authorised me to bring in all enemy alien women in the area . . .'

'But I'm not an enemy alien,' protested Elsa. 'I'm not even a grade A, I'm only a grade B . . .'

'I'm sorry.' The constable shrugged his shoulders and buttoned his notebook into his breast pocket. 'But orders are orders.'

'Now, dear, if you'd just get yourself ready,' soothed the WVS officer, all efficiency and professionalism.

'Get ready . . . ?' repeated Elsa, so stunned that she could hardly believe this was happening to her. How could they think she was any danger to this country? Why, she hadn't even set foot in Germany since 1935!

'You're allowed one suitcase, plus anything else you can carry,' explained the woman. 'If I were you I'd take plenty of warm clothing, and a rug or blanket if you have one. Oh, and a bar of soap.'

'Warm clothing? Why? Where are you taking me?'

'Sorry, miss, can't tell you,' replied the PC. 'Strictly hush-hush.'

Elsa looked from the WVS to the policeman and back again, silently beseeching them to admit that this was all some terrible mistake.

'But I can't go,' she argued. 'My Duchess – how on earth will she manage if you take me away?'

Martha smiled; a smile not of sympathy but triumph.

'The mistress and I will manage, ma'am. We managed well enough before you ever came.'

'I'm sorry,' repeated the constable. Elsa felt profoundly irritated by him. Sorry – was that all he could say?

'I have no right of appeal?'

'At this moment in time – no.'

'I've done nothing wrong,' protested Elsa, though she knew protesting was useless. She might as well have been talking to a brick wall.

'I don't doubt it, miss, but there's a war on.'

'Now, dear,' cut in the WVS lady. 'There's no use getting yourself all worked up about this, is there? I'll wait here with Constable Green while you go upstairs and pack your case.'

It was the morning of 27 May 1940, and Grethe Herzheim was returning from work.

She was tired but there was money in her handbag; she and her little son Emil would celebrate with a good meal tonight. Perhaps she would buy him a bar of Five Boys as a special treat. Pete at the Spotted Cow could get you anything you wanted, shortages or no shortages.

Grethe walked quickly down the road, aware that she must look out of place in her fur jacket, red dress and high-heeled, strappy shoes. Not that she cared what the rest of Streatham – or the rest of the world – cared about her. Whoring wasn't her choice, but it brought in a good living for her and Emil.

Turning the corner into Rosier Walk, she nodded a brief good morning to Mr Curtis. Jimmy Curtis was an understanding man, and extremely useful too. He kept a very discreet little private hotel, solely for the use of 'passing trade'. Grethe had taken more clients there than she cared to remember.

'Morning, Grethe – good night?'

'Not bad.' She thought briefly of the darkened doorways and the dingy rooms where she conducted most of her business, then shut the thought out of her mind. The best way to survive as a brass was just to get on with it; if you didn't think about it it couldn't hurt you. 'Made a bob or two.'

'I'll be seein' you later then? With my cut?'

'Maybe. Or maybe tomorrow.'

'Mind you don't forget then.'

'I won't.'

Grethe had a long-standing arrangement with Mr Curtis, paying him a pound a week for the regular use of one of his rooms. Last night, however, she hadn't needed to use Curtis's dingy boarding house, nor the doorway of the butcher's shop near the common. Last night she had been taken home for a whole night by a real toff.

You didn't get many over-nighters now, mostly just soldiers with the price of a half-hour's fumble. He hadn't given her his real name, of course – well, would you, in his position? But he was obviously something important, a judge or a magistrate or what have you. And he'd paid her well.

Quite right too, she told herself. She might be thirty-nine now, but she was still a looker. Her bottle-blonde hair was neatly tonged into tight curls, her heavy make-up not masking her handsome features. Her clothes were just the right side of tarty – bright, expensive, unapologetically clinging to her curves. As she walked she swung her hips, and the skirt of her dress swirled against her knees and thighs, revealing the smooth line of a pair of enviable legs.

At the far end of the road was the house in which she and Emil shared a flat with her friend Claire. It was a turn-of-the-century villa, red brick with fancy weatherboards and terracotta mouldings, and it must have been quite a house in its day. Now, it was divided up into small flats. Almost all the tenants were working girls like Grethe – girls doing what they could to make a living. And in many cases it was a good living too – better than working in some dreary shop, anyway.

What was that? Grethe's practised eye caught the hint of uniform blue long before she actually reached the house. Police blue. Her heart skipped a beat and she hesitated for a split second. Why would the police be waiting for her at the house? She wasn't soliciting, just walking down the street like any respectable woman. Maybe they weren't waiting for her at all. Or maybe something had happened to Emil . . .

She quickened her pace and turned into the driveway. There were not one but two police constables waiting on the doorstep – or to be precise, one constable and a WPC, a chunky, homely-looking girl who looked as if she'd be more at home in a pair of Land Girl's jodhpurs.

'Morning, Constable,' said Grethe coolly as she swept past.

'Miss Herzheim?' enquired the WPC, equally coolly.

Grethe stopped and swung round.

'You should know,' she smiled sweetly. 'You've arrested me often enough.'

'I'm afraid we're going to have to take you in, Grethe,' said the constable, almost apologetically. Grethe regarded him with a mixture of annoyance and pity. He might not be a bad-looking young man if he got out of that uniform and got himself a real job, relaxed a bit.

'Oh yes? And what am I supposed to have done this time? Because as you can see, I'm just coming home after a night with a . . . friend.'

The WPC's sour face remained unchanged but the PC's lips twitched as he tried to suppress a smile.

'No, Grethe, it's not soliciting – not this time.'

'What then?'

'You're being interned as an enemy alien.'

'What!'

'You heard,' said the WPC. 'You're registered as a B-grade alien, and we're empowered to take you into custody for the sake of national security.'

'Fuck national security,' replied Grethe. 'I'm not going. You can't do this. I've got a son to look after . . .'

'Where is he?' asked the PC.

'At school. My friend Claire sends him off every morning and I collect him in the afternoon . . .'

'Something will be arranged.'

31

'Look, you can take me if you want, but I'm not leaving Emil behind.' Grethe was fighting mad now. If there was one thing in the world she truly cared about, it was her little boy.

'Come on, Grethe, get a move on,' snapped the WPC. 'You've got precisely half an hour to pack a suitcase and come with us.'

'I told you, I'm not leaving Emil . . .'

'And I told you, something will be sorted out.' The WPC's mouth curved into a sneer. 'Anyway, women like you shouldn't be allowed to have kids. What sort of a mother sells her body on the street?'

Grethe returned her gaze with a look of utter contempt.

'And what sort of bitch takes a mother away from her kid and puts her in prison?'

'Now, now, Grethe, that's enough of that,' said PC Mackintosh, who didn't much like the way things were heading. 'Your boy will be taken care of. Now, best pack your things and come quietly.'

It was about six o'clock the same evening when Claire Hodges turned into Rosier Walk.

After sending Emil off to school, she had spent the day up West. Claire preferred to work the daylight hours, and there were plenty of soldiers in the West End right now, not just the poorly paid Tommies but Canadians, Aussies, Polaks, all sorts. Life could be a lot worse. Why shouldn't she make a lonely lad happy for half an hour and earn a living at the same time?

She and Grethe Herzheim had shared the Streatham flat for about eighteen months. It was common for working girls to share – it cut costs and it was safer. What's more, sharing meant they could take turns at looking after Emil. Grethe wouldn't hear of him being evacuated, war or no war.

Claire walked briskly up the street towards Rosier Mansions. If she got a move on she might just catch Grethe before she went out.

But something wasn't quite right. She knew that as soon as she reached the house. Emil was sitting on the front steps, his little face streaked with dirt and tears. That was odd – Grethe doted on the boy, sometimes to the point of suffocation. She'd never leave him outside on his own, especially not upset like that.

She half walked, half ran up the driveway.

'Emil . . . what's up? What you been up to, eh?'

The small boy leapt to his feet, ran towards her.

'Claire, Claire, me ma's gone an' left us!'

Puzzled, she stroked Emil's tousled, mid-brown hair.

'Come off it, kid. This a joke, is it? Where's your ma, Emil? You been in trouble and she give you a rollicking, did she?'

Emil shook his head vigorously.

'The police has took her, Auntie Claire! Mrs Jones seen 'em.'

Claire held him at arms' length.

'You telling the truth, my lad? 'Cause if you ain't . . .'

'It's the truth, honest it is. There's a letter for you.'

'A letter?' Claire couldn't take all this in. 'But why . . . why would they take your ma? She ain't done nothing.' Ever since the Tribunal last year, Grethe had been even more careful than usual, taking no chances, paying all her fines . . . 'You better show me, okay?'

Emil led her by the hand upstairs to the flat. Wardrobes stood open, drawers pulled out. A suitcase was gone, a couple of blankets, Grethe's best coat. And on the kitchen table lay an envelope, addressed to Claire in a hasty scrawl. Claire tore it open and read.

'Claire, the police came to intern me. Look after the boy. Grethe.'

Chapter 3

There were six women in the cell at Streatham South Police Station: three Austrian housemaids, a middle-aged nurse, a German deaconess – and Elsa Nadel.

Elsa wriggled uncomfortably on the hard wooden bench. Spring sunshine filtered into the room through the high window, casting a pattern on the tiled floor as it shone through the bars. It felt peculiar to be locked up. Even back in Germany, when she and Max had been active socialists, she had never actually ended up behind bars. What's more, it wasn't an experience she ever wanted to repeat.

'It's a disgrace, that's what it is,' sniffed the nurse. She was still wearing her uniform, having been arrested in the middle of giving a patient a bed-bath. 'I mean, there I am doing useful work, and what do they do? They arrest me.'

'Do you think we'll be here for long?' asked one of the housemaids, a very young, very pretty and very blonde girl called Mathilde. A real Aryan *mädchen*, thought Elsa.

'They can't keep us here like this,' replied the nurse. 'Not six to a room.'

'It's disgusting,' added Mathilde's sour-faced friend, Inge.

'I expect they're going to move us somewhere soon,' suggested Elsa.

'I expect so,' sighed Mathilde, fiddling with the strap of her handbag. 'I wonder how Mrs Fitzroy is. She always has morning coffee at eleven-thirty.'

'Well, she'll have to get her own today,' commented Olga, the third housemaid; a brown-haired woman somewhere in her early thirties. 'Fat cow could do with the exercise.'

Silence fell over the assembled women. They were a curious combination, with very little in common. The three housemaids were frivolous, jingoistic and resentful by turns, the nurse quietly furious and the deaconess serenely aloof from it all. Elsa worried about the Grand Duchess. How was Marie-Louise going to manage with Martha? Would the WVS lady keep her promise, and make sure that she was looked after?

'Where do you suppose they'll take us?' asked Inge.

'I heard they were going to ship us to Canada,' cut in Mathilde.

Nurse Imhof shook her head.

'No, Australia. I definitely heard Australia.'

'We're probably all wrong,' pointed out Elsa. 'I mean, why should they tell us where they're taking us?'

'Wherever it is,' declared Olga, 'I shall make life hell for them.' She wrinkled her pretty nose. 'The English are led by Jews, you know. They do say even Churchill has Jewish blood.'

Elsa's blood was boiling, but she said nothing. What point was there in starting an argument? If they were all going to be locked up together for goodness knows how long, their differences would soon become all too painfully apparent.

'What do you do, my dear?' asked the deaconess, turning to Elsa.

'I was trained as a pharmacist,' she explained. 'But I've been working as companion to an old lady. The only way I could get into Britain was on a domestic permit.'

Mathilde cut in:

'So why did you come here at all? You don't look Jewish.'

'I'm not.' She paused. 'I came here a few years ago with my brother. He's an artist.' She didn't add that Max's work had been declared 'degenerate' by the Nazi government, or that both of them had been blacklisted as socialist sympathisers, and consequently couldn't obtain any work. They had been faced with a fairly simple choice: leave the country, or starve.

'An artist! How exciting,' enthused the deaconess. 'You must tell me all about his work.'

But Elsa was saved from further explanations by the sound of a key turning in the lock. Six pairs of eyes turned to watch the heavy door swing open.

'I've brought you some company,' said WPC Bailey, ushering the latest arrival into the cell. 'I'm sure you'll find plenty to talk about.'

As the door clanged shut and the bunch of keys rattled in the lock, Grethe Herzheim surveyed the watching women. She could see from the expressions on their faces what they made of her, with her peroxide hair and high-heeled shoes.

'No need to ask her what she does for a living,' observed Fräulein Imhof with distaste. 'You'd think they'd have the good grace to keep women like her away from decent folk.'

'Her?' enquired Grethe icily. 'Who do you think I am – the cat's mother?'

'More like a five-shilling tart,' replied Olga.

'Five shillings, darling?' enquired Grethe with a smile of contempt. 'Is that all *you* charge? Still, with a face like yours . . .'

Olga sprang to her feet. Mathilde clutched at her shoulder but she shook her off.

'I'm not spending another minute in this cell with that filth.'

'I don't think we have any choice,' pointed out Inge. But Olga was already hammering on the cell door.

'Let me out. Unlock this door and let me out.'

A distant, weary voice called out in reply.

'Shut yer row in there, will yer?'

'Do calm down, ladies, let's not be uncharitable,' said the deaconess, but there was no friendliness in her eyes. If Grethe had had some infectious disease she could not have been less welcome.

'Come and sit by me,' suggested Elsa, sliding a little

37

further up the bench so that Grethe could squeeze in by the door. It was a tight fit for seven complete strangers who hadn't the slightest desire to get to know each other.

'Ta very much, I'm sure.' Grethe was grateful, but wary. Why should this woman give her the time of day? It was pretty obvious that she was no prostitute. 'Mind if I smoke?'

No one said anything. They were all ignoring each other now, turning their resentment of this ridiculous situation into resentment of one another. Elsa shook her head.

'No, don't mind me.'

Grethe slipped a silver cigarette case out of her handbag. 'Want one?'

'No thanks, I never acquired the habit.' Elsa's eyes travelled around the cell. 'But if this goes on much longer, I probably will.'

She looked at Grethe's hand and noticed how, for all her brassy self-assurance, the fingers trembled as she lit a match.

Grethe took a long pull on her cigarette, blew a smoke ring and sat back, resting her head and shoulders against the cold tiled wall.

'Grethe,' she said. 'Grethe Herzheim. I'm a whore.' She turned her head to look at Elsa. 'And you are . . . ?'

'Oh – Elsa, Elsa Nadel.'

They shook hands briefly, with an awkward formality which was very English. Funny how, when you had lived in a country for a while, you began to change, adapt to fit that country. After all these years Elsa had almost come to think of herself as English – how strange to be reminded that she was an 'unfriendly alien'. Stranger still to be shaking hands with a prostitute – and find yourself liking her.

'So how did you end up in here, then? You don't look like an "undesirable".'

Elsa eased herself into a slightly less uncomfortable position.

'When I went before the Tribunal last year they couldn't decide if I was a "friendly" alien or not, so instead of C they graded me B. My brother, too.'

Grethe drew on her cigarette.

'Interned too, is he?'

Elsa shrugged.

'I wish I knew. I haven't heard from him in months. And then there's the Duchess . . .'

'Who?'

'The old lady I've been working for as a companion. But I suppose she'll manage . . .'

'Bastards,' hissed Grethe, and for the first time Elsa saw anger flash across the world-weary eyes. 'Heartless bastards, that's what they are. Do you know what they did? They made me leave my Emil behind, my little boy. Two minutes to write a note, that's all I had.'

She threw back her head and shouted, so loud that the sound echoed round the cell.

'Bastards!'

Elsa touched her arm.

'Getting upset won't help.'

'What do you expect from a woman like that?' sniffed the nurse. 'Guttersnipe.'

'At least I'm not a frigid bitch,' snarled Grethe.

At which point Sergeant Greenwood arrived, shirt-sleeves rolled up and a half-eaten pilchard sandwich in his hand. His paunch wobbled over the belt of his uniform trousers.

'What's all this about, ladies?'

'Where's my son?' demanded Grethe.

'All in good time. Now, if you'll just follow WPC Bailey, there's a coach waiting for you outside.'

'What's happening?'

WPC Bailey appeared in the doorway.

'Hurry up now. We're transferring you to Holloway Prison.'

Rachel Kotkin was knitting socks for soldiers. It was what she did for most of each dull prison day. Great khaki-coloured things they were, huge and woolly, but knitting seemed to take her mind off her anxieties about Reuben. It pleased the prison wardresses, too, helped to persuade them that she really was what she said she was: a helpless refugee who hated Nazi Germany even more than they did.

At least one aspect of the Holloway regime had improved. A few days ago, the Governor had agreed that cell doors would be left unlocked during the daytime, so that the internee women could socialise.

And so it was that Rachel Kotkin and Sarah Rosenberg were sitting talking in Rachel's cell.

'I wonder what it's like outside.' Sarah climbed onto Rachel's bed and peered out through the high, barred window. 'Is it sunny?'

'Looks beautiful. I can only see the sky, but it's deep blue. I wish we had more than an hour's exercise a day. I wouldn't even mind walking round that revolting yard.'

Rachel's fingers moved swiftly, click-clacking her four needles together as yet another sock took shape. Sarah turned and jumped down, sitting beside her.

'The British may be short of guns but they won't be short of socks,' she commented.

Rachel glanced down at her knitting and laughed.

'It keeps me busy. Stops me thinking about . . . you know.'

'Those Nazi women on the next landing?'

Rachel nodded.

'Sometimes, in the night, I can hear them singing – the Horst Wessel Song. It makes me think of Berlin . . .'

Sarah patted her arm.

'I'm sorry, I shouldn't have reminded you.' She stood up and paced up and down, glancing out of the door. One or two other women were walking between each other's cells, but apart from the low buzz of conversation all was quiet. Strange how easily some people adapted to captivity.

'I can't stand this,' she said, turning back to look at Rachel, still clicking away. 'I don't know how you can be so patient, really I don't.'

Rachel looked up.

'What else can we do?' Sarah's fidgeting made her nervous, made the old panic stir in her belly, but she said nothing. She knew it was the other woman's way of coping.

'When do you think they'll let us go free?'

'Soon,' nodded Rachel. 'I'm sure it will be soon. The Chaplain said they are going to move us, take us out of this prison.'

'But will we be *free*?'

Rachel didn't answer. She'd been asking the same question, but everyone was being very evasive. Wild rumours were circulating about being transported to the Dominions, even that the women were going to be put on a boat and made to go back to Holland. It was best not to think.

Sarah put her head close to Rachel's.

'Johanna Birnbaum says they're putting something in that horrible tea they give us.'

Rachel's eyes widened.

'What sort of thing?'

'Something to calm us down. Bromide.'

'Will it harm my baby?'

'No. No, I'm sure it won't. They're just worried we'll get hysterical and make trouble for them.'

'I don't want any trouble,' said Rachel, laying down her knitting needles. 'I just want to make them see that they are wrong about us.' She smiled. 'Oh, and I wouldn't mind a huge bowl of oranges!'

'Oranges!'

Rachel patted her stomach.

'I have such a craving for them,' she confessed. 'But goodness knows when any of us will see an orange again.'

The motor coach drove away, and the latest contingent of internees looked up at their new home.

Elsa Nadel felt a chill of horror creeping over her flesh. This was Holloway Prison, where they put all the murderesses.

She glanced at Grethe Herzheim as they were led inside.

Outwardly she seemed calm, even self-assured, but she was pale beneath her make-up.

'I've never been in a prison before,' confessed Elsa.

Grethe grunted.

'Then it's high time you joined the club, *liebchen*.'

'You've . . . ?'

'Of course.'

'More than once?'

'I've lost count. It's an occupational hazard in my line of work, see. I've never been in Holloway, though. My patch is south of the river.'

The women were led through interminable echoing corridors, and up a long flight of stairs to a landing. Somewhere in the distance Elsa made out a long line of open doors, and a woman standing in a doorway, watching them. Cells with open doors?

'After you have been searched, you will bathe and then the doctor will examine you,' announced an enormous wardress in prison grey. 'Go into the cubicles and undress.'

'Searched?' Elsa looked questioningly at Grethe, who shrugged her shoulders in resignation.

'You get used to it.'

'I don't intend to!'

Else felt degraded and abused. It wasn't the fact of being searched; it was the humiliation of having another woman's hands on her, another woman looking at her nakedness. She hadn't experienced anything like it since boarding school.

Two wardresses carried out the search, one writing down each possession or item of clothing. Shivering in a prison robe, Elsa watched them sorting methodically through her suitcase.

'French knickers, artificial silk, five pairs.'

'Knickers, five pairs,' intoned the younger warder, writing everything down in a rounded, childish hand.

'Shoes, two pairs.'

'Shoes, two pairs.'

'Books.' The wardress picked one of Elsa's books out of the suitcase.

'Please be careful,' cut in Elsa. 'It's very special to me.'

It was a first edition of a Thomas Mann novel, given to her by Max on her eighteenth birthday. Elsa winced as the wardress flicked open the cover, leafed through the pages, shook them then threw the book back into the suitcase.

'One book, German,' she commented, then turned to the next. 'One textbook, English, *Clinical Applications in Pharmacology*. One pair of trousers green, one sweater blue. Silk stockings, three pairs . . .'

Elsa listened to it all as though it were a dream, watching as her jumble of possessions was sorted through – clothes, books, family photographs, her diplomas from university. Could her whole life really be so hurriedly condensed into the contents of one battered suitcase?

'Full name?' enquired a prison nurse as she lined up for her medical examination.

'Elsa Constanze Nadel.'

'Date and place of birth?'

'Heidelberg, fifteenth of February nineteen hundred and five.'

'Do you have any medical problems?'

'None that I'm aware of.'

'Good. Occupation?'

'I've been working as an old lady's companion, but I'm a qualified pharmacist.'

'Is that so? I'd have thought you'd be doing useful war work.'

You and I both, thought Elsa with some bitterness. You and I both.

Grethe looked around the cell with a sense of *déjà vu*. All prison cells were very much the same: a hard bedstead, a table and chair, blank tiled walls and a lock on the door.

Mind you, it was a novelty to find herself in an unlocked

cell. Evidently the Home Office was squeamish about locking up women whose only crime was not being English. Not that it made much difference in practice. A prison was still a prison, and right now she didn't feel much inclined to 'associate' with anyone. Not even Elsa Nadel, who seemed less of a bitch than most.

A toothbrush, a nightdress and a copy of the Bible – that was what the warders had given her. The first she already had, the second she never bothered with, and as for the Bible: well, she couldn't see herself having much use for that either. Repentance wasn't high on her list of priorities.

Grethe took out her powder compact, flicked it open and began reapplying her make-up. At least they hadn't taken that from her. Thoroughly showered and scrubbed, she felt naked without it. She knew she wore too much, but it was an essential barrier between her fragility and the harshness of the outside world. Few realised how vulnerable Grethe Herzheim often felt. Concealing her emotions had become second nature, an important safeguard against hurt.

'Hello.'

Grethe heard the knock on the door and the soft voice, but did not look up.

'Hello. I saw you arrive.'

'Really,' commented Grethe, concentrating on the scarlet ox-bow of her lips.

'My name's Rachel.'

'That's nice.'

'Can I come in?'

Grethe sighed impatiently. Obviously her unwanted visitor wasn't going to get the message. She put away her lipstick and turned to face the door. She was surprised to see an obviously pregnant woman, a mass of dark hair framing a thin, rather pale face. She looked unfeasibly young, scarcely more than a schoolgirl.

'Yes, I suppose so.'

The girl gave a nervous smile.

'It gets lonely in this place.' She rubbed her aching back as she sank down onto Grethe's bed.

'You've been here long?'

'Not quite two weeks. Reuben and I . . .' Her face darkened for a moment. 'We escaped from Holland with some other Jewish families. We were very lucky to get away, but . . .'

'But you didn't reckon on fetching up in this place, right?' Grethe leaned back on the hard wooden chair. This really was no place for a pregnant kid, what were the authorities thinking of?

'They kept saying we were German. We showed them our papers, told them we had no citizenship, but they wouldn't listen.'

'They generally don't,' agreed Grethe. 'So what's happened to your man – Reuben, is it?'

'I don't know. They separated us, took him away in a police van. I keep asking, but they won't tell me anything.'

'They'll have to tell you sooner or later,' said Grethe. It hardly seemed right to frighten the kid.

'I suppose you're right. And you – you are German?'

'Used to be, a long time ago. I haven't been back to Berlin in, oh, fifteen years. If I'd bothered to get myself naturalised, maybe I wouldn't be in this mess.' She looked Rachel up and down. 'Is it your first?'

Rachel blushed.

'Yes.'

'When's it due?'

'Two months, maybe a little more. I'm not sure of my dates . . . it wasn't planned, you see.'

'Mine neither.'

'You have children?'

'A son.' Grethe flicked open her powder compact and started dabbing at the shine on the end of her nose. She didn't want Rachel to see the depth of her feeling. 'Emil. He's six.'

'They wouldn't let you bring him with you? But I thought . . .'

45

Grethe turned her face away, hiding the brightness of tears gathering in her eyes. Yes, she too had heard that interned women were to be allowed to keep their children with them. The Governor had listened, been patient, kind even, but the answer had still been the same: arrangements would be made, but if Grethe wanted her boy with her she would have to go through the 'proper channels'. And everyone knew how long that could take . . . Her only consolation was that she could trust Claire to take good care of the kid.

'I'll get him back,' she vowed. 'I'll get him back, no matter what it takes.'

'Poor Rachel,' said Elsa, as she and Grethe sat in Elsa's cell. 'The kid must have been through hell. She's lost everything and now she doesn't even know where her husband is. And her with a little one on the way.'

Grethe fiddled with the rough blanket on Elsa's bed.

'She'll get through. We all will.' She surprised herself by adding, 'Maybe we can help her. If she wants us to . . .'

Elsa knew what Grethe meant. When all was said and done they were Germans; why should Rachel trust them or value their friendship?

'We'll help each other,' said Elsa. 'It makes sense.' After all, she thought to herself, we've all lost something. Grethe's lost her child, Rachel's lost her home and her husband, and I don't have the faintest idea what's happened to Max.

'If anything makes sense in this stupid war,' retorted Grethe.

It was late afternoon on 27 May, and Cora Quine was out walking on Bradda Head with her friend Fenella Kneen.

Bonzo scampered ahead, darting into patches of heather and gorse after the tantalising scent of rabbits. Cora knew just how he felt. As they stepped out in the blustery May sunshine, she could feel the tension beginning to ease from her shoulders.

It was blissfully good to be free of the *Bradda Vista*, even for an afternoon.

'Your grandad all right, is he?' Fenella's long legs made easy work of the springy heather. 'And your Uncle Harry?'

'Oh, Grandad's fine. Harry's away at the fishing.' Harry Kerruish was Cora's maternal uncle, a bachelor from Port St Mary, who spent his summers 'at the herrin''. With most of the crew joining the Merchant Navy, the *Mary Jane* needed every hand she could get. 'So how's your dad these days?' Fenella's father was a tenant farmer just north of Port Erin. 'I haven't seen him since Christmas.'

'Oh, much better since the doctor gave him that new medicine for his chest. He's keeping me busy on the farm.' Fenella spied on Cora out of the corner of her twinkling brown eyes. 'How's your *friend* James then? Has he asked you to marry him yet?'

Cora giggled.

'Don't tease.'

'I'm not. He's sweet on you.'

'You think so?'

''Course he is.' Fenella took long strides, the breeze tugging at her long brown plait. 'He can marry me if he likes,' she added. 'If you don't want him.'

'Now, did I say that?'

'No, you didn't, Cora Quine – and you're blushing.'

Laughing, they walked on together, the dog snapping at bees and midges hovering tantalisingly about his head.

'Are you bringing James to the Young Farmers' dance over Arbory way next week?' enquired Fenella, picking up bits of stick to throw for Bonzo. As she drew back her arm he ran in circles around her feet, barking wildly.

'I doubt I'll be there at all. What with all this business with the internees.'

'But you love your dancing.'

'I know,' Cora sighed. 'And I used to have loads of time

47

when I worked at the shop. But now, with all these German women coming . . .'

'They're saying there will be thousands,' remarked Fenella. 'Just think of it; all those foreign women on this little island. And then there's all the men they're sending to Douglas and Ramsey . . .'

'At least your farm's outside the wire,' Cora pointed out. 'They're sending me sixteen women and children, you know!'

'Rather you than me.'

'And I don't know how they expect anyone to feed a grown woman on a guinea a week.'

'I heard Mrs Costain saying she was going to give hers nothing but kippers and bread,' commented Fenella. 'She says it's all they deserve.'

Cora sniffed.

'I never did like that woman. It's no wonder no one ever comes back to her place two years running. She'll have a riot on her hands if she's not careful.'

Cora and Fenella walked on together, enjoying the fine weather. The headland was so high that the sky seemed only a hand's reach away. Looking back over her shoulder, Cora could make out the huddle of cottages and boarding houses around Port Erin bay, and the dark, green-brown swell of the Calf of Man beyond. It was so perfect. Was it all about to change?

'I hear the women are supposed to be arriving the day after tomorrow,' commented Fenella.

'That's what I've been told.'

'Have you got everything ready?'

Cora nodded.

'I've locked away all Grace's best things, just in case. Oh, and I've moved the radio into the upstairs flat. Apparently the women aren't allowed to hear the news or see newspapers, at least at first.'

'I suppose that's in case there are spies,' mused Fenella.

Bonzo ran up, barking, and Cora bent to scratch his head.

They were almost at the crest of the hill, and she wasn't sure that she wanted to go any further.

Beyond lay the boundary of the new Rushen Camp – a line stretching from Fleshwick Bay in the west across to Gansey Point in the east, cutting off the villages of Port Erin, Port St Mary and Cregneash. Soon that line would become a permanent barrier, a double row of barbed wire slung between wooden posts. Not for the first time, Cora wondered who the Government was trying to imprison – the internees or the locals.

'Come on, Fenella,' she said, clipping on Bonzo's lead. 'Let's go back. It's turning a bit chilly.'

Chapter 4

'It's not right, Rachel.'

Rachel lay on her side on the hard prison bed, listening to Sarah. She understood why Sarah was so angry, how could she not? But she could not share that anger.

'I was only talking to them, Sarah. There is no harm in talking.'

'But to them? They're not our kind. They're Germans.'

'I know.' I of all people should know, thought Rachel. The Germans took my home, my life, my family away from me. I should hate them all, and in my mind I do. But in my soul . . .

'You know how much they hate us. You've heard those Nazi women singing their songs. They would kill us if they could.'

Rachel thought of Elsa and Grethe. How could she explain to Sarah that these two women were not like that?

'I'm sure Elsa and Grethe aren't Nazis. Grethe has a child . . .'

Sarah laughed, humourlessly.

'Ah yes, Grethe's son. I wonder if she knows which man was the father.'

'Sarah!'

'Grethe Herzheim is a *shmatte*, Rachel. A cheap street-walker. Is that the sort of woman you want as a friend? The sort of woman you could bear to have near you when your baby is born?'

Rachel made no reply. Her head was spinning with whys and wherefores. What Sarah said might be true, but some deeper instinct told Rachel that Grethe was more, and better, than she seemed.

'And as for Fräulein Nadel,' continued Sarah. 'A communist . . .'

'A socialist,' Rachel corrected her. 'She and her brother had to leave Germany, it wasn't safe for them.' But Sarah was already in full spate.

'A communist, like the communists in Russia. And the Russians have always hated Jews. You said they drove out your Reuben's grandfather . . .'

With some effort, Rachel struggled into a sitting position.

'I don't think you are very fair, Sarah. I cannot hate Grethe and Elsa just because you tell me I should. We're locked up like criminals – even the Jewish refugee council can't help us. We must find friendship where we can . . .'

'Friendship!' Sarah's dark eyes were filled with an angry pain.

'What are you doing?' Baffled and slightly alarmed, Rachel watched as Sarah's fingers fumbled to unfasten the buttons on her blouse, pulling it out of her skirt, half tearing it open.

'Look at me,' said Sarah quietly, pulling open her blouse. 'Go on, look. The SS did this to me – don't you admire their handiwork?'

Rachel tried to turn away, but she could not stop looking at the long, pink burn scars which ran down from Sarah's neck over her breasts, arms and torso.

'Take a really good look,' said Sarah. 'And then tell me if you still want Germans as your friends.'

It was the end of the afternoon and Cora was helping out in Evie Bannister's haberdashery shop.

'It was so good of you to come,' smiled Miss Bannister, very small and neat in her fitted costume and lace-up shoes. Her cheeks dimpled with pleasure as she smiled.

'It was the least I could do – after having to hand in my resignation at such short notice.'

'I quite understand, dear.' Miss Bannister leaned closer and lowered her voice. 'And it's very kind of you to help train Daphne. She's very willing, but . . .' She sighed. 'Let's just say she still has a lot to learn.'

Daphne was the sixteen-year-old daughter of George Corless, the local postman. As Cora watched her struggling with a bale of pink printed cotton, she thought back to her own first days in the shop. She'd been so sure that she'd never get the hang of it.

'Oh no, I've done it all wrong,' announced Daphne, with a squeal of dismay.

'What is it now, dear?' fussed Miss Bannister.

'I've cut it in the wrong place.'

'It's all right, Daphne,' said Cora, doing her best to be encouraging. 'Lay it down on here and measure out another one and three-quarter yards.' She gave the customer an apologetic smile. 'You don't mind it in two separate lengths, do you, Mrs Jones?'

'No, no, that'll be quite all right.'

Miss Bannister watched approvingly as Cora calmed Daphne down, showed her how to cut and fold the fabric, and cleared up the mess. She let out a sigh of relief as Mrs Jones left the shop, the doorbell jingling behind her.

'Go and put the kettle on would you, Daphne?'

'But it's not time . . .'

'Now, Daphne. If you wouldn't mind. And this time, don't forget the milk.'

Miss Bannister closed the door behind Daphne.

'A nice girl,' commented Cora.

'Very nice. But she's all fingers and thumbs, poor thing. Not like you, dear,' added Miss Bannister. 'You were always so efficient.'

Cora laughed.

'That's not how I remember it.'

'Such a terrible thing, this war. You know, I'd always hoped you'd stay on, and buy the business when I retired.'

'So had I. But with William and Grace away . . .'

'I know, dear, duty calls. But you're very much missed.'

'Well . . . perhaps when the war's over I'll be able to come back,' volunteered Cora.

She didn't dwell on her frustration at having to give up her job. It might not be much to Grace, but Cora had loved her job in the shop. She'd been working there for years, knew the business inside out. She'd been saving hard against her dream of one day buying the business herself.

Not that William or his stuck-up wife had cared a jot for her plans, thought Cora. They were too busy thinking about their own.

'Mrs Killip's daughter's expecting, you know,' commented Miss Bannister, folding a set of damask napkins and putting them away.

'Really?'

'It's due in October, apparently, and she was only saying the other day how she wished you were here to help choose a pattern for the matinee jackets.'

'Oh, I'm sure she can manage very well on her own. Eileen Killip has excellent taste.'

'Ah, but then there's all the material to find for Helen Joughin's bridesmaids' dresses . . . She's so terribly particular, and in wartime one needs to be so much more resourceful.'

Cora laughed. It was nice to be heaped with praise.

'Oh, you just need to be firm with her,' she smiled. 'Or she'll only keep insisting on the pink, and you know how self-conscious that poor red-haired niece of hers is! The emerald-green would look pretty.'

'Yes, but Helen Joughin's mother won't have anything green in the house. Her husband brought home the first car in the village and she made him send it back because it was green. It's the bad luck, you see.'

Cora chuckled.

'Ah well, who'd get married?' Not me, she told herself, I value my independence too much. But whenever she thought of James McArthur she wasn't quite so sure.

'I had offers,' nodded Miss Bannister, 'but, well . . . by then I had my own life to lead. Ah – here's Daphne with the tea. Be careful with that tray, those cups seem rather over-full . . .'

After tea and a long chat, Cora consulted her watch. 'I'd best be on my way. There's tea to cook, and Bonzo to take for his evening walk, and we're expecting the internees tomorrow, you know.'

The smile faded slightly from Evie Bannister's face, and she took hold of Cora's hand.

'Now you will be careful won't you, dear?'

'Careful?'

'Just don't be too trusting. I'm sure there are some good ones among them, but there's a war on, and you really can't trust anyone any more.'

'I'll be fine, really I will,' Cora assured her. 'And besides, I need the money to keep the old place going.'

She stepped out into the stillness of the evening air, and breathed in its salty tang. The sun was beginning to set, sinking in a haze of pink and orange over the western sea.

'Thank you for the tea, Evie.'

'My pleasure.' She paused. 'I hope you don't mind my saying, dear, but I did think it was unfair of Grace, leaving you in the lurch like that.'

'I'm sure she had her reasons,' replied Cora, mentally cursing her sister-in-law.

'Well, of course your brother would feel it was his duty to join up,' agreed Miss Bannister. 'But I did think Grace might have stayed to help you . . .'

Cora was almost glad she hadn't. The thought of Grace *helping* was even worse than having to muddle through on her own. At least like this, she could do it *her* way. And to judge from the state Grace had left the books in, she couldn't do much worse.

'Good night, Evie.'

'Good night, Cora – and remember what I said.'

Cora strode out along the seafront, heading towards the *Bradda Vista*.

It was so very quiet, almost unearthly save for the regular swish of the distant sea, glittering copper under the dying rays of the sun. Soon, when night fell and the blackout curtains were drawn, all would be darkness and silence. Up to now, even with the threats of invasion, the war had seemed very far away, but tomorrow it would be brought right here, to Port Erin.

Right here on Cora's own doorstep.

At about the same time, James McArthur was closing up the surgery. Evening surgery had been the usual procession of children with sick rabbits and sticky sixpences. James made it a rule never to charge a child more than sixpence – a rule which had led to acrimonious arguments with his senior partner on more than one occasion. But Gerald was away on war service now, so James could run things the way he wanted.

It was good to have an evening off at last. Alastair Goodwin, Gerald's father, had come out of retirement to help keep the practice going, and he was on call tonight. Locking the door, James walked round to the dog pen at the back.

'Hello there, Fergus, hello boy.'

The sole occupant of the pen was a dog of enormous size and indeterminate breed – a great shaggy thing with tatty ears and a hairy mop of a tail. At James's approach it got to its feet and wagged an enthusiastic welcome.

'I suppose I'd better take you for a walk, you old fleabag.'

Fergus licked his hand and he fastened on the leash.

'Poor old feller.' Fergus cocked his head on one side. You'd swear he understood every word. 'Miss your master, do you? C'mon then, let's go and see if the sea's still there.'

The sun was setting rather prettily over the sea, but then beautiful sunsets were commonplace on the western side of the Island. A few fluffy clouds made dark blotches in a sky which ranged from soft apricot to deep blood-red at the horizon.

Fergus pulled at the leash, his big floppy tongue lolling out of his mouth as he panted his enthusiasm.

'Steady on, boy, you'll drag me over,' muttered James, finding it hard to keep up.

The beach was almost deserted, the few walkers anonymous silhouettes against the sparkling sea. But one shape he thought he recognised – the figure of a woman, laughing as she played chase with a little black dog.

'Cora?' he called. The woman turned and started walking towards him, the dog haring off up the beach after some imagined shadow.

'James!' As she got nearer he saw her face. She looked pretty like that, her features picked out in light and shade and her hair glossy. And that skirt and jumper hugged her so tightly that it was impossible not to notice what a nice figure she had.

'Hello, Cora. I see Bonzo's in fine form.'

She laughed.

'He's a little monster and he knows it. He and Archie are always fighting now Archie's better.' She peered at Fergus. 'What on earth is *that*?'

James grinned.

'This is Fergus. Say hello to Miss Quine, you old reprobate.'

Right on cue, Fergus presented a paw to be shaken.

'Charmed I'm sure.' Cora gave Fergus a good scratching, and he registered his pleasure with a lick of appreciation. 'But where on earth did you find him? Is he one of your patients?'

'Not exactly. He belonged to an old chap up at Niarbyl, Ned Garew. The old chap took ill last week and died before they got him to hospital. They called me in and . . . well, no one else wanted this ugly old brute, did they, Fergus?'

'Poor thing! You'll keep him yourself then?'

'It looks as if I shall have to. No one else will have him, and

57

we've such a problem with unwanted dogs just now. What with this war, people are afraid they won't be able to feed themselves, let alone a dog. But we'll manage, won't we, Fergus?'

Turning, Cora shouted at the top of her voice.

'Bonzo, come here this minute!'

A little bundle of black fur came scudding up the beach toward them.

'You've got him well trained,' observed James.

'He only does it when he wants to!' Cora bent down and scooped Bonzo into her arms. 'Have you eaten?'

'Not yet. I thought I'd have a sandwich at the Station Hotel.'

'Why don't you come back and eat with Grandad and me? There's plenty for three.'

Elsa Nadel wasn't much given to outbursts of temper, but then she wasn't used to prison life, either – and this was the final degradation.

'I'm quite capable of going to the lavatory on my own,' she snapped.

'I'm sure you are, miss, but rules is rules,' replied the wardress.

'You could at least let me have a little privacy.'

'I'm sorry, but like I said, rules is rules. If the Governor says you have to leave the lav door open, you'll have to leave it open. Or if you're so prissy you can't face that, you'll have to wait till lock-up and use the bucket in your cell.'

'I'll die first,' Elsa muttered under her breath.

'What?'

'I said, I've never peed in a bucket in my life and I'm not about to start now.' She tried a different approach. 'Look . . . couldn't you turn your back? I mean, it's not as if I'm going to escape or anything, is it?'

'Just get on with it, will you? I'm off in half an hour, and I want you all safely locked up and packed, ready for tomorrow.'

58

'Packed? Why?' Elsa looked blankly at the wardress. 'What's happening tomorrow?'

The wardress contemplated her with folded arms.

'Didn't they tell you? They're moving you out, that's what.'

Grethe was bored. Bored, bored, bored. Whenever she'd been in prison before, she'd shared a cell. It was all right having the cell doors open, but that presupposed there was someone you wanted to visit. Elsa was OK she supposed, so was the frightened little Jewish kid, but how could she expect them to understand how she was feeling?

And she was anxious too. Really worried, though she kept it under wraps, afraid to let it explode into the violently protective love she felt for her son. Emil would be all right, she kept telling herself that over and over. The police had promised, the Governor had promised. She had to believe them. Claire would take good care of Emil, she always did.

She tried to force the black thoughts out of her head. They'd be coming to lock the doors soon, and in a way that would make her feel more secure. Being in a prison for breaking the law and being locked up, that she understood. All this other stuff, about being an 'unfriendly alien', that seemed like nonsense.

She hadn't been back to Germany in years. The apartment she'd lived in, the club where she had been a young singer, they probably didn't even exist any more. Germany was an irrelevance, and so was this bloody stupid war.

Grethe's eyes lighted on the neat pile of things on the table. A cup, a comb, a toothbrush, knitting needles and a couple of balls of dung-coloured wool. Knitting! Did they seriously expect her to sit here and knit balaclavas? In a fit of temper she picked up the needles and flung them to the floor.

It was in the silence, as she bent to pick them up, that Grethe heard the sound. It was very quiet, very muffled as though whoever was making it was trying to suppress it.

Grethe listened, her ears instinctively tuning themselves to the sound even though she was telling herself that other people's problems were none of her concern.

The sound of crying. It was the unmistakable sound of a young girl crying.

She walked out onto the landing. The door of the next cell – Rachel's cell – stood ajar. Others must be able to hear, but they were all studiously ignoring her. Bloody typical.

Grethe hesitated. Rachel's friend Sarah had already made it perfectly clear how she felt about Grethe. But Grethe had never cared about other people's opinions. She stepped forward, raised her hand, knocked softly on the door.

'Rachel? Rachel, *liebchen*, are you all right?'

The sobbing seemed to falter for a moment, but there was no reply.

'Look, tell me to go to hell if you want. I won't mind. I'm just a nosy cow who can't keep out of other people's business.'

Rachel was lying on her bed, her knees drawn up and her face pressed into the blankets.

'I'm just going to sit down here, okay?' Grethe drew up a chair and sat down. Waited. If nothing else, the life she led had made her good at waiting and listening. 'If you want to tell me about it, I'm here. If not, it doesn't matter.'

Rachel lifted her face, wiping away the tears.

'I'm sorry,' she said. 'I should be strong.'

Grethe gave a dry laugh.

'There are lots of things I should be, but I'm not.'

'But I should be strong. Not for me, but for the baby.'

'What's this all about, Rachel? Why don't you tell me?'

Rachel smoothed the dark, straggly hair back from her face, sat on the edge of the bed and wiped her eyes.

'It's Reuben's birthday today.' A tear escaped, unbidden, and ran down her cheek to the corner of her mouth.

'Oh. Oh, I'm sorry. You miss him?'

'If only I knew where he was. I don't even know if he's alive!'

'Of course he's alive!'

'How can you be so sure?'

'Rachel, the English may be many things but they aren't murderers. They don't kill people for nothing.' Leastways I hope not, thought Grethe. For Reuben's and Emil's and all our sakes, I hope not. 'He'll be fine, just you wait and see. And I don't think he'd be very pleased if he knew you were making that baby of yours miserable with all that crying!'

'No.' Rachel blew her nose loudly, and a smile twitched the corners of her mouth. 'You're right. He's always telling me I should sing happy songs to the baby, so it will be born happy . . .'

'Go on then,' said Grethe. 'Sing.'

'But what? I don't know what to sing . . .'

'It's Reuben's birthday, isn't it? Why don't we both sing Happy Birthday to him?' And she began, in her husky contralto: 'Happy birthday to you . . .'

'Oh, I couldn't!'

'Come on, Rachel. Happy birthday to you . . .'

'Happy birthday, dear Reuben . . .'

'Happy birthday to you!'

Rachel's voice tailed off, half in laughter, half in tears.

'Thank you, Grethe. I shouldn't feel so sorry for myself. You're good at cheering people up.'

I should be, thought Grethe to herself. After all, it's my job.

'Rubbish,' she said, sitting down on the bed next to Rachel. 'It's you, cheering yourself up. Now, what shall we sing next?'

Chapter 5

Joe Grimes, owner of Grimes's Reliable Coaches, stood outside the gates of Holloway Prison and scratched his head. This was the first time he'd ever been called upon to do a job like this, but then war was a funny business all round and you never knew what you might be asked to do next.

Three coaches were parked and ready, awaiting their cargo of humanity.

'Nice to see you again, Joe,' commented Sergeant Porteous, snatching a quick smoke while he had the chance.

'Pleasure, Sarge. Always a pleasure to 'elp the boys in blue, you know that.'

The Sergeant produced a packet of Woodbines and offered one to Joe.

'Much obliged, Sarge. Ain't got a light, 'ave you?'

His cigarette lit, Joe felt much more at peace with the world.

'These 'ere women . . .'

'What about 'em?'

'They dangerous, are they?'

Sergeant Porteous considered for a good long moment. He liked to be the centre of attention.

'Well, depends on what you call dangerous, don't it? I daresay the Chief Constable wouldn't have ordered us to round 'em up if they wasn't dangerous.'

'That's true.' Joe Grimes blew a smoke ring and glanced at his watch. 'It's 'alf-past. Quarter-past, I was told.'

'They'll be here soon.'

'Do you s'pose it's true, what you read in the papers? About fifth-columnists an' such?'

'Stands to reason, don't it?' pontificated Sergeant Porteous. 'If you was British and you was living in Germany, which country would you be rootin' for?'

'Britain o' course.'

'Like I said, stands to reason. Now, I ain't saying they're all bad, but that geezer in the *Daily Mail* was right: you 'ave to collar the lot, just to be sure you've got all the troublemakers.'

'S'pose you're right at that. 'Ang on though, I heard some of 'em was refugees; you know, Jews as Hitler'd kicked out of Germany.'

'Might be,' replied Sergeant Porteous enigmatically.

'Meanin'?'

'Meanin' maybe they are an' maybe they ain't. Maybe that's just what they *want* us to believe.'

'Oh.' Joe thought for a moment, mulling over the implications. 'Spies, you mean?'

'Spies, saboteurs, *agents provocateur* . . . who knows? Now, who'd suspect a woman with a kiddie, you tell me that? It's the perfect disguise. At any rate we can't take 'em at face value, can we? There's a war on. If they're innocent they'll have plenty of opportunity to prove it.'

At that moment the front door of the prison opened and a warder stepped aside to let the women out. They stepped into the grey of the afternoon hesitantly, weighed down by their suitcases and bundles.

'Luggage in the back, ladies. Hurry up, please, we haven't got all day.'

They moved slowly and for the most part quietly. Some muttered to each other in their own language, others spoke in English; some just looked plain stunned.

'Onto the coach now, do get a move on, *please*.'

'Where are you taking us?' called out one of the older women. Joe noticed with some surprise that she had a South London accent.

'Sorry, ladies, can't tell you that. Strictly hush-hush. Now *do* get along . . .'

Joe watched them file onto the coaches; old women, young women, pretty women and pregnant women. On one of the other coaches, there were even mothers who'd brought small children with them. For the most part you wouldn't look twice if you passed them in the street – these women were just plain ordinary. It was that ordinariness that struck him most of all, and he found it quite unsettling.

Because, whatever these women might be, they didn't look like spies or desperadoes.

Elsa sat huddled at the back of the coach, squashed between Inge Stresl and an enormous woman in a mink coat. Rachel and Grethe were sitting near the front, Rachel looking paler than ever and Grethe tight-lipped and furious.

'I trust when we arrive we shall be offered some place of safety for our valuables,' boomed the fat woman.

'I don't really have any valuables worth mentioning,' replied Elsa. The fat woman regarded her for a few seconds, her bejewelled earrings quivering with disbelief.

'Nonsense, my dear, of course you do. You're clearly a woman of good background.' She tapped the side of her nose. 'But of course, one might not wish to broadcast one's wealth to others less . . . ah . . . fortunate than oneself.'

'This is unforgivable,' spat Inge, her handsome face distorted by hatred. 'Locking us up with filthy Jews and their revolting children . . .'

Elsa stiffened.

'If we're all going to be locked up together, we might as well make the best of it,' she said quietly. But Inge only regarded her with contempt.

'I might have expected you to stand up for them,' she sniffed. 'Olga told me you're a communist. In Germany, they send traitors like you to Buchenwald.'

Not for the first time, Elsa felt bleak and alone. Oh, at least she wasn't entirely destitute like Rachel – she had what little money she had managed to bring with her – but that wasn't much consolation. The Nazis disliked her for not siding with them, Rachel's friend Sarah feared and despised her. How on earth were they all supposed to get along together?

She craned her neck to peer out of the coach window, but she didn't recognise where they were. She'd been in London five years, but she'd hardly ever crossed the river to north London.

Wait, though – there was the railway line, and what looked like a big main line station beyond. They were heading towards it. She recognised it vaguely, remembered the imposing stone arch.

'Euston,' someone said. 'It's Euston Station. You know what that means.'

'What?' asked her companion.

'We must be going north.'

The line of coaches drew up outside a back entrance to Euston Station, and the women disembarked.

Elsa collected her suitcase and bundle of books, and joined the long line of women and children filing into the station. Some of the smaller children looked tired and fractious, their eyes heavy-lidded. One or two of the older girls were still wearing school uniform – sixteen-year-olds interned at their boarding schools that very morning.

'It's my birthday today,' one dark-haired girl told her, as they were ushered towards the waiting train. 'I can't believe it . . .'

'We'd just finished Games,' her friend cut in. 'Rosie and me. We'd only just changed back out of our gym kit when the policewomen came. And we were going to have a party for Rosie tonight, in the dorm . . .'

'Never mind,' said Elsa. 'We'll have a party when we get there.'

'Where?' asked Anna. 'Where are they taking us?'

'We'll find out soon,' Elsa assured them. She looked ahead, wishing Grethe were here. Grethe was good with people, much better than she was, though people often seemed to cast her in the role of leader or spokeswoman. It wasn't a role she particularly relished.

Once on the platform, a large-bosomed WPC had to shout to make her voice audible above the hissing of the engine.

'Into the carriages, quick as you can now.'

Clouds of greyish-white steam swirled about the engine and the leading carriages. The train was painted in the livery of the GWR but that didn't mean anything. This was wartime. They might be going anywhere.

On a neighbouring platform a group of sailors were jostling and laughing; fresh-faced boys for the most part. Elsa wondered if they had any more idea of where they were headed than the internee women did. And thoughts of responsibility made her think of the people they – and she – had left behind: mothers and sisters, half frantic with worry, not knowing what had happened to their brothers and sons.

Elsa thought of her twin brother for the tenth time that day. Max was no longer an adolescent boy, but that didn't stop him being irresponsible. Vulnerable too, though he'd hate to know that was what she thought of him. Where was he now? Why had her letters been returned unopened? Had he been interned, too? If only she knew . . .

When her time came Elsa scrambled into a carriage with the others. Out of the corner of her eye she saw Grethe and Rachel getting into the next carriage. Rachel looked fragile; it wasn't right, making her travel on a crowded train in her condition.

'Here you are, *Fräulein*, you sit here by me.'

'*Danke schön*.' Elsa squeezed onto the end of the long bench seat. It was a compartment made for six to sit comfortably, three on either side, but right now it held ten adults and two children. They belonged to the woman who had invited Elsa to sit down – a babe in arms and a brown-haired boy of about five, smartly turned-out in a blue sailor suit with knickerbockers and buckle shoes.

'It is like a mad-house!' commented Frau Ziegler, the harassed-looking young mother. 'If we only knew where we were going . . .'

Inge snapped from the seat opposite:

'As long as it is far away from this *Judenschule*, I couldn't care less!'

'Mutti, Mutti, what is a *Judenschule*?' piped up the small boy. Flustered, his mother ruffled his hair.

'Never you mind, Fredi. Just you keep still now. We'll soon be there.'

'Are we going to Pappi now, Mutti? Will we go where they have taken Pappi?'

Elsa saw the young woman turn her head away, as though she did not want her child to see her lie.

'Soon,' she soothed the child, her voice soft and distant. 'Soon we'll see your Pappi again.'

'Want to sit down, want to sit down.' The boy scrabbled at his mother's skirts.

'Here, you can sit on my knee,' said Elsa, holding out her hands. The boy climbed up onto her lap without a moment's hesitation, too young to have learned the habit of mistrust.

Somewhere in the cacophony of chatter and argument and hissing steam, a whistle sounded. Police uniforms moved about in the corridors, shadowy figures barking out orders. Elsa thought she heard someone say the word 'Liverpool', but it was hard to make out what anyone was saying over the thump and slosh of the blood pounding in her veins.

Then she felt the train lurch and, looking out of the window, saw the platform beginning to recede into the distance; at first slowly, then faster and faster until at last it had disappeared from view.

The deep royal-blue of twilight had almost faded to the

blackness of night as Minnie Driver walked home through the Liverpool streets.

She was almost thirteen; impatient to be old enough to leave school and get a proper job. Already she helped out in her parents' pub, collecting empties in return for pocket money. *And* she had a sweetheart, though her mam would've slapped her face if she knew about Eddie . . .

Humming softly to herself, she turned into Cooper Street and noticed that a crowd had gathered; twenty or thirty standing near the far end of the street, others standing on their doorsteps. Everyone was still, silent – unnaturally so. Even the kids had stopped playing. Beyond the front row of people Minnie could see the distinctive shape of police helmets. She walked up to a woman in a red turban and asked:

'What's goin' on, Ena?'

The woman folded raw, red arms.

'Comin' this way, aren't they?'

'Who?'

'The Nazis. Them German women they've rounded up.'

'Oh.'

'Our Gary's mate's a copper,' cut in a thin teenage girl, standing next to her. 'He says they're puttin' them on a boat tonight. They're marchin' them down to Pier Head from Lime Street station.'

'Good bloody riddance an' all,' commented a woman two doors down. 'I got two boys an' a husband in France.'

The door of the 'Flying Angel' pub opened and four or five men in shirt sleeves swaggered out, pint glasses of beer in their hands. They joined the group at the end of the street. Minnie glanced around, feeling suddenly very uncomfortable. It was like standing in the middle of a lynch mob, you could feel the hatred buzzing in the air.

'They're 'ere, I can see 'em coming,' announced one of the men, balancing the beer glass in his right hand as though weighing up its possibilities as a missile. A woman next to him had a bowl of rotten fruit. The intention was obvious.

69

Minnie felt very cold. She didn't want to be here any more, yet she couldn't just turn and walk away. There was a horrible fascination which kept her rooted to the spot. Minnie didn't know a lot about the war, but she guessed where the women must be headed. Everyone knew that internment camps were being set up on the Isle of Man. She wondered if the internee women knew, too . . .

More people had gathered now, pushing and shoving to get a better viewpoint, so that she was forced forward.

'Calm down, calm down,' boomed a policeman's voice.

'Get out the way, an' let us at 'em,' shouted a woman from the back. The crowd surged forward, throwing Minnie against a man in front. The police linked arms, forming a barrier between the crowd and the column of women walking, heads down, towards them.

'That's right, let us 'ave 'em and we'll teach 'em a lesson they won't forget.'

'Nazi bitches!' screeched a woman's voice.

'Now come on, why don't you all go home, eh?' urged an elderly police sergeant. 'There's nothing to see.' But soothing words fell on deaf ears. 'Get back, get back, will you?'

All at once, Minnie felt very sorry for the women she saw before her; some carrying children and suitcases as the police forced a way for them through the crowd of boorish men and hostile, snarling women. War was war, that was what her dad was always saying, but this didn't seem right, it really didn't.

Rachel had been afraid many times in the last few years, but fear did not get any easier to deal with.

They had spent what seemed like years on that darkened, overcrowded train, stopping and starting so many times that Rachel had begun to wonder if the whole journey was some never-ending nightmare. When, finally, they'd arrived at their destination she had been utterly exhausted, almost fit to drop.

'Come on, Rachel, it won't be long now. Give me your suitcase.'

'No, Grethe, it's all right really, I can manage . . .'

'Give it here.' Grethe was not one to take no for an answer. 'I can easily manage both.' She turned to the WPC walking almost alongside them. 'Look, officer, my friend here is worn out, you can see she's expecting a baby . . .'

The WPC took Rachel's arm.

'You all right, dear? You do look pale. Do you need an ambulance?'

Rachel stiffened. No, no, not that. She wasn't being parted from Grethe, no matter what.

'I . . . I'm fine. Just a little tired. Must we go much further tonight?'

The WPC shook her head.

'Not too far.'

'But where . . . ?'

'You'll soon find out.'

The march through the streets of Liverpool, down to Pier Head, was relatively uneventful until they turned into Cooper Street. Half the town seemed to be waiting for them there, the crowd surging forward in a tidal wave of hatred.

'Nazi bitches!' screeched the woman close to Grethe. Grethe turned and stared her straight in the eye, daring her to say it again. She put her arm round Rachel's shoulders.

'Come on, don't listen. She's an ignorant cow.'

But the whole crowd was joining in now, voices mingling in a chorus of blame and intolerance.

'Let us at them!'

'Spies!'

A man in the crowd spat at them, and a blob of frothy white spittle hit Grethe on the cheek. She did not even dignify his action by wiping it away, simply walking on, trying not to look or listen.

'Traitors!'

'Lock 'em up . . .'

71

Head down, Rachel huddled against Grethe's shoulder as soldiers with fixed bayonets forced a path for them through the crowd.

'Nazis, Nazis, filthy Nazis . . .'

A hand clawed at Rachel's shoulder, the voice chanting mockingly in her ear. It was more than she could bear.

'No!' Rachel swung round, her dark eyes aflame and her pale cheeks red with anger. 'We are not Nazis, I am a Jew, *Ich bin Jude*, don't you understand?'

'Nazis, filthy Nazis . . .' the chant went on.

'Why don't they understand, Grethe, why don't they?'

'It's all right,' replied Grethe, with a grim cheerfulness which masked her own angry pain. 'We'll make them understand, just you see if we don't.'

Piet de Maas watched with mixed feelings as a long line of women and children boarded the *Princess Josephine Charlotte*.

Only weeks ago, the Belgian cross-channel steamer had been making routine trips between Britain and the Low Countries, carrying on as normal despite the threat from Hitler's armies.

She had been berthed in Ostend harbour on the day Belgium fell. Almost at the last moment, the Belgian government had ordered the captain of the *Princess*, Master Aspislorch, to take on refugees and sail for Britain.

And so it was that Piet found himself stranded far from home, far from everything he had ever known or cared about. Whatever else he might have expected from the war, he hadn't expected to be making repeated trips across the Irish Sea, delivering internees to their imprisonment on the Isle of Man.

He looked at the children and it broke his heart to see them clutching their mothers' hands, trusting as only children trust, not understanding about war and its savagery. Piet had children too: two boys and a girl, left behind with their mother Antje in Bruges. And now he had no way of knowing if he would ever see them again.

A cold wind was blowing up the Mersey, churning the sludge-coloured waters into spiky-crested waves. It would be a choppy crossing tonight, he told himself, feeling the vessel move beneath him. A difficult crossing, and a stormy dawn.

It was pitch-black when the *Princess Josephine Charlotte* left the mouth of the Mersey estuary and began its journey across the open sea.

Grethe stood alone at the stern of the boat, not really noticing the salt spray as it lashed her face, turning her blonde hair into thin wet strands which whipped her bare skin like wire.

Looking down in the darkness, she could just make out the ship's wake, a creamy mass disappearing into the blackness as they left land far behind. It was certainly rough on the sea tonight, the ferry rising and falling on a mountainous swell as it cut a furrow through the dark water. Rachel had been sick, and for a little while Grethe and Elsa had been very concerned about her, but at last she had drifted off into a deep sleep, huddled below decks under one of Elsa's blankets.

Grethe was glad that Rachel had Elsa to look after her, too. Somewhere deep inside herself, Grethe was very afraid of not being strong enough. There was always someone who needed to be cared for, someone who depended upon you to be strong.

Like Emil. She bit her lip as the ache of separation gnawed at her again. She was violently angry with herself for not foreseeing that this would happen, not making the proper provisions to ensure that he would be safe. She knew that Claire would do her best for him, she had promised, but even so, there were dangers . . . And it was so very hard for any mother to entrust her child to the care of another, even a friend as good as Claire. Soon, young Rachel Kotkin would understand that too.

'Grethe . . . cold . . . inside.'

Only a few of the words actually reached Grethe's ears, so strong was the buffeting wind, but she turned round, leaning her back against the rail. Elsa was standing on deck beside her, one hand holding her coat tightly closed and the other trying to prevent her hat from flying away.

'Grethe, what are you doing out here? You'll catch your death of cold, come inside.'

'I'm all right. I just wanted some fresh air.'

'Fresh!' Elsa laughed, the wind catching her laughter and throwing it into the encircling night. She stood beside Grethe, and they gazed into the darkness, picking out the occasional star as the gusts of wind parted the clouds.

'How's Rachel?'

'Still sleeping. Her friend Sarah's watching her, just in case, and one of the German midwives says she'll be fine.'

'That's good.'

'So – where do you suppose we're going? Ireland?'

'Not Ireland. Why would they send us there?'

'Ireland is neutral.'

'True, but the English don't trust the Irish. They believe they're all spies, in league with the Germans.'

'They see spies everywhere,' sighed Elsa.

Grethe looked at her sharply.

'Do you blame them? Really blame them? After what is happening in Holland, Belgium, France . . . ?'

'No. No, I suppose not. So where do you think we're going, then?'

'Scotland, perhaps.'

'Scotland! My brother Max was in Scotland, when I last heard from him. Do you suppose . . . ?'

'Or the Isle of Man.'

'The Isle of Man!'

'I heard they were thinking of sending some of the men

there. So why not send us there too? Keep us all locked up on the same island, out of mischief?'

The Isle of Man, thought Elsa to herself. I don't even know where it is, let alone what it's like. But maybe I soon shall . . .

Chapter 6

Cora yawned as she drew back the curtains. She hadn't slept well, despite the toddy of whisky and hot water her grandfather had prescribed. Thomas Quine was a great advocate of the restorative properties of whisky, and always kept some in an old medicine bottle beside his bed.

'Storm's died down,' announced Thomas, as she came into the kitchen. 'There's sea-wrack and dead jellyfish all over the beach. I'll take a bucket down later – the wrack's terrible good for the garden.'

'It must have been a rough crossing last night,' remarked Cora, gazing out through the kitchen window at the fluffy remnants of cloud scudding across the watery blue sky. She thought of poor Uncle Harry, his apprentice Petey and the rest, crewing the *Mary Jane* – one of the thousands of 'little ships' that had answered the call to rescue British soldiers from the French beaches.

'Aye, I'd as soon not have been out on the sea on a night like that,' conceded Thomas, rummaging in his waistcoat pocket for his tobacco pouch.

'I wonder if the internees arrived safely in Douglas.'

Thomas shrugged, affecting not to care one way or the other. At almost seventy-five years of age, Thomas Quine reckoned to have seen just about everything – wars, revolutions, four different monarchs. He'd been in the merchant navy during the first lot, when the Jerries were interned over Knockaloe way, and he still reckoned that a man who could sit out the war in an internment camp was a lucky man.

It wasn't quite so easy to harden his heart to the women and children, even if they would most probably sell their own grandmothers for the sake of the Fatherland. Thomas had made up his mind to hate them all, especially after hearing what was happening at Dunkirk. These women deserved worse than being locked up. And yet . . .

Thomas turned to the back page of his newspaper.

'We'd have heard on the radio if they hadn't.'

'You're probably right.' Cora reached down her apron from its hook on the back of the door, and slipped it on over her head. 'Goodness knows, I've had a few rough crossings to Liverpool in my time. Now, you'll be wanting your breakfast . . .'

She walked into the pantry and opened the meat safe, watched with interest by Bonzo.

'Shoo, boy, you'll get yours in a minute.'

Inside the meat safe reposed two pairs of kippers and a few rashers of fatty bacon. It was hardly enough to feed a houseful of internees; still, until everything had been properly sorted out with the camp authorities, they'd all have to make do. But she'd heard that some of the women were Jewish. What if they insisted on kosher food? And what if they brought in meat rationing, like on the mainland? Her head reeled with the enormity of what she'd taken on.

'Bacon or kippers?' she called into the kitchen.

'Nice piece of fat bacon would go down a treat.' There was nothing Thomas Quine liked better than a thick slice of belly-pork, or bacon so fatty the meat was scarcely more than a couple of pink streaks. 'Lines your stomach of a morning, so it does.'

Cora brought out the greaseproof packet of bacon and took a frying pan from one of the kitchen cupboards. It gleamed, like everything else in Cora's kitchen. Lighting the gas, she dragged the pan onto the hob, dropped in the bacon and stood back, wiping her hands on a tea-towel.

'I'm sure it can't be good for you, all that fat,' she

commented. 'And it's so horrible and salty!'

'Nonsense, sticks to your ribs, keeps out the cauth,' insisted Thomas. 'And salt bacon's a wonderful thing if you're taken with the seasickness.'

Cora wrinkled her nose. If she was feeling seasick, the last thing she'd want would be greasy bacon.

'Aw, gel, it's the truth. Salt bacon and ginger beer, that's the stuff to settle your stomach when the sea's a bit rough.'

A knock on the door interrupted Thomas in full flow. Turning down the gas, Cora went to open it. Outside stood village postman George Corless.

'Mornin', missus.' He nodded in Thomas's general direction. 'Tossie.'

'Good morning, George. You're early today.' Cora accepted the letters and slipped them into her apron pocket.

'Aye, well, with the first lot of internees coming today, and all the road blocks, it's a real palaver. I thought I'd best finish my round while I can.' George sniffed the air. 'Now that's a fine bit of bacon I can smell, and no mistake . . .'

Cora laughed.

'Missed your breakfast again did you, George?'

'To tell the truth, missus, all this fresh air and exercise fair sharpens your appetite.'

'Then you'd best come in and have a bite to eat.'

'That's very civil of you, missus, very civil.'

Leaning his bicycle up against the yard wall, George wiped his boots on the scraper and stepped into the warm and fragrant kitchen. He could see at a glance that Cora had been busy. That Grace Quine wasn't much of a housekeeper, and none too friendly either, but you could see that Cora believed in doing things properly. The lino on the floor was clean and polished, and the paintwork – although yellowed with age – had obviously been washed to within an inch of its life. The old pine table had been scrubbed, and there was a jam-jar of wild flowers on the windowsill.

'Come in, George, and shut the door. There's a terrible

draught in here,' grumbled Thomas.

'Ah, 'tis fine to take the weight off my old feet,' beamed the postman, accepting a cup of tea and a slice of bread. 'Thanking you kindly, missus.' He eyed up the precious sugar ration in its china bowl then took a slurp of unsugared tea. 'That's grand, just grand.'

Cora dropped another rasher into the frying pan.

'How's Dora, George? And the girls? I saw Daphne at the shop last week.'

'Mustn't grumble. Though Dora's not happy about all this barbed wire, I can tell you.'

Cora nodded. She knew how inconvenient things were going to be, not just for the residents of Port Erin and Port Mary, but for anyone who lived just outside the camp perimeter and needed to use the village shops.

'I suppose it must be difficult for Daphne too. She'll need a permit to go and see her friends in Castletown.'

'And then there's all these extra mouths they're askin' us to feed.'

'You'll be all right though, George, with your garden?'

'Aye, most likely. Though I'd as soon not have a load of Germans taking the food out of the kids' mouths.'

Finishing off the last of his bacon sandwich, Thomas ran his finger round the plate and licked off the greasy crumbs.

'At least you don't have to share a house with 'em,' he pointed out.

'No.' George drank up his tea and wiped his mouth with the back of his hand. 'All ready for them, are you?'

'I hope so.' Cora started clearing away the dishes. 'We've moved extra beds into the rooms, and got extra bedding from the laundry . . .'

'And locked up the valuables,' added Thomas, not without satisfaction.

'Aye, well, better safe than sorry,' agreed George, jamming his cap back on his head. 'Thank you kindly, missus, and I'll bring you a couple of wood-pigeons next time I'm passin'.'

'Right you are, George, and thank you.' Cora watched George's retreating back as his bicycle wobbled off towards the main road. Then she closed the door and felt in her pocket for the mail. 'There's a letter from Great-Aunt Jane,' she said, handing it over to Thomas. 'Oh, and one from Banbury. It must be from Grace.'

She sat down at the table and slit open the envelope without enthusiasm. Cora wished she could see eye to eye with her sister-in-law. After all, Grace had had her troubles. But why did she have to be so unpleasant?

She unfolded the letter and began reading.

Dear Cora
    We are both well. William is a sergeant instructor at the training camp here and has the chance of a promotion. He is very well thought of.
    I am staying at Mum and Dad's until the promotion comes through and we can afford something better.
    Hope you are taking good care of the *Bradda Vista*. Naturally we would have found someone more experienced, but war is war and you can't always have what you want, can you?'

Quite, thought Cora. How was it that Grace managed to sound as if she was doing her a favour? And how come – war or no war – Grace always managed to do exactly as she pleased?

'How is she?' grunted Thomas, belching into his napkin.

'Same as usual,' replied Cora.

It was a little after seven in the morning when the *Princess Josephine Charlotte* began unloading its passengers onto the quayside.

Elsa, Grethe and Rachel walked up the companionway onto the deck, blinking in the morning light. It was a cool morning at the end of spring, the light clear and bright, with pale sunshine illuminating the dark mass of Douglas Head.

Elsa put down her suitcase and leant over the rail.

'It's so . . .'

'So quiet?' Grethe stood beside her, surveying the broad sweep of the bay: the long, curving promenade with its neat line of Victorian hotels; the jumble of the town, spilling back from the seafront; and the hills beyond, green-brown shapes against the morning sky. Seagulls cut across the bows of the ship, wheeling and crying as they swooped in search of food; but there was little to disturb the peaceful stillness of this May morning.

'Where are we?' asked Rachel. 'What is this place?'

'It's the Isle of Man, didn't you know?' A middle-aged internee with an Italian name and a Scottish accent pushed to the front. '"The Isle of Man for Happy Holidays", that's what the posters used to say.'

Mrs Effie Pantin knocked at the door and waited.

'Come.'

She pushed open the door and stepped into the office of Dame Joanna Cruickshank, recently appointed Commandant of the women's internment camp.

'Good morning. My name is Mrs Pantin. I have an appointment to see the Commandant.'

The woman behind the desk stood up and accepted Effie's proffered handshake.

'Miss Arnold, I'm one of the Commandant's assistants. I'm afraid Dame Joanna is busy at the moment. Perhaps I can help you.'

Effie sat down on one of Dame Joanna's very hard wooden chairs.

'You have internee women arriving today, I believe?'

'That is correct.'

'I am a member of the Society of Friends,' she explained. 'The Aliens' Emergency Committee in London has asked me to offer my services to the women's camp as a voluntary welfare worker.'

'I see.' Miss Arnold brushed a speck of dust from the sleeve of her immaculate white blouse. 'Well, as you know, the camp is under the jurisdiction of the Home Office, and we already have a staff of five highly trained administrators . . .'

'Do you really believe that a staff of five is adequate to care for several thousand women?'

'Well . . .'

Effie leaned over the desk, getting into her stride now. For a pacifist, she had quite an aggressive streak.

'And can you honestly say that administrators are qualified to deal with the personal problems of all these women?'

Miss Arnold secretly agreed with Effie Pantin, but was equally sure that Dame Joanna would not. Dame Joanna had nursed in the Great War, and had great faith in the military approach.

'And there will be problems,' added Effie. 'You can be very sure of that. There is bound to be resentment, fear, anger, a sense of injustice . . .'

'Perhaps so. But we must remember that these women are being detained in the interests of national security. Whilst some may be innocent refugees, others are undoubtedly Nazi sympathisers.'

'Nevertheless,' said Mrs Pantin quietly, 'they are all human beings. They have a right to our compassion and our prayers.'

The little steam train chugged tirelessly between Douglas and Port Erin with its cargo of internees; sliding slowly past trees and fields and hills and stations – Port Soderick, Santon, Ballasalla, Castletown . . .

Nazis, non-Nazis and Jews were squashed and jumbled together in the tiny carriages, tempers fraying from time to time into hostility.

'I don't see why they had to lock us inside the carriages,' remarked Elsa. 'We're on an island. It's not as if we could get

83

very far even if we tried to run away.'

'But it is our duty to make things as difficult as possible for them,' replied Frau Zeller, wife of a high-ranking German diplomat. 'They realise that, and they are treating us as prisoners of war.'

'You may see yourselves as prisoners of war,' retorted Grethe. 'But some of us are just trying to get by.'

'Yes, and we all know how *you* get by,' sniped Inge. 'So you needn't go trying to lecture decent people on how to behave.'

Grethe just glared. She was fed up with this internment business, fed up, scared and furious. Although she would never have admitted it, the pro-Nazi women frightened her with their bravado and their talk of resistance. It was particularly irritating that, since they had signed a declaration of loyalty to Germany, they had become entitled to special privileges normally reserved for prisoners of war.

'Oh just shut up, will you?' snapped Rachel, who had almost reached the end from exhaustion. Her eyes were red with tiredness but she could not cry. 'Just shut up, all of you! I can't bear it . . .'

The carriage fell silent for a few moments. From the next carriage floated the sounds of laughter and a German folksong.

'We're slowing down,' said one of the women, pressing her cheek hard against the glass of the carriage window. 'I think we're coming into a station.'

Sure enough, the grating of brakes announced their arrival. Fields gave way to buildings, then the dark, red-brick shape of Port Erin railway station.

'Well, it looks as if we're here,' commented Grethe. 'Wherever here may be.'

It was a long time since St Catherine's church hall had held so many people. As Dame Joanna Cruickshank stood up to address the internee women, Elsa felt as though she were back at school, being given a stern talking-to by the headmistress. Even with an interpreter, there was too much to take in all at once.

'We regret the need to detain you . . .'

'I bet,' grunted Mathilde.

'. . . but the exigencies of war demand that we must all make sacrifices. Whilst you are here at Port Erin you will be allocated to a house. You will be free to move about within the camp between the hours of eight in the morning and eight at night . . .'

'Free to move about?' Sarah was bewildered. 'Does she mean inside the house?'

'Shh. I don't know.' Rachel placed a hand on her arm. 'Listen. I'm trying to understand what she's saying.'

'You are not, however, permitted to associate with male residents of the village . . .'

Grethe could not suppress a low chuckle. She had already encountered other prostitutes from her south London 'beat', and wondered how many of them would heed the Commandant's instructions. And if they didn't, what could the Commandant do – put them in prison?

'Mr Newell here is an Anglican curate. He will be visiting all the houses to offer pastoral care . . .'

Grethe looked him up and down. He was young – too young to be a priest. Too young to know anything. And in any case, what did God have to say to her? They hadn't seen eye to eye for years.

'Miss Arnold will be allocating accommodation to each of you. She will give you each a slip of paper bearing the name of an hotel or guesthouse. You will go there directly . . .'

Grethe pushed forward.

'What about our children?'

Dame Joanna looked surprised.

'I beg your pardon?'

'Our children. Some of us were forced to leave our children.'

Miss Arnold took Grethe's arm and led her to one side.

'You have a child?'

'A boy – Emil. They made me leave him in London.'

'Arrangements will be made.'

'What sort of arrangements?'

'Arrangements will be made to bring your child to the camp. In fact, all the children who have been parted from their mothers.'

'When?'

'Soon. I cannot say exactly when, but soon. You have my word.'

At the other side of the hall, a small, thin woman in a tweedy suit was handing out slips of paper. Grethe took hers and read: *Empress*. Frau Zeller stepped forward, swathed in mink. Her piece of paper read *Empress* too.

'I absolutely refuse to be sent to the same place as this degenerate,' snarled Frau Zeller.

'Don't worry, I'd rather share with Adolf Hitler,' retorted Grethe, screwing up the piece of paper and throwing it on the floor. 'Send me somewhere else.' The tweedy woman's lips pursed in annoyance.

'Ladies, please, if you would just be patient . . .'

Elsa held out her piece of paper.

'Rachel and I have been given *Bradda Vista*. Couldn't Grethe come with us?'

'Please.' Rachel looked so small and perilously pregnant that the official felt her iron resolve softening. 'Grethe has been very kind to me.'

'I will go to the *Empress* in your place,' volunteered Nurse Imhof.

'Oh very well! But your landladies *must* inform the camp office of any transfers between houses . . .'

Relieved, Rachel turned to look for her friend Sarah. But Sarah had crossed the hall and was talking very earnestly to a group of Jewish students, refusing to look at her. Rachel walked across to her and touched her on the shoulder.

'Sarah.'

Sarah gave her half a look then glanced away.

'Please, Sarah.'

She felt Sarah tense then relax. Their eyes met.

'I've been given *Bradda Vista*, Sarah. Where are you going?'

'The *Rowany Glen*.'

'Why not come with us? I'm sure we could persuade them to let you.'

'Rachel, you will be all right now. You're safe. You have your new . . . friends.'

'Why do you hate them so much?'

'I don't hate them. If you can be friendly with them, then that's your affair. You saw what their kind did to me.'

'If that is really how you feel . . .'

'It is. And anyway, they say the *Rowany Glen* is a kosher hotel. You're not kosher, you and Reuben are liberal. You'll be happier where you are.'

'Yes. Yes . . . but we'll still be friends, won't we? We went through so much . . .'

On impulse Sarah took her hand.

'Of course. Now you look after yourself, you hear? Look after yourself for Reuben, or I'll want to know the reason why.'

Port Erin had never seen anything like it. Hundreds of women, some with children in tow, were wandering about, trying to find the right hotels.

Elsa, Grethe and Rachel made their way onto the promenade. Port Erin was hardly bigger than a largish village, but it extended along and around a wide, almost square bay. To the left was Mull Hill, rising above the Marine Biological Station and the remains of the old Victorian breakwater. In the distance, to the right, were Spaldrick Bay and Bradda Glen, and further on the imposing, rocky mass of Bradda Head, with Milner's Tower standing sentinel over the little town. The morning sun glinted off a calm, green-blue sea which lapped gently at the ribbed golden sand of a wide, sandy beach.

'I don't believe this,' said Elsa. 'They lock us up like criminals and then suddenly they let us loose to find our own way, without so much as a map. It's almost like . . .'

'Like being free?' suggested Grethe. 'But walk a mile or two in any direction and there's barbed wire. And on this side,' she gazed out to sea. 'Nothing between here and Ireland. So if you were thinking of swimming for it, I'd give it a miss.'

'But the air smells so fresh and sweet.' Rachel threw back her head and filled her lungs. 'If only Reuben . . .'

'I know.' Grethe gathered up Rachel's bags and parcels. 'Come on, eh? Let's find out where that dreadful woman has billeted us.'

'He promised,' said Rachel softly. 'He promised we'd be together when the baby's born.'

'And you will be,' said Elsa firmly. 'If he's promised he'll be with you, I'm sure he will.'

Bonzo stood on the window-ledge in the front parlour of the *Bradda Vista*, his front paws scrabbling against the pane and his breath misting the glass.

Cora stood beside him, scratching his ear. Normally she would have told him to get off her nice clean windowsill, but today wasn't a normal day. They were both looking out at the same thing: the long, straggling procession of women and children heading towards them.

Her heart thumped like a bass drum. She'd thought she was prepared for this moment, but of course she wasn't. Questions tumbled over and over in her brain. Would they understand English? Would they be hostile and unco-operative? Would they refuse to comply with all the rules Dame Joanna had laid down for their behaviour?

She went out of the parlour into the front hall and called up the stairs:

'They're here, Grandad.'

Thomas didn't reply, though she knew he could hear her perfectly well, even with the Light Programme on full blast.

He had shut himself in the upstairs flat all day and Cora knew better than to try and prise him out.

Voices and the squeak of the front gate made her turn back to the door.

'Is this the place?' a voice asked.

'The *Bradda Vista*. See, it says the name over the door.'

'But I am a professional woman, I cannot be expected to live in such a place!'

A fourth voice cut in, a South London twang blending with the clipped German vowels.

'Well, Frau Feldmann, if you'd sooner go back to prison I'm sure it can be arranged.'

'You are *unmenschlich*, Elsa Nadel.'

'That may be,' retorted Elsa. 'But I'm also hungry, and Rachel's almost dead on her feet. Ring the doorbell.'

Cora stood in the hallway, almost hypnotised by the shadowy figures. There seemed so many, a menacing crowd. She glanced in the hall mirror. Ridiculously, it seemed more important than ever to look presentable. As the doorbell jangled, she took a deep breath and opened the door.

'Welcome,' she smiled, with only the faintest hint of a tremor in her voice. 'Welcome to the *Bradda Vista*. My name is Cora Quine. Won't you come in?'

'*Guten Tag*,' replied Frau Feldmann, pushing into the house ahead of the others. A waft of expensive perfume followed her as she swept into the hallway in her couture suit and extravagant hat. Another three well-dressed women followed close behind; it was obvious that they were friends. Cora disliked all four of them instantly. 'I shall of course be requesting a transfer to more suitable accommodation in due course.'

'You'll . . . ?' For once, Cora found herself at a loss for words.

'I am a wealthy woman with many society connections, *Fräulein*. Surely you can see that I cannot be expected to remain here.'

'There is a war on, madam. We must all accept less than perfect arrangements.'

This did not please Frau Feldmann one jot.

'I am accustomed to the best and I will have the best, *Fräulein* Quine.'

'I'm sure the Camp Commandant will be very interested to hear what you have to say,' replied Cora, wondering what Dame Joanna and Frau Feldmann would make of each other. 'But in the meantime, we'll all have to put up with each other.'

Now all the women were pushing their way into the house, jostling with suitcases and bundles, everyone talking at once – some in English, some in German, some in a language which Cora assumed must be Yiddish. A small child began to howl loudly, burying its face in its mother's skirts. Cora knew just how it must be feeling.

'*Fräulein*, my valuables. I must have a place of safety for my furs, my jewellery . . .'

'Miss Quine, my little Heini has had nothing to eat since last night . . .'

'My husband, I must know where they have taken my husband . . .'

'Who do I see about finding my brother . . . ?'

'. . . my son . . .'

'. . . my sister . . . ?'

'Is it true, *bitte* – that we may come and go as we please? That we may bathe in the sea?'

Cora held up her hands, raising her voice to be heard over the babble.

'Ladies, please!'

Fourteen pairs of eyes turned on her, all expecting the answers they wanted to hear.

'Please, you must be patient. I will try to answer all your questions, but first I shall show you to your rooms. Then we shall have lunch in the . . .'

'Miss Quine, please, Rachel is exhausted.'

Cora turned to see a small, dark-haired woman, almost lost in the babbling throng. Heavily pregnant, she was leaning against a woman with bobbed brown hair, her eyes half-closed and her face as white as paper. A blonde woman, heavily made-up, was standing beside them.

'She needs help. Poor kid's had all she can take.'

'Are you all right?' asked Cora, her heart going out to the pregnant girl. 'Do you feel ill? Shall I fetch a doctor?'

The eyes flickered open. They were dark as jet, bright and apprehensive. A child's eyes.

'Thank you. No, I am not ill. Just a little tired . . .'

And then quite suddenly, as if she knew she had reached the end of her journey, Rachel's last reserves of strength ran out. Silently she slipped from Elsa's encircling arm, her thin frame making hardly a sound as she fell to the ground, into the darkness and comfort of oblivion.

Cora knocked on the door of Room Four.

'It's Cora. Miss Quine. May I come in?'

She pushed open the door. Inside the room was rather cramped – it had never been designed to hold three people, after all – but at least it was cosy. Somehow, two double beds had been squeezed into the small space. Originally the plan had been for four women to share, two to a bed, but those who were pregnant or had small children were to be allowed a bed to themselves.

Elsa was sitting on one of the double beds, reading a book, and Rachel was propped up in the bed nearer the window, her dark hair unbound and falling over her shoulders in tangled strands. She looked tired, but not pasty-white as she had done a few hours before. There was no sign of the blonde woman.

'Are you feeling any better?' asked Cora, stepping inside and closing the door gently behind her. Not that there was much chance of giving Rachel any peace and quiet. What with arguments, banging doors, and the sounds of women

91

running up and down the stairs, the *Bradda Vista* was beginning to sound like a mad-house. She wondered what Grace would make of it all.

'Thank you, yes.' Rachel's smile made a welcome difference to her pallid face, smoothing out the hollows in those too-thin cheeks.

'Doctor Jefferson thought we should send you to the hospital,' began Cora, but Rachel's smile disappeared.

'No, please, don't send me there. You won't make me?'

Cora shook her head.

'Not if you don't want me to. But for your health's sake, for the baby's sake—?'

'I don't want them to take me away! I want to stay here.'

'It's all right, Rachel.' Elsa put down her book and went over to sit on Rachel's bed. 'No one's going to make you do anything you don't want.' Her eyes searched out Cora's. 'Are they?'

Cora sighed.

'No one wants to do that. But if you're taken ill again, Rachel, you must do whatever Dr Jefferson advises. You wouldn't want the child to come to any harm now, would you?'

Reluctantly, Rachel gave a nod of acceptance.

'I've saved you some food. Would you like something to eat now?'

'Later perhaps.'

'Some soup?'

Rachel laughed.

'You sound like Reuben. Always he is trying to make me eat. "For the baby's sake," he tells me. "For our baby's sake you must do this!"'

'Reuben is your husband?'

Rachel nodded, suddenly silent again.

'She doesn't know where he is,' explained Elsa. She wanted to add that she didn't know where Max was either, but it seemed a selfish thing to do when Rachel's problems were a

92

thousand times worse than hers. 'She needs to know – wants him to be with her when the time comes for her to have the baby. Is there some way . . . ?'

'I don't know,' Cora admitted. She knew that many male aliens had already been interned in camps on the Island, but there were also many more thousands in camps on the mainland. In any case, the Home Office had decreed that – for the time being at least – the women should have no access to newspapers, radio or even letters. Even between internment camps on the Island there was no provision for communication. It seemed a harsh thing to do, harsh and foolish – the stuff of which rumours were born; but it wasn't Cora's place to question Home Office policy, just to carry it out. 'You would need to ask the Commandant . . .'

She got up to go.

'You must come and find me if Rachel needs anything.'

'You are very kind.'

Elsa and Cora exchanged glances, weighing each other up, each wondering if they could afford any small measure of trust. With the war going so badly for Britain, and a different invasion scare every single day, it was hardly surprising that suspicion should have become a way of life.

'Where is your other friend?' enquired Cora.

'Grethe?' It still surprised Elsa to think of Grethe as her friend, yet the unlikely trio seemed to have been thrown together for good or ill. 'She has gone to put her money in the camp bank.'

Cora had heard that the authorities were going to allow the Isle of Man Bank to open a special branch in Port Erin, for use by the internees.

'I see some of the others have gone shopping already!' she commented.

Elsa shrugged.

'There are some who have money to waste.' She glanced at Rachel knowing full well that she had nothing beyond two Dutch silver guilders, wrapped up in a twist of paper. 'But the rest of us must save what we have. When will we be free to earn our living again?'

When indeed? thought Cora. When would any of them know freedom again?

Chapter 7

As May melted into the warm days of early June, several more boatloads of internees arrived on the Island. Almost overnight, the little villages of Port Erin and Port St Mary found their populations increased four times over. The *Bradda Vista* and the *Ben-my-Chree* were full to bursting, with women sharing three or four to a room. Hardly surprising, then, that all was not sweetness and light.

That was what Cora told herself as she came out of the chemist's shop with a bottle of embrocation for Rachel Kotkin's aching back. If everyone was like the occupants of Room Four, things wouldn't be so bad – but it had soon become obvious that a few internees were determined to make life difficult for the rest.

She pushed open the door of the butcher's shop on the corner of Station Road.

'Morning, Bobby.'

Bobby Knox looked up from his chopping board, wiped his hands on his apron and came across.

'Mornin', missus. What can I do for you today?'

'Half a pound of that salt bacon if you have it. The sort Grandad likes so much.'

Bobby laughed.

'Ach, 'tis terr'ble greasy, wouldn't touch it myself.' He flipped the rashers onto the scales then wrapped them up. 'I put a couple extra in there, seein' as you're good customers.'

'Thank you. Oh, about the meat order for the internees.'

'Somethin' wrong with it?'

'No, nothing wrong. Only, could you send me an extra pound of mince and not so many sausages?'

Bobby scratched his head.

'Mince is more expensive.'

'Yes, I know. But one or two of the women can't eat pork, you see.'

'You'd've thought they'd 'a' took what they was given an' be grateful.'

If only it was that simple, thought Cora, searching her purse for an elusive silver 'Joey'. She found it and added it to the small pile of change on the counter.

'You'll send it round on Thursday?'

'The boy'll bring it round before the shop opens. Now, anythin' else, is there? Couple of white puddings? Fresh-made today . . .'

The door bell jangled and Cora glanced around to see Fenella Kneen, rosy-cheeked in muddy boots, check shirt and dungarees.

'Morning, Bobby – morning, Cora, wondered where you'd been hiding yourself.' Fenella dumped a basket of eggs on the counter. 'There you are, Bobby, four dozen hen and a dozen duck. Dad says you can pay him Saturday week.'

'Much obliged, Fenella. You'll take a cup o' tea with the wife? She's only out the back.'

Fenella shook her head.

'Can't stop, Bobby, have to get back to the farm.'

'Be seein' you then, gel.'

Cora and Fenella left the shop together.

'How's life?' asked Cora. 'I haven't seen you since before the camp opened.'

'Oh you know, not bad, not bad. And you?'

'Sometimes I feel more like a referee than a landlady.'

'Trouble with the women?'

'Most of them are fine, all they want is to get on and make the best of it. But there are one or two complete bitches. All they seem to enjoy is giving the others a hard time. And me,'

96

she added, pulling a face. 'Two of them had a fight in the dining room last night – I had to practically pull them apart.'

'Sounds bloody awful. I don't know how you stick it.'

'I suppose I'm just muddling through.' Cora chuckled. 'I'll say one thing – Evie's glad the internees are here.'

'Evie Bannister? Why?'

'Because they've been spending so much money in her shop! There's hardly anything for them to do, so they've all started knitting and sewing.'

'I thought they were allowed to go swimming and go for walks and things.'

'Oh, they are. But you can't spend every day on the beach, can you?'

'It's a pity there's nothing useful for them to do.'

'Well, there's the cooking. They get paid for that, so of course everyone wants to do it. We had a few burnt offerings before we found somebody who really could cook.'

'Actually I'm glad I bumped into you,' said Fenella as they strolled back to where she had parked the farm van. 'I've got some news.'

'It's not your dad is it? He's not ill again?'

'No, no, he's fine. And since he took on two more men he doesn't really need me. So I've decided to get off my backside and see a bit of life.'

Cora looked at her quizzically.

'Life? What do you mean?'

'I've signed up for the ATS as a driver.'

'You've leaving the Island?'

'Next week.'

Cora was stunned. She'd been at school with Fenella Kneen, had never imagined her as anything other than Farmer Kneen's daughter.

'Don't look so horrified! You know I love driving, and I'm fed up with Dad telling me farming's men's work – after all I've done to help him keep the farm going. I want to show him what I can do.'

'You're sure you're doing the right thing?'

'Who knows?' shrugged Fenella. 'But there's a war on, and I'm damn well not staying here to rot.'

'It was your turn to wait at table,' sniffed Mathilde Kohl, noisily dumping a pile of dirty dishes on the draining board in Cora's kitchen.

'I did it yesterday,' retorted Inge Stresl, pushing back the cuticles on her pretty nails. She cast a disdainful glance at the girl who was busily scraping leftover food into the pig-bin. 'If you ask me, the *Saujuden* should do all the dirty work around here.'

The girl turned to face her, eyes blazing.

'Don't you dare speak to me like that!'

Inge's lip curled into a smile; she was pleased that her words had provoked such an instant reaction.

'Like what, *Saujude*?'

'Don't call me that word!'

'What word is that, Jew-pig?'

'My name is Lena.'

'Oh, so it speaks, does it, the little Jew-pig?'

Inge was really enjoying herself. All the bitter resentment she felt at being cooped up in the back of beyond came spilling out. Decent women, locked up with tarts and Jews and dissidents – it wasn't right.

Lena returned her contemptuous sneer with a look of pure venom.

'I don't have to listen to this,' she said quietly. 'Not from some jumped-up Austrian parlour maid.'

That was enough to turn hostility into hatred. Inge took a couple of steps forward, but Lena stood her ground.

'You should count yourself lucky the Führer threw you out of Germany when he did,' hissed Inge. 'You know what they do to your kind in Germany, don't you?' Her voice was quietly taunting. '*Don't you?*'

Lena turned away, determined not to let her rage lead her

to acts of folly, but Mathilde's hand seized her by the shoulder and spun her round.

'Look at your betters when they're talking to you, *Saujude*,' snapped Mathilde.

'Get your hands off me! Off, do you hear?' In a violent outburst of utter revulsion, Lena pushed her away. But Mathilde pushed back, forcing her against the sink. A plate slipped from the pile on the draining board and fell to the floor with a clinking of broken china.

'Don't you cheek me, you little . . .'

'Little what? Go on, tell me.'

'You know what you are. Your sort disgust me. You deserve to be put down, like the animals you are.'

'That's right,' agreed Inge. 'Already Germany has driven the British out of France. How long do you think it will be before France falls? And then Britain?'

Mathilde gave Lena a second push, catching her off-balance so that she had to save herself from falling by catching at the corner of the table. Inge looked on, laughing. Neither of them noticed Elsa coming into the kitchen with a tray of teacups.

Elsa dumped the tray on the table with a cry of outrage.

'Leave her alone – *lass doch*, do you hear? *Sofort!*'

Mathilde and Inge turned, their game checked as much by surprise as by any sense of guilt. Inge took several steps toward Elsa.

'Well, well, if it isn't the Jew-lover.'

'You should be ashamed of yourselves. Get away from her, leave her be.'

'What's it got to do with you? You're the one who should be ashamed. Traitors like you make me sick.'

'I said, leave her be.'

Lena looked from her tormentors to Elsa and back again.

'I can speak for myself,' she said, pushing away Mathilde. 'I can take care of myself.'

Elsa stared at her.

'But I was only . . .'

'Keep out of this. Please. Don't you understand? It's got nothing to do with you.'

'I'm sorry, I thought . . .'

'Well, don't think. I don't need your help, I don't want your help. Just leave me alone, *all of you*. Leave me alone!'

Cora burst into the kitchen like an avenging angel, only to be greeted by a sudden silence, so thick and acrimonious you could have cut it with a knife.

'What's going on in here?' she demanded. She looked around the kitchen. Lena was on her knees by the sink, picking up pieces of broken china. 'Lena?'

But Lena avoided her gaze.

'I broke a plate. I am sorry.'

'That girl's so clumsy,' commented Inge. 'You should make her pay for it.'

Cora felt exasperation rising inside her like some suffocating gas. She wasn't blind and she wasn't stupid. She knew the tensions in this place were never bubbling far beneath the surface. But how could you even begin to sort things out if people wouldn't speak to you?

'Won't anyone tell me what happened?' Her eyes sought out Elsa's, imploring rather than demanding an explanation. 'Elsa?'

Elsa felt Inge's blue eyes boring into her. But it took more than some boneheaded girl to frighten her. No, what made her hesitate before answering was the look on Lena's face.

'It was nothing. Really . . . just a private disagreement.'

Cora looked at her quizzically. She'd known Elsa Nadel for only a few days, but long enough to think of her as a potential ally. Someone sensible and educated. Certainly not someone who'd side with the likes of Inge Stresl. Cora folded her arms across her chest.

'I know you must think of me as an enemy,' she began. 'But I'm just trying to do my best for everyone. It's not easy for any of us . . .'

'But we are prisoners,' said Lena, getting to her feet. 'And you are free.'

Free? thought Cora. Living behind barbed wire? Hardly.

'I'm sure it won't be for long,' she hazarded.

'How long?'

'I don't know. Until it's safe for you to be released. Or until the war is over . . .'

The distant jangling of the doorbell gave Elsa the chance she had been looking for.

'I'll go,' she said hastily, glad of the chance to escape.

James McArthur stood on the doorstep of the *Bradda Vista*, Fergus at his heels.

This was the first time he had come to visit Cora since the internees had arrived, and he scarcely knew what to expect. Subconsciously, he realised that he had been keeping his days as full as possible, avoiding this first encounter with the enemy.

The news from the Continent was disturbing: British soldiers trapped like rats on the beaches, Manx ships lost in the rescue operation, and Alfie Gawne's younger son among the dead. James glanced down at the walking stick which accompanied him everywhere.

Soon, when his damned leg got better, he'd be in uniform with the rest of them. But soon wasn't soon enough.

He rang the bell. He could hear women's voices, and suddenly realised how quiet the boarding house had been before. Footsteps came along the hallway and he heard the latch click back. Even before the door was properly open Fergus was inside, his hairy bulk barging into the house.

'Hello, Cora, sorry about Fergus's muddy feet. I just thought . . . oh, hello.'

Turning back, he saw that it wasn't Cora who had opened the door. A tall woman in her mid-thirties was standing behind it.

So – this must be one of Cora's internees. She was certainly very different from Cora, James mused. Whereas Cora wore her wavy, golden-brown hair shoulder-length and neatly rolled, this stranger's nut-brown locks were dead straight and bobbed at the jawline. The cropped style was severe and boyish, but it suited her strong features. Her clothes were different to Cora's, too – not neat and flowery and feminine, but simple and practical. She was wearing green fitted trousers and a plain beige sweater which showed off her athletic figure.

'Good evening,' she said, in perfect English with a cultured German accent. 'Can I help you?' Her eyes were fixed on Fergus's ungainly antics as he rolled about on the hall carpet. James followed her gaze.

'He has no manners, that dog.' He tugged at the leash and reluctantly Fergus rolled over onto his belly and sat up on his haunches, panting enthusiastically. James held out his hand, the gesture tentative and awkward. 'James McArthur. I've come to see Miss Quine.'

Their eyes met. Of course, he had seen the women walking about the village, but seeing wasn't the same thing as meeting. Elsa accepted his handshake. Her touch felt warm yet hesitant.

'If you will please wait here, I will find Miss Quine for you.'

'Thank you.' He watched her walking back down the hallway towards the kitchen. From upstairs he could hear the sounds of women arguing noisily in German, and the impatient grizzling of a tired child. How on earth was Cora coping with all this?

A few moments later Cora appeared, taking off her apron. Her face flushed with pleasure as she saw him.

'James! I wasn't expecting you.'

'I thought I'd pop in and check up on Archie. Well, to be honest I was wondering how you were getting on.'

Cora raised her eyes to the ceiling.

'Teething troubles. Some of them hate each other, but I suppose that's inevitable.' She beamed at James, genuinely delighted to see him. 'What did you make of Elsa then?'

'Elsa?'

'Elsa Nadel – the woman who let you in. She's a pharmacist, you know. She's wasted locked up in this place.'

James nodded thoughtfully.

'Still, I suppose the Home Office has its reasons.' He wondered what they were. Enemy or not, there was something he'd liked about Elsa Nadel.

'She's talking about organising some educational classes for the women,' Cora explained as they walked up to the flat she shared with Grandad Quine. 'Perhaps you could help by giving them a talk about animals or something.'

'Perhaps, I don't know.' James followed one step behind, still not quite sure how he felt about all this. 'But I suppose I could think about it . . .'

Chapter 8

'How about you, Grethe?'

Elsa tucked her blouse into the top of her shorts and turned back to look at Grethe. The solitary figure in the double bed groaned, grunted and rolled over. A hand emerged and pulled back the bedclothes, just a fraction.

'What time is it?'

'Almost seven. I've been awake for hours. It's a beautiful day.'

Grethe pulled a face.

'Get up before ten? Never!'

'You'll miss breakfast,' commented Rachel, who was knitting by the open window.

'Then I shan't be missing much,' retorted Grethe.

'You should count yourself lucky we have a decent landlady,' Elsa chided her. 'At the *Rowany Glen* they get fed nothing but macaroni and kippers.'

Grethe kicked back the blanket.

'I'm awake now, I'll never get back to sleep.'

'Good! You can come down to the beach with me for keep-fit.'

'No fear. You can punish yourself if you want, I'll stay here and keep Rachel company.'

Grethe slid her long legs out from under the blanket and sat on the edge of the bed. She leant forward, examining her hair in the dressing-table mirror.

'My roots are showing. Do you suppose I could get some peroxide anywhere?'

'Why not let it grow out? It might suit you dark.'

Grethe greeted this suggestion with horror.

'*Liebchen*! I've been a blonde since I was seventeen, I'm far too old to change now.'

'Well, please yourself.' Elsa slipped an Alice band over her hair, to keep it out of her eyes. 'Oh, by the way – are there any points you want me to raise with the Commandant? Now you lot have elected me house representative, I have to prepare an agenda for the first weekly meeting.'

Grethe chuckled.

'It'll be a big agenda. I heard Frau Feldmann saying if we didn't get better food soon, she was going to complain to the International Red Cross.'

'She can complain till she's blue in the face,' replied Elsa. 'But the fact is, we have to try and keep on the right side of the Commandant if we want to get anything done.'

And that was why she'd reluctantly accepted the job of house rep – *very* reluctantly, she reminded herself, thinking back to last night's chaotic house meeting. She glanced at Rachel, but Rachel was looking out of the window, her fingers click-clacking as the length of knitting grew. 'How are you feeling, Rachel?'

The dark-haired girl turned back towards Elsa and patted her stomach.

'Stronger, thank you. Though this heat tires me out. I shall be glad when the baby's born.'

'What did the doctor say about the hospital?'

Rachel's expression darkened.

'I told him I won't go. Not unless Reuben is with me.'

'And you've still heard nothing about Reuben?'

She shook her head.

'But, Rachel,' cut in Grethe. 'Even if Reuben was here, they wouldn't let him go to the hospital with you.'

'He will be here. He promised he would.'

'I know.' Elsa tried not to let doubt creep into her voice. 'But you should do the best for you and the baby. Reuben will want both of you to be well and strong.'

'We will,' said Rachel determinedly. 'When my Reuben gets here.'

Grethe and Elsa exchanged looks.

'I'm going,' said Elsa. 'You're sure you won't . . .?'

'*Liebchen*, there are so many more interesting ways to exercise the body . . . if only we had men . . .'

Elsa thought fleetingly of the young veterinary surgeon who had visited the house a couple of days before. She wondered why he had popped into her thoughts. Probably because he'd shown an interest in the education scheme she was helping to develop. Yes, that would be it.

'Well we haven't, so that's that. You'll just have to come to keep-fit.'

'I'd rather die.'

'It's your loss.'

Elsa stepped out onto the landing and ran down the stairs to the ground floor. The front door was standing ajar, and an invigorating salt breeze was wafting into the hallway. She stood for a moment on the stairs, just breathing it in. She adored the early morning, with its soft light and the stunning patterns of colour drifting across the sea.

She hurried to the end of the road and trotted down the steep slope to the promenade. About thirty women of varying ages, shapes and sizes were assembled on the beach. A couple of bored-looking WPCs were sitting nearby but that was the only sign that this was no ordinary holiday resort.

Elsa ran down to join the other women. Standing in rows on the sand, they were a motley band. One or two, like Elsa, had been fortunate enough to beg, borrow or steal shorts or a gym-skirt. Most were wearing dresses or trousers, with a few of the hardier ones in bathing costumes.

At this time of year the sea was still icy-cold but so inviting that many of the women went swimming every day – one or two of them in the nude. This titillating fact – much reported in the Manx press – had raised so many eyebrows that the

107

authorities had been forced to provide bathing costumes as a matter of urgency.

'Touch your toes, ladies, stretch and bend . . .' The Finnish instructress's voice boomed out across the beach.

Elsa took her place, not paying much attention to the women standing near her. She enjoyed losing herself in physical effort; it made it harder to worry about Max, about the Duchess, about the war – the distant war which had changed every one of their lives beyond all recognition.

Afterwards the women mingled and chatted, some going straight back to their hotels, others bathing or lounging about on the beach. There was nothing to hurry back for but the next roll-call, so Elsa sat down on the sand. She found the regular ebb and flow of the sea hypnotic and calming.

Lost in thought, she hardly registered the arrival of another body by her side.

'Elsa. Elsa Nadel?'

'Hmm?' Still half daydreaming, Elsa turned her head to the woman sitting beside her on the sand.

'Don't you remember me, Elsa?'

The breath caught in Elsa's throat.

'Marianne? Marianne von Strondheim?'

The woman threw back her head and enjoyed the play of sunshine on her half-closed eyelids. She was blonde, beautiful, elegant – and knew it.

'I knew you'd remember me. We used to be such *good* friends.'

Completely taken aback, Elsa drew herself up, curling her legs underneath her.

'Marianne – I didn't know you were here! Why haven't I seen you?'

'I only arrived the day before yesterday. They arrested me on Tuesday, damn them. I was beginning to think they'd forgotten all about me, and it was only Alexander they wanted.'

'Alexander?'

'Alexander Cage-Hampton. My husband. I married him a couple of years ago. That's when I came to live in this godforsaken hole of a country.' She sniffed. 'The trouble with the English is, they are too soft, they don't understand the value of discipline. Everything is hopelessly disorganised.'

'I think they're doing their best,' said Elsa lamely.

Marianne threw her a sidelong look.

'I've been hearing disturbing things about you, Elsa. One of the girls in your house tells me you take Jews as your friends.'

'I . . . share a room with a Jewish girl and a German – why?'

'Jews and whores.' Marianne shook her head. 'How can you do such a thing? Why, Elsa?'

'Why not?'

'Still a hopeless idealist, Elsa? I was hoping you'd have changed your politics.'

'You obviously have,' replied Elsa, her eyes fixed squarely on Marianne's. 'When we were at university, you believed in socialism every bit as strongly as I did.'

'University?' Marianne gave a dry laugh. 'That was a long time ago, Elsa, we were just stupid kids. I grew up. It seems you didn't.'

'If that's the way you choose to see it.'

'The Führer is a great man, Elsa. He's been the saviour of Germany, made the Fatherland great again. Wasn't that what we wanted when we were young?'

'He hasn't made Germany great, Marianne, only powerful. It's not the same thing.'

'Germany is your country, Elsa! How can you slander the country of your birth?'

Marianne's words knifed into her with painful precision. Elsa had been called many things in her time, but she had never expected to be called a traitor.

'Germany hasn't been my home for a long time, Marianne. Not since Max was thrown out of the country and I had to go with him because no one would employ me.'

'You're still a German, Elsa. Would you rather the world was ruled by a Jewish conspiracy?'

Elsa started getting to her feet. She didn't feel any inclination to go on talking to Marianne. It was clear they had nothing whatsoever in common any more, if indeed they ever had. And that thought pained her, because once, not so very long ago, they had been close.

'Look, Elsa, don't go.' Marianne reached up and took hold of Elsa's wrist. 'We used to be best friends, don't you remember?'

'You were different then.'

'Stay and talk, Elsa, just a little longer. Please, for old times' sake.'

Reluctantly, Elsa sat down again. She tried a different subject.

'Your husband – he's English?'

Marianne nodded.

'We met at a rally near Berlin.'

'He's . . .'

'A Fascist? Of course he is. He is one of Oswald Mosley's advisers. Surely you don't think I'd marry some hopeless English liberal?' Marianne's expression changed quite suddenly from disdain to bitterness. 'They took him nine months ago, at the beginning of the war.'

'Took him?'

'Interned him. He was on an M15 list of known Nazi sympathisers. One postcard, that's all I've had. They won't let him write to me.'

Elsa heard the anguish in Marianne's voice, and for a moment she almost felt sorry for her.

'I haven't heard from Max in almost two months,' she said.

Marianne looked at her in surprise.

'Max? He's been interned?'

'I don't know. All I know is that he said he was going to Scotland, then all of a sudden my letters started coming back marked "Not known at this address".'

Marianne made circles in the wet sand with her carefully manicured fingertip.

'Max was always the irresponsible one, even when you were kids. He's probably just done one of his famous disappearing acts.'

True enough, thought Elsa. They might be twins, but Max had never quite grown up and Elsa had had to try and protect him from his worst excesses. In some ways Max Nadel was terrific fun; a free spirit and a charming seducer of beautiful women. But he could also be a liability, not least to himself.

'But he was graded B at his tribunal. At the very least there would be restrictions on his movements . . .'

Marianne shrugged.

'Then either he has run away or they have interned him, just like they have interned my husband. Who knows? He might even be in a camp on this very island, and you would never know.'

'Here? On the Island? Is that possible?'

'There are internment camps for men on the Isle of Man, I know that much. At Douglas, Onchan, Ramsey . . .'

'But surely if Max were here, on the Island, I would have been told. Wouldn't I?'

'Why should they tell you? You're just another Nazi bitch like me.'

Elsa's heart was beating so fast that she paid no attention to Marianne's insult.

'But . . . but that would be so unfair. For us to be so close and not even to know!' She thought of Rachel's husband Reuben. Might he be on the Island, only a few miles away yet so far out of reach?

'They won't let us have newspapers or radios. They won't even let us receive letters. Why should they treat us fairly? We must simply live with the injustice until we triumph. As we surely shall.'

Elsa was not quite convinced by the hard edge in Marianne's voice.

'I heard one of the policewomen say yesterday . . . about the male internees . . .'

'Say what?' Marianne looked up sharply.

'That they may be deported. To the colonies.'

Marianne shook her head, flinging back her blonde curls, trying to shake the thought out of her head.

'No, that's not possible. They wouldn't waste their ships on deporting aliens. And anyhow, my Alexander is a British citizen. He has rights . . .'

But not my Max, Elsa thought to herself. Max is German. And she wondered how on earth her feckless brother could possibly cope.

'No,' said Marianne decisively. 'It is just another of these stupid rumours.' She moved a little closer to Elsa. 'Jewish rumours.'

'Marianne . . .' protested Elsa, but Marianne continued, her tone more urgent now, almost pleading.

'Why don't you see the Commandant and demand that you are transferred to my hotel? There is a room next to mine, a good room . . .'

'I'm happy where I am.'

'With those . . . degenerates?'

'With Rachel and Grethe. They're my friends.'

'If you persist in this foolishness you will suffer, Elsa – don't you see? You will be shunned by your own kind *and* their kind.'

'Are you threatening me?'

Marianne's ice-blue eyes sought out Elsa's.

'I wouldn't do that, Elsa. I *care* about you, about our friendship. We go back a long way.'

She touched Elsa's bare forearm, and Elsa recoiled as though from an electric shock. There was something in that touch which made her afraid. Pushing Marianne away, she got to her feet.

'I have to go now. I'll . . . see you around, I expect.'

'Elsa, you're making a big mistake.' Was there a slight

note of menace in that silky-smooth voice? Elsa met her gaze.

'I don't think so, Marianne.' And she turned and walked back to the *Bradda Vista*.

Grethe Herzheim wasn't accustomed to idleness. Back in London there would have been more than enough to keep her occupied – but here in Port Erin she had too much time to think about Emil.

Was Claire looking after him properly? Was he well – and was he missing his mother? So many questions demanded answers, and still there had been no letters from home. The camp authorities blamed it on the difficulty of setting up two post offices in the village, one for the locals and one for the internees, but Grethe was sure they simply didn't want the internee women to know anything. After all, weren't they supposed to be spies?

She walked up the promenade towards Spaldrick. It was a clear June day but not warm, a little breezy and chilly even for Port Erin, which so often received the worst of the winds and storms. Nevertheless, there were women playing on Rowany Golf Course, and she could hear the shouts and laughter of others swimming in the open-air bathing pool. For some, this was undoubtedly the holiday of their lives. For Grethe, it meant anxiety, frustration and boredom.

Lost in thought, she did not notice the young man keeping step beside her.

'Good afternoon . . . Miss Herzheim, isn't it?'

She turned to see Adrian Newell, the Anglican chaplain. Too young for cynicism, his energy and enthusiasm seemed boundless, puppy-like.

'Hello, Reverend.'

'Please, call me Adrian.'

They walked on in silence for a little while, heading towards the peculiar domed structure of Collinson's Cafe.

'So – what can I do for you, Re . . . Adrian?'

'Nothing really. I was just wondering how you were getting on.'

Grethe observed him with raised eyebrows. He was so wet behind the ears he probably hadn't even worked out what she did for a living. If he had, he'd be less eager to spend time with her.

'I'd be getting on better if I knew what had happened to my boy,' she replied.

'You have a son?'

'Emil. I had to leave him behind in London.' She looked him in the eye. 'Not by choice.'

'No, no, I'm sure.'

'I want him back. I *must* have him back. They promised they would bring him to me, but they've done nothing.'

'Perhaps I can do something.'

'Why would you want to help me?'

Newell ignored the question.

'How old is he?'

'Six.'

'And is his father . . .?'

'His father has nothing to do with him.'

'So . . .?'

Grethe laughed.

'You don't know, do you?'

Newell gave her a puzzled look.

'Is there something I *should* know?'

'Let's just say I'm not exactly the respectable type who comes to your church every Sunday.'

'You don't have to be "respectable" to come to church. God welcomes everyone.'

'Not me. God and I don't get on.'

'All the more reason to come along and tell Him so.'

Grethe paused for a moment, then asked:

'Did you mean what you said? About trying to help me get Emil back?'

'Of course. Though I can't promise anything. But I do

know that there are quite a few ladies here who had to leave their children behind when they were interned.'

'And are they tarts too?' asked Grethe archly. 'I'm sorry,' she added. 'I shouldn't have said that.'

'You should say whatever you want to say.'

They stopped outside Collinson's Cafe, overlooking the bay.

'Do you really think the Home Office is going to send me my child?'

'You're a mother. And a child should be with its mother. I'll speak to Effie Pantin about this.'

Reverend Newell continued on up the hill towards Bradda West. Grethe went inside, still musing on what he had said.

The cafe had been 'donated' to the camp and was rapidly taking shape as a social centre. Elsa and some of the other professional women were busy trying to set up classes, particularly in English, which was at best a second or even third language for many of the women.

Grethe had intended having a cup of coffee before returning to the *Bradda Vista*, but as she walked across the cafe she saw a familiar figure sitting hunched at a table in the corner. On a mad impulse she started walking towards the corner.

'Sarah Rosenberg? Are you all right?'

The figure showed no reaction, the woman simply staring out across the sea to the distant horizon.

'Mind if I sit down?'

At the sound of the chair scraping the wooden floor, Sarah glanced at Grethe.

'I can't stop you.' Her voice was flat and expressionless.

'Want to talk about it?'

'Why would I want to talk to you?'

Ask a silly question, thought Grethe.

'I don't know. Cigarette?'

'Oh. Yes, all right.'

Grethe noticed how thin Sarah's fingers were as she took the cigarette from the packet.

'Are you eating properly?'

Sarah stared at Grethe in amazement.

'What did you say?'

'I asked if you were eating proper meals.'

'Why should you care?'

Grethe gave a heavy sigh.

'Okay, okay, I'm sorry. Forget I spoke. But if they're not treating you right you should complain. Get your house representative to see the Commandant.'

'Complain!' Sarah's voice held a note of sarcasm. 'And you think we haven't already done that?'

'Then do it again. Make a bloody nuisance of yourself. I've heard what the owners are like at the *Rowany Glen*. All they care about is making money out of you. They feed you muck and they treat you the same. Get yourself transferred to another house . . .'

'And you really think that would change everything, do you?'

'It's a start, *liebchen*. And you could tell me what's on your mind.'

Sarah looked at her, eyes searching her face; and for a moment Grethe thought she was actually going to open up. But she turned away, pushed back her chair and got to her feet.

'Oh, what's the use?' she snapped. 'What's the use of trusting anyone? Sooner or later they all end up betraying you.'

'You want the rest of that stew, or what?'

A broad Cockney voice cut into Max Nadel's reverie and he handed the billy-can to his neighbour.

'Go ahead, Ernst,' he said. 'I've lost my appetite.'

And no wonder, he thought, gazing at his surroundings. Never in his wildest drunken imaginings had he ever dreamed he would end up in a place like this.

Warth Mill was, quite simply, hell on earth. A disused and

116

derelict cotton mill near Bury in Lancashire, it had been pressed into service as a holding camp for male aliens. The plan had probably been that no one would spend more than a night or two there, but in wartime things seldom went according to plan. Some of the men had been here for weeks now, and in the suffocating June heat it was not a pleasant experience. When the sun blazed down and the breeze blew from a certain direction, the stink from the canal was so thick it was almost visible.

Around two thousand men were crammed into the main mill building, with another five hundred camping in the hall. Looking up Max peered disconsolately at the broken glass roof – complete enough to magnify the noonday heat, but so shattered that it allowed the rain to pour in and collect in oily pools on the rotting floors.

'Not bad stew this,' commented Ernst, tipping up the billy-can and catching the last drops of gravy in his mouth.

'Oh God, Ernst, I don't know how you can,' groaned Max. He'd never been an especially fussy eater, but this place was enough to turn anyone's stomach.

'It wouldn't be so bad,' cut in an elderly academic, 'if only there were tables and chairs. Eating standing up like this gives me indigestion.'

They were a strange assortment, mused Max: Jews and Germans and Czechs, Austrians and Finns, everything from professors to road sweepers, actors to rat-catchers. And they certainly needed the rat-catchers, he told himself as his foot accidentally nudged the corner of a straw palliasse and a fat brown rat went scurrying across the floor.

'Your turn to queue for water,' announced Ernst Müller, plonking a large tin jug in Max's hands.

'I gave you my dinner,' protested Max.

'More fool you!' retorted Ernst's father Willi. 'Turn and turn about, Max, that's what we agreed.'

Grudgingly Max joined the water queue. There were only a few cold taps in the whole of the mill and clean, cool water was a must in this nauseating heat. If you wanted the toilet, well, you crossed your legs as long as you could, because all the camp had to offer two thousand men was a row of metal buckets in the yard. The soles of his shoes slipped slightly on the floor, and the stench of warm oil rose up, filling his lungs. If only he knew what he was supposed to have done to deserve *this*.

'All right, Max?' asked the man behind him in the queue.

'As all right as anyone could be in the circumstances.'

'What I'd give for a beer! A nice cold pilsner . . .'

'Shut up, Erich, you sadist! It's bad enough being here without you going on about cold beer.'

'And pretzels, and a good big plate of bockwurst and sauerkraut . . .'

'I'd rather have my girl,' remarked a young lad, as the queue shuffled forward.

'Pretty is she?' enquired Erich.

'*Wunderschön,*' grinned the lad, miming a perfect hourglass figure. Erich responded with a low whistle.

'Don't suppose she's got a sister for me?'

The mention of sisters made Max think of Elsa. He had had no communication with her for months now – everything had happened so quickly. Admittedly he'd never been a good letter-writer, but there had seemed no special urgency to keep in touch. And now it was too late: he didn't even know if she was all right.

Guilt stabbed him in the guts every time he thought about his twin sister. If it hadn't been for him they might never have got thrown out of Germany. Elsa had always been more discreet about her political convictions.

He'd been up in Scotland when war broke out, working on a private commission. When the local tribunal had graded him 'B' he'd been slightly annoyed but not surprised. Not everyone regarded his socialist principles sympathetically, and when all was said and done, he was still a German by nationality if not conviction.

The restrictions which had been placed upon him had not been too terrible. They'd made him report to the local police station at regular intervals and had forbidden him to own a bicycle, but what did that matter to him when the lady of the house where he was working was happy to ferry him anywhere he wanted to go, in her beautiful new Hispano-Suiza? The war had seemed a very faraway thing to Max Nadel; all he'd cared about was getting on with his painting.

And then, quite suddenly, everything had started to go horribly wrong. He was taken before another tribunal, and, without any satisfactory explanation, regraded 'A' – an enemy alien. Max Nadel, public enemy number one! In hindsight, it was just as ludicrous as it had seemed the day the police had come to take him away and intern him 'for the duration'.

He knew why, too. It was his employer's jealous husband, telling lies about him to the tribunal, to get him out of the way.

'I hear it's definite about the deportations,' commented Erich, as he filled his jug from the tap.

'Deportation? Where to?'

'British colonies, I suppose. Australia . . . Canada, maybe.'

'But they can't make us, can they?'

Erich shrugged.

'They can do anything they want with us. We're enemies of the state, remember?'

'How will they choose who goes and who doesn't?'

'Maybe we'll all have to go.'

'No!' Max filled the heavy jug and started walking back towards the main hall. 'But what about old Willi? He must be pushing seventy. How will he manage?'

How will any of us manage for that matter, he wondered as he carried the water back. And how will Elsa manage on her own – wherever she is?

Chapter 9

'Right! That's it. I've had about as much as I can stand.'

Elsa looked up from the common-room table to see Cora standing in the doorway, arms folded and eyes blazing.

'I'm sorry?' she began.

'It's all right, Elsa, it's not you. It's *them* again. Those two can pack their bags. I'm having them transferred to the *Erindale*.'

'Inge and Mathilde?' guessed Elsa. It wasn't exactly a long shot. The two Austrian girls had been nothing but trouble ever since they'd arrived. They seemed to thrive on unpleasantness.

'If I've read them the Riot Act once I must have done it twenty times. It's no good, they have to go. I only wish I'd had the guts to do it sooner.'

Cora came into the common room and flopped into a sagging armchair. It was good to have an ally, someone she could talk to; and Elsa seemed so understanding, so helpful.

'You know, I went into the kitchen to feed Archie and found that poor Czech girl in floods of tears. I just don't understand it . . .'

'Would you like me to speak to them?' Since Elsa had been elected house representative the weight of other people's expectations was pressing heavily on her shoulders.

'No, no, there's no need. Besides, you have enough on your plate with all these classes you're organising.'

Elsa laughed.

'You mean *trying* to organise. It's amazing how many

121

people think of ten other things to do when you ask them for help. And these work rotas I'm trying to draw up.' She pushed the piece of paper away in disgust. 'Just when I think I have everything worked out, I realise I've missed something out.'

Cora sat down at the table with Elsa and scanned the paper.

'It looks very complicated.'

'It wouldn't be if everyone took their turns. People keep swapping round and then things don't get done at all. And I caught Frau Feldmann paying those two schoolgirls to clean the toilets for her . . .'

'How about the cooking?' Cora peered at Elsa's jottings and crossings out. 'Any more volunteers?'

Elsa chuckled.

'Plenty! The knack is finding the ones who can cook.'

'Well, I think I shall leave all this to you,' smiled Cora. 'You're obviously much better at it than I am.'

'But this cleaning rota's a complete mess . . .'

'Ah, but you have the knack of persuading people to do things even when they don't want to.'

'I only wish I had the knack with Dame Joanna. At the meeting of the house representatives, I asked her when we would find out what had happened to our brothers and husbands, and she said . . .'

'Go on.'

'She said "Fräulein Nadel, if our own soldiers' wives do not know where they are, why should you know where your menfolk are?"'

'She's a bit of a martinet. But it will all work out right in the end, I'm sure it will.' Cora got to her feet. 'I hear you're organising classes at the Marine Biological Station.'

'Yes, it's a programme of guided study for anyone who's interested. And lectures, of course.'

'Oh yes. Isn't James McArthur involved in some way . . .?'

'Yes, Mr McArthur's offered to give us a talk about his

work as a veterinary surgeon. It's very kind of him.'

'Oh, I'm sure he'll enjoy it.' Cora smiled to herself. James had taken quite a lot of persuading, but she knew he could make a real success of it. 'He's a very good public speaker, very entertaining.'

'I'm really looking forward to it,' nodded Elsa.

Quite how much, Elsa hardly dared admit.

Claire Hodges took a deep breath and marched purposefully towards the door of Streatham South Police Station.

She had seen the inside of plenty of police stations, but seldom voluntarily. Still, necessity could make you do some funny things, and she had Emil to think about now.

Inside the police station a gaggle of three black-clad Italian women were arguing noisily with the desk sergeant, who contemplated them with a kind of compassionate desperation.

'Please, Sergeant, you cannot take my Tony away, he is good man. What will I do without him?'

'Come along now, ladies, it's no use getting yourself all worked up like this . . .'

'But, Sergeant, without my Tony how shall I feed my children?'

'She has the cafe to run, and no one to help her. What will become of us all?'

'We are not your enemies. We have lived in your country for twenty-five years . . .'

Sergeant Greenwood put down his pencil.

'I'm sorry, Mrs Bertorelli, you know I am. But I can't do anything – it's out of my hands.'

'There must be something you can do to help us. You can't let them take him away from me, he is all I have . . .'

'And her son is in the Army, Sergeant. Fighting for this country. You should be ashamed to intern a good man like Tony Bertorelli!'

'Like I said, I didn't have anything to do with it. I was just carrying out my orders from the Chief Constable.'

The sergeant felt distinctly unhappy about the way things had turned out. The Jerries, well that was one thing; real thugs some of them were and you couldn't be too careful. But the Italians – it didn't seem right somehow. Young Arturo Bertorelli was a corporal in the Tank Regiment, doing his bit for Britain. And the sergeant had been a regular at Bertorelli's Cafe for years. Wonderful sandwiches they did.

'Why is it that you do this to us?'

'I really am sorry, madam, but war is war. And if your Tony had got himself naturalised, none of this would have happened. I'm afraid you'll have to take it up with the authorities.'

Claire watched and waited. She felt extremely uncomfortable. On 10 June Italy had finally declared war on Britain, and the arrests had started immediately. The violence too, with riots up and down the country all night as mobs attacked Italian businesses and terrorised innocent families.

Streatham had come off better than some places, but even so the Italian community was in turmoil. The front of Bertorelli's Cafe was covered with sheets of plywood where bricks and stones had shattered the windows. It made Claire feel ashamed. The Bertorellis had been part of the local community for years. Old Mrs Bertorelli deserved better than to see her business destroyed and her husband dragged off to be interned.

The declaration of war had come so suddenly that there had been no time to classify the Italians living in Britain and so all sorts had been rounded up: young and old, enemy and friend. It had been a haphazard business, with ample scope for injustices. But with Italy in the war and panic at its height as Paris struggled to hold out against the might of the German army, was that any wonder?

As the three sobbing women left the station, Claire stepped up to the desk. The sergeant went on scribbling in the day book.

'Sarge?'

He paused but did not look up.

'What is it? Come to pay off your last fine?'

Claire felt a stirring of anger, but now wasn't a good time to lose her temper.

'Come on, Sarge, you know I ain't been in trouble for a couple of months now.'

'No.' He laid the pencil down on the polished counter and scrutinised her from head to foot. 'And if I didn't know you better, Claire Hodges, I'd be wondering what you're up to.'

'I ain't up to nothing. I need your help, that's all.'

'What's up? One of your clients been knocking you around, has he?' Sergeant Greenwood's tone was not unsympathetic, just world-weary. He'd seen it all in twenty years in the Force, and the war wasn't making his job any easier or pleasanter.

'Not that.' Claire's fingers fiddled nervously with the strap of her shoulder bag. 'It's Grethe.'

'Grethe Herzheim? You were sharing a place with her, weren't you?'

'Could be,' replied Claire evasively. Admit nothing, that was the safest thing to do. Every working girl knew you could be had up for running a disorderly house, just because you shared rooms with another tart. 'We're not now. She's been interned.'

The sergeant nodded, calling that particular day to mind. It wasn't easy, what with so many passing through the station in the last couple of weeks. Men, women, children; Germans, Austrians, Czechs, Italians . . . it was hard to remember every face. But Grethe stuck in his mind. He'd arrested her often enough to have developed a soft spot for the woman.

'What about it?' he asked.

'I need to know where she is.'

The sergeant laughed.

'Well, there ain't much chance of that.'

'Why not?'

'Well, for starters it's a matter of national security. And in any case, I don't know where they've taken her.'

Claire wasn't so easily fobbed off.

'C'mon, Sarge, don't give me all that. You must know where they've took her.'

The sergeant considered for a moment, remembering the day they'd brought Grethe in. Some of the others had wept, sworn at him, even tried to scratch his eyes out, but not Grethe. For a tart she had dignity. He respected that.

'Even if I did know, I couldn't tell you. And anyhow, wherever they took her, she won't be there now. They just take 'em to a holding camp first, see, then transfer them somewhere permanent.'

'I read in the paper they was sending all the women to the Isle of Man. Is that where they've took her?'

'Could be,' he admitted.

'Well, I need to contact her. It's important.'

'Why?'

Claire thought of Emil, playing at soldiers in the scrubby back garden behind the flats they'd moved to.

'That's my business.'

'It wouldn't be about that boy of hers, would it?'

Claire stiffened, her heart skipping a beat.

'Why?' she demanded cagily.

'By rights, he should have been taken to the children's home,' replied the sergeant. 'If I was doing this by the book, I really ought to report . . .'

'You ain't takin' the kid from me!'

Sergeant Greenwood shook his head sadly.

'Did I say I was?'

'You said . . .'

Out of the blue, the sergeant leant across the desk and patted Claire's hand.

'Look, I can't help you but I won't let on about the boy. So just you take good care of him, understand?'

News had a way of filtering through, thought Cora as she walked back from Bessie Teare's boarding house, Bonzo pulling and panting on the end of his leash.

'Morning, Cora,' called George Corless as he wobbled into view on his overloaded bicycle.

'Morning, George.'

''Tis terrible news from France.'

'It certainly is. Looks like we're on our own now.'

George cycled off with his load of letters and parcels. There were none yet for the internees, but the Commandant had promised that some sort of postal system would be set up as soon as possible. Cora was relieved. Without news from outside, some of the women were becoming tetchy and troublesome, some withdrawn and demoralised. Some had taken to a butterfly existence of golf, swimming and idle chit-chat. Others were finding the boredom just too much to bear, especially the women who had been parted from husbands and children.

The camp authorities might try to prevent the internees from having access to newspapers or the radio, but how could it possibly work when they were living among the locals? A careless word here, an eavesdropped conversation there – it was impossible to keep them entirely in the dark. Only the other day, Grandad Quine had caught one of the internees' children listening outside the door of his room, ear pressed up to the keyhole to hear the late news on the Home Service.

Anyhow, the news was out and that was all there was to it. Three days before, on 14 June, Paris had fallen.

Of course, everyone was still in shock. James especially. She should have known he would take it badly. As Cora thought of him, sadness and frustration mingled in equal measure. She knew she cared for him, and deep down, sensed that he had begun to feel more than friendship for her too. But since his accident James had become less open, more withdrawn. Now every time she felt she was getting close to him, he seemed to shut her out. If only he could understand that she didn't see him as any less of a man, just because he couldn't fight . . .

Stepping down onto the beach, she let Bonzo off the leash

and watched him scamper across the sand like an animated hearthrug. He, at least, was spared all this worry.

She walked past a group of German women, bright-eyed and laughing. They were talking and singing in their own language, paying her no attention – well, why should they? The Germans had taken Paris, France would surely make peace any day now, and Britain was standing alone. It was little wonder they were celebrating. What was that they were singing?

'*Wenns Judenblut vom Messer spritzt . . .*'

She tried to close her ears to the jubilant hatred in the women's voices. Marianne von Strondheim was standing in the middle of the circle of women, conducting as they sang at the tops of their voices. Cora didn't need to understand the words to guess the meaning of their song.

'*. . . gehts uns noch mal so gut . . .*'

Hands in the pockets of her light summer jacket, Cora turned her back on the women and walked along the margin of the sea. Only a few were like that, she told herself. A hard-faced, vociferous minority who did their best to make things tough for everyone else.

A small boy was toddling in the shallows, his fat pink legs and arms splashing delightedly in the water. Cora felt the joy of his innocence as the child's mother swung him up in her arms and covered his laughing face with kisses.

Such a lot had changed in such a short time. A few months ago Cora had had her whole life neatly plotted out: working at the shop, saving to buy the business when Miss Bannister retired, enjoying the monthly dances and the cycling club. Enjoying James's company too. The war had seemed so far away.

Reaching into her pocket, Cora took out Bonzo's old tennis ball and threw it for him, flinging it with the full power of her frustration. How could everything have gone so wrong, so quickly?

First, James had had his accident. Before, things had been

going really well for them, she'd been so sure they were drawing steadily closer to each other. But these days, she hardly recognised James as the carefree young man who'd so loved his dancing, his hill-walking and his rugby.

Cora kicked the toe of her shoe into the wet sand. As if all that wasn't bad enough, William and Grace had announced that they were going to the mainland – leaving her at the helm of the *Bradda Vista*. But even then, Cora had scarcely imagined that things would turn out like this.

She bent to pick up a piece of driftwood. Straightening up, she was struck by the sheer beauty of this place. Early summer sunshine struck diamond-bright sparks from the crests of each wave, gulls swooping down over the sea with cries as bright and sharp as the morning light.

In the far distance to her left was the Marine Biological Station, its squat brick buildings dark against the blue sky, and a jagged line marking the ruined breakwater. To the right, sheltered by the cliffs, lay the lighthouse, beach cafes and the Traie Meanagh open-air pool, with the long white row of boarding houses lining the clifftops behind. Fluffy white sheep dotted the steep, green-brown slopes beyond, free to wander where they wished, oblivious to the turbulent world about them.

Beautiful, yes. Perhaps the most beautiful prison in the world.

A few days later, James McArthur found himself walking down to the Marine Biological Station with Cora, a sheaf of lecture notes tucked under his arm. He was beginning to regret offering to give the very first afternoon lecture to the internees.

'Are you sure this is a good idea, Cora? They'll most probably be bored rigid.'

'They'll love it,' Cora assured him, slipping her arm through his.

'Well, I hope so! I haven't felt so nervous since I took my viva at university.'

'Your what?'

'My viva – you know, the oral exam. They show you a bone or a pickled spleen or something, and you have to say what the poor beast died of.'

'Sounds revolting.'

'It's a bit nerve-wracking. I remember old McCluskie handing me something and I just stared at it – I couldn't think for the life of me what it was.'

'And what was it?'

'Part of a cow's rumen – it was easy really, my mind just went blank. It'd better not happen now,' he added. 'I'm not used to this sort of thing.'

'Of course it won't, you'll be fine. Just tell them some of the stories you've told me. You're clever, you'll get by.'

James laughed.

'Clever? You're the cleverest person I know, Cora Quine, keeping that wreck of a guesthouse from falling down, and making sure your lot don't kill each other over whose turn it is to cook the dinner . . .'

'You're making fun of me,' said Cora. 'I wish you wouldn't.'

'No I'm not. I couldn't do what you do. I'm all right with animals, but people . . .' He put his arm round Cora's waist and gave her a squeeze. 'You're strong, you know. Stronger than me.'

'Me? Strong?'

'Yes, you! I don't know how you stand being cooped up with the internees, what with the war going so badly.' He fiddled with the handle of his walking stick. 'I should be out there fighting, you know.'

Cora sensed his mood darkening and changed the subject. Today was supposed to be a happy day, a day when they could enjoy each other's company. She didn't want to risk spoiling it.

'It's Grandad Quine who gives me more trouble than anyone. You must come and see him; apart from George, you're the only person he listens to.'

'It's a bit busy at the moment . . .'

'Why not come for a meal one evening?'

He slipped his arm round her waist.

'I'll see what I can do, I promise.'

They walked into the Marine Biological Station together, Cora taking a seat near the back and James going off to prepare his notes. Despite the fine weather plenty of the women – and some children too – had come to hear the local vet. Among them were Grethe, Elsa and Rachel, and the two schoolgirls from the *Bradda Vista*.

Cora felt a surge of vicarious pride as James stepped up to the lectern and began to speak. He was good-looking, intelligent, everything she'd ever admired in a man. If only he recognised all the good qualities in himself, instead of dwelling on the bad. If only he could rid himself of the bitterness, open up to her, let himself be the man whose laughter and love of life had so attracted her when they first met.

The talk went well, as Cora had known it would. Afterwards she intended to go over and congratulate James. But Bessie Teare was in the mood for a long and cosy chat, and by the time Cora got to the front James was already talking – to Elsa Nadel.

Cora hung back, reluctant to interrupt; listening to their conversation.

'Mr McArthur, I wanted to thank you. Your talk was most entertaining.'

'Thank you, Miss Nadel.' James paused. His first instinct was to maintain his distance – this woman was supposed to be an enemy wasn't she? – but his response to Elsa was friendly and warm. 'It's very kind of you.'

'Not at all. I was especially interested in what you had to say about the use of sulphonamide drugs.'

'Ah yes.' He remembered what Cora had told him. 'You're a qualified pharmacist, I believe?'

'Unfortunately I haven't been able to practise since nineteen-thirty-five. My brother and I were thrown out of

131

Germany, and the only way I could work in Britain was as an old lady's companion.'

James shook his head.

'That's a very great pity. Not to be allowed to use your skills – it seems such a waste.'

'It is very frustrating – I would like to be doing really useful work, medical work. Like you,' she added, her eyes fixed on James's.

'And you should be allowed to do exactly that.'

'But what can I do? I am here and so are lots of other women who shouldn't be. But that is war . . . no one ever said it was supposed to be fair.'

'I'm sure you will be able to work soon – when the present emergencies are over.'

'I hope so.' Elsa warmed to James's smile. She was beginning to realise how much she liked that smile. With an effort she dragged her thoughts back to James's lecture. 'Tell me, Mr McArthur, what are your opinions on the treatment of diabetes in animals . . .?'

Cora stopped a few yards away from James and Elsa. They hadn't noticed her standing there and she wasn't sure now that she wanted them to. All of a sudden she felt shut out.

It wasn't that they were deliberately excluding her from their conversation but what had she to say that could possibly interest them? She wasn't unintelligent but she wasn't an intellectual either. Cora had never really felt her lack of education up to now, but seeing James and Elsa together, so obviously enjoying each other's company, made her feel uncomfortable.

And, perhaps, just a little jealous.

Chapter 10

'Move, you bloody useless creature!'

'Come on, that's it . . .'

'Go! *Sofort!* You can do it!'

'Ach! What's the use?' Ernst Müller sat back on his haunches, wiping the sweat from his brow with the back of his hand. He glared at the cockroach, but still it wouldn't move. It just stood its ground and seemed to be staring back at him. Its companions – happy to be liberated from matchboxes and upturned cups – scurried off across the oily floor of the disused mill, towards the safety of the shadows. 'And to think I had two cigarettes bet on him, the idle bugger.'

Max Nadel laughed and nudged the cockroach with his finger.

'You're sure it's not dead, Ernst? Or maybe it's a Nazi cockroach.'

'Watch the Professor's go,' whistled young Erich. 'You been using some special training tactics, Professor?'

The elderly Oxford academic tapped the side of his nose and chuckled.

'That's for me to know and you to guess. Now, are you boys going to settle your debts or not?'

Old Willi Müller gave a disgruntled cough as he reluctantly handed over his stake.

'Cockroach races! Whose damn fool idea was it anyway?' Another spasm of coughing racked his thin old body, shaking him like a dog with a rag doll in its mouth. 'To think we've come to this!'

'Sit down, Willi, for goodness' sake. Have a drink of water.' Max took Willi by the shoulders and practically forced him to sit down on an improvised bench the men had made from some wooden crates and discarded sacks.

'I'm all right,' grumbled Willi. 'Never had a day's illness in my life. It's just this heat . . .'

If nothing else, Willi Müller was right about the heat. The smouldering warmth of late June turned discomfort into agony, and the stench from the canal was more overpowering than ever. Men were getting dysentery, going half-crazy. And the food – when it came – was unappetising stodge. Boredom and inactivity left ample time to brood, and the thought uppermost in everyone's mind was simply getting out of this place.

Ernst Müller leant against one of the rusty iron pillars which held up the remnants of the glass roof, reached into his pocket and took out his tobacco tin. He watched as Max picked up a crumpled piece of paper and the stubby end of a pencil, and began sketching.

'Still scribbling, Max?'

Max spoke without glancing up, keeping his eyes fixed on the middle distance where a young lad of perhaps sixteen or seventeen was gazing out of a barred and shattered window, past the guards with their guns and fixed bayonets, towards the distant moors.

'When this is all over and they let us out, I want to paint this place – so everyone knows what it was like.'

'If they find you've been drawing, they'll confiscate your pictures,' commented Ernst. 'They'll think you're a spy, and then where will you be?'

Max paused for a moment then went on drawing.

'Same place I am now, I expect.'

'Don't you care?'

This time Max did look up.

'Of course I bloody care, Ernst, you cretin. For a start-off, I care about the bastard who got me rounded up and put in this place.'

134

'Steady on, Max,' said Ernst, stuffing tobacco into the bowl of a battered pipe. 'We don't like it here any more than you do.'

'No, but you all got grade B, didn't you? They gave me A. What chance do I have of getting out?'

He looked down at the sketch in his hand; it wasn't how he wanted it. Nothing was. In a fit of temper he screwed up the sheet of paper into a tight ball, flinging it with a roar of fury across the vast hall.

'Damn you. Damn you all!'

He sensed all eyes looking at him, and felt immediately ashamed of himself. Max was a great bear of a man, powerfully built and filled with even more powerful emotions. Reddish-brown, wavy hair worn slightly long framed a bearded face dominated by wild grey eyes that could glitter with joy, with sorrow, with rage. His 'artistic temperament' had got him into trouble more times than he cared to remember – and not just him, either. His stubbornness and his tantrums had brought trouble for his friends, his parents, his sister.

His lovers too. And there had been many lovers in Max Nadel's life: colleagues, friends, chance acquaintances, even his last employer's wife – which was where his troubles began. Women were his great passion, and they in turn were drawn by his zest, his charm, his vibrant sensuality.

'Sorry,' he said.

'Max,' began Ernst.

'What?'

'Could we have a word? Alone?'

Puzzled, Max nodded.

'Whatever you say.'

'Come with me. I need to talk to you.'

Max got up from his makeshift seat and followed Ernst across the hallway to a quiet place where rain and snow had soaked into the floor, weakening the timbers.

'Careful where you stand. Don't want you falling through the floor.'

'Quite.' Max chose his spot carefully, leaning up against the brick wall. 'So what did you want to talk about?'

Ernst looked down at the scuffed toes of his boots.

'You know they're going to deport some of us in a few days' time?'

'I heard that the first contingent had been selected, yes, poor bastards. Why?'

'I've been chosen to go.'

'Oh.'

'I didn't tell you because I didn't want Willi to know. I don't know what to do, Max.'

'That's terrible, but what can I do?'

'You could help me, Max. They'd never know.'

Ernst's eyes searched Max's face, pleading with him to understand what he was asking.

'Don't you see how?'

A lightning-flash of realisation arced across Max's brain. When he spoke, it was slowly and deliberately, like a man awaking from sleep.

'You mean you want me to go in your place?'

'I know it's a lot to ask . . .'

Max gave a disbelieving laugh.

'Ernst, you're asking me to get myself deported. I'd say that was a lot to ask, yes.' He thought. 'I can't see how it would work.'

Ernst took hold of his wrist, willing him to see that it could, would work.

'Others are doing it – fathers and sons, brothers who don't want to be separated. They've found others who are willing to go in their place. They exchange documents, registration papers and tickets for the voyage. No one will know – we're about the same age, the same build. You could shave off your beard. They won't check.'

'I don't know.'

'Max, *please*. At least you'd be getting out of this place. You said yourself there's not much chance they'll release you.'

Max's gaze drifted across the smelly, overcrowded hovel he had called home for week upon tedious week. Somewhere beyond the crumbling walls and the armed guards were fresh air, countryside and freedom.

'Where are they deporting the internees to?'

'They won't say. But I heard Canada. They say there may be more freedom over there, not so many restrictions – work even.'

Canada. Max thought of the open spaces, the mountains, the crystal-clear rivers; of all the beauty just waiting to be drawn and painted. And his conscience niggled inside him, reminding him that Willi Müller was an old man, sick and frail. He'd done nothing wrong and he didn't deserve to be parted from his son.

'All right, you win.' When all was said and done, what did he have to lose? 'I'll go.'

'You mean that?'

'I need my head examining, but yes, I mean it. What if it doesn't work out, and they find out who I really am?'

'I'll tell them it was me behind it, I forced you into it – anything you want me to say.'

Max let his breath escape in a long sigh of release. It was only now that he realised how much anger had become pent-up inside him with each shallow, uneasy intake of air. A fat, sleek rat sat on a nearby ledge, watching him with its beady black eyes as it cleaned its whiskers. That was one aspect of Warth Mill that Max certainly wouldn't be sorry to see the back of. That, and about a thousand others.

'When do I leave?'

'A few days, I'm not sure exactly. We'll exchange papers just before. Oh – and I think you should have this.' Ernst rummaged in the pocket of his threadbare trousers and took out a white postcard.

Max took it.

'What's this for?'

'It's a special card for contacting your family; all the

137

deportees were given one. It's not much but it's better than nothing.'

Max examined the card. Ernst was right – it wasn't much. But it was the first chance he'd had to let Elsa know he was even alive. He scanned the instructions:

'NOTHING is to be written on this side except the date, signature and address of the sender. Erase words not required. IF ANYTHING ELSE IS ADDED THE POSTCARD WILL BE DESTROYED.' Underneath, were a series of phrases: 'I am (not) well'; 'I have been admitted to hospital'; 'I am being transferred to another camp'.

Transferred, yes, thought Max. But to where? It wasn't as if he could tell her where he was going. And in any case, he didn't even know where Elsa was. Was she still safe and free, working for the Grand Duchess, or had she too been interned? And if he sent a card to her at the house in Streatham, would it find its way to her?

'Come on, Kotkin. The starving millions are baying for their dinner.'

Reuben Kotkin looked up from his book, closed it and put it to one side.

'*Shalom*, Goldman, I was miles away.'

'*Na ja, schon wieder*. Not brooding again?' The older man looked him up and down. 'How's the black eye?'

Reuben explored it gingerly with his index finger.

'I'll live.'

'That'll teach you to brawl with German sailors!'

Reuben joined in the uneasy laughter. Both of them knew the reality behind Reuben's black eye and the bruise on his cheek. Here at Huyton Camp, an empty housing estate on the outskirts of Liverpool, there was a strong contingent of Nazi merchant seamen, who had done just about everything they could to defy the authorities and run the camp the way they wanted. They had taken charge of the administration office, and were trying to prevent those internees they did not approve of from having access to privileges.

This rankled with Reuben. For weeks he had reined in his anger, keeping faith with his pacifist principles, but one evening it had spilled over into violence. It had started as a trifling dispute over the allocation of rooms, not even something which affected Reuben directly. But when insults had turned to violence, Reuben had found himself at the centre of a very large punch-up. The result had been ten days in solitary detention, but Reuben had never much minded spending time on his own. And since his release back into the camp, the Nazi contingent had treated him with noticeably more respect.

'Come on, Kotkin, I'm starving.' Goldman thrust his hands in his pockets and set off down the stairs, followed by Reuben.

'Why me?' protested Reuben.

'Because you're the only one who knows what to do with this muck they give us to cook! I'd rather eat your boiled salt cod every day than put up with Papiermeister's burnt offerings. For a tailor you're a fine cook, Reuben Kotkin.'

They descended the stairs and walked along the corridor to the kitchen of the small terraced house, where two middle-aged men with rolled-up sleeves were peeling potatoes.

'Sachs, Papiermeister.' Reuben nodded to the two men and contemplated the day's rations, arranged on greaseproof paper on the table. A little margarine, some beans, bread and cooking fat. He prodded a small mound of uninspiring greyish flesh. '*Jaj istenem.* Whatever is this?'

'I don't know. Dogfish maybe?' suggested Goldman.

'Dog more like,' retorted Sachs.

'Snoek,' said Papiermeister darkly. 'It's filthy stuff.'

'But Kotkin will turn it into oysters and champagne,' declared Goldman. 'Oysters in champagne sauce. I remember once, I was dining at the Strand Palace Hotel . . .'

'Oh shut up, will you?' Sachs threw a dishcloth at him but he ducked and it hit the wall, slithering wetly to the floor.

'And be grateful you're not living in a tent, like the Italians they've just moved in.'

Although Huyton Camp was centred around a half-finished housing estate, there were too few houses and two many internees for everyone to enjoy the benefits of bricks and mortar. Most of the houses had been allocated to internees with special needs – the elderly or infirm, with a couple of 'youth houses' for those under twenty-one. Thousands of the others were having to manage in old Army bell-tents; which might be all right in the summer, mused Reuben, but what if they were still here at Chanukah?

'I wish my Hannah was here,' mused Papiermeister. 'Such *gefillte* fish she makes.'

'Have you heard anything?' asked Reuben. Here, his personal tragedy was nothing out of the ordinary. All the men here had been parted from wives, families, friends.

Papiermeister shrugged.

'Only that she has been interned and taken to the Isle of Man. The Commandant told me that all the interned women are being taken there. And you, Kotkin? What news of your Rachel?'

'Nothing at all. I hoped she would be free by now, with her so near her time, but do you think she has perhaps been sent there too? To this Isle of . . .?'

'Man. Isle of Man. It is between England and Ireland. If she has been taken there, she will be safe.' Papiermeister dropped a peeled potato into the pan. 'At least there she will be far from the bombing, if it comes.'

'It will come,' said Sachs. 'It came for us in Belgium and it will come for us here.' A penniless young writer, Sachs had only just succeeded in getting out of Brussels before the Blitzkrieg came.

'If it comes for you, Sachs, I'm sure we shall all be very grateful for the peace and quiet,' snapped Goldman, watching Reuben's glum expression out of the corner of his eye. 'When is the baby due, Reuben?'

'Sometime in July. It is hard to know exactly . . .'

'She'll be in good hands,' Goldman assured him. 'Go to the Welfare Officer and explain. He will find out for you, ask that you can write to her so she knows that you are safe.'

Reuben nodded.

'I will,' he promised. Inside, he was thinking; but I wanted to be with her, I promised I would be with her when the baby comes. What will she think of me if I let her down now? A sinking feeling in the pit of his stomach told him he might not have any choice. 'I have to go outside,' he announced, slipping on his jacket. 'To the washroom.'

'What about the snoek?' protested Sachs.

'I won't be long. Put the beans on to boil.'

He stepped outside, grateful for a breath of fresh air and an escape from all the well-meaning questions. He coped better on his own, and was glad to have the washroom as an excuse. Although the men were lucky to be living in a house, the bathroom had not been completed and during the daytime they used a purpose-built wash-block nearby.

Hands in pockets, he walked briskly across the road and past the youth house, where a group of lads were kicking a ball about in the road. Further on, a man in overalls was up a ladder, fixing a broken slate. It was a peculiarly normal scene – until you looked beyond the houses to the lines of tents, and the double row of barbed wire slung between stout wooden posts.

'*Shalom uv'rachot*, Reuben,' called out a young Jew, as they passed in the road. 'You are well?'

'Peace and blessings, Isidore. Very well – and you?'

'Better since they let my college send my books on to me. Now I have much to occupy my mind.'

Reuben walked on towards the washroom block, standing aside for a moment to let two elderly men come out before he stepped inside.

As he washed his hands at the sink he looked at the wall above. It was covered with graffiti, some words scrawled, others carved into the plaster by internees. He read their names: 'Itsaak Cohn, 1940; Kretzmer; Moishe Feldman; Bomzer, a prisoner of conscience . . .'

He felt a curious sense of affinity with all these other men, many of whom he had never met. Already some had passed through the camp, on their way to wherever the Government thought they ought to be. Feeling in his trouser pocket, he fetched out the pencil stub he'd been using to jot down notes on his book.

'REUBEN SAMUEL KOTKIN,' he wrote on the crumbly yellow plaster above the sink. 'AN INNOCENT MAN.'

The twentieth of June was Cora Quine's birthday – but she wasn't in the mood for celebration.

'Thirty!' she moaned, avoiding looking at herself in the hall mirror. She was sure she would see new grey hairs that had sprung up overnight. 'I'm thirty years old!'

'What's so bad about that?' shrugged Grethe Herzheim, following her along the corridor with a second bale of dirty laundry. 'And who needs to know? In my mind I am seventeen for ever.'

'In Port Erin *everyone* knows. They've all known me since I was a baby.'

'Then you should have a party. A *big* party, celebrate it.'

Cora laughed at the ridiculousness of the idea.

'Celebrate getting old?'

The two women hauled the laundry into the kitchen, ready for collection, and Thomas contemplated them from the depths of his newspaper.

'What's that?' he grunted.

'A party,' said Grethe. 'It's Cora's birthday, she should have a party.'

'More like a wake,' he commented. 'With the face she's got on her this morning. Anybody'd think the gel was as old as me.' He nodded towards an envelope on the kitchen table. 'Somethin' from Grace and William.'

Cora's heart sank. She'd hoped it might be a card from James. But why should he remember her birthday? She allowed herself a small flicker of resentment. These days, James seemed more interested in persuading the authorities to let Elsa come and work in his surgery than in spending time with Cora.

She slit open the envelope and took out the card. It was a very small card, so Grace must have chosen it. The figure '30' leapt out of it in gloatingly bright red. 'Happy birthday, Grace and William,' it read, in William's handwriting.

'Something nice?' enquired Grethe.

'Not really.'

The kitchen door opened and a face peeped round it. It was Elisabeth, one of the schoolgirls.

'The first floor toilets are blocked,' she announced.

'Oh damn,' groaned Cora.

'And Fredi's been sick all over the bathroom floor.'

'That's all I need.'

Offering up a small prayer for patience, Cora had taken three steps up the stairs when the front doorbell rang. She was in half a mind to ignore it, but Grethe was already opening the door.

'Mr McArthur, hello. Cora is just . . .'

Cora stopped and turned on the stairs.

'James!'

He was standing there in his best sports jacket and flannels, his hat and stick in one hand and a huge bunch of flowers in the other. He stepped into the hallway, a big silly grin on his face. Cora's heart fluttered into happy life.

'Happy birthday, Cora. Did you think I'd forget?'

She stood and stared, on the point of giggling like a silly kid.

'Oh, James, they're lovely.'

'Well, don't just stand there, get your gladrags on. I'm taking you for a birthday picnic.'

* * *

143

They drove north through Dalby, turning west towards Niarbyl and the vast, sparkling expanses of the sea.

Parking the Austin Seven by the side of the road, they scrambled down over the rocks to the beach. Niarbyl Bay spread out before them; the long rocky peninsula stretching out into the sea to the north and, to the south, magnificent views of the south-western coast of the Island. Rocky headlands and bays extended into the far distance, and on this clear day Cora could see as far as Bradda Head and the Calf of Man.

The bay was deserted, the only sign of life a couple of fishermen's cottages nestled in the lee of the rocky cliffs. Their whitewashed walls were almost painfully bright against the dark greys and mossy greens of the rocks.

Letting Fergus and Bonzo run free, they unpacked the picnic from the back of the car.

'Happy birthday,' grinned James.

'You've said that already.'

'I suppose I just like birthdays.'

Cora stood on tiptoe to peck a kiss on his cheek. He held her lightly for a moment, and she breathed in the scent of him, the light tang of sweat. It thrilled her to feel so close to him, even for a few brief seconds.

'This is lovely, James, really lovely. And such a surprise.'

'I like surprises too. And we haven't had a picnic since last summer. Do you remember – up at the Curraghs?'

'Yes, the ants got into all the sandwiches, but Bonzo ate them anyway,' laughed Cora, spreading a cloth on the rocks at the margin of the beach. How could she forget? It had been a perfect day, she'd wanted it to go on for ever. 'You know, I think I'm too excited to eat anything.'

'I persuaded Mrs O'Hara to make us one of her seedcakes.' James unpacked a cake tin and prised off the lid.

'Well, maybe just a slice . . . or three.'

'Oh, and there's some of Bessie Teare's gorse wine.' Out came a lemonade bottle, washed and refilled with a clear, pale yellow liquid. 'George Corless grew the radishes, and even

Tossie let me have a lettuce from his precious garden. Oh, and Evie Bannister insisted on making some scones, but you don't have to eat them if you value your digestion.'

James's fingers made contact with hers as they knelt on the sand, setting out the plates. He seemed in no hurry to break the contact. It felt good.

'I can't believe all this,' she said. 'I truly can't!'

'As soon as I mentioned the idea to Bessie Teare, everybody wanted to donate something.'

'But why?'

'People like you, Cora.' He brushed a wisp of hair off her face, warm from the sun. 'They really do.'

Max Nadel was just one more anonymous figure in the procession of men who arrived at Liverpool Docks on 1 July 1940. How many other men had swapped papers, he could only guess; but he knew four or five others who had come to an arrangement and were travelling on somebody else's documents.

Ernst had been right, of course. With well over a thousand men forming this contingent, the guards had become careless. No one bothered to question if the man carrying Ernst Müller's papers was really Ernst Müller.

They were a mixed bag: Germans and Italians, Nazis and Fascists and Jews. Supposedly, all the men being deported were Nazis, prisoners of war or Italian fascists, a danger to British security, but that was patently untrue. There were seventy-year-olds and sixteen-year-old boys too young to grow a beard – and even a group of Italian socialists who had spent years leading the struggle against Mussolini. The whole exercise felt like the result of panic rather than good planning.

Max's neighbour nudged his arm.

'I heard the last contingent were shipped to the Isle of Man,' he said. 'That's where they've taken the women. Maybe I'll see my wife and sister there.'

'Maybe,' said Max. But he took one look at the ship they

were to travel on and knew instantly that they must be going a lot further than the Isle of Man.

The *Arandora Star* was a fifteen-hundred-tonner, a fine ocean-going liner before the war but now refitted as a troop ship. This was no pleasure-boat, it was a ship designed for long-distance travel. Clearly Ernst had been right about this, too: they must be headed for Canada at the very least, maybe even Australia.

As his turn came to board the ship he glanced up. A swastika pennant was flying below the white ensign, signifying that the ship was carrying German prisoners of war. He looked away, the old rage twisting his guts as he wondered at the irony of it all. The Germans had threatened to put him in prison for being a socialist, and now the British had jailed him for being a Nazi. It if hadn't been so personal, he could almost have laughed.

'Single file, hurry along now.'

A corporal from the Pioneer Corps ushered them towards the gangplank and Max stooped to pick up his suitcase – the bearer of all his worldly goods, his hopes and dreams. An unexpected surge of optimism quickened his step. Maybe life in Canada really would be better after all. It could hardly be much worse than Warth Mill. He just wished Elsa could be there to share his good fortune.

Chapter 11

Harry Kerruish was a changed man. Dunkirk had made sure of that.

Cora's bachelor uncle had always been a man of few words, a man who kept himself to himself; but she noticed how tired he seemed as she ushered him upstairs into the flat. Older too, much older than his forty-seven years.

'Welcome home, Uncle Harry. Welcome back to the Island.'

He nodded a greeting, took off his cap and stuffed it into his jacket pocket.

''Tis good to see you again, gel.'

Cousin Juan was three paces behind Harry, a gangly youth of seventeen with the first sproutings of a downy beard. Full of life and energy, that was Juan: everybody's friend and just about everybody's cousin. It was plain to see the difference between him and Harry – but then, Juan hadn't been on the *Mary Jane* as she cut and ran through the gunfire and out of Dunkirk. Young Petey Faragher had gone in his place, and Petey hadn't come back.

'Sit down, Juan, help yourself to sandwiches. Tea, Uncle Harry? Or would you prefer beer?'

'Tea'll be grand.'

Harry chose a hard chair by the window and sat down. He was never very happy with polite company or comfortable furniture. A life spent out in all weathers had given him skin like weathered walnut, and a taste for simplicity.

Thomas wiped crumbs off his bristly top lip.

'You're a brave man, Harry, I'll say that for you.'

'Or a bloody fool,' replied Harry. 'Depends how you look at it.' Praise did not sit well with him.

'Well, I think you're brave, Uncle Harry,' piped up Juan. 'I wish you'd let me come with you to Dunkirk.' Harry threw him a pitying look.

'Boy hasn't the sense he was born with. Pass them sandwiches, will you? Ham, are they?'

Cora handed him the plate of sandwiches. She knew Harry must be inwardly squirming. He hated being the focus of attention.

'So how are you, Uncle Harry?'

Harry chewed and swallowed, taking his time answering.

'Well enough. In one piece at any rate.'

'And Davey?'

'Doc says he was lucky. Bullet passed right through an' missed the bone.'

An awkward silence fell over the gathering as they all thought of the two crew members who hadn't been so lucky. Poor Padraig O'Keefe, the Irish pacifist, and Petey Faragher – only seventeen, a couple of months younger than cousin Juan. Both brave, like Harry. Both dead and gone.

Cora busied herself with the tea tray, topping up cups and handing around food.

'I hope you don't mind eating in here,' she said brightly. 'We're having to use the front parlour as a common room for the internees. Still, Grandad and I are quite cosy up here.'

Grandad Quine snorted his disagreement.

'Cosy now, is it? Poky more like. 'Tisn't natural, a man of my age being kept out of his own front parlour – and by a load of Germans an' all.'

'Oh, stop grumbling,' urged Cora. 'Those two nice schoolgirls baked you a cake last week.'

Grandad Quine stirred his tea discontentedly.

'What's the use of cake with saccharine in it?' Whatever were things coming to? The Manx Government had already rationed his sugar, and no doubt the tea and the milk would come next. And then what? Water? Air?'

'Better than no cake at all,' replied Harry, draining his tea-cup in a single draught. 'Fine cup of tea, Cora.'

'Too weak by half,' complained Thomas.

'Now, Grandad, you know we're having to cut down.'

'Don't seem right, tea with no tea in it.'

Harry shook his head.

'Tossie always did like it so's you could stand the spoon up in it.'

'And so I do,' agreed Thomas. 'A good cup of strong tea's proper sustainin'.'

'Tossie Quine, I'll bet the inside of your belly's tanned like a pair of my old boots. And at least I don't ruin my constitution with ropey old baccy.'

'Ropey? That's Morley's Royal Mixture – one and eight an ounce!'

'Then old man Morley must've seen you coming!'

'Switch the wireless on will you, Cora?' Thomas sniffed. 'I'd rather listen to Lord Haw-Haw than have Harry bletherin' on.'

Cora went across to the wireless and switched it on to warm up. Downstairs she could hear the internees laughing and dancing to the old wind-up gramophone she'd let them use. At least some of them seemed to be making the best of things.

'Put it on the Light Programme, gel,' urged Thomas, sucking on the stem of his empty pipe. 'Let's have some music to liven us up.'

'It'll take more than music to liven you up,' commented Harry.

'Sh, Harry, I'm listening.' Juan leaned forward, straining to hear the faint sounds from the radio as the valves began to warm up.

As the radio hummed into reluctant life, music faded into the background and the cultured voice of an announcer cut through the chatter.

'. . . This is the Home Service. And now for the early evening news . . .'

'That'll do,' grunted Thomas. 'Turn it up, gel.'

Cora turned the knob and the voice grew louder, filling the room.

'Germany has demanded that the United States remove its diplomatic missions from Belgium, Holland, Luxembourg and Norway. At home, the maximum price of milk is to be raised to fourpence a pint . . .'

'Scandalous,' tut-tutted Tossie, sucking on his pipe.

'. . . Tonight it is reported that the merchant vessel the *Arandora Star* was torpedoed by a German U-boat early this morning, off the west coast of Ireland.'

'Poor buggers,' grunted Thomas.

Cora felt a shiver of sorrow, as though the war was reaching out and touching her with its cold finger. She had never heard of the *Arandora Star*, yet she sat down on the chair nearest the wireless and found herself listening intently.

'The *Arandora Star* was deporting enemy aliens and prisoners of war to the Dominions, and was flying a swastika pennant. She is reported sunk with many hundreds of lives lost . . .'

The other items rolled past: tragedies and victories, losses and gains; but somehow none hit home like the loss of the *Arandora Star*.

Juan shook his head slowly.

'How could they do that? Attack their own . . .?'

'Times is strange, boy, that they are.' Thomas Quine took out his tobacco pouch and pushed a few threads of orange-brown tobacco into the bowl of his pipe. 'But thousands of our boys was killed at Dunkirk. There'll be some as say 'tis a just retribution . . .'

'But why? Why do a thing like that?'

Cora looked across at Harry, wondering what he must be thinking. Was there a quiet satisfaction beneath that impassive façade? Was he secretly glad that so many Germans and Italians had died?

'Perhaps they didn't believe it was true,' said Harry, his expression not changing.

'Believe what?' asked Cora.

'That the ship was carrying aliens.'

'But the swastika flag . . .?'

'Aye, well, in the first lot we had what they called Q-ships. All done up like passenger ships they was, but when the Jerry U-boats got close our men'd whip the covers off the guns an' open fire. Maybe they thought this was a trick too.'

Husbands and sons and fathers, Cora thought to herself. Each of those aliens was some poor mother's son. And she thought of all the women living here at the *Bradda Vista*. Had any of them had fathers, husbands, lovers on the *Arandora Star*? She tried hard to banish the thought. Once you gave the enemy a face, how could you go on hating him?

As though in answer to her thoughts, Harry spoke up.

'I've done a few bad things in my times,' he began. 'No doubt about that.'

'But, Uncle Harry . . .' protested Cora. He put his hand up to silence her.

'Hear me out, gel. I've done bad things and I've done good, but I never killed an innocent man in cold blood.' His face creased as though with the memory of some remembered pain; and Cora knew he must be reliving the horrors of Dunkirk.

'Innocent,' grunted Thomas. 'I'd not call a bunch of Nazis innocent.' Harry paid him no heed.

'Whatever else happens in this war, gel,' declared Harry, 'we must do what's right. An' we must never turn out like that.'

'Elsa.'

At the sound of her name, Elsa turned on her heel. A woman with short brown hair and thick ankles was walking down the promenade towards her. She recognised her vaguely as Olga Wissel, one of the Nazi women from the *Erindale*. An uneasy feeling stirred in the pit of her stomach. What could this woman possibly want with her?

'Elsa Nadel?'

'Yes.'

Elsa stopped and waited for Olga to catch up. It was a beautiful morning, fresh with the winds that gusted in across the Irish Sea, but with the warmth of an early July sun to take the chill away. Out on the sea a fishing boat was bobbing, heading back toward Peel harbour with its catch.

'*Guten Tag, Fräulein Nadel.*'

Elsa nodded a wary greeting.

'*Guten Tag.*'

'I have a message for you.'

Elsa's heart sank as she saw the envelope. Another letter. No question who it was from. Reluctantly she took it.

'A message?' she forced herself to say coolly. 'From whom?' But she could guess.

'I am just the messenger, *verstehen Sie?*'

'Oh, I understand,' replied Elsa with a hint of irony. 'I hope you are paid well for your trouble.'

Olga turned and did not look back. As she watched her walk away, Elsa wondered why she bothered to play along with this childish game. She should simply rip up the letter, envelope and all, and drop it over the cliffs to fall, confetti-like, into the frothy waters swirling about the rocks below.

So why didn't she?

Or she could take the letters to the Commandant, complain that she was being harassed. But it was rumoured that Dame Joanna Cruickshank favoured the Nazi women. And even if that was untrue, how could Elsa tell her troubles to a martinet who walked around the camp with a riding crop, ordering people to keep off the grass? It was bad enough being persecuted by Marianne von Strondheim, without being on Dame Joanna's blacklist as well.

Sitting down on a bench overlooking the sea, Elsa tore open the envelope. Inside was a single sheet of flimsy paper. Obviously even Marianne had to make do with less than the best when times were hard.

'Elsa,' the letter read. 'Why will you not see sense? Why must you persist in this bone-headed stupidity? You betray your Fatherland and your race by consorting with degenerates and Jews. How can you collaborate and cooperate with the enemies who have imprisoned you . . .?'

It was the same rubbish as the last time, repellent yet painfully personal. Why couldn't she bring herself to tear it up and throw it away? Taking it to heart was exactly what Marianne wanted her to do. But she couldn't force herself to look away. She and Marianne had once been as close as sisters, closer. Could she truly have changed so much?

'. . . Why betray our friendship? Why betray yourself, Elsa? Forget your misguided idealism. I have powerful friends, I can protect you. You must understand the dangers of betrayal.

'You are German, Elsa. Have you no honour . . .?'

Anger engulfed Elsa. She wanted to stand and scream her rage into the buffeting wind. Instead, she screwed the paper up into a tight ball and thrust it deep into her pocket.

Lies. Evil, pernicious rubbish – that was all it was. If only she wasn't so afraid. Afraid she might start believing it was true.

Reuben Kotkin's heart soared. He knew nothing about the Isle of Man, not even where it was, but the very fact that he had been brought here was enough to lift his spirits.

She must be here, he kept on telling himself. Here, on this island. The Commandant at Huyton had promised that it was so, had even arranged for him to be on the next transport to the Island. In some ways he had been almost sorry to leave Huyton, where he had begun to settle into a sort of dull routine; but for a chance to be reunited with Rachel he would have walked barefoot to the ends of the earth.

The old *Victoria* docked in Douglas Harbour early in the morning, and the few hundred men disembarked, subdued after a night on the boat from Liverpool. After perfunctory police checks, they were formed into a long column and marched, under guard, along the promenade towards Broadway.

To Reuben, it felt good just to breathe in the air and see the bluey-green of the sea, the softer greens and browns of the hills. This place was as strange to him as Dover had been, then Huyton, but this time he felt less fear, more anticipation. Curious, he took in the long curve of boarding houses, wired off here and there into compounds; the mast of land-based HMS *Valkyrie*, the double row of rails which marked where the 'toast rack' horse trams had run before the war. And he wondered in which of these houses Rachel was living; how long it would be before the British authorities let him see her.

Drexel Sachs walked beside him, uncharacteristically edgy and quiet.

'Where are they taking us, Kotkin?'

'I don't know. To a new camp. "P Camp", the soldier called it, I think. It will be a better place, you will see.'

'I hope for both our sakes you are right,' replied Sachs. Generally cast as the joker in any gathering, he did not feel particularly like joking today. Right now, he felt quietly furious at being treated like a commodity to be shunted from place to place.

'Get off your *toches*, will yer?' grumbled a voice that was considerably more Bermondsey than Berlin.

'All right, all right.' Sachs transferred his heavy suitcase to the other hand. 'Keep your hair on, Finkel.' He turned back to Reuben. 'I'm going to get out of here, Kotkin.'

Reuben regarded him with faint surprise.

'We all want to get out. We will get out. Some have been released already – the old, the sick.'

Sachs snorted.

'But I am neither old nor sick, Kotkin, and I don't intend

staying here until I am! First chance I get, I'm volunteering for the Pioneer Corps – and if you're wise, you'll do the same.'

The long column of men wound its way up the hill towards Hutchinson Square, weighed down with suitcases and packages. Reuben looked around him with interest. Some of the men he recognised from Huyton, others had been brought here from other camps on the mainland.

'Look, there's Samuel Green, and that nice old gentleman who used to teach anatomy at the university.'

Sachs followed Reuben's pointing finger, and pulled a face.

'And that *yentzer* who cheated Papiermeister at cards. I tried to warn him, but would he listen?'

They were a mixed bag all right, thought Reuben. Where else but in an internment camp could you meet Yiddish-speaking Chassidim, Spanish Civil War veterans, Prussian ex-ministers, a Protestant pastor from the German Resistance Church, University professors, refugees, artists, crooks and even a condom salesman called Liebe; all in the space of half a square mile?

One man had brought a portable typewriter with him, another had even brought his dog, trotting along beside him quite contentedly on the end of a length of string. Behind him shuffled a man struggling with a cello in a heavy wooden case. Each had brought with him the most important symbol of his life outside the wire. And what had Reuben brought with him? He too had brought what mattered most in the world to him: the love of his wife Rachel, deep and warm and constant in his heart.

At last they came to the gates. Hutchinson Camp – or 'P Camp' as it was officially known – was centred on a square of houses off Broadway, a steep road which wound up from the promenade to Upper Douglas. At the centre was a terraced lawn, surrounded by streets of typical Victorian boarding houses which had been hurriedly requisitioned for the new

155

intake of internees, and enclosed with double rows of barbed wire. Outside the perimeter soldiers patrolled with fixed bayonets. Turning to look back beyond the wire, Reuben could see the broad, sweeping panorama of Douglas Bay.

The gates opened and they filed in. There were a few occupants there already, men who stood outside their houses and watched the newcomers with interest.

'Is there any news?' called one.

'How goes the war?' asked another.

'Quiet. Quiet, gentlemen, *please*.' The Camp Commandant stepped forward to take charge of the motley band. They shuffled to a standstill, their chatter subsiding to a low buzz as they waited to hear what he might have to say. 'You will all be allocated to houses. Are there any of you who are kosher?'

A few hands were raised and heads nodded.

'You will go to house fourteen.'

A voice spoke up from the back.

'I wish to apply for repatriation.'

The Commandant focused on the figure, a tall man in a suit.

'All in good time.'

'I have waited long enough. First I am told I must fill in a special form, then I am told there are no forms to be had . . .'

'You will be dealt with. You will *all* be dealt with in due course.'

The Commandant could see this job was going to be far from trouble-free. Aliens had a right to apply for repatriation – not that there was much immediate chance of their getting it. But once they had applied, they would also have the right to certain privileges. It was a complication the Commandant could have done without, but when all was said and done, you had to treat these men in a civilised way, the way you would hope to be treated if the situation was reversed.

'Sar'nt Major.'

A dapper-looking sergeant stepped forward.

'Sir.'

'Allocate these men to their houses and appoint house captains. I will see the captains with any requests or complaints they may have.'

'Right away, sir.'

Reuben and Sachs found themselves counted into a group of about thirty men, destined for House forty-one. This was one of the boarding houses just behind the square; a big, white-painted building of three storeys, plus two attic rooms at the front, their dormer windows jutting out of the roof like a frog's eyes.

Two old men were playing cards, sitting outside on deck chairs stamped 'Douglas Corporation'. They scarcely looked up as the newcomers filed past.

'How is it here?' asked Reuben. 'Is this a good place?'

One of the old men scratched his bald pate.

'Good if you like herring, not so good if you don't,' he commented with a dry chuckle, and went back to playing cards and continuing his conversation with his companion. 'I wrote to my wife and I said, "Broche, get yourself interned. You've never had it so good!"'

Reuben and Sachs followed the others up three stone steps and into the hallway of the boarding house. The first thing they noticed was how bare it was, with hardly any furniture and very old, yellowing lino instead of carpet.

'I see they're not taking any chances,' commented Sachs.

'Chances?'

'With us. The owners obviously don't trust us – they've taken out all the good stuff and left us with nothing.'

Samuel Green, very self-important after being appointed captain of the house, set about organising everyone.

'There will be four to a room,' he announced, 'two to a double bed.'

'A double bed!' The Oxford academic shook his head in dismay. It had not been like this at Keble . . .

'At least here we *have* beds,' retorted Oskar Vischer. 'At

Huyton, all I had was a stinking straw palliasse in a leaking tent!'

Reuben and Sachs were more fortunate than most, in that they had only to share with each other – though their attic room was tiny, with a ceiling so low that Sachs had to stoop to avoid banging his head on the eaves.

Samuel Green stood in the doorway.

'Here you are then, your new home. What do you think of it?'

Reuben threw his case down on the bed and sank down after it, his eyes scanning the room. It was hardly the height of luxury, with its peeling yellowed wallpaper, marked here and there with lighter rectangles where pictures had been taken down. It was dark and dingy, and the old iron bedstead creaked alarmingly as he sat down.

'*Riboyne Shel O'lem*!' exclaimed Sachs. 'There is no table. Not even a chair! Where will I do my writing?'

Samuel Green sighed. Less than an hour in the job and already he was starting to see its drawbacks.

'Most men want to eat and sleep – he wants to write! There are chairs downstairs, you can do your scribbling there.'

Reuben paid little attention to Sachs's complaints. He was glancing first at the window, then up at the single lightbulb dangling from a bare flex.

'Samuel . . .'

'What is it now?'

'Why is the window painted blue and the lightbulb painted red?'

Samuel shrugged.

'It is for the blackout. They say the blue and the red mix together and no light will show through the glass. So we cannot send signals to German aeroplanes . . .'

'They think we are spies?'

'Of course. The British are so afraid of invasion that they think everyone is a spy.'

'Oh they do, do they?' Reaching up and taking the lightbulb out of its socket, Sachs began scratching off the red paint with his thumbnail.

Reuben got slowly to his feet. It was an effort: he was suddenly and incredibly tired. But a single thought kept driving him on, cutting through his exhaustion.

'Samuel, you are captain of this house. The Commandant said that we must direct all our requests through you.'

Samuel leant up against the doorpost.

'What is it, Kotkin? You can't be complaining about the food already – you haven't had any.'

'It's my wife, Rachel. I know she's here and I want to see her.'

Samuel's gaze drifted upward to a spider, walking slowly across the ceiling.

'Every man here wants to see his wife or his girl, Kotkin. What makes you so different?'

'She's expecting our first child.'

'When?'

'I'm not sure, it's difficult to be certain. In a few weeks' time, I think. I promised her I would be with her when the baby comes. And now I'm so afraid I won't be . . .'

Samuel nodded, not unsympathetically.

'I'll speak to the Commandant, but . . .'

'Samuel, I promised her. And she doesn't even know I'm here. I asked to be brought here precisely because I heard that she was on the Island.'

'I wish it was that simple, Reuben.' Samuel sat down on the bed next to him. 'The women's camp is miles from here. There's no communication between our camp and theirs. They've promised meetings soon . . . but when, I don't know.'

Marshalling all his strength, Reuben got to his feet.

'You don't understand, Samuel,' he said firmly. 'I have to see Rachel. And I will see her. And if you will take me to see the Commandant, I will tell him so.'

* * *

Grethe slept fitfully, her dreams filled with images of little Emil; his face tear-stained and his arms reaching out to her. But he was always just out of reach.

Surfacing once more into wakefulness, Grethe rolled onto her side. Elsa was sleeping next to her in the big old double bed, her face turned away and her knees drawn up, like a slumbering child. Grethe wondered if she was dreaming about that good-looking Scottish vet who seemed to be taking such an interest in her welfare; and what Cora Quine thought about it all. Not that it was any of Grethe's business, of course. She knew the value of discretion.

As she reached out for the glass of water on the bedside table, she heard Rachel call out:

'Reuben. Oh, Reuben, why don't you come to me . . .?' And then a little sob, stifled by the blanket half-obscuring her face.

Thinking Rachel was dreaming, Grethe took a sip of water then lay down again. She was hot, too hot. Pushing back the sheet she lay in the darkness, listening to the regular sound of Elsa's breathing. This July night was so oppressive – and it must be so much worse for Rachel, poor girl.

Her thoughts drifted back to her own pregnancy, not so many years ago. She had faced a tough decision: to keep the child or visit the old woman who performed abortions for the price of a bottle of whisky. Looking back, it seemed crazy that she had ever thought of getting rid of the baby; but she had been so alone. Different and yet not so different from Rachel Kotkin.

As she lay there she heard Rachel call out again. Only this time, the voice sounded different. Instinctively Grethe sat up, half wishing that Elsa would wake up and take over.

'Rachel?' she whispered. 'Are you all right?'

Rachel didn't reply instantly, but Grethe could hear her moaning softly in the darkness. She got out of bed, sliding her bare feet into her satin mules, and padded across to Rachel's bed.

'Come on now, *liebchen*, what's the matter? Missing Reuben, are you?'

She reached for Rachel's hand. It felt cold and sweaty; and when she felt Rachel's brow that was wet with perspiration, too.

'Grethe. I want Reuben . . .'

'I know, sweetheart. I know.' She sat on the edge of Rachel's bed and took her hand. She was astonished at the tension in the young girl's body, as though she was straining every muscle not to cry out. 'What's the matter? Do you feel ill?'

'I have . . . to be . . . strong. For Reuben.'

'You *are* strong.'

'Grethe, please. Help me. It hurts!' And in the next second Rachel let out a thin, high cry, drawing up her knees to her chest and rolling onto her side so that she was facing Grethe. 'No, no, it can't happen yet!'

Grethe's heart was thumping in her chest.

'Rachel – answer me. Does it hurt very much?'

'Yes. It comes and goes.'

'*Mein Gott*,' Grethe whispered to herself. She wasn't ready for this – but then neither was Rachel Kotkin. It looked as if she was going to have to try and be strong for both of them.

Across the room, Elsa stirred in her bed. Her voice was sleepy, not yet quite awake.

'Grethe . . . is that you?'

'Get up, Elsa.'

'W-what? What is it?'

'Elsa, hurry up, will you?' Grethe felt Rachel's hand clasp hers as tightly as a vice grips metal.

Elsa slipped sleepily out of bed, groping for her robe.

'What's the matter?'

'You'd better go and wake Cora,' said Grethe, surprising herself with her own calmness. 'Tell her to bring the midwife. And quickly!'

'There's something wrong with Rachel?'

'She's having the baby, damn it! She's in labour.'

'Are you sure? It isn't due . . .'

'How many times have *you* given birth, Elsa Nadel? Now, tell Cora to fetch the midwife before it's too late!'

Chapter 12

Cora knocked at the door and opened it a fraction. Inside, she could see the German midwife – a Protestant deaconess – gliding about with stern, effortless efficiency.

Swamped by the huge double bed, Rachel was fast asleep, propped up on pillows. Her once-white face was flushed with effort and her dark hair plastered in damp tendrils to her forehead and the side of her face.

Adjusting a corner of the sheet, the midwife glanced towards the door and gave a curt nod.

'Five minutes, no more.'

Cora stepped inside, closing the door behind her.

'Is she . . .?' she began in a low whisper, afraid of waking Rachel.

'She is very tired, as you can see. But it was a short labour and she is well.'

'And the child?' Cora hardly dared ask the question on everyone's lips. Every single inhabitant of the *Bradda Vista* had been on tenterhooks since early morning, when they had heard the news that Rachel Kotkin had gone into labour.

'A little girl. She is also doing well.'

The deaconess inclined her head towards the end of the bed. The scene almost broke Cora's heart. The child was swaddled in a pillowcase, lying in a drawer taken from the dressing-table and padded out with squares of torn-up sheeting. There had been so few preparations for the birth that there had been no cot, no baby clothes, no nappies, nothing to welcome the little child into the world.

She stepped a little closer, and looked down at the baby. It was so incredibly tiny, its sleeping face as red as a beetroot and its hair a mass of jet-black fuzz – not exactly beautiful, yet wonderful all the same. A tiny miracle in the middle of such horrors and sadness.

'Do *try* not to wake the infant,' said the midwife.

Cora stood very still, hardly daring to breathe. She found the baby quite astounding in the perfection of fragile fingers and toes, that squat little button nose, those silky eyelashes.

All at once she was transported back to the day when she had first seen William and Grace's baby – a little boy, blond and fat. Billy, they had called him, after his father. Everyone had been so proud, even Cora, who had hardly known what to do when William lifted the child into her arms and introduced her to her brand-new nephew.

So happy, and so proud. Who could have foreseen what would happen to Billy, to Grace, to the whole family?

'Cora?'

She turned to see that Rachel had woken up and was hauling herself up into a sitting position.

'Please, Rachel, don't tire yourself,' said Cora.

'Yes, you must rest.' The midwife patted down the sheets. She seemed more concerned about creases in the bedclothes than her patient's wishes.

'Nurse, I would like to hold my daughter now.' Cora sensed a new maturity in the girl who had seemed scarcely old enough to be a mother. 'Please bring her to me.'

The midwife hesitated.

'Now, please.'

'Very well, *Frau Kotkin*. As you wish.'

She lifted the baby out of the drawer and carried her across to Rachel. The child did not cry, but awoke and made little gurgling noises as the midwife placed her in her mother's arms.

Rachel held her daughter very close, cradling her in her arms, mesmerised by the blue eyes which gazed so unblinkingly

164

up at her. Her joy was so intense that it was almost a physical pain.

'My daughter,' she kept whispering over and over again. 'My own daughter . . .'

'She's very special,' said Cora, drawing up a chair and sitting beside the bed. 'Perfect.'

'Reuben will be so proud.' Rachel tried to disguise the tremor in her voice.

'I'm sure he will.' Cora shifted on her chair, not sure what to say. 'You caused quite a stir last night, you know!'

'I did?'

'Dame Joanna's furious that we didn't call her when you went into labour. When I rang her this morning, she said: "I am a trained nursing sister, and I am quite capable of delivering an infant".' She managed a passable imitation of the Commandant's forbidding tones.

'Oh, Cora, I'm sorry, I didn't mean to cause trouble for you.'

Cora laughed and shook her head.

'Don't be silly. I couldn't care less what Dame Joanna thinks. The only thing that matters is that you're both all right. And besides, how could you stop baby coming when she'd made up her mind to be born?'

Rachel's eyes met Cora's.

'Would you like to hold her?'

'No. No, not yet awhile – when she's a little older. I'm not very good with little babies, I'm all fingers and thumbs.' She put out a finger and tentatively stroked the child's face; it was delicate as priceless porcelain. 'Now, Rachel, how are you feeling?'

'Tired and sore – but good.'

'Well you must tell me if you need anything. Do you promise to do that?'

Rachel nodded. At that moment another knock at the door drew a gasp of exasperation from the midwife.

'Come.'

The door opened and two faces appeared in the doorway. 'Can we come in?'

'Elsa, Grethe!' Rachel's half-smile brightened.

'One visitor only,' said the midwife sternly. 'Frau Kotkin is very tired.'

'Please, nurse, I want to see them,' insisted Rachel.

'It's all right.' Cora got to her feet. 'I have to go anyway. There's the laundry to supervise, and I expect the ambulance will be here any time now, to take you to the hospital.'

'Must I go?' Rachel's dark eyes pleaded, but the midwife cut in before Cora's better judgement had a chance to weaken.

'Of course you must go to hospital. You want the best for your baby, don't you?'

Rachel said nothing, but she looked glum.

'The "Jane" is a wonderful place,' Cora reassured her. 'Brand spanking new, and the best of everything.'

'I'd much rather stay here.'

'But you'll have a lovely rest, away from this place.'

Making brief goodbyes, Cora got up and left, nodding a greeting to Elsa and Grethe as she closed the door quietly behind her.

'She's looking worn out,' remarked Elsa. Grethe raised her eyes heavenwards.

'Of course she's worn out, Elsa, she's just had a baby! And when you've had one, you'll know what hard work is. Now, Rachel, are they taking good care of you?'

'Very.'

'You're sure?'

Rachel couldn't help laughing.

'Quite sure. You're like a mother hen.'

'Well, somebody has to make sure you're being looked after.' Grethe exchanged a glare of mutual animosity with the midwife. 'You and the baby.'

Elsa came forward. Bending over the bed, she gently

pushed back the blanket which had half slipped over the baby's face.

'Hello, little stranger,' she whispered. 'Welcome to the world.' And what a world it is, she thought.

'Thank you,' said Rachel, looking from Grethe to Elsa and back again. 'Both of you.'

'What on earth for?' Grethe sat down on the edge of the bed, arms folded.

'For everything . . . for what you have done for me. Not just last night, but ever since we came here.'

Slightly uncomfortable with Rachel's gratitude, Elsa tried to wave her thanks away, but Rachel touched her hand and held it fast.

'Without you, I would have been so alone. You helped me to be strong.'

Elsa smiled, but in the pit of her stomach there was a funny, hollow feeling; and she couldn't quite empty her mind of Marianne von Strondheim's letter, her softly treacherous words, trying so hard to insinuate themselves into her heart.

'We're going to have such a party when you come back from the hospital,' said Grethe cheerily.

'One of the new Italians is a pastry-cook,' butted in Elsa, 'and we're all going to save up our rations so she can bake a cake.'

'Couldn't you come to the hospital with me?'

Elsa shook her head.

'Don't worry, you'll be fine.'

At which point the door opened yet again, and Cora looked in.

'There's another visitor for you, Rachel,' announced Cora.

'Out of the question,' snapped the midwife, reaching out her arms to take the child from Rachel's arms. 'Give her to me, all this commotion will wake her up.'

Rachel snapped back:

'Thank you, nurse; I think I know what is best for my own daughter.'

'Your visitor's here with me,' said Cora.

'Who is it?'

'Would you like to see her now?'

'Y-yes. I suppose so.' For a single, crazy split-second, Rachel had almost believed that her visitor might be Reuben.

The last person she expected to see was Sarah Rosenberg.

'Sarah.' The word escaped from her lips in a startled outrush of breath.

Sarah walked into the room. She was less gaunt than the last time they had spoken, several weeks ago; smartly dressed with her black hair neatly brushed and coiled into a bun. She hesitated as she saw Grethe and Elsa, her expression wary; then she addressed a silent nod of acknowledgement to them and walked towards the bed.

'Rachel.' As she got closer, Rachel saw that she was shaking. 'I heard . . . about the baby.'

Rachel stared at her, dumbfounded. Sarah had been ignoring her for weeks, had made it clear that she wanted nothing to do with her – and now here she was. For a moment she wanted to blurt out all the pain she had felt, how much it had hurt to be rejected by a woman she had wanted – and needed – as a friend. But the angry words would not come.

'Come and sit by me, Sarah.'

'I wanted to see how you were.'

Rachel nodded.

'I'm fine. We're both fine. See, I have a daughter – isn't she beautiful?'

She held out the child.

'Go on, Sarah. Take her. Hold her.'

Sarah cradled the child and she opened her eyes and began to whimper. But as Sarah rocked her, she kicked her legs in pleasure.

'What are you going to call her?' asked Sarah.

'Esther Kotkin. Esther *Sarah* Kotkin.'

That afternoon, when Rachel had been safely transferred –

under police guard – to the Jane Crookall Maternity Home, Cora set about reorganising the house.

Rachel's newborn daughter had set the whole of Rushen Camp buzzing. The birth of a child seemed to signify that there would be, must be, a better tomorrow just around the corner.

'The two Italians will have to go in the attic,' Cora declared, pausing for a moment to glance out of the back kitchen window. On the patch of grass behind the boarding house, the two schoolgirls, Rosie and Anna, were playing with Bonzo. His little short legs were a blur of activity as he tore round after his old tennis ball. 'I can't think of any other way to fit everyone in, now that Rachel needs a room to herself.'

'It'll come right, gel,' grunted Thomas. 'And this house'll be a darn sight quieter once that Inge and Mathilde have gone.'

Cora couldn't help agreeing. It had taken an age to get those two transferred to the *Erindale*, but today – at long last – they were going. Even Archie seemed to appreciate this, rubbing his head against Cora's ankle.

'Mind my stockings, Archie. They're my last decent pair.' That'll teach me to try and impress James McArthur, she thought.

'I hope that dog keeps off my carrots,' commented Thomas darkly, peering out at the lawn. Most of the garden had been dug up to provide fresh vegetables, and Thomas was engaged in stiff competition with George Corless to see who could win more prizes at the annual produce show.

'Do try not to get so worked up,' urged Cora. 'It's bad for your blood pressure. Now, I wonder how they're getting on with moving that furniture . . .'

Bustling out of the kitchen, she almost walked straight into James, who was helping Harry Kerruish to manhandle a chest of drawers up the stairs.

'James!' scolded Cora. 'You said you'd only move little things, and here you are lugging furniture around!'

'Don't fuss, Cora, everything's fine,' panted James, looking over his shoulder as he guided the chest up the stairs.

'But you promised! I wouldn't have let you help if I'd thought you were going to do this.'

'Don't worry, gel, I'm takin' most of the weight,' Harry assured her, pausing for a moment to mop his perspiring brow. 'Now then, Mr McArthur, if you'd just shift your end over a bit . . .'

The chest of drawers disappeared up onto the first landing, and Cora heard it deposited safely in its new location. Voices were chattering over the bangs and crashes of wood on wood, but she could just make out Elsa's voice over the top of it all, directing and encouraging operations.

'That's right, can you manage? You will watch out for your poor leg, won't you?'

Taking off her apron, Cora set off upstairs. She couldn't help feeling peeved. James knew very well that another accident might set back his recovery, but he would insist on trying to do more than he was capable of. And of course he wouldn't listen, would he? It was like talking to a tree . . .

'Put it down over there, boy,' called Harry. 'Just over there, by the window.'

'Just here? If you could . . . oh!'

Cora entered the room at the very moment when James lost his grip on the chest of drawers and it slipped down, crashing against his leg. Before she had a chance to open her mouth, Elsa Nadel was at his side.

'Oh, James, are you all right? Have you hurt yourself badly? Here, James, lean on me.'

Cora held her breath, waiting for James to bite Elsa's head off. That was what he always did when anyone tried to fuss over him. To her annoyance, he smiled.

'Don't worry. Just gave myself a bit of a clout on the shin, that's all. That'll teach me to be clumsy!' He looked across and saw Cora standing by the door. 'Hello there. Anything wrong?'

'No,' replied Cora, tight-lipped. 'Everything's perfectly

fine. You're obviously being *very* well looked after.'

She turned on her heel and walked out, passing Grethe on the landing and cutting her dead.

'Cora.'

She looked over her shoulder to see Elsa hurrying down the stairs after her. Without stopping she responded:

'What?'

'Is something the matter?'

'Why should anything be the matter?'

'I don't know . . . you just seemed angry. Did I do something wrong?'

Stopping half-way down the stairs, Cora took two deep breaths. She could feel her heart thumping in her chest.

'No,' she said, forcing herself to smile as she turned to look at Elsa. 'Of course you haven't.'

But perhaps *I* have, she thought to herself. Perhaps I have . . .

The Jane Crookall Maternity Home was all that Cora had promised it would be, and more. Rachel couldn't believe how well she was being treated. The nurses were polite to her, she had her own room – and even a bell to ring if she needed anything.

'Now, Mrs Kotkin, you understand English, I believe?' Curate Adrian Newell peered at her benignly.

'Yes.'

'The doctor will be coming soon.'

Rachel's face registered alarm.

'There is something wrong with my baby?'

'No, no, there is nothing wrong. The nurses tell me she is perfectly well. But we must make sure that both of you stay that way.'

'Why? Why are you doing all this for us?'

Newell stared back at her, clearly bewildered.

'Why, my dear? Because every mother and child deserve the best care we can give.'

'Then, will you do something for me? Please?'

'If I can.'

Rachel leaned forward and took hold of the priest's hand.

'Please find my husband, Father. Find my Reuben and bring him to me.'

Grethe left Inge and Mathilde arguing in the hallway of the *Bradda Vista*, and walked down to the end of the road. It was good to be out in the fresh air again.

The promenade was dotted here and there with women in shorts and bathing costumes, with children in home-made sun-hats and the occasional old man, dozing in the afternoon sunshine. It was hard to believe that four out of every five people she could see were not holidaymakers, but internees.

It had been quite a day – quite a night, too. Now that the excitement was all over, it felt like an anticlimax. And the birth of Rachel's child had reawakened the ache of separation inside Grethe.

She felt in her pocket for the brief note she had at last received from Claire, together with a card which Emil had made and drawn himself. At least she knew now that Emil was safe – but it wasn't enough. Everywhere she looked there were women with children. Why couldn't the authorities keep their promise and bring her son to her?

The sand was warm and powdery, grains of it working their way into her sandals, and in between her toes. Stopping, Grethe bent down; unbuckling her sandals, she took them off then walked on.

She looked across towards the breakwater. On the beach below the jetty stood a familiar figure; shoulders hunched, hands in pockets, gazing out to sea.

Harry Kerruish was a man who never quite fitted in with his surroundings. Wherever he was, whoever he was with, he seemed set apart: the sort of man who would be lonely even in a crowd. Like me, thought Grethe. And yet not like me . . .

Grethe had hardly exchanged half a dozen words with

Harry on his occasional visits to the *Bradda Vista*, but there was something about him which intrigued her, drew her attention. He looked preoccupied and sad, as if there was something he longed to talk about but had vowed to keep firmly locked inside.

After a moment's thought, Grethe started padding across the sand towards him.

'Mr Kerruish?'

His back stiffened and he glanced over his shoulder then turned away.

'Oh, it's you.'

'Mr Kerruish – is something wrong?'

Harry said nothing. Grethe almost gave up and walked away, but decided to give it another try.

'I thought perhaps . . . I could help.'

He grunted.

'I bet you did.'

The penny dropped, and Grethe felt the old anger bite.

'Oh, you think I'm touting for business, do you? You think just because I'm a working girl that's all I ever think about?'

Harry stared down at his boots.

'S'pose not.'

'Well you suppose right.'

She moved so that she was standing right next to Harry and he couldn't ignore her. He cast a sidelong glance at her.

'You'd better not let them see you talkin' to me out here,' he commented gruffly. 'They'll put you in jail.'

'Jail! What do they think this is?'

'Still, you don't want a night in the police cells.'

'If Elsa Nadel can talk to that vet, I don't see why I can't pass the time of day with you.'

All right, so Elsa had special permission to 'liaise' with James McArthur about the adult education classes; but that still didn't make it right for there to be one law for Elsa, and a different law for everyone else, now did it?

'Well, be it on your own head, gel.'

Grethe stooped to pick up a shell from the edge of the water.

'I couldn't stay in that house,' she said, turning the shell over and admiring the many-coloured opalescence of its inner surface. 'Not with Inge and Mathilde screaming at each other and the dog chasing the cat and Cora in a mood. Is that why you came out here, too?'

Harry squinted at a far-distant speck on the horizon: perhaps a fishing boat, perhaps a passenger ferry to Ireland.

'A man needs to be alone with his own thoughts sometimes.'

'I'm sorry. I'll go.'

'Stay if you like.'

'You don't mind?'

'I'll say so if I do.'

They stood there, side by side, saying nothing. Those moments seemed to last forever, the two of them strangely separate from everything around them. In the end it was Harry who spoke first.

'You got a man then, gel?'

'No. But I have a son.'

'I never married.'

'Nor did I.' Grethe allowed herself a wry smile. 'My sort don't.'

'Ah. No.' Harry considered for a moment. 'Your lad's not with you then?'

'They made me leave him in London. My friend's looking after him.'

'I always thought I'd marry. But you can't read the future, can you?'

'No,' agreed Grethe. And it came from the heart. 'Mr Kerruish . . . is something wrong?'

'What's it to you if there is?'

'Oh . . . nothing. I just thought you might want to talk about it.'

'No.' Harry shot a glance at Grethe. 'Not yet.'

* * *

174

Cora stood in the hallway of the *Bradda Vista*, watching Inge and Mathilde dragging their suitcases down the stairs.

'I hope you'll be happier at the *Erindale*,' she said. The further away the better, she told herself.

'At least there we shall not have to share our meals with Jews and communists,' snapped Inge.

Cora shrugged. She wasn't about to tell them that, frankly, she preferred Jews and communists any time to spiteful housemaids who'd never raised a finger to make themselves useful.

'Goodbye,' she said cheerily, and took great pleasure in crashing the door shut behind them. 'And good riddance,' she muttered in the peace and quiet of the empty hallway.

Cora leant back against the door and let all the tension drain out of her in one long breath. What a day. Italian arrivals, Austrian departures and a baby born – what else could happen before the day was out? There was just time to make the attic room comfortable before the next batch of Italians arrived. She climbed wearily up the stairs, followed by Bonzo, hopefully carrying his tennis ball in his mouth.

She looked away as she passed Inge and Mathilde's old room, but it was no use trying to suppress the thought. Secretly she couldn't help wishing that Elsa was leaving too.

Chapter 13

It was 10 July, and it seemed as if it had always been summer in Port Erin.

A hot, white sun blazed down out of a brassy blue sky, and the beach was thronged with sunbathers and swimmers, with tiny tots digging holes in the sand and older children playing games.

But under the surface tensions bubbled like hot fat, threatening to burst to the top at any moment. The news of the sinking of the *Arandora Star* had come as a bolt from the blue, a horror too terrible to sink in at first. The repercussions had only become clear later, as fragments of news filtered through and one by one, women were told that they had lost sons, fathers, brothers, husbands. Rushen Camp was reeling from the blow.

Sarah Rosenberg pushed the sleeves of her dress up to her elbows. On this sultry, sticky afternoon she was busy helping to put the finishing touches to the new camp nursery.

'These walls need painting,' she announced, stepping back to admire her handiwork. The patch she had just washed looked several shades lighter than the rest of the wall.

'So we'll paint them,' shrugged her companion, Nan, a rotund, matronly woman in her fifties.

'Where will we get the paint?'

'We'll ask the Commandant, say it's essential for the health of the little ones. You don't get anything in this place if you don't fight for it.'

Sarah started sponging the next section of wall.

'Perhaps, when the walls are clean, we could get someone to paint pictures on them for the children. Animals, birds . . .'

'There is a woman at the *Breakwater* who was an artist. We could ask her. She could draw the outlines, and we could get some of the others to fill them in.'

'You have such good ideas.'

'I must keep myself busy. Or I will think . . .'

Footsteps on the path outside made Sarah look out through the window.

'Who is it?' asked Nan.

'Elsa Nadel. Why can't she just leave us to get on with our work? Why does she think she must organise everybody?'

The conversation was cut short by Elsa's arrival, her arms full of toys and games.

'*Guten Tag*, ladies. See what lovely things we have been given. Mrs Pantin arranged a collection of toys from the local children, and there are more to come. There is even a train set . . .'

'That's good,' said Sarah. 'Please put them on the table over there, out of the way.'

'Oh. All right then.' Elsa felt disappointment at Sarah's lack of enthusiasm. She'd thought briefly, when Sarah came to see Rachel and the baby, that things might be all right between them. But here she felt like an intruder. She tried again.

'Hello, Nan.'

On her knees washing the floor, Nan dipped her brush again into the bucket of soapy water, then leant forward and went on scrubbing vigorously.

'Hello.'

'Did you hear anything . . . about your Joseph?'

Nan paused for a fraction of a second, then went on working.

'Yes.'

'Was the Commandant able to tell you where he is?'

'Only that he was on the *Arandora Star*.'

'No! Oh, Nan, I'm so sorry. But – perhaps he was rescued . . .?'

Nan sat back on her haunches. Elsa knew from the angry stiffness of her back that she'd made a big mistake.

Sarah turned round, eyes sparking a warning.

'*Fräulein Nadel*, I don't say that you are a wicked woman . . .'

'I beg your pardon?'

'I don't say that you are wicked, or trying to stir up trouble, but stupid?'

'I'm sorry, really I am. I didn't know.'

'No. Of course you didn't.' Elsa could tell Sarah thought she was lying.

'Nobody is sure of anything,' said Nan, her voice very faint. She scrubbed obsessively at the bare floorboards. 'Nothing. They tell me my husband was on the ship, but they don't know if he is alive or dead.'

'Do you know how that feels?' demanded Sarah. 'Do you?'

'Sarah, don't do this,' said Nan quietly. 'It doesn't do any good.'

'No good? Someone has to tell these arrogant German bitches they can't lord it over us and expect us to be grateful for their "sympathy".'

'Look, Sarah,' said Elsa.

'No, you look, *Fräulein*. There is only one good thing about the *Arandora Star*, and do you know what this is? Hundreds of Nazis died on that ship, hundreds of Germans. Just like you.'

Elsa wanted to reply, retaliate, placate – something. But she opened her mouth and no sound came out.

'Leave her alone,' said Nan. Wiping her hands on her overall, she got to her feet and put her arm round Sarah's shoulders. 'It's not worth doing this to yourself for.'

'No, *she's* not worth it. Not worth a damn thing. Not her, not any of her godforsaken race.'

Elsa took a step forward.

'I'm sorry you feel that way. Truly sorry.' Yet suddenly she

179

felt angry. Why cast her as the villain? Why expect her to take the blame for something which had nothing to do with her? Something she hadn't wanted to happen?

'Just leave us alone,' snapped Sarah.

'I think it's better if you go,' said Nan.

'I'll leave the toys here with you.'

Elsa turned to go. Could Sarah and Nan feel the anger and the hurt in her? Right and wrong, hatred and love were so easy for them. Did they know what it was like to be condemned not just by one side but both in this godless, worthless war?

Outside, she leaned her back against the hut and took long, deep breaths. She must be calm. But her fingers were tensing against the hot, rough wood, her back bracing as the heat throbbed and pulsed into her.

The sun shone fiery red through her closed eyelids; red as the anger she had felt back there in the nursery. Whatever was happening to her? To the mature, calm, professional woman she had always found it so easy to be?

She mopped her forehead with her handkerchief, and felt in her pocket for the postcard she had received that morning. The very first word she had had from Max. And it said so very little: that several weeks ago he had been at some place called Warth Mill, and that he was expecting to be 'transferred to a new camp'. But where to? She hardly dared hope that they might be bringing him to the Isle of Man.

But at least she had something to be happy about. Max was alive and safe and well; and his name was not on the passenger manifest of the *Arandora Star*.

Cora, Bessie and Evie Bannister were spending Saturday afternoon together, doing war work in the church hall.

'I wish we could do more,' declared Cora, picking a tiny piece of metal off the floor and dropping it into one of the pudding basins lined up on the long trestle table. 'These poor fighter pilots need all the help they can get.'

'You're already doing more than your bit,' retorted Bessie.

180

'You've got the *Bradda Vista* to look after, and all those women, and the Spitfire Fund, and this bit of war-work . . .'

'And she still finds time to help James McArthur on his rounds,' remarked Evie, casting a glance at Cora over the top of her reading glasses.

Cora scooped another handful of aeroplane rivets onto the table. Once sorted, the rivets would be collected and taken to RAF Jurby, where they would be used to service and repair the planes stationed there.

'How *is* James?' enquired Bessie innocently.

'He's . . . fine.' Cora went on sorting the rivets into different sizes, using an old shove-ha'penny board. 'Actually, I haven't seen very much of him lately.'

'Such a fine young man,' mused Miss Bannister. 'Lovely manners, and it was such a nice idea of his to give you a birthday picnic.'

'How is his leg?' asked Bessie.

'I'm not sure. A little better I think.'

Please, please stop talking about James, Cora pleaded silently. Right now she was finding it extremely difficult to cope with her feelings towards him. On the one hand she counted the days to their next meeting; on the other, she could hardly ignore the fact that James now spent most of his time working with Elsa Nadel. Elsa had even been given permission to accompany him on a few of his calls . . . and try as she might, Cora couldn't suppress her jealousy.

'I heard he has that nice German pharmacist helping him in his dispensary now,' commented Bessie.

'Yes.' Cora smiled and offered up silent curses.

Elsa *was* nice, and that only made it worse. Nice, sensible, clever . . . attractive? She wondered if James thought Elsa was more attractive than she was. No, that was silly, or course he didn't. Hadn't he asked her to a party in Douglas next month? *Only because Elsa Nadel wouldn't be allowed to go with him*, whispered a treacherous little voice in her head. No, no, she mustn't allow herself to think like this; she was behaving like a child.

'Hand me that jam-jar, would you, dear?'

Cora picked up the jar, painted with 1/32 on the side in green paint, and handed it to Evie.

'Thank you, dear. Mrs McKechnie's daughter told me Miss Nadel was helping to set up a nursery for the internees' children.'

'She must be very resourceful,' remarked Bessie. 'Such a pity they couldn't find something for her to do, instead of locking her up.'

'Quite,' muttered Cora.

'Well, the country needs all the skilled workers it can get,' pointed out Miss Bannister, rummaging in the pile of rivets. 'She'll probably be released before long.'

'I do hope so,' said Cora, brightening at the thought. And she carried on sorting with a new enthusiasm.

Elsa arrived back at the *Bradda Vista* just as Grethe was on her way out.

'Hello. How was the nursery?'

Elsa shrugged.

'Oh, coming along . . .'

'Cora had a phone call today. Seems Rachel and the baby are doing well. They should be back here in a few days' time.'

'If I was her I'd be trying to stay away as long as possible.'

Grethe studied Elsa quizzically.

'What's eating you?'

'Nothing. Don't mind me. Where are you off to, anyway?'

'Nowhere special.'

Grethe wasn't normally secretive, and when all was said and done she was only going down to the jetty for a little chat with Harry Kerruish – but the fewer people knew about her new friendship, the better. They wouldn't understand. She wasn't even sure she understood herself.

'Well mind you're back for roll-call, or there'll be no end of trouble.'

'You're not my mother, you know,' observed Grethe loftily, sashaying past her and down the steps in a rather nice blue frock. I'm sure that's a new dress, thought Elsa with a flicker of interest. Then she turned away with a shrug and stepped into the hallway, closing the front door of the boarding house behind her.

'*Guten Tag, Fräulein Nadel*,' breezed Rosie, one of the schoolgirls, bounding down the stairs two at a time. 'Have you heard the news?'

'What news?' The only news Elsa had heard lately had been about the *Arandora Star*, and that was hardly any cause for celebration.

'Me and Anna, we're being released. The telegram came today, from the Home Office. We can go back to boarding school in September, and everything!'

'Congratulations.'

'You are not happy, *Fräulein*?'

'Of course I am. I'm very pleased for you.' Elsa watched the girl jump down the last three steps and head out towards the sea, crashing the door shut behind her. How long is it since I had that sort of zest for life? she asked herself. And the answer came to her, quick as a flash.

Not since the last time James McArthur came to call . . .

Grace Quine was alone in her upstairs room. These days she seemed to be alone all the time.

Her parents' house on Casson Street had been her home since William's posting to Banbury. It had seemed then that they would manage to sit out the war quite comfortably together – William with his nice cosy training post at the Army camp, and Grace doing the odd bit of typing in her uncle's office.

She sat on the bed, listening to her mother and father arguing downstairs, then picked up Cora's letter and re-read it.

'Everything is fine, tell William not to worry about the

Bradda Vista. Is he still at the camp?'

If only he was, thought Grace. William's overseas posting had come out of the blue, and turned Grace's whole world upside down. And now, with German planes making raids on the south of England, she found herself stuck here, not even knowing where William was and just waiting for the bombs to fall. She was beginning to wonder if it had been such a good idea after all, coming back to the mainland. Even the Isle of Man might have its compensations.

She read on.

'The house is about as full as it can get. With four to a room there are a few troubles, of course, but nothing that can't be worked out.

'There was a real drama here last week. Rachel Kotkin gave birth in the middle of the night . . .'

Grace put down the letter, unable to read any more. But she was glad for the girl. She hoped she understood just how irreplaceable that new life was, and how fragile.

She knew Cora thought she was a cold-hearted bitch, and perhaps she had reason. But how could you open up without letting the pain overwhelm you? How could you explain how your whole world fell apart when that tiny, precious life was gone?

'*Na ja,* there you are, Sachs! Now tell me, have I lost my touch?'

Reuben held out his friend's jacket for his inspection. Sachs took it from him and turned it over and over in his hands, checking it minutely.

'Not bad, not bad,' he conceded.

'Not bad, he says!' Reuben raised his hands in disbelief. 'I take his old pile of rags and turn it into a jacket, and all he can say is "not bad"!'

Sachs grinned as he wriggled his arms into the jacket. You could hardly see the jagged rip that had extended diagonally across the right-hand pocket. Reuben Kotkin was a regular magician with a needle and thread. He'd been doing a roaring trade in garment repairs since they'd arrived at Hutchinson Camp.

'It'll do.' Vaulting lightly over the stone wall, he flopped down on the steps of the house, next to Reuben. 'I suppose you'll want paying now?'

'Fair exchange is no robbery.' Reuben picked up the next garment from the pile beside him. He tut-tutted as he held up the ancient pair of black serge trousers: worn so thin that you could actually see right through them in places. '*Oy!* Does he think I am a miracle worker, that I should resurrect them from the dead?'

Sachs reached into his capacious trouser pocket and took out a very fresh, very green apple, which he had laid on the warmed stone of the step with a flourish. A second followed from the other pocket, then a third.

'Apples!' Reuben nodded appreciatively.

'It's the first time the camp shop has had them since we arrived. I had to fight off Benny Finkel to get these.'

'I shall save them for Rachel,' Reuben decided, putting down his needle for a moment.

'You have heard from her?'

'Not yet, but the Commandant gave me a special paper to write to her. She is definitely at Rushen Camp, praise God.'

'And she is well?'

'I wish I knew for sure.' Reuben held the two edges of the tear together, and began sewing. 'It must be very near to her time now. And no one will tell me if I can be with her when she has the child . . .'

Sachs drew his knees up and rested his chin on them. At the end of the street he could see Hutchinson Square, with its neat terraced lawn where two improvised teams were kicking a football about. A group of black-clad Orthodox Jews walked by, deep in discussion over their Talmuds. At the edge of the grass an artist was sitting cross-legged, sketching the scene.

'This is such a strange place,' commented Sachs. 'I have

never met so many different people in all my life. Rabbis, students, artists . . . have you met that man Neunzer?'

'Neunzer? Oh, you mean the one who calls himself Blick? The lion-tamer?'

'That's the one. What a character. He's scratched pictures of animals into the blue paint on his bedroom window. Giraffes, elephants, all sorts. God alone knows what the Commandant makes of it.'

'Isn't Neunzer the one who catches mice with a lasso?' Sachs chuckled.

'The very same. Funny what people do to pass the time.'

'Yes,' said Reuben, mending the threadbare cloth with the tiniest, most invisible of stitches. 'At least I have my trade. But you – you're stuck here, away from your books.'

'Oh, I get along all right, don't you worry. I'm scribbling a little, and I'm helping set up a camp library, did I tell you that? And the lecture programme's getting off the ground at last. Oh, and Maryan Rawicz is giving a piano recital . . .'

'Kotkin, Sachs!' A breathless figure came running up the street towards House forty-one, a huge grin all over his red, perspiring face.

'What gives, Oskar?' demanded Sachs. 'You look like a dog with two tails.'

'And so I should, *boychik*, so I should. The meeting with our womenfolk.' Vischer gasped for breath. 'The one they have been promising for so long . . .'

Reuben set down his work, hardly daring to hope; not after so long.

'The meeting? What about it, Oskar?'

'It is going to happen! The Commandant told me so!'

'Ach, that is what they always say,' scoffed Sachs.

'No, I tell you it is true! Next week, or the week after, they will take us to Port Erin to meet our wives. I shall see my Ruth again!'

And I shall see my Rachel, thought Reuben, his heart

soaring towards the blue of the afternoon sky. At last, I shall see my Rachel!

'Rachel, Rachel, you are looking so well!'

'And the baby . . . oh look at the baby, isn't she the prettiest little thing you ever saw?'

'Did they look after you at the hospital?'

'How are you feeling?'

Rachel Kotkin stepped out of the ambulance and into a gaggle of at least a dozen well-wishers, who had come to the *Bradda Vista* to welcome her back. She felt pleased yet bewildered and faintly embarrassed to be the centre of so much attention, and clutched the child protectively to her breast.

Cora came down the steps of the boarding house, intent on shooing the onlookers away.

'Ladies, please – poor Rachel can hardly breathe!' She took Rachel's arm and guided her gently towards the front steps, turning back to smile at the happy crowd. 'You can see her later, but one at a time! Mum and baby need their rest.'

'Really, Cora, I'm quite all right,' protested Rachel as Cora took her inside the house. 'I'm just tired of being told to rest!'

'Ah,' said Grethe, emerging from the common room. 'But up to now you've been in the hospital, with the nurses taking care of you and the baby. From now on, it's just you and little Esther – I think you'll be glad of any rest you can get!'

'Grethe, it's good to see you.' Rachel accepted a kiss on both cheeks, and blushed with pleasure to see how Grethe fussed and cooed over the baby. 'Isn't she perfect? I can't stop looking at her, I still can't believe she's mine!'

'A regular beauty queen,' smiled Grethe. 'She'll break a few hearts when she's older, you see if she doesn't.'

'Where's Elsa?' asked Rachel as they walked together towards the stairs.

'Out somewhere. Organising something or someone – you know Elsa, she never stops.'

'No.' Rachel was determined not to show her disappointment. She had wanted both Grethe and Elsa to be there when she came 'home'. They had helped to bring Esther into the world. It only seemed right.

'Just you wait until you see your new room,' breezed Cora, leading the way up the stairs.

'New room? Am I not sharing with Elsa and Grethe?'

Cora laughed.

'I don't think they'd take too kindly to little Esther waking them up in the middle of the night, do you? Besides, you need privacy for yourself and the baby. We've found you a lovely room just along the corridor . . .'

And it *was* a lovely room, as Rachel discovered when Cora threw open the door. A lovely corner room with a big bay window, a double bed, chair, baby's cot and dressing table. There was even a square of carpet on the floor!

'Oh, Cora!' Rachel could feel tears prickling her eyes as they welled up, unbidden. She gazed around the room, at the stack of little packages piled up on the candlewick bedspread. 'What are all these . . .?'

'Presents,' explained Grethe. 'Presents for you. Everyone in the house has made something for the baby.'

'Everyone?' gaped Rachel, disbelieving.

'Everyone. Even Signora Mentoni on the second floor, who's always moaning about the noise. Everyone. Elsa made some little bootees, Frau Kessler bought some nappies, and I . . .'

'Don't spoil the surprise,' laughed Cora. 'Why don't you open them yourself, Rachel?'

Rachel sat down on the edge of the bed, suddenly quite exhausted and overwhelmed.

'You're so kind,' she repeated, over and over again. 'So incredibly kind . . .'

'Nonsense,' said Grethe. 'Nothing but the best for little

Esther. It's bad enough being born into the middle of a war, without any aunties and uncles to make a fuss of you, isn't it, Esther?'

As if she understood, the baby gurgled and blew bubbles.

'There's a huge cake for you downstairs,' said Cora. 'Signora Bertorelli's done you proud. Later, we're going to have a little party.'

'But that's not the only surprise,' smiled Grethe. 'There's something else.'

'What . . .?'

'Why don't you open the drawer of the bedside cabinet and have a look inside?'

Rachel looked at Grethe questioningly.

'Go on, Rachel. I think you'll be glad you did.'

Rachel slid open the drawer, hardly knowing what to expect. Inside lay a single yellowish-beige envelope, marked with a censor's stamp. She reached out trembling fingers for it. It couldn't be real. It couldn't. She'd waited so long that it seemed an impossibility for her dreams to come true.

Her fingers curled about the envelope and she took it from the drawer. She did not need to read the sender's name and address on the back to know who it was from. One glance at the wild, sloping scrawl was enough to send tears of joy coursing down her cheeks, splashing onto the ink and making it blur.

It was from Reuben.

Chapter 14

Cora peered through the window of Evie Bannister's drapery shop with raised eyebrows. It looked as if a plague of locusts had passed through, pausing only to buy every single length of fabric in the place.

'What's been going on?' asked Cora as she stepped inside, the little shop-bell jingling as the door closed behind her.

Miss Bannister rose to greet her from rearranging the depleted display of ribbons and trimmings. Behind her head hung a lopsided notice proclaiming: 'P & B Wools – scarce but worth looking for.'

'Oh, my dear, you simply wouldn't believe how busy I've been!' she gasped, straightening up.

'Don't tell me, the internees have been out looking for dress material?'

Miss Bannister surveyed the virtually empty racks which had held bales of fabric.

'Anything they can get, my dear – even sheeting and ticking, and blackout material too! It's as if every woman in Port Erin wants a new dress!'

'They probably do,' replied Cora, taking off her white summer gloves to help tidy the shop. 'You see, there's a meeting of husbands and wives at the end of the month.'

'Here? In Port Erin?'

'I think so – or Port St Mary. At any rate, the women are really excited about it. They've all been sewing and knitting and having their hair done for days now.'

'Well, I don't say I'm not glad of the custom, only I do wish they'd try and understand. I have to keep to the proper procedures.'

'Procedures?'

'If they want to spend more than five shillings, they choose what they want and I give them an invoice. That goes to the camp bank, which pays out the money. Then they bring it to me, and I give them the goods. It's very long-winded.'

'But I suppose it helps to stop them spending more than they can afford.'

'Speaking of which, how are you managing on what you're paid by the Home Office?'

'It's very tight,' Cora admitted. 'Still, we've got a wonderful new cook. She's Italian, used to run a cafe in London. Even Grandad has cheered up since Mrs Bertorelli started cooking for us.'

Miss Bannister leaned back against the counter. She loved a 'lil cooish', the more scandalous the better.

'They tell me the food has got so bad at the *Rowany Glen*, the poor women are having to boil nettles instead of cabbage!'

'No! Really?'

'It's those Costains. All they care about is money. They think if they skimp on food, they can put a bit by for themselves.'

'But that's awful!'

'I quite agree. You can't treat people like that, even if they are . . . well, you know. Not quite . . .'

'British?' ventured Cora.

'Indeed.'

Miss Bannister began sorting reels of coloured cotton into their boxes.

'Did you see Fenella Kneen's picture in the *Mona's Herald*? Her father must be very proud of her, passing out top of the whole ATS intake.'

Cora started to tidy away a jumble of dressmaking patterns. She was so used to working in the shop that it felt odd, just being a customer.

'Yes, Mr Kneen's telling anyone who'll listen all about his clever daughter,' she chuckled. 'When she comes home on leave, he'll be showing her off all over the Island. As a matter of fact, I had a letter from Fenella last week.'

'Is she still stationed at Aldershot?' enquired Evie.

'She mentioned something about going to London and driving staff cars for senior officers. She can't say too much – you know how it is. But it all sounds rather glamorous, though I suppose it isn't really.'

Evie nodded.

'Well, be sure and give her my best when next you write.' She finished putting away the boxes of cotton reels, and slid the drawer shut. 'Anyhow, my dear, what can I do for you?'

'I just wondered if you had any pink baby ribbon. Everyone seems to have made something for Rachel's baby, but I've been rushed off my feet . . .'

'Let me see. Everything's in such short supply.' Miss Bannister stepped behind the polished wooden counter and started rummaging in boxes, pulling out the glass-fronted drawers until she found what she was looking for. 'Oh. No pink left, only blue or lemon, I'm afraid.'

'I'm sure lemon will do.' Cora opened her handbag and took out her purse – a purse considerably lighter than it had been in the days when she worked for Evie Bannister. Still, no sense in moping.

'Half a yard?'

'Best make it three-quarters. I'm going to use it to trim a bonnet and a little matinee jacket.'

'Ah, babies.' Miss Bannister's face registered a wistful nostalgia. 'Time was . . . but it's no use dwelling in the past, is it?'

'Not in my experience, no.'

Cora's thoughts turned briefly to James. She couldn't help wondering how things might be now if there had been no war; if James hadn't broken his leg; if Elsa Nadel hadn't come to the *Bradda Vista* and taken up so much of his attention . . .

'Something wrong, dear?' Miss Bannister looked concerned.

'No, nothing.' Cora took a handful of coppers out of her purse.

'You're looking very nice today,' commented Evie as she wrapped up the ribbon. 'Been busy with the sewing machine?'

Cora glanced down at the beige floral dress with its pretty lacy bolero.

'Oh, this dress? It's years old! I just ran up the bolero from some old net curtains I found in the rag-bag.'

'Well it looks lovely, dear. And very economical.'

'Actually it was Rachel who suggested it. She and her husband had a tailoring business before the war.'

'How interesting. Now, will you join me in a cup of tea?' Anticipating a good long gossip, Miss Bannister pulled up the heavy flap of the counter so that Cora could come through to the back of the shop.

Cora glanced at her watch.

'I'd love to, Evie, only I'm supposed to be at Dora Corless's by ten-thirty. The Ladies' Committee is trying to organise a summer concert in aid of the Spitfire Fund.'

'My, you are keeping yourself busy. I don't suppose you see much of James these days?'

'Not as much as I'd like.'

And not as much as Elsa Nadel does, thought Cora. That's for sure. And she could have bitten off her tongue for her silly jealousy.

'Come to think of it, I haven't seen you two out together as much as I used to. And you seemed to be getting so . . . well . . . friendly . . .'

Cora picked up the ribbon and put it into her handbag.

'Ah well, that's the war for you,' she replied. 'There'll be time enough for friendship when it's all over and done with.'

Thomas Quine buried his head in the *Daily Sketch* and tried to close his ears to the racket. The *Bradda Vista* was alive with the sounds of laughter, tears, arguments and running feet.

If this was what it was going to be like every time a meeting was arranged between the internees and their husbands, Thomas hoped it wasn't going to happen too often. His morning pair of oak-smoked kippers sat heavily on a stomach unsettled by days of to-ing and fro-ing, noise and clutter.

With a grunt of irritation, he put the paper over his head and tried to go to sleep.

Downstairs in the common room, there were swathes of fabric, dresses with the sleeves ripped out and the hems let down, pins, needles and scraps of fancy trimming all over the floor. Over by the window, Maria Bertorelli was doing a thriving trade as a hairdresser, snipping and preening chic new styles from tired locks.

In the middle of all this chaos stood Rachel Kotkin, skilfully pinning and tucking as a girl from the *Ben-my-Chree* stood in front of her, trying not to wriggle as the pins scratched and tickled. For the first time since her arrival in Britain, Rachel was really coming into her own. An accomplished tailoress, she knew dozens of different ways to take old clothes and make them look brand new.

'Ow, Rachel, that went right into me!' The girl rubbed her side.

'It's your own fault for moving, Petra. Now keep still, I'll be as gentle as I can.'

Elsa put her head round the door. She wasn't going to go inside, but Grethe – sitting in the corner nursing Esther – spotted her and called out:

'Come in, Elsa. Join the madhouse.'

Half-reluctantly, Elsa walked in. Rachel nodded and smiled to her with a mouthful of dressmaking pins. Signora Bertorelli murmured a peremptory 'Ciao', then went back to the absorbing business of cutting hair. Everyone was so busy, so preoccupied, thought Elsa. So *happy*.

'Hello, Grethe. I just came to see if anyone wants to come to the Biology class this afternoon, at the Fish Hatchery.'

Grethe laughed softly, rocking the child in her arms.

Despite all the chatter – not to mention the gramophone playing Frances Langford's 'The Man I Love' – Esther seemed completely serene. Utterly unaware of the turmoil that the world had got itself into.

'Now really, Elsa; do you honestly think anyone's going to want to go to one of your lectures on a day like this?'

'I suppose you're right.' Elsa sat down next to Grethe, and absent-mindedly stroked the baby's tiny hand.

'And besides, with the meeting in a few days' time, every woman in the camp wants a new outfit!'

'I wish I had something to want a new outfit for,' said Elsa.

'You and me both, *liebchen*.' Grethe began singing softly, her warm contralto blending well with the husky voice on the record. 'I used to be quite a little singer, you know,' she said, out of the blue. 'Had a regular spot in a nightclub, and everything.'

'You?' Elsa looked at Grethe, glimpsing a new aspect to her. 'A professional singer? I never guessed.'

'I wasn't always a cheap tart.'

'Sorry, I didn't mean . . . well, I'm just a bit surprised, I suppose.'

'It was in Berlin, oh, back in the 'twenties. I was going to be the biggest star in the whole world!'

'What happened – or shouldn't I ask?'

Grethe shrugged. She had been over this old ground so often in her mind, in her dreams, that it no longer hurt to talk about it. Or at least, that was what she liked to think.

'I fell for a man, *liebchen*. A real bastard. He brought me to England, told me he was going to make me a star. Then kicked me out onto the street when someone prettier came along.'

'I'm . . . sorry.' It sounded a bit weak, but what could you say?

'Why should you be sorry? It's not as if it was your fault. I was just a kid, it wasn't difficult to fill my head full of nonsense. If anyone should be sorry, it's him. But then men like him don't know what sorry is.' She looked down at the baby, bent over and kissed her lightly on the forehead. 'Have you heard from your brother?'

'Not since the postcard.'

'He'll turn up like a bad penny, they always do.'

'I just wish I knew where he'd been transferred. I mean, he could be here, on the Island, and I wouldn't even know!'

'At least you had the postcard, so you know he's all right.'

'Yes, at least there's that.'

'And it's not as if you're the only one, is it? There's poor Nan, who lost her man on the *Arandora Star*. And there are all the other women who don't know where their men are. And there's . . .'

She stopped abruptly, that vision of Emil surfacing in her mind. Always he was there, his little face upturned and his arms reaching out to her. To his *Mutti*, who had abandoned him. That must surely be how he saw it. He was too young to understand.

'Oh, Grethe, you're thinking about Emil aren't you? I'm sorry, I didn't mean to be so selfish.'

'It's all right. Besides, I've heard from Claire and she says he's well. And he sent me a picture he'd drawn.'

'That's good. And they're talking about bringing the children over to the Island. Soon . . .'

'Soon,' echoed Grethe. 'Even if it was today it wouldn't be soon enough.' She gave a dry laugh. 'If I was Manx I suppose I would say, "Traa-dy-liooar".'

'Traa-dy-what?'

'Liooar, it means "time enough". They say it all the time. It's probably why nothing ever gets done.'

Elsa regarded Grethe archly.

'You've been coming out with a lot of homespun Manx philosophy lately. I don't suppose this would have anything to do with a certain Harry Kerruish . . .?'

'I don't know what you're talking about.' Grethe's heart skipped a beat. A simple conversation between two people could provide so much ammunition for anyone who wanted to cause trouble – and the last thing she wanted to do was cause trouble for Harry. 'Anyhow, if that isn't the pot calling the kettle black, I don't know what is!'

'What's that supposed to mean?'

'Come on, Elsa, don't think I haven't noticed how much time you spend with that young vet.'

'We're just colleagues,' protested Elsa. 'The Commandant gave me special permission to work with him, you know that!'

'Yes, yes, I know. Keep your hair on.' Grethe gazed across at Rachel, so transformed by the joyful anticipation of seeing her husband again. She and Petra were waltzing round the parlour in time to a record, the mannequin still covered with pins and giggling every time they stumbled over each other's feet. 'But you'll be careful, won't you?'

'What's there to be careful of?'

'He's . . . he's Cora's friend. If you ask me, she's in love with him.'

'Why should that be of any interest to me? I told you, we're just colleagues. We work well together, that's all.'

As Reuben Kotkin sat on the motor-coach, he hardly knew what to feel. He was excited, restless, ecstatic and terrified, all at once. Were he and hundreds of others from the men's camps in Douglas really being taken to a place called Port St Mary, where they would meet their wives? It scarcely seemed possible, after all that had happened and all they had been through.

He glanced around the bus as it rolled and rumbled through the Manx countryside. Ordinarily he would have noticed how pretty it was, but today all he could think about were the miles that still lay between him and Rachel, the miles that were eaten up so very slowly.

Every man on this coach had a story to tell, a story of separation and loss. Perhaps some of them cared more about their wives than others did, but all shared the same silent, terrified anticipation of what was to come. Were their wives as desperate to see them as they were to see their wives? Could the old closeness return after so many weeks and months apart?

Some had brought small gifts with them, little things they had made in the camp workshop, and in several cases bizarre bouquets of dandelions and any wild flowers they had been able to scavenge within the perimeter fence of the camp. Reuben had nothing; nothing but his love. He hoped it wouldn't matter, that Rachel wouldn't think any the worse of him.

He knew – all the men knew – that the real purpose of this meeting was to persuade them and their wives to accept deportation to the British dominions. Reuben couldn't think of a single man who would be crazy enough to volunteer – not after the *Arandora Star* disaster – unless tempted by the promise of greater freedom and a chance to live with his spouse as man and wife.

In any case, all Reuben could think of right now was how much he had missed her and how much he longed to hold her in his arms again.

'We are almost there.' The old man in the seat next to Reuben's nudged his arm, and Reuben turned to look at him.

'How do you know?'

'I came to this Island once, in the 'twenties, when I had just arrived in Britain. I worked here in the summer season, as a porter in a hotel. Over there, on the right, that is Port Erin, where my Johanna is. And soon, on the left, we shall come to Port St Mary.'

The old man's travelogue meant little to Reuben, beyond the fact that he had seen Port Erin, if only from a distance. That was where they were keeping his Rachel, the place where he longed to be above all places, just to be by her side.

'My wife is having a baby,' he said, the words just spilling out.

'Your first?'

'It shows?'

The old man laughed and nodded.

'Believe me, my boy, they will take good care of her. Better by far than they would care for any of us in Germany. I count myself fortunate to be here in safety.'

Reuben looked at him, surprised.

'You don't wish to be free?'

'Free? What is free? To have enough to eat, a warm place to sleep, that is freedom enough for me. And when you are old like me you will know that this is so.'

The coach rattled on along the great empty sweep of Shore Road, with its magnificent, glittering views over the sea, and into the village of Port St Mary.

'That is it,' said the old man excitedly, wagging his finger at a building in the middle distance. 'The big white building with the four square towers. That is the Ballaqueeney Hydro, a very fine hotel.'

'You know it?'

'Everyone on the Island knows the Ballaqueeney, my boy. And besides, I worked there.'

Chatter subsided into murmurings, and then into a dense, suffocating silence as the convoy of coaches rolled into Port St Mary and stopped outside the Ballaqueeney.

'Everybody out,' announced a middle-aged corporal with slick, brilliantined hair and a nose like a squashed tomato. 'Everybody out and assemble on the grass.'

They piled out in shambolic order, much to the irritation of the corporal, who had spent weeks trying to instil some sort of sense of military discipline into his charges. After all, he told himself, if they were ever to be persuaded to join the Pioneer Corps or the Jewish Brigade, they would first have to understand the value of discipline. So far, it hadn't worked at all.

'Alphabetical order,' barked a sergeant with a clipboard.

'What's he say?' demanded an elderly man, his hand cupped round his ear.

'Alphabetical order,' shouted Reuben.

'What's that? I don't read.'

After much jostling and rearranging, the men were finally sorted into a long column, arranged in alphabetical order. Slowly they were marched inside the hotel and filed into the ballroom.

'Aarons, A.' A man walked forward, a woman rushing towards him, a shout of pleasure, a kiss . . .

'Bauer, P; Becker, G W; Berghaus, O T; Bloom, L . . .'

Reuben scanned the crowd of women and children in the ballroom. He couldn't see her there, not anywhere. She wasn't there! Panic rose in his throat and he wanted to scream Rachel's name. What had they done to her, where had they taken her? Maybe she had got sick, maybe the baby had died inside her . . .

'Green S; Heinrichson, T; Henreid, G S; Ishmael, S . . .'

Tension made Reuben shake all over. He felt such an idiot; never had he shaken with such fear, not even when Holland had been invaded and they had been fleeing for the coast, just hours in front of the Nazi invaders.

'Kotkin, R S.'

At the sound of his name, Reuben froze. He heard the blood rushing through his veins, the crazy drum-roll of his thundering heart.

'Get a move on, Kotkin, we haven't got all day. Don't you want to see your wife and kiddie then?'

The corporal gave him a shove and he took an involuntary step forward, then a second and a third. His mouth was dry and he was struck dumb: paralysed by the sight of a woman pushing her way through the crowd to the front. Walking towards him. Smiling.

A woman carrying a tiny baby in her arms.

'Reuben! Oh, Reuben!'

Rachel half ran, half threw herself forward. Her hair was smoothly coiffured and she was wearing a pretty new dress, but Reuben did not notice anything but her face: her radiant, lovely face with its beautiful dark eyes and smiling mouth. There was the sparkling trail of a tear on her cheeks and all he wanted to do was kiss it away – if only he weren't so ashamed of his own weakness, the tears pricking unbidden at the corners of his eyes.

'Rachel, my darling . . . *liebe* Rachel, *bubeleh* . . .'

'You have a daughter, Reuben – see, is she not lovely? Is she not the most precious thing in the whole world?'

Then her arm was round his waist and he found himself holding his child, his daughter – oh, God be praised, such a beautiful daughter. He wept so freely that his whole frame shook uncontrollably, his tears flowing unchecked now, and unashamed.

They kissed and the salt of their tears mingled, melting away the distance, the fear, the separation. For these few, precious moments at least, neither the war nor the wire existed.

Only the love.

'It's gettin' late.'

Harry Kerruish was sitting on the sea wall, gazing out across Port Erin bay at the first blush-pink tinge of sunset. He didn't look round as he spoke, but inclined his face slightly towards Grethe. She smiled but did not move.

'Not so very late.'

Harry took the battered old watch from the pocket of his waistcoat.

'Curfew's at nine.'

'Do you want me to go?'

There was a long silence, as though Harry were trying to summon up the strength of will to lie convincingly. He failed.

'No.'

'Then I'll stay until one minute to nine and run *wie das Wind* so I get there just before they lock the door.'

'And if you don't?'

Grethe kicked her heels against the wall. She knew she

was playing a dangerous game, but if the prospect of 'getting into trouble' hadn't influenced her in the past, why should it now?

'Then I'll get a dressing-down, won't I?'

This time, Harry did turn to look at her. Sometimes she felt that he avoided her gaze, almost as if he were afraid of what he might find there.

'You're a bold one, Grethe.'

'I am what I am.'

'It's what you are that bothers me.'

'A whore, you mean?'

Harry gazed out to sea, clearly discomfited.

'No, not that. I don't care about that.'

The penny dropped.

'German?'

'I shouldn't be talking to you like this.'

'No.'

'I shouldn't be talking to you at all.'

'That's very true. I might be a spy.'

'For God's sake, gel, do you have to keep agreein' with me?'

She smiled again, and he didn't want to look at her smile; only it drew him in and seemed to understand.

Grethe seemed to understand so much about him. Perhaps that was what had drawn them together in this curious, ill-matched companionship. He didn't need to tell her things, she just . . . *knew*. They were so different – enemies, that was what they were supposed to be – but how could you not be drawn to someone who was the echo of your every thought and feeling?

They had been meeting once a week to talk; sometimes just to sit and listen to the sea. It wasn't easy, it wasn't sensible, and in his heart of hearts he knew it was wrong . . . but how *could* it be wrong? The Manx fisherman and the German prostitute; whenever he thought about it it seemed ludicrous, so he had tried to stop thinking about it. She filled the emptiness in his heart, and that was something he could not – would not – deny.

'So we shouldn't talk.' Grethe shrugged. 'But what's the harm? What's the harm of two people just sitting next to each other on a wall and looking at the sea?'

Harry didn't reply, but his hand sought out hers, at first hesitantly then with greater deliberation; their fingers interlacing in the comfort and warmth of a silent, unspoken understanding.

Chapter 15

'How is he, Nurse Wilson?'

The young doctor stepped up to the head of the bed and looked down at the sleeping patient.

'A little better, Dr Knight. The sedative seems to have calmed him down.'

Dr Knight checked the chart and sat down on the chair by the bed.

'Well, that's something, I suppose. Let's just hope he's more coherent when he wakes up.'

This particular patient was posing a serious problem. Of the eighty or so injured survivors from the *Andora Star* brought to Mearnskirk Emergency Hospital, almost all had been deeply shocked on arrival in Scotland. But whereas most of the others had recovered and many had already been shipped out to Australia, this one was still in the grip of a persistent delirium.

His head injuries had been horrific, but time was mending his body. Dr Knight only wished he could say as much about the patient's mind. It was just as well they'd found his identity papers still on his body when he was rescued, otherwise they might never have found out who he was. In the terrible tragedy and confusion, so many victims and even survivors had still not been identified.

'Let's take a look at the wounds while he's out for the count.'

Nurse Wilson drew back the counterpane and sheet. Under the bed-cradle the patient's left leg was still bandaged, the result of burns sustained from burning oil from the torpedoed liner. The right leg was intact but heavily bruised, and there was a clean break of the left wrist. Dr Knight performed a quick examination, nodded and the bedclothes were replaced.

'Coming along nicely,' he said. 'His body should make a complete recovery. It's that nasty head wound I'm worried about.'

'But you think he'll recover – in time?'

'We have no way of knowing.'

The man in the bed stirred in his sleep, his body tensing then relaxing; a few inaudible syllables escaping from his parted lips.

'When he is awake – he is still confused?'

'Yes, Doctor, he's still having the delusions. One minute he accepts that he's Ernst Müller. And then he starts rambling . . . he starts dreaming he's an artist called Max.'

Bessie Teare was weary of the hot July sun. It faded the red velvet curtains in her parlour, made the flowers in her garden wilt, and seemed to make some people more tetchy than usual.

Her sister Ida Quilliam had always had a temper on her, of course, but with her two eldest children away at the war, Ida had become more difficult company than usual. Bessie was glad that Evie Bannister had decided to join their 'knitting bee'.

Knitting jumpers for evacuees might not be a very exciting occupation, but it made Bessie and her friends feel useful. What with the knitting, the war-work and the internees to keep an eye on, she had scarcely a moment to herself – which was how Bessie liked it.

Miss Bannister cast off a sleeve and held it up to the light. It was rainbow-striped, made from odds and ends of different-coloured wools she'd been left with in the shop, or unravelled from old sweaters.

'What do you think, girls?'

'Very colourful,' nodded Bessie. 'And warm.' She glanced out of the front window, at the brassy sea and sky. 'Though I can't imagine ever being cold again, can you?'

Ida tutted as her needles clacked their way along yet another row. With four children and a husband to knit for, she'd had so much practice that she no longer needed to look at what she was doing.

'Come the winter, when it's bitterly cold, those children will be glad of a warm jumper,' she scolded.

'Yes, Ida dear.' Bessie carried on working, sewing up the tiny pink cardigan she had just been making. It was so sweet, so utterly irresistible, that she found herself imagining it on one of her internees' little girls. Or how about Cora's Rachel? She had a beautiful little daughter . . . 'Do you think Rachel would like this for her baby?' she asked Evie. Miss Bannister stopped casting on stitches to take a look at the little pink cardigan.

'Oh, Bessie, it's adorable. I'm sure she'd love it.'

Ida piped up indignantly.

'Bessie, I'm surprised at you, really I am. These garments are meant for the benefit of poor children. Poor *British* children.'

'Well, they don't come much poorer than Rachel Kotkin,' retorted Bessie. 'From what Cora told me, the girl turned up with not a stitch to her name.'

'You must do what you think is right, I suppose,' sniffed Ida.

'Don't worry, I shall.'

The distant sound of the doorbell had Evie levering herself up out of her armchair, but Bessie waved her back into her seat.

'Don't bother yourself, dear. Rebecca's in the kitchen. She'll get it. She's been such a help to me.'

Sure enough, the sound of feet clumping heavily on lino announced that Rebecca – one of Bessie's internees – was on her way down the hallway to the front door. And then the

207

sound of voices, just audible from Bessie's first-floor sitting room.

'Please?'

'Is Miss Teare in?'

'Please do come in.'

Miss Bannister's face lit up with pleasure.

'I'll swear that's Cora Quine.'

Bessie nodded.

'She did say she might call on us this afternoon. She has one or two things she wants to chat to me about.'

A moment later, there was a knock on the sitting-room door.

'Come in.'

Rebecca popped her head into the room.

'Miss Teare . . . there is someone . . .'

'It's all right, let her in. Cora, how nice to see you! You're looking lovely – isn't she looking lovely, Ida?'

Ida looked up with a smile and a nod, pleased to see the new arrival. She approved of Cora Quine. She dressed presentably, kept herself to herself and had her feet firmly on the ground. Mind you, time marched on and Cora Quine was no spring chicken. If she didn't get a move on, she might not make the good match a girl like her deserved.

'Very nice, Cora. Such a neat little summer frock, if I may say so.'

'Thank you, Mrs Quilliam.'

'Please – call me Ida.'

'Let me take your jacket, Cora.' Bessie stepped forward. 'And would you like a glass of parsnip wine?'

'I'd love some.' Cora's eyes wandered from Miss Bannister's rainbow jumper to Ida's sensible mittens and the baby's cardigan lying, almost finished, on Bessie's knees. 'I hope I'm not interrupting. You're obviously very busy . . .'

'Nonsense.' Bessie poured Cora's drink. 'It's a relief to put my knitting down. Now, won't you tell us all your news? How's your brother and his wife?'

'William's training ATS catering recruits in Banbury, and Grace is staying with her parents, just down the road from the camp.'

Doreen looked up.

'And how is she – your sister-in-law?'

'She seems well . . . from her letters. Though she doesn't say much.'

Cora had long since stopped trying to understand Grace. There had been too many wounding words on both sides for there to be any warmth between them.

'Such a tragedy it was.' Doreen Bannister shook her head slowly. 'About Grace . . . and the child dying like that.'

'Some might say it was a tragedy,' replied Ida. 'Of course, there were some who said it wasn't an accident.'

'Ida!' snapped Bessie.

Ida shrugged and went back to her knitting.

'It was certainly a tragedy for the child,' she commented quietly.

Bessie threw her sister a withering look, but Ida ignored it.

'Now, Cora, what was it you wanted to talk to me about?'

Grateful for the change of subject, Cora launched into the main reason for her visit.

'Mrs Pantin mentioned that the Government are thinking of setting up an information bureau in London,' she began.

'An information bureau? Whatever for?' asked Ida.

'You know, so that internees and their families who've lost touch can find each other again.'

'It sounds like an excellent idea,' said Bessie.

'But you don't know anything about it?'

'Nothing more than rumours, no. But I'd certainly support the idea. There are so many who've lost touch with their loved ones. Take poor Olya and Rebecca – two of my ladies. Olya's husband is dead, and Rebecca doesn't know if any of her family are still alive. War is such a terrible thing.'

'It is a terrible thing for the British,' pointed out Ida. 'For our boys at the front, our fighter pilots . . .'

'Yes, of course it is, Ida,' said Bessie. 'But surely we can feel for these poor innocent refugees too.'

'For those who *are* refugees, perhaps. But how can we know who are our friends and who are our enemies?'

'Some of us trust our instincts, Ida . . .'

'The thing is, Bessie,' cut in Cora, eager to defuse an argument before it began.

'What, dear?'

'It's Elsa – you know, our house representative.'

'The pharmacist?' asked Miss Bannister. 'The one who's been helping Mr McArthur in his surgery?'

'Yes.' Cora forced herself not to sound as if she minded. 'Yes, that's right. Anyhow, Elsa's terribly worried about her twin brother, Max. He was interned before her and they lost touch. The last she heard, he was at a camp near Bury. He told her he was going to be transferred to another camp, and she's heard nothing since.'

'Well, you know how it is,' said Bessie. 'Ever since they set up two post offices, the internees' mail has been getting mixed up with ours. Max has probably written to her and the letter's got delayed somewhere. He may even be on the Island by now.'

'It's possible,' agreed Cora. 'But Elsa can't get information out of anyone. The thing is, she's worried the Government may deport Max. And after what happened to the *Arandora Star* . . .'

'Does she really think they would?' asked Miss Bannister.

'He's a Category A alien. It's a distinct possibility.'

Ida gave a dismissive shake of her head.

'Category A? Then he is an enemy alien and a danger to national security.'

'Elsa believes he was wrongly graded. There was a mistake . . .'

'Then the truth is bound to come out in the end.'

Cora allowed herself a despairing sigh. Ida Quilliam could be very hard work when she got on her high horse. She would insist on seeing everything in black and white, with no shades of grey.

Bessie stood up.

'There – I've finished.' She held up the fluffy pink baby's jacket. 'What do you think?'

Cora admired it.

'It's beautiful. Somebody's baby is going to be very lucky!'

Glancing at Ida, Bessie held out the jacket to Cora.

'Actually, Cora, I thought you might give it to your Rachel, for her new little girl.'

Emil Herzheim limped up the street, pausing to pull up his socks and wipe his nose on the back of his hand.

It wasn't fair, it wasn't. Thumping the living daylights out of him just because he had a German name. He was South London born and bred, like them. But he mustn't blub, because that was a girlie thing to do and you shouldn't blub in front of your Auntie Claire.

She wasn't his auntie really of course, but that didn't matter because he liked her. All those things the other boys said, they were just wicked lies and anyway, he didn't really understand what the words meant. He would have bunked off, only his Ma had told him he had to work hard at school, no matter what, and he loved his Ma too. He wished he could understand why they'd taken her away from him like that.

Reaching the corner, he gave his nose a really good blow on the cuff of his shirt. Better to get a clip round the ear for dirtying your shirt than have her see you'd been crying. He set off up Mabberley Street, hands in pockets, trying not to limp even though his kicked shins were giving him gyp.

It was just his luck that Claire was standing on the front steps of the big old house, talking to Mrs Perks. He didn't like Mrs Perks. She had big brown teeth and a gap at the front when she smiled. Sammy Carter said she ate babies for breakfast, but of course Emil didn't believe that. Well, not all the time.

He tried to dodge round the side of the house, but Claire had already spotted him.

'Emil? What you bin up to this time?'

'Nuffink.'

'Emil, come 'ere this minute.'

He shuffled reluctantly up the path to the front steps. Mrs Perks treated him to one of her horrible smiles.

'Well, well, ain't you bin in the wars, then?' She reached out and gave his face a tweak. He winced. 'Looks like 'e's bin fightin', proper little bruiser ain't yer, Emil?'

'I ain't,' he protested. 'I ain't bin fightin', Auntie Claire.' He paused, his brain working frantically to think of an excuse to get him off the hook without telling the truth. 'I fell over.'

'Is that a fact?' Claire didn't know whether to shake him or hug him. Poor little bugger, she thought, looking him up and down. Shirt all torn, smears of blood on his knees and a big graze on his arm.

'Let's look at you, you little sod,' she said, somewhere between smiles and tears.

'Ow,' protested Emil as Claire turned him round, assessing the damage.

'Lovely shiner 'e'll 'ave in the morning,' observed Mrs Perks serenely.

'I'll tan your backside, Emil Herzheim, you see if I don't,' exclaimed Claire. It wasn't easy, this mothering business. And the more you did it, the more you got attached to the kid, even though he wasn't your own. 'Now, you'd best come inside and we'll get you cleaned up.'

She pushed him through the door and up the stairs to their flat on the second floor. It wasn't quite as nice as the flat they'd shared with Grethe, but Claire couldn't afford that now with her the only breadwinner. What's more, taking decent care of Emil had seriously curtailed the hours she could work the streets; but she'd promised Grethe she'd look after the boy, and look after him she would, as best she could.

Inside the flat, she closed the door behind her and leant her back against it.

'Now tell me what really happened.'

'I told you, Auntie Claire. I fell over, didn't I?'

'Don't give me that, Emil. Them big boys bin pickin' on you again, have they?'

Emil stared at the scuffed toes of his boots. He didn't like lying, so he said nothing.

'Come on, Emil. You don't get two black eyes fallin' over.'

He looked up at her, his round blue eyes clouded with righteous indignation.

'They was sayin' things.'

'What things?'

'About you. An' Ma . . .'

'Oh, they was, was they? Well, just you listen to me, Emil. They can say all they like but you don't 'ave to listen, do you?'

'It's 'ard, Auntie Claire.'

She knelt down in front of him and put her hands on his shoulders.

'I know it is. But what's the sense in lettin' them get to you like this, eh? Next time you take no notice – you walk right past, you hear?'

Emil looked glumly defiant, his bottom lip jutting in a telltale pout.

'I said, do you hear?'

'I s'pose.'

'Now, let's get you washed before your tea. Auntie has to go out later on.'

'Aw, Auntie. Do yer 'ave to?'

'If I don't go out an' earn us some money, there'll be no sausages for tomorrow's tea.'

She brought a bowl of water and some antiseptic from the kitchenette, and started bathing Emil's war wounds.

'That's right, take your shirt off – what there is left of it. Honest, kid, I don't know what you do to your clothes.'

'Ow. Ow, don't!'

'Stand still, yer little terror, or I won't tell you what I 'eard today.'

'What's that?' Emil stopped wriggling and listened.

'It's a secret.'

'Aw, Auntie Claire!'

'Oh, all right then.' She smiled. 'Now, you miss your Ma, don't you?'

'Yes, Auntie Claire. Is she comin' 'ome?'

'Not yet, but listen. You know Sergeant Greenwood promised to tip me the wink if them do-gooders come wantin' to put you in a children's home?'

Emil nodded.

'Well, he told me today the Government's thinkin' of sending all the kids to the place where your Ma's bin taken. That'd be good, wouldn't it?'

She was surprised by the look on Emil's face.

'What's up, kid?'

'Would it mean I never saw you no more?'

''Course not. Just till all this mess is over. There'll be other kids there – an' a beach to play on, an' sea . . .'

'I ain't never seen the sea.'

'I know you ain't.'

'Is it ever so big?'

'Ever so. Now, go put a clean shirt on and wash your 'ands. If you're a good boy maybe you'll see your Ma again soon.'

Chapter 16

'It all seems so long ago,' mused Rachel. 'And it was only a week ago.'

Anya laid a hand on her shoulder.

'You'll see Reuben again soon. There'll be other meetings, the Commandant promised.'

Rachel shifted her position on the warm sand and shaded her eyes, gazing out to sea. Such a vastness stretched out towards the horizon, glittering and enticing. It was good to enjoy the summer sun on the beach with her friends from the other houses, but hard not to relive every moment of that brief reunion with her husband.

'It is so hard to be patient when all you want is to be free.'

'We all feel the same as you do,' said Anya's room-mate Katarina. 'Before the war, when I worked as a housemaid in London . . .'

'Free?' Sarah jabbed a stone into the sand. 'I have forgotten what it is like to be free. Perhaps there is no such thing as freedom any more.'

Rebecca, a jolly girl with dark, dancing eyes and braided chestnut hair, leapt to her feet.

'Come down to the sea. It is such a beautiful day – we mustn't sit here being sad.'

Rachel yawned.

'Ever since little Esther came along, I feel exhausted all the time. She thinks her *mamaleh* shouldn't sleep!'

'Ah, but the little ones are worth every sleepless night,' smiled Katarina.

Rachel thought of Esther, watched over by Grethe as she slept in her cot, and her heart filled with warmth.

'She is worth everything I can give. I should be with her now . . .'

'You must have time to yourself,' said Katarina firmly. 'Enjoy it while you can. The baby is safe, someone will come for you if she wakes.' She called out to a small girl playing happily near the sea's edge. 'Don't go too close, Marta.'

Her friend Anya smiled.

'Wait till your Esther is walking. You will need eyes in the back of your head.'

'By then we shall be far from here.'

'How can you be so sure?' said Sarah. News had leaked through of the fierce battle raging in the skies over southern England. 'What if the Luftwaffe breaks the spirit of the British pilots? The British are alone. How can they hold out against an invasion?'

'You mustn't talk like that,' cut in Anya.

'Why not? It's the truth.'

'This is a beautiful day and we are happy,' said Rebecca. 'Don't spoil it. Let's eat.'

'What have you brought?' asked Rachel.

'Bread and cheese,' replied Katrina. 'Mrs Costain gives us so little, but we have saved up our rations.'

'Miss Quine is good to us,' said Rachel. 'She gives us more food than she has.'

She unwrapped sandwiches, cake, fruit, feeling almost guilty to be at the *Bradda Vista*. Everyone in Port Erin knew about the Costains' meanness.

'Have some bread and cheese, Sarah. Or some fruit.'

Sarah hesitated, uncomfortable with the idea of charity, then took an apple. It was the first time she'd tasted fruit in quite some time.

'Thank you.' Sarah bit into the apple; it was crisp and sweet. She had almost forgotten how good food could taste. Flopping down on her belly in the sand, she propped

216

herself up on one elbow as she ate.

'You'll give yourself indigestion,' scolded Rachel.

Sarah allowed herself a smile.

'I don't care. Could I . . . can I have another?'

Rachel held out the bag of fruit.

'Eat as much as you like. There is plenty.'

'When they let us out,' began Katarina, eyes closed and daydreaming, 'I'm going to go to London. I'm going to work and save all my money, and buy myself the biggest meal *ever*!'

'Chocolate,' giggled Anya. 'Lovely, dark chocolate, all melty and sweet.'

'And *lox*,' murmured Rebecca, joining in the sweet sensuality of this communal daydream. 'There is *such* a baker's shop in Whitechapel. Lupowitz's . . . they sell fresh-baked bagels, still warm, smothered in cream cheese and *lox* . . .'

'Paradise,' breathed Anya, wriggling her toes into the sand as she ate.

'I had nothing when I came to England,' Rebecca went on. 'A few pfennigs only. And Itzchak Lupowitz sees me standing outside his shop with my face pressed up against his window, and he says, "What is wrong?" And I say, "I have no money to buy bagels." "Then I will give you a bagel," he replies. "Next time, when you have money, you will come back to my shop and buy bagels from me." That was the best meal I have ever tasted . . .'

They ate and talked and laughed, old tensions easing in the sunshine. Sitting on the beach below the high cliffs, they were sheltered from the lively breeze which ruffled the grass at the top of the slope. This was a good day, thought Rachel. A good day, with good friends. Sarah seemed happier too, as though she were at last beginning to leave the nightmares behind.

'*Was haben wir hier?*' A German voice, loud and vulgar, rang out across the quiet corner of the beach. Rachel froze in the middle of laughing at little Marta, playing in the sand.

Rachel had already seen the group of German women coming towards them, and felt Sarah's body stiffen.

'Ignore them, Sarah. They just want to make trouble.'

But the newcomers didn't want to be ignored. Inge Stresl spoke again, more loudly this time.

'What have we here – on *our* part of the beach?'

This time, Rachel turned her face towards the group. Two of them she recognised instantly as Inge Stresl and Mathilde Kohl, the two Austrian housemaids who had moved to the *Erindale*. The others, she knew only as hangers-on of Marianne von Strondheim. Bad news, all of them.

'Since when was this your part of the beach?' Katarina asked calmly.

'What was that?' enquired Mathilde, with an exaggerated pantomime of pretending to hear something. 'Did I hear something? Did I hear a pig squeal?'

Inge's lip curled into a cruel sneer of perverse pleasure; and she started sniffing like a dog trying to pick up a trail.

'Am I imagining it, or is there a bad smell around here? A bad *Jewish* smell?'

Sarah's eyes blazed with hatred.

'Leave us alone.'

'Listen how the little Jew-pig squeals,' mocked Inge. It was too much for Sarah to bear.

'*Paskudnika,*' she hissed. 'If there is a bad smell on this beach, it is the smell of your own stinking filth.'

'Easy, Sarah,' urged Rachel. 'No need to make a *gevalt* . . .' She got to her feet, brushing sand off her dress, surprising herself with her own composure. 'There is a woman police constable up there.' She nodded towards the promenade. 'Go away and leave us alone, or I swear I will scream at the top of my voice.'

Inge laughed.

'And you think they'll pay attention to your squealings, do you?'

'If you don't go away we shall both find out.'

Mathilde tugged at Inge's sleeve.

'Let's go. We're wasting our time around scum like this.'

Rachel stood her ground and watched them turn and walk away towards the open-air swimming pool. Inside, she was jelly; but she felt surprisingly strong. She was learning that Reuben could not fight all her battles for her. Esther's birth had made her grow up fast.

She sat down again on the sand as if nothing had happened, and picked up a plate.

'Won't you have one of these rock cakes? Mrs Bertorelli made them specially.'

Thomas Quine opened the door of his sitting room and took a peep outside. Nobody about. He heaved a sigh of relief.

Shutting the door quietly behind him, he set off across the first-floor landing and down the stairs, taking special care to avoid the squeaky tread.

Over the last few weeks, Thomas had become increasingly furtive. He no longer blustered and barged his way around the house, no longer barked commands from the top of the stairs. These days he crept around like an unsuccessful spy.

He reached the bottom of the stairs and took a quick glance around. It was lucky it was such a nice day. Almost all the women were either out sunning themselves or fully occupied with domestic chores. Relaxing a little, he sauntered along the passageway towards the kitchen.

A sandwich, that's what he'd have. What with rationing, and not half enough sugar for his tea, he found himself frequently peckish. What he really fancied was a nice plate of roasted herrings, but he supposed he'd have to make do with bread and scrape.

Pushing open the kitchen door a couple of inches, he took the lie of the land. All seemed peaceful – and mercifully deserted. Six loaves had been set to rise next to the gas range, and there was a lovely yeasty smell of baking. He stepped inside and closed the door.

Archie and Bonzo were curled up together, as close to the side of the warm oven as they could possibly get without actually getting inside. Thomas deigned to bend his arthritic back and tickle Archie behind the ear.

'Now then, boy, you want to watch yoursel', or you'll scorch all your fur off, you daft beast.'

Now to eat. Rubbing his hands, Thomas took the lid off the blue and white enamel bin. There was just the end of a wholemeal loaf and a wedge of soda farl – his favourite. Eagerly he scooped it out and went hunting for the butter. He knew Cora had some somewhere, and sure enough it turned up behind a pack of that nasty hard margarine.

Just as the knife was sinking into the butter, he heard the kitchen door open. Oh no, it couldn't be. But it was.

'*Signor* Thomas. My poor *Signor* Thomas!'

He froze like a rabbit caught in headlights, too late to escape. Signora Bertorelli had him in her clutches and she wasn't going to let go of him easily. Silently he cursed his growling stomach. It was coming to something when a man couldn't even get a bit of bread and butter in his own kitchen!

'I was just going,' he said lamely. But the big Italian woman – and my, she *was* big – just grinned at him, her plump cheeks dimpling with delight.

'You are hungry, *Signor* Thomas?'

'Well . . .' It seemed a bit daft to deny it, seeing as the butter-knife was still in his hand. He tried edging away, but she just came after him, wagging her finger at him as though he were a schoolboy.

'You are very naughty man, *Signor* Thomas. Very naughty man. You hungry, you see Maria Bertorelli, yes? She make you lovely, lovely food – right food for hungry man. No?'

'No,' protested Thomas. More fool him for letting her corner him here, in her domain. He should have known she'd track him down in the kitchen.

'You no like my food?'

'Aye, well, 'tis ter'rible good, but . . .'

'I cook for you, yes? I make you beautiful meal.' She kissed her fingertips to show exactly how beautiful. There was a glint in those sloe-black eyes, mused Thomas, and he didn't like it. Didn't like it at all.

He reached out and tried to seize the chunk of soda bread but to his surprise and horror she slapped his fingers.

'I tell you, you very bad! You wait and Maria, she cook you food to make you good and fat. Yes?' She squeezed Thomas's arm. 'You too thin. Maria make you fat.'

Thomas regarded Maria with horror. Even Archie was sitting up on his haunches, gazing at her with wide-eyed astonishment. Maria Bertorelli was definitely not Thomas Quine's ideal woman. For a start-off she was sixty if she was a day, and twice his size; a fearsome matron with strong red arms and a bust made to suffocate unwary males. Worse still: there was the unmistakable light of passion in her dark and roving eye.

'You give Maria little kiss, eh? Little kiss to thank her for cooking you beautiful meal . . .'

Maria made a grab for him and pinned him against the back door. He swallowed hard.

'Mrs Bertorelli, you're a married woman!'

Maria gave a dismissive shrug of her shoulders.

'My husband, he far away, in a camp in Onchan.' Her plump fingers pinched Thomas's cheek affectionately. 'What he not know, he not care about, yes?'

'No!' insisted Thomas. But he had the feeling his goose was already cooked.

That evening, Cora and James went to the pictures in Douglas. It was only a repeat screening of *The Lady Vanishes*, but that didn't matter to Cora. It felt so good just to be out with James again.

'That was a lovely evening,' sighed Cora as James stopped the car high on the cliffs and they looked out over the starry sea. 'I had a really good time.'

'Me too.' James leant back in the driver's seat and breathed in the fresh night air.

'It's been too long.'

'Much too long. We'll do it again soon.'

'Promise?'

'Promise.'

They didn't speak for a few moments, each feeling the awkwardness of a relationship which had gone beyond casual friendship but never quite fulfilled its early possibilities. Cora opened her mouth to speak but said nothing. There was so much she wanted to say – things she should have said a long time since – but there were always too many good reasons not to say anything.

It was James who broke the silence.

'I'm sorry we haven't seen much of each other lately,' he began.

'It's all right, I understand.'

'It's been so busy at the practice. I've had a lot on my mind.' For a brief moment Elsa's face flashed into his mind but he pushed the image out of his thoughts.

Cora cleared her throat.

'We don't have to see each other if you'd rather not. I mean, if you're too busy . . . or if you don't enjoy my company the way you used to . . .'

Her words startled James.

'Of course I enjoy your company! Whatever made you think . . .?'

'Oh, nothing really.'

James clicked open the driver's door.

'Let's get out and go for a stroll, shall we?' James got out of the car and opened Cora's door for her. She slid out as elegantly as her tight skirt would allow, James taking her hand and helping her to her feet. 'You know, you look lovely tonight. That colour really suits you.'

Cora felt her cheeks redden with pleasure. She let her hand rest in James's for a few moments, then slipped it through the crook of his arm. He pressed it close to his side, and she felt his warmth, steady and strong.

'Come on then, let's walk down to the sea. I want to count the stars – like we used to. Do you remember?'

'Of course I do.' He thought of the sweet, simple times before the war came, when everything had seemed so easy and you could just get on with life, without really thinking about it. 'Funny how things have changed, isn't it?'

'Well, if you'd told me a year or two ago that I'd be running a boarding house full of internees, I'd have thought you'd gone mad.'

'Were you very angry when William and Grace dumped the *Bradda Vista* on you?'

'Furious. I had everything planned out, see. I was going to save up and buy Evie Bannister's shop when she retires.'

'You still can, when all this is over.'

'I . . . don't know.'

'Come on, Cora, she'd have you back like a shot. The last time I saw her, she kept saying how much the customers were missing you.'

'No – what I meant was, I don't think I'd want to go back, not now.'

'Why not?'

'Like you said, things have changed. Sometimes I feel . . . well, restless. I can see why Fenella decided to join up – everybody needs a challenge.' Even me, she told herself. Even I can't stand still forever.

'And do you feel like that, too? Would you leave the Island?' James held his breath, not even admitting to himself how much he wanted to hear her say no.

'I've got the *Bradda Vista* to think about. But after the war, perhaps.' She looked across at James, his face half in shadow, wishing she could read his thoughts. 'It might depend on whether or not there's anything to stay for.'

They walked on a little further. Questions burned to be asked. Cora took the plunge.

'How about you, James? What do you want to do with your life when the war's over?'

James considered for a moment.

'Work hard, I suppose, maybe become Senior Partner one day . . .'

'You'll stay on the Island? You wouldn't go back to Scotland?'

She couldn't see his face in any detail, but the starlight made James's eyes glitter as he turned towards her.

'There are . . . reasons why I'd like to stay.'

Cora's heart was thumping, a flood-tide of wanting building up inside her. She longed to tell him all she felt, all she hoped; but she was so afraid of spoiling everything, of him driving away.

A reckless impulse stirred within her.

'James . . .'

'Yes?'

'James, we've been . . . friends for quite a while now. Good friends.'

'Oh, it must be what – a couple of years, since we met?'

'More. And we've had some good times together, haven't we?'

'The best.'

'You see, James, I just wanted to say – oh, it's no good, forget I spoke.'

He stopped, took her hands in his, made her look into his shadowy face.

'No, go on.'

If only she could see his face properly. Maybe then she'd know how much of a fool she was about to make of herself.

'You mean a lot to me, James. I've wanted to tell you so for such a long time, but I was afraid you'd laugh in my face.'

'You really think I'd laugh about something like that?' Cora heard a nervous catch in his voice; but it was too late to go back now. What she'd said could not be unsaid.

'James . . .' she began. 'Will you answer me one question?'

'Of course. Anything.'

'You do care about me too – don't you?'

The silence was no more than a few seconds, but to Cora it seemed an eternity. Had she gone and ruined a perfectly good friendship by opening her big mouth?

Then James spoke again. His voice trembled slightly, but it was suffused with a quiet warmth which made her dare to hope she had not been mistaken.

'Of course I care about you, Cora. You know I do. And I always will.'

Planting a kiss upon her forehead, he slid his arm about her waist, and they walked together slowly back towards the car.

Reuben Kotkin was feeling distinctly brighter. Oh, the old frustration was still there – but things had changed. He had found Rachel again, kissed and held her. And he had become a father! Suddenly the grim, embattled world didn't seem quite such an awful place after all.

'Have you seen that fellow over there?' Sachs nudged his arm as they strolled together in the square.

'The wild-looking *mensch* with the terrible scar? He arrived a couple of days ago, from Scotland. Seems he was on the *Arandora Star*, poor fellow.'

Sachs shook his head in disbelief.

'That such a thing should happen! Is it any wonder the man is half out of his wits?'

Reuben looked across the grass at the man sitting alone on a bench. His fingers were fidgeting nervously with a pencil and a scrap of paper, as though he could almost – but not quite – remember what he was supposed to do with them. His whole body looked shrunken somehow, as if he had too little flesh to hang on his broad, once-powerful frame.

'What is his name?'

'Müller. Ernst Müller. Why?'

'I thought to have words with him.'

'But why, Reuben? He's German.'

'So he's German. He's a sick German.'

'The poor *shnuk* will not thank you for it. He's *meschugge*.'

Reuben shrugged.

'So he's a little sick in the head. Perhaps if people talked to him instead of leaving him alone, his wits would mend.'

'Since how long have you been a doctor, Reuben Kotkin? Why not leave it to the psychiatrists to sort him out?'

Reuben looked across at the man with the wild hair, straggly beard and scarred face. He appeared to be scrawling something over and over again on his scrap of paper, his lips moving silently in time to the moving of the pencil. *Meschugge* or not, he cut a pathetic figure and Reuben's heart went out to him.

'It could have been me, Sachs.'

'God forbid!'

'Or my Rachel even.'

'Whatever do you mean?'

'Rachel and I – we escaped from Holland in a lifeboat. It was terrible, the sea was throwing us all over the place. What if the Germans had attacked us? What if the boat had capsized?'

'Well, just you watch yourself, Kotkin,' cautioned Sachs, grudgingly approving. 'And mind he doesn't turn nasty and take a swing at you.'

Reuben set off across the square towards the stranger. What was he going to say? What crazy arrogance made him think, even for a moment, that he could do anything when the doctors had so manifestly failed?

'*Guten Tag, Herr Müller,*' he said hesitantly. The man looked up, at first seeming not to recognise his own name.

'*Guten Tag.*'

It was a start. Encouraged, Reuben felt the conversation worth pursuing.

'May I sit down?'

'As you wish.'

Reuben sat down next to him on the bench. Müller seemed not so much mad as confused – constantly searching for something in the dusty vaults of his mind; something that kept eluding him.

'How are you? I heard you were in the hospital.'

'Oh, not so bad. Not so bad.'

'How do you like it here?'

Müller ignored the question, his eyes roving over the square, the rows of identical boarding houses, the figures walking and talking. Searching for something . . .

'If I could just . . .'

'Just what?'

'If I could remember.' He looked down at the piece of paper in his hands and Reuben followed his gaze. 'Who am I? Can you remember?'

'You're Ernst Müller,' said Reuben.

Müller kept on looking at the piece of paper. On it was scrawled the same word, over and over again.

Max. Max. Max.

'Then who is Max?'

'I don't know. But you're Ernst Müller. Don't you remember?'

Müller passed his hand over his brow, wiping the sweat away. He shook his head slowly, uncomprehending.

'Not yet,' he said. 'I don't quite remember yet . . . But I will. I will remember.'

Chapter 17

It was a fresh morning in the middle of August and Elsa Nadel was happy to be out of doors.

At the other end of the beach she could hear the other women enjoying early-morning gymnastics. But now Elsa found that increasingly she preferred her own company to that of people who couldn't accept her as she was.

Last night had seen a wild electric storm, leaving behind a messy jumble of driftwood, sea-wrack and the odd dead jellyfish. But the storm had swept away the stifling heat and left the air exhilaratingly clear. On a day like today, you might see all the way to the Mountains of Mourne and believe you could walk there across the glassy sea.

Wading in, she gasped as the chilly water rose up her legs. In the morning sunshine it looked so inviting – a glassy blue-green, crystal-clear to the pale sand beneath. The iciness took her breath away, making her skin sting and tingle.

She plunged in, letting the pleasure of her swim sweep away her frustrations and anxieties. A couple of policewomen were stationed up on the promenade, but it wasn't difficult to imagine she was as free as the kittiwakes wheeling in the sky overhead.

Elsa was a strong swimmer and it was a good half-hour before she decided to turn and swim back to the shore.

James McArthur was enjoying a rare morning off. He liked to take Fergus for a good long walk whenever he had the opportunity, and the exercise helped to work the stiffness out of his slowly mending leg.

He let Fergus off the lead and watched him go zig-zagging down the cliffside path which led to the beach, through grass and shrubs. James followed more cautiously, taking care not to slip on the loose stones.

To his left, a group of internee women were doing morning exercises on the beach. Their perfect physical precision irritated him, and he looked away to the right. No one was up the north end of the beach – no one except a single figure, swimming slowly but powerfully towards the shore.

He walked down towards the bottom of the cliff path. Fergus was already there, tearing around like a whirligig with a tangle of seaweed hanging from his jaws.

'Come here, boy, leave it alone.'

Fergus trotted up, presented the mass of wet seaweed to his master then tore off again, splashing into the sea and getting a thorough soaking.

James ignored him. Something else had caught his eye. No, not something – someone.

She hadn't seen him yet, but he had seen her. Standing in the shallows, she was shaking the water from her dark, bobbed hair, and sparkling droplets were falling through the air, some onto her shoulders, making wet, glittering trickles that ran down over her bare arms and legs.

He caught his breath, astonished at the sudden excitement inside him. It was Elsa. Intelligent, sensible, mature Elsa Nadel. He'd known her, worked alongside her at the surgery for weeks now – but he'd never seen her like this before. Her body was a revelation to him.

Maybe he'd never quite seen her as a woman before. The tailored trousers and plain shirts she favoured didn't do justice to the athletic beauty of her body, the clean lines of breast and waist and hip so perfectly revealed by the ruched black bathing costume with the halter neck.

Her breasts were full and firm beneath the wet, semi-transparent fabric; her thighs long, slender, smooth as silk. Trails of water dripped down them in long, slow caresses as she came towards him, wading out of the water. He held his breath.

And then, almost to his regret, she saw him. Recognised him. Stopped. And smiled.

'Hello . . . James.'

He hoped his voice didn't betray his inner turmoil as he replied:

'Lovely morning for a swim.'

'Yes.' She slicked back her wet, dark hair and a spray of water droplets sparkled in the sunny air.

The awkwardness surrounded them like a thick fog. It was like being in a dream, wanting so much to run but your legs and arms won't obey. Gauche as a blushing adolescent, James searched around for something to say.

'You'll be coming to help at the surgery tomorrow?' He wondered if she'd noticed him staring at her, drinking in the smooth lines of her semi-naked body. What would she think of him?

'I promised I would.'

'Yes, but . . .'

'I want to. Would you rather I didn't come?'

'No. No, of course not. I'll . . . look forward to seeing you.'

'I might be a little late. I promised I'd see someone in the afternoon. About the classes . . .'

'Yes, yes, of course. I mean, if the surgery's getting too much, what with all the other things you have to do . . .'

Elsa silenced him by laying her hand on his arm. It felt cold and moist through his shirt sleeve and he prayed she couldn't feel the shiver of pleasure that ran through him.

'I told you, I want to help. Oh, I'm sorry!' she smiled. 'I've made your shirt sleeve all damp.'

'My pleasure,' replied James. And he meant it.

Cora couldn't remember a time when she'd felt less glamorous. She didn't have to look in the mirror to know she looked a fright in her patched overall and rubber gloves, with her hair tied up in an old tea-towel.

'Oh dear,' said Bessie Teare, standing with her at the back of the *Bradda Vista*. 'You *did* catch the worst of the storm last night.'

'And don't I know it.' Cora had to stop herself retching as she lifted the inspection cover and peered into the overflowing drains. 'Ugh! What a horrible stink.'

'Er . . . yes.' Bessie held her breath and took a step back.

'Just my luck,' sighed Cora, dragging the cover back over the drain. 'Half a dozen tiles blown off the roof *and* blocked drains!'

'Do you think the women have been putting . . . you know . . . things down the lavatory?'

'Who knows? The thing that's worrying me is how I'm going to get all of this sorted out. I'd ring nice Mr Corkish, only he says he won't come near Port Erin since he had that run-in with the Commandant. She seems to have a knack of getting up people's noses.'

'I expect it comes of being an Army nurse,' replied Bessie. 'She just can't bear things to be disorganised. I don't know how that Mrs Pantin puts up with her.'

'I wish Mrs Pantin could help Elsa find her brother,' mused Cora. And perhaps if she did, she thought to herself, it would distract her from being quite so friendly with James . . .

'No luck in tracing him yet, then?'

'Not a word since he wrote to say he was being transferred. And no one seems to know where he was transferred to. That's the war for you.'

'It's all such a muddle,' nodded Bessie. 'Anyhow, what are we going to do about your drains, dear? I'm sure they can't be hygienic. Perhaps you should ask Mr McArthur to help . . .'

The thought was tempting. Since that night when they'd talked together by the sea, she'd longed for a chance to see him again, to talk about the things that remained unsaid. But James was busy and Cora wasn't some helpless little kid. She rolled up her sleeves.

'You know, Bessie, there are some old drain-rods in the cellar. I don't see why I can't unblock them myself . . .'

'Hello, Ernst. How goes it?'

Ernst Müller looked up from his mug of soup to see Reuben and Sachs walking towards him. He didn't speak, but inclined his head in their direction. Sachs exchanged a nod with Reuben, and they sat down at the table, opposite Müller.

The 'Artists' Cafe' hadn't long been established, but already it had become Hutchinson Camp's most popular social venue. It had been set up in a basement laundry room by a famous Austrian pastry-cook, and attracted not only artists but anyone who enjoyed coffee and cake.

'How are you today?' asked Sachs, as breezily as he could. He still had reservations about this crusade of Reuben's, but Kotkin's heart was in the right place even if his brain wasn't. 'Feeling better?'

He didn't really expect a reply, but Müller surprised him.

'All days are much the same here.'

'Still,' cut in Reuben, 'there are things to do – people to keep you company. Why don't you come to one of the talks with us?'

'There's one on tonight,' said Sachs. 'Professor Marcus is talking on modern art and society. It doesn't cost anything – all you have to do is take along a chair to sit on.'

'You like art, don't you?' asked Reuben cautiously. Everyone in the camp had become accustomed to the shambling figure with his scraps of paper, forever sitting scrawling, scrawling, scrawling meaningless words and squiggles.

'Why do you say that?'

'I . . . well, I just thought you did, that's all.'

'I don't know.'

'Don't know what?'

'I don't know if I like art. I thought I did. I'm not sure now.'

'What did you do for a living, Ernst?' enquired Sachs.

'Before you came to this rotten hole? I was a writer,' he added with a grin. 'A very bad and very penniless writer.'

Müller reached into the inside pocket of his jacket and drew out a set of papers, the ink and paper much damaged by seawater. He opened up the beige card booklet that Reuben recognised as an Alien's Registration Document.

'Ernst Müller,' he said, reading the words. 'Born Bremen, nineteen-oh-seven. Clerk.' He lifted his eyes to meet Reuben's. 'But I don't remember, see.'

'You don't remember anything at all about your life?' Reuben glanced at the grainy, stained photograph on Müller's identity card. It wasn't a very good photo, and hours soaking in seawater hadn't improved the likeness. There was no beard either, but if you screwed up your eyes it almost looked like him.

'I can remember a few things – just flashes really, hardly anything. And the things I do remember don't make much sense.'

'Such as?' enquired Sachs.

'I remember pictures, lots of pictures. And a lot of hills and water. And a tall woman with short dark hair. I have these dreams . . .'

'Your wife?'

Müller shook his head.

'No. I don't know. I can't even see her face properly!' His right hand curled into a fist of tension, and he slammed it down on the table, making the cups rattle.

Sachs sipped his coffee.

'Steady on, it'll come back.'

Reuben nodded.

'You've had a bad knock on the head, these things take time. You have to be patient.'

'I could draw . . . I'm sure I could draw . . .'

'But you can't now?'

Müller looked down at the scrappy paper on the table. It was covered with squiggles and what looked like abortive attempts to draw scenes, things, people.

'I can't make my hand do what my brain wants it to. Perhaps they're right, perhaps I am mad.'

Sachs looked at Reuben.

'No,' he said. 'Of course you're not.'

'The thing is . . .' he began, then shut up abruptly.

'What?' asked Sachs.

'I can't.'

'Tell me.' Reuben made him look him full in the face. 'No one will think anything bad of you. Who are we to judge?'

Müller took a deep breath and let it out in a long, shuddering gasp. Reuben noticed that there was a fat blue vein pulsing rhythmically on his temple, just underneath the deep, disfiguring scar that ran up the left side of his face from chin to scalp. A severe blow to the head could do terrible things to a man's mind, thought Reuben, make him believe all sorts of implausible things.

'I'm not who they say I am.'

'But you have your identity papers . . .'

'I know. I must be this Ernst Müller – but this picture . . .' He fingered the blurred photograph on the identity card. 'Is it really me?' There were unshed tears at the corners of his grey eyes.

'You know it is.'

'I can't . . .' He shook his head, as though trying to shake the truth into it.

Reuben looked down at the messy doodles and despaired of ever finding the right words to say. How could you tell a man that he was deluding himself? If, of course, he was . . .

'Max,' whispered Müller, almost inaudibly. 'Who is Max?' He looked at Reuben, his eyes begging him for answers. 'Perhaps he could help me find out who I really am.'

'And you'd better behave yourself, Grethe Herzheim, this is no laughing matter.'

Grethe glared at the woman police sergeant as she was

marched unceremoniously up the stairs to the camp office.

'What's it to you what I do?' she snapped.

'They've sent me to this bloody island to make sure you behave yourself, and I'm damned if I'm going to let you run wild like some mongrel bitch.'

'Darling,' Grethe smiled sweetly. 'I love you too.'

The sergeant knocked on the door and a voice answered from within.

'Come in.'

'Just count yourself lucky it's not Dame Joanna dealing with you,' hissed the sergeant. 'She knows what to do with slags like you.'

The door opened and Grethe stepped inside. Miss Arnold was working at her desk and looked up at the new arrivals.

'Grethe Herzheim, madam.'

'Thank you, Sergeant Curtis. If you'd just wait outside for a few moments.'

'You wouldn't prefer me to stay, madam? In case of any trouble?'

'I will call you if I require assistance.'

'Very well, ma'am.' The sergeant threw Grethe a filthy look but it was lost on her.

Miss Arnold waited until the door had closed behind Sergeant Curtis, then opened a buff folder on her desk.

'Miss Herzheim?'

'You should know.' Grethe stared back dispassionately.

'This is a very serious matter.'

'If you say so.'

'You are aware, I am sure, of the regulations which state that internees must not speak or in any way communicate with the local male residents?'

'I've done nothing wrong.'

'According to camp rules . . .'

'So I got caught. I don't see why I should apologise. It's not as if I'm sorry.'

Miss Arnold counted slowly to ten in the silence of her

head. Maybe she should have sent this one to Dame Joanna to be dealt with, after all. But she'd miscalculated, thought this one would see reason.

'Look, Grethe, I'm not unsympathetic. But rules are rules.'

'They're your rules, not mine.' Grethe's temper flared. 'And you said you'd send my kid to me. Remember that?'

'That's nothing to do with me.'

'Really? So it's all right for you to break the rules, is it? As long as we do what we're told and don't make a fuss.'

'You were seen talking to a Mr Kerruish . . .'

'You mean, someone who's got it in for me *told* you I'd been talking to him.'

'You deny that you have been associating with this man?'

'*Associating*? You mean, have I been screwing him?' Anger ripped through Grethe, turning her face deathly white.

Miss Arnold remained silent, purse-lipped, letting Grethe's fury run its course.

'No, I haven't,' spat Grethe. 'But I don't expect you to believe that. I mean, once a tart always a tart, isn't that right?'

'No one is accusing you of any moral impropriety.'

'That makes a change.'

'But you have broken one of the camp rules and must be punished for it.'

'Punished? For *talking*?'

'If you have no regard for your own welfare, then at least think of Mr Kerruish's reputation. He too could be punished for your indiscretion.'

Secretly, Grethe felt a surge of relief. It was a stroke of good fortune that Harry had gone off 'to the fishing'. At least he was spared the humiliation of a lecture from a crabby old spinster who wouldn't and couldn't understand that even whores needed friends.

But Grethe felt guilty too, guilty for the taint that had touched him because of her. He had brought her nothing but goodness and kindness; and look how she was repaying him for his friendship.

'You realise, Miss Herzheim, that you could receive a custodial sentence for this type of offence.'

Grethe managed a wry smile.

'Prison? I'm terrified.'

'Listen to me. I am prepared to be lenient, but you will not speak to Mr Kerruish again, do you understand me?'

Grethe shuffled her feet on the squeaky linoleum.

'I understand.'

Oh, she understood all right. She understood perfectly. But understanding wasn't the same thing as accepting. She would move heaven and earth to protect him; but in her heart she knew it would take more than a slap on the wrist to keep her away from Harry Kerruish.

Chapter 18

August darkened into September, and the skies over London were filled with the sounds of German bombers.

The first daylight raids on the capital were all the more shocking because they had been so long in coming. Londoners reeled, momentarily unable to grasp the devastation around them; then got on with their lives with a grim and joyless determination.

At the flat on Rosier Walk, Claire was busy trying to talk some sense into Emil.

'If I say you'll go to school, you'll go to school.'

'I don't want to.'

Claire Hodges stood in the doorway of the kitchenette, trying hard to look stern.

'You 'eard. Once they've mended the bomb damage you'll be there every day, or I'll know the reason why.'

'Sid Dukes ain't goin' to go to school no more,' said Emil hopefully. ''Cause of the war.'

'I don't care what Sid Dukes does. You're going and that's all there is to it.'

'You can't make me. You ain't my Ma.'

Emil's jaw was set in that stubborn way that so reminded Claire of Grethe. She sat down at the table, next to Emil.

'Your Ma wants you to 'ave a proper education.'

'Why?'

''Cause she wants you to 'ave better than she 'ad, that's why.'

'I want to stay 'ome with you. If they drop more bombs on us I could protect you.'

Claire half smiled. He was too young to understand the terror that had swept London in the wake of the first daylight raids. The children kept on laughing and chattering, turning the whole thing into some sort of game.

'Don't you worry about me. Just eat up, then you can go round to Mrs Perks's. She'll keep an eye on you while I'm out.'

'But she smells funny and she's got no teeth!'

'She's a nice kind old lady an' it's good of her to mind you.'

Emil pushed his cereal round his plate.

'I don't like Shredded Wheat.'

'Well, that's just tough, kid, 'cause that's what you're 'aving.'

'It wouldn't be so bad if there was sugar on it.'

'There ain't no sugar. It's on the ration now, remember.'

'Why?'

'Because the Germans are sinkin' the ships what carry it, that's why.'

'Oh.'

Claire bit her tongue. She wished she hadn't mentioned Germans. She knew what would come next.

'My Ma's German, ain't she?'

'Yes.'

'An' that's why they took 'er away an' put 'er in a prison?'

'Well – yes. It ain't really a prison though.'

'But she ain't a bad person?'

''Course not.' Claire put her arm round the little boy's shoulders. 'Your Ma's a good person, an' she loves you very much.'

Emil chewed thoughtfully.

'Why can't she come 'ome an' be wiv us, like before?'

Claire sighed.

'I don't know, Emil.'

'When will they let me go to the prison an' stay wiv her, then?'

'Soon. Sergeant Greenwood says they're sending the kids over to the Isle of Man any day now.'

'When?'

'Soon. I don't know. Now, eat up that Shredded Wheat or else.'

'Or else what?'

'Or else you'll get a clip round the ear. Now just pipe down an' be grateful for what you got.'

Claire ruffled his hair and went back into the kitchenette to make tea. She retied the belt on her housecoat as she put the kettle on the gas ring. It wouldn't do for the kid to see her not looking decent, no matter what she might be in other people's eyes.

Thoughts of Grethe preyed on her mind. Grethe; all those miles away and without the little boy she doted on. And yet, at least Grethe was miles and miles away from the bombs. It felt like the whole world was in prison now, only Grethe's prison was less horrible than most.

Claire looked round the door into the living room.

'Ain't you done yet?'

Emil pulled a face.

'I've ate one of 'em.'

'Oh, go on then. Get your coat and go down to Mrs Perks.' She picked her handbag off the table and felt inside for her purse. 'Here's a couple of bob to give to her for minding you, and a shillin' for your dinner.'

She watched Emil pocket the money carefully, putting the florin and the shilling into the back pocket of his shorts.

'Now on your way, you 'ear? An' don't you go givin' Mrs Perks no cheek, nor running off nor nothin'.'

'I won't do nuffink, Auntie Claire.' He grinned up at her. 'I'm a good boy, ain't I?'

'If you're a good boy, Emil Herzheim, I'm Max bloody Miller.' She glanced at the clock. Time was getting on and she

241

had to get out and try and earn a bit of money, bombs or no bombs. 'Hurry now, your Auntie has to go to work . . .'

The sound of heavy shoes clumping up the stairs from the ground floor stopped her in mid-sentence. She'd know the sound of a copper's boots anywhere. And there was another sound, too – the lighter tap-tap of a woman's shoes on the bare wooden staircase. Claire's heart skipped a beat.

Rat-a-tat-tat.

'Auntie Claire. Auntie Claire, there's someone at the door. Shall I let 'em in?'

'No, you stay here. I'll get it.'

A second knock, louder this time.

'Open up, please. It's the police.' She brightened as a sudden thought hit her. Emil! They must have come to take Emil to the Isle of Man. And she'd hardly started packing his case . . .

She opened the door. Outside on the landing stood Sergeant Greenwood, looking hot and embarrassed. Next to him stood a woman in her early forties, respectable and faceless in her dark brown costume and clumpy lace-up shoes.

'Who is it, Auntie Claire?' called Emil from the room behind her.

'No one special. Wait in the bedroom a minute.' She stepped out on the landing and closed the door softly behind her. 'What's all this then? You come to take Emil to his Ma?' She looked at Sergeant Greenwood, wondering why he looked so ill at ease. 'You could have given me a bit of notice . . .'

'This is none of my doing, Claire,' said the Sergeant gruffly. Claire stared at him.

'What . . .?'

The woman cleared her throat.

'You are Miss Claire Hodges?'

'Who wants to know?'

'My name is Miss Charteris.' She consulted a clipboard. 'Emil, such a nice name. I hear he's quite a bright boy, if a little unruly.'

'He's a good boy, he's fine. I couldn't sleep easy in my bed if I didn't do the best for Grethe's kid.'

'Ah yes, Miss Herzheim.'

'So – have you come to take him to his mother, or what? It's about bloody time. The poor kid never stops talking about her.'

'Not exactly.'

'Then what, *exactly*?'

'We at the council are concerned about the boy's welfare. Not only is his mother classified as an enemy alien, Emil is being cared for . . . well, in circumstances which are hardly ideal.'

Claire sneered at Miss Charteris's studied politeness.

'You mean he's got a tart for a mother and a tart taking care of him?'

'As I have said, we are concerned for his moral welfare.'

Claire's lips pursed.

'Then get off your backsides and send the kid to his Ma,' she snapped. ''Ave you any idea how the poor woman feels, locked up with 'er boy the other side of the country?'

'Look, Claire,' urged Sergeant Greenwood. 'You've done your best, but it's time to let the boy go. You want the best for him, don't you?'

'What do you think?'

Miss Charteris carried on talking, perfectly unruffled.

'Pack a bag for the boy, Miss Hodges, we haven't got all day.'

'Just hold on a mo, Miss high-and-mighty. Where d'you think you're takin' him?'

'London isn't safe. Emil will be much happier with a nice foster family in the country.'

'You can't do this. You can't bloody do this. You promised to send him to his mother!' Claire threw Sergeant Greenwood a look of pure venom. 'You bastard. I should have known better than to believe a word you said.' She turned back to the woman from the council. 'Send him to Grethe. She's his mother, she's got a right . . .!'

Miss Charteris framed her words carefully.

'I'm so sorry. I'm afraid that won't be possible. Now, Miss Hodges, if you'd just tell Emil to pack his things, we'll be on our way.'

'Eat up. You know what Potato Pete says. Waste not want not.'

And you know what Potato Pete can go and do to himself, thought Grace Quine, chasing a forkful of bullet-hard peas around her plate.

'Yes, Father,' she replied, her voice flat to disguise her irritation.

'Such a pity William isn't here,' commented Grace's mother, Iris Pope. 'He has a lovely light touch with a pie.'

'I suppose,' muttered Grace. William this, William that – why didn't anybody give a damn about her?

'*Such* a nice man, William.'

'So you keep saying.'

'Kind and considerate. The reliable type . . .'

Reliable! thought Grace. That's just plain laughable. With a grimace she pushed her plate away from her. 'I can't eat this.'

'Grace!' exclaimed her mother. 'Are you ill?'

'No, Mother, I'm not ill,' replied Grace with the slow, measured tones of exasperation. 'I just don't like eating pigswill.'

Eric Pope stopped munching and looked up.

'You'll mind your manners while you're under this roof, my girl,' he growled. But Grace couldn't care less any more. William had been posted, she was alone and bored and practically imprisoned here with her parents. Things hadn't worked out at all the way she'd planned.

'I'll say what I think.' She pushed back her chair and got up. 'And I'm not staying here to listen to you going on about

William as if he's God or something. I'm going to my room.'

'You'll stay where you are until we've all finished, then you'll help your mother do the dishes.'

'I'm not a child! You can't order me around the way you used to do when I was at school!'

'Perhaps if I'd taken my belt to you a bit more often, you wouldn't have gone and done what you did,' replied Eric.

'Eric, dear . . .' hazarded Iris, but Grace and Eric were squaring up to each other, eyes blazing.

'What exactly is that supposed to mean?' demanded Grace.

'It means you never did listen to a word we said, and look where that got you! You ruined that young man's life . . .'

Tears stung Grace's eyes but she wiped them ruthlessly away.

'*His* life? William's life? That's all you damned well care about, isn't it, your precious William? You'd rather have him than your own daughter!'

'Don't be silly, Grace,' urged her mother.

'Oh, it's all right, Mother, I know. I know Dad always wanted a boy. It was a real disappointment when you had me instead, wasn't it?'

'Not as much of a disappointment as you turned out,' retorted her father. 'Flaunting yourself like that – going out dancing every night. No decent young girl would have behaved the way you did. You looked like a tart, that's what you looked like.'

'So that's what you think, is it? That I'm some sort of whore!' Grace thought back to those days, not so very long ago, when she had been a carefree kid with nothing on her mind but the pursuit of fun, fun, fun.

'If the cap fits.'

'What!'

'Painting yourself up like that. It's no wonder William was tempted . . .'

'William, William, William! That's all you ever bloody talk

about. He was twenty-five, Dad, and I was seventeen – or have you forgotten that?'

'I'll grant you he should have been more careful, at his age,' conceded Eric. 'But that was no excuse . . .'

'Let her alone, Eric,' pleaded Iris. 'She doesn't mean it.'

'I was just a kid. A kid! What did I know about men? Nothing, because nothing's what you told me.'

'We wanted to keep you pure, sweetheart . . .'

'William told me it'd be all right, do you know that? "Don't worry," he said, "trust me. You can't get caught out the first time you do it." And do you know what? I believed him!' Scrunching up her table napkin, she threw it on the floor. It wasn't much of a gesture, but any gesture seemed pretty futile.

Eric stood in silence for a few minutes, then sat down again at the table.

'Finish your dinner.'

Grace looked across the table at him with eyes that had flooded with unshed tears. She knew her father, too, was thinking about what had happened after she'd fallen pregnant. Not about the furious rows, or the rushed wedding, or the reluctant move to the Island; but about what had happened afterwards. What had happened to the child . . .

'I said, sit down, shut up and finish your meal.'

Grace just stood and wept tears that burned and corroded, the rage of injustice and resentment eating away at her guts. How could her parents shut themselves off like this, how could they blame her for everything, with their cold, accusing eyes? She knew their sudden silence was their way of dealing with the tragedy of Billy's death, but how was she supposed to deal with it? Why oh why couldn't she have her old life back, become a person again?

'You don't give a damn about me, do you? Either of you.'

Silence.

'Well, that's just fine by me, because I hate you. In fact, I wish you were both dead.'

Neither her mother nor her father answered and, in a paroxysm of fury, Grace seized the dinner plate and hurled it across the room. It seemed to smash in slow motion, leaving a trail of peas and gravy on the beige floral wallpaper as the fragments slid down to the skirting-board. Iris and Eric just stared at it, unblinking, unresponding.

Grace wanted to scream at them, but no sound would come. Turning on her heel, she stormed out of the dining room and ran upstairs to her bedroom, locking the door and throwing herself face-down on the bed.

William's photograph smiled at her from its silver frame above the fireplace. Suddenly she hated him for his calm, his composure, that quality in him which made other people love him. Even her.

On the radio downstairs, somebody was crooning about love.

Grace buried her face in the eiderdown and wept. People said time was the great healer, but that was a lie. Why couldn't she be forgiven, or, at least, forget?

Early September brought more changeable weather to the Island. But on this particular afternoon the air was caressingly warm and soft; with that peculiar stillness which so often comes before a storm.

'I'm glad you came,' said Marianne.

Elsa kept her distance, mistrustful and angry.

'This isn't a social call.'

'If you say so.'

'This business of harassing the Jewish girls can't go on. I've come to try and sort things out, once and for all.'

They walked together in the mottled green twilight of Bradda Glen, past the cafe and the bandstand. Elsa didn't really know why she'd agreed to come and talk to Marianne. The woman made her flesh creep, they had nothing at all in common. Nothing. But as house representative of the *Bradda Vista*, it was her job to try and sort out the women's problems

– and everyone knew that Marianne von Strondheim and her acolytes were making the Jewish women's lives a misery.

'We have to talk,' began Elsa.

'I'm always happy to talk to you, Elsa, you know that.' She smiled. 'Why don't we talk about you moving into the *Erindale* . . .?'

Marianne's attitude maddened Elsa.

'Look, Marianne, I'm not here to play games and I can't stay long. I should be getting back to the *Bradda Vista*. There's roll-call and then I have to work on a paper I'm writing. And there's something else I promised I'd do.' She felt oddly reluctant to admit exactly what that something was.

'Really? What?'

'I said I'd be with Grethe Herzheim when she talks to Mrs Pantin about her boy. The Home Office is sending over the children soon, and she wants to be sure Emil's with them. All the mothers are desperate to see their children again.'

'Well, well, you *are* public-spirited, aren't you?' There was heavy sarcasm in the smooth, Germanic tones. 'Though nobody in their right mind would put a whore in charge of a child!'

'Grethe's his mother. She has a right,' protested Elsa.

'Some people shouldn't be allowed to have children. In Germany . . .'

Elsa put up her hand to stop her.

'Please, Marianne. You know my views. I was hoping you'd be willing to see sense, but it's obvious I shouldn't have bothered coming.'

To her surprise, Marianne's reply was conciliatory, almost crestfallen.

'I'm sorry, Elsa.'

'And so you should be. Those letters you sent me – those threats you made . . .'

'I never wanted to threaten you, only to make you see how wrong you are. I wanted us to be close again, like when we were at university together. Don't you remember? We used to go for long hikes – you and me, and Minna and Katrine.'

'I remember.' Elsa felt a pang of sadness. 'Things were very different then.'

'Please, Elsa. Let's sit down and talk.'

Finding a bench overlooking the sea, Marianne sat down, stretching her long legs out in front of her and leaning back against the wooden back of the seat.

Elsa hesitated, sick at heart. There seemed to be two equal and opposing forces, the one pushing her forward and the other dragging her back. She hated everything Marianne von Strondheim stood for, yet the ties of the past were so strong.

Marianne patted the seat beside her.

'Come on, what's the harm? You look like a scared rabbit.'

That decided Elsa's mind for her. She sat down. Her heart was racing – she wondered why.

'I'm not afraid of you, Marianne. You should know that by now.'

'Really?' Marianne's voice became softer, less combative. 'We were good friends, back in Leipzig.'

'It was so long ago. I hardly remember.'

'Why would you never admit to yourself what you felt for me?'

'I don't know what you mean,' said Elsa stonily.

'You mean you don't want to.'

Elsa half got up to go, but Marianne laid a cool hand on her arm and all the strength seemed to drain out of her.

'It hurts me too, you know,' said Marianne. Elsa turned to look at her, in surprise.

'What?'

'It hurts me that you turn away from me like this, that you betray everything . . .'

'If anyone's a betrayer, Marianne, it's you. You believed in equality as strongly as any of us . . .'

'I was a child. So were you. But I grew up.'

'I told you, Marianne, I don't have to stay here and listen to you insulting me.' Elsa covered her pain with anger, afraid that Marianne might see her weaken, sense her need to belong again . . .

'No. I'm sorry.' Marianne half turned her face and looked through the trees, across the bay, towards the distant brownish smudge of the Calf of Man. 'But you must know what I felt for you. You must know that I loved you.'

Panic rose, a choking, nauseous pain which turned Elsa's blood to ice. No, no, no, screamed a voice inside her head. Don't say it, it's not true. She shook as she edged away, suddenly afraid.

'There was never anything between us but friendship, Marianne. Girlish friendship. And now it's gone.'

'No, Elsa. Look at me! Will you look at me?'

Marianne seized both her hands and Elsa was forced to look her full in the face. She didn't want to. Marianne's ice-blue eyes were bright as though they brimmed with tears she would never allow herself to shed.

'I loved you then, Elsa. I love you now . . .'

'No!' She tried to draw away. 'Let go of me.'

'Stay, Elsa. Listen to me. I loved you and you loved me too.'

Elsa pulled her hand away, violently, like one who has touched some foul thing and fears that she is tainted.

'Don't say these things, Marianne.' There was real fear in her voice. 'Don't say it, it's crazy, it's not true. How can you believe such a thing?'

Marianne said nothing for a few seconds. Elsa tried to look away but she could not. She was hypnotised by the beautiful blue eyes that, moments before, had seemed so cold. Now they seemed to burn with a secret flame, kindling a treacherous spark within her, reawakening guilty feelings she had believed long forgotten, long dead.

'Because you love me still, Elsa. I can see it in your eyes.'

'Marianne – Alexander . . . your husband . . .'

'I never loved him the way I love you.'

For a moment, Elsa could not remember why she had felt

so afraid of Marianne, so repelled by her that she could scarcely bear to be next to her. Had it really been repulsion? Or had it been fear – fear of what she really was and could not admit to being?

Marianne's slender fingers stroked her bare arm, coaxing, pleading.

'Elsa, you know it's true.'

'Marianne, no!'

All at once the fear and the hatred and the disgust came crashing back like a great black bow-wave, and Elsa pushed Marianne away.

'Get your filthy hands off me.'

Marianne stared back, deeply shocked, her voice almost a whimper.

'Elsa, don't go. You know you want to be with me.'

'No.' Elsa closed her mind to the guilty ache of need. 'No, Marianne. It may be what you want but I'll never feel that way about you.'

Marianne took a step towards her but she was already backing away, hot with anger and shame.

'I'm going back to the *Bradda Vista*. I have things to do . . . Just leave me alone, will you? Leave me alone.'

Marianne did not try to follow her as she turned and half walked, half ran out of Bradda Glen and back towards the promenade. But Elsa thought she heard her voice calling out behind her:

'You'll come back to me, Elsa. You'll come back to me.'

She didn't look back. But although she wiped Marianne's caress from her skin, it lingered like the scent of her own sweet corruption.

Rachel Kotkin bent over the pram, rearranging the canopy so that baby Esther's face was shaded from the sun. Her own face was a picture of radiant pride, the once-pale cheeks now rosy and the joy plain for all to see in her dark eyes.

'Oh, thank you, *Frau* Schultz,' she smiled. The older

woman smiled and nodded in return.

'Think nothing of it. My Putzi is old enough to walk now. You are welcome to use the pram to take Esther out.'

'It is very good of you.' Just how good, Rachel knew only too well. Karin Schultz was interned in one of the patriotic German houses. She had no cause to show friendship or favour to Rachel Kotkin or her child. But not every German was a bad German, as Rachel had discovered. Why, you only had to look at Grethe and Elsa to know that.

'Just watch those filthy seagulls, that is all I ask,' laughed Frau Schultz.

'Don't worry, I shall. I'll polish the pram up like new before I bring it back.'

She set off along the promenade, pausing to show off her new acquisition to Thomas and Cora Quine, who happened to be walking back towards the *Bradda Vista*.

'A Silver Cross!' exclaimed Cora. 'She looks like a princess in there.'

Thomas allowed himself a quick peek under the hood.

'I've seen worse,' he conceded. Praise indeed from Grandad Quine, thought Cora, particularly since his experience with Signora Bertorelli had made him rather less well disposed towards the internees.

'Where are you off to?' enquired Cora.

'To the *Ben-my-Chree*. Rebecca left her sewing behind when she came to visit us yesterday.'

'Give Miss Teare my love. And tell her I'm so sorry to hear about the trouble they had last night.'

Rachel's smile faded slightly. She too had heard about yesterday evening's 'trouble'. Apparently several windows had been put through at the *Ben-my-Chree*, and everyone suspected troublemakers from the *Erindale*, though nothing had been proved.

'I will.'

She set off towards the *Ben-my-Chree*, slightly wary about what she might find. As she approached, she saw that two of the first-floor windows had been broken and were now boarded up with black-out screens. The sight shocked her more than she had expected, bringing back memories of Kristalnacht, and the breathless flight first from Germany and then from Holland.

Rachel almost turned back, but no. Reuben would not think much of her if she could not face up even to this small fear. She stepped up to the door and knocked.

A few moments later, heavy footsteps sounded within and the door opened. It was Bessie Teare.

'Hello, my dear. Oh, you've brought baby to see us!' Bessie's face creased into dimples of delight. Bessie Teare adored babies.

'Frau Schultz lent me her pram.'

'That was kind of her, dear. Won't you come in?'

Rachel felt a tiny contraction inside her, like a hand squeezing her heart. It was the familiar sensation of fear – a stupid feeling, but she couldn't ignore it. Nor could she quite trust Bessie, kind and sensible though she undoubtedly was.

'I . . . no, thank you.' Rachel bent down and took Rebecca's sewing bag from the little shelf under the pram. 'Rebecca left this at the *Bradda Vista*.'

'Ah yes, of course.' Bessie nodded. She didn't press the point about inviting Rachel in. She could see just from looking at her that the poor kid was scared, and frankly she couldn't blame her. Anya and Rebecca were uneasy too, what with the broken windows and the bullying. And there had been trouble at the *Rowany Glen*. 'I'll make sure she gets it.'

Rachel meant to turn and go, but she couldn't stop staring up at the broken windows.

'There was . . . trouble . . .'

'Yesterday, yes. Some stupid, ignorant woman. Dame Joanna will find out who it was.'

'Why do they do these things?'

'Oh, my dear, I wish I knew. And I wish I knew who'd done this, because I should like to tell that what I think of them. And goodness only knows when we shall get any glass to put in the windows, what with the war and all this bombing in London . . .' She stopped suddenly, realising that perhaps she shouldn't be discussing such things with an alien, however friendly. 'Anyhow,' she said breezily, 'we shall manage. And perhaps soon you'll be released!'

'You think that Reuben and Esther and I . . .?'

Bessie smiled and shook her head.

'It's not for me to say, dear. But they've released some already, haven't they? And now the Government's saying it'll release more if they're special cases.' She smiled down at the gurgling baby in the pram. 'Now, there's a special case if ever I saw one. I'll bet your husband's proud, isn't he?'

Rachel forgot her fears for a moment and beamed with joy. She only had to close her eyes and she could still see the expression on Reuben's face, the first time he had set eyes on his brand-new daughter.

'I think so.'

'Of course he is!' laughed Bessie. 'And now there are going to be monthly meetings for husbands and wives, he'll be able to see her growing up.'

'I wish he could be with me.'

'I know, dear.'

'I wish the war would go away, so we could be a family and be free. Peace, that is all we want. It has been so long . . .'

Bessie looked into the pram. Esther was fast asleep, her pink mouth open and her tiny eyes screwed tight shut. For her, at least, the war was a complete insignificance.

'We all wish that,' she said softly, thinking of the bombs falling on London; and her own niece and nephew, caught up in the war with so many other Manxmen and women. 'But all we can do is try our best, and pray. Who knows what tomorrow will bring?'

Elsa hardly slept at all that night. She lay in bed beside Grethe, listening to her rhythmic breathing, praying that

Grethe would not wake up and ask her what the matter was.

Every time she closed her eyes she saw Marianne's face, felt her touch, smelt her perfume. She longed for the memory to go away, to turn into some ugly dream, but it had been real and Elsa wondered how she could ever forget, or ever feel clean again.

Waves of disgust turned her stomach over as she thought about what Marianne had said. Was it really disgust, or fear? The fear that Marianne had been right, and she was stifling a real self she couldn't bear to acknowledge?

No, no, that was rubbish. Just so much malicious rubbish. Marianne von Strondheim would say anything to destroy her ideals, to unsettle her and make her vulnerable to her propaganda. Playing on their old friendship had led Elsa to a mad moment of weakness, that was all; a moment of confusion in which she had forgotten who she really was.

She wasn't like that. She couldn't be. She *wouldn't* be.

Elsa breathed a sigh of relief as the clock ticked around to seven o'clock. Grethe muttered something in her sleep as Elsa got out of bed, but did not wake, much to Elsa's relief. The last thing she wanted was another third-degree.

She dressed quickly and went downstairs, nodding a brief good morning to Rachel and some of the others who were assembling for roll-call.

'Where's Grethe? Still asleep?'

Elsa nodded.

'She'll catch it if she doesn't turn up again.'

'That's not my problem.'

Frau Metzner threw her a curious look but she ignored it. She wished people wouldn't talk to her, not today. Afterwards the others headed off towards breakfast, but she turned aside.

'Not eating today, Elsa?' asked Rachel, the baby gurgling in her arms.

'Not today.'

'You're looking very pale. Is something the matter?'

'I'm fine. I have to go to the surgery now, I promised I would help Mr McArthur.'

Rachel watched Elsa walk away, wondering what could possibly be the matter. In recent days Elsa had seemed less friendly, but not like this. She looked so haggard and upset.

Elsa walked quickly through the village towards James McArthur's surgery. The first bite of autumn was in the September air, the moist chill of a sea-mist like white smoke over the water.

It was a relief to get away from the *Bradda Vista*, but then again she didn't feel much like helping at the surgery either. Really she just wanted to be alone. No, not alone. She wanted Max to be here with her, so that she would have an excuse to be strong for him and forget about herself.

Reaching the back door of the surgery, she glanced at her watch. She was very early – there was a whole hour before morning surgery. She knocked.

'Elsa, you're bright and early. Come in. Here, let me take your coat.'

The sight of James's open, smiling face almost made her weep. If only she could tell him, she so much needed to share her fear with someone. But he would be every bit as disgusted with her as she was with herself. She felt so alone, belonging nowhere, isolated and afraid of what might become of her.

'Thank you.'

'You look frozen,' commented James as he led the way into the dispensary at the back of the house.

'Oh, I'm all right, really. It is just a little chilly outside.' She did her best to sound breezy and efficient, though all she truly wanted was the comfort of tears. 'Now, you must tell me what you wish me to do today.'

'Well, there's a long list of treatments to make up. Old man Gawne's sheep need dosing again, and there are those pills for Miss Quine's dog.'

James handed her a sheet of paper. As she took it from

him, his eyes searched her face.

'Is something the matter?'

'No.' She turned her face away, finding it too painful to endure his gaze.

'Your eyes are all red.' James took a step nearer. 'You've been crying.'

'Please,' she said softly, fighting to stop the tears coming again. 'Please don't.'

'If there *is* something – you know you can tell me, don't you?'

She lifted her face slowly, turning to look at him. As their eyes met she felt a shiver pass through her, an electric shock of recognition, of understanding.

'James . . . I'm afraid.'

'Afraid?' He looked puzzled, his grey-green eyes crinkling at the corners as he frowned. 'What of?'

'I can't tell you. I can't tell anyone.'

All at once she started shaking, not just with fear and shame but with something else. With need. Could he feel it, too? Could he understand how much she wanted him, suddenly and brutally and irresistibly?

James looked into her eyes, his head mixed-up and his instincts in utter confusion. This was crazy, crazy, crazy. This was dishonourable and disloyal and dangerous. He thought of the peaceful happiness of that evening with Cora; counting the stars over Spaldrick; his kiss on her brow. And then he remembered how he had felt that morning on the beach, when he'd seen Elsa coming out of the sea, the water dripping down over her bare thighs and firm breasts. Now he was feeling it all over again . . .

'James.' Elsa's voice was soft and husky. 'I want you so much, James. I want you to kiss me.'

For a moment he did not answer. He could not. Her words had stabbed him in the gut with jackknife precision, leaving him speechless. Then he stepped back, shaking his head slowly, afraid of the sweet temptation of her parted lips.

'Don't be crazy, Elsa. Let's just pretend you never said that.'

'I said it. And I meant it.'

Her desire had become reckless now, an unstoppable hunger she could no longer control, even if she had wanted to. There was no pleasure in it, only desperate need.

She stepped closer. How could she not have realised before just how desirable he was? Perhaps it had taken her nightmare experience with Marianne to make her realise how much she desired him.

'Don't you want me, James?' Her voice pleaded with him, trembling with need.

He was in agony, his body racked with guilt and hunger. Of course he wanted her, of course he bloody well did. He was flesh and blood, he was frail and fallible and yearned for the physical comfort of lovemaking. He had wanted her since the day he saw her standing before him in her wet bathing costume, wanted her in the uncomplicated way that one animal wants another. But it was wrong, so very wrong to feel this way.

'You're talking madness, Elsa . . .'

'I don't care.'

All at once she was in his arms and their lips pressed together, hot and hungry. Her kiss burned but he craved more as she clung to him, pressing her firm, athletic body against his.

She was his for the asking and he ached for her; but he pushed her away, suddenly horrified by what he had allowed himself to do. Cora's sweet, kind, happy face was in his mind, his soul, his guilty heart. He hardly knew what he wanted any more, only that he had made an enormous and irrevocable mistake which could only bring them all pain.

'No, Elsa.'

'James!' Elsa's eyes were pleading with him.

'I'm sorry if you thought that was what I wanted. Really sorry. It's my fault . . .'

'James, please . . .'

'No.' He turned away, mechanically wiping the back of his hand across his mouth. What had he done? What had he *almost* done . . .?

She touched his shoulder but he shook her gently off and walked across to the medicine cabinet. Unlocking it, he took out a canister of pills and handed them to Elsa.

'Perhaps you could make up the prescription for Miss Quine's dog? I have to go and get ready for morning surgery.'

Chapter 19

The tiny tot frowned in concentration as she lisped her way through her party-piece.

'On the good ship Lollipop . . .'

'Oh, isn't she adorable!' exclaimed a doting mother, clasping her hands together in an ecstasy of pride. 'My little Sonja has such a talent!'

'Mmm,' said Grethe Herzheim, sitting next to her in the audience and trying not to wince as little Sonja squealed and tapped her way through the rest of the number.

'. . . where bon-bons play,
On the sunny beach at Peppermint Bay . . .'

It was a fine day, and Bradda Glen was packed with mothers who had come to watch their children put on a show. The 'stage' was improvised from a bandstand, circular in shape like a giant dovecote with a canopy of thatch. A medley of assorted sheets had been painted and hung up to make curtains and scenic backdrops, and the audience of mothers, sisters and aunties sat on the grass in front, some on folding chairs brought from their houses or borrowed from the Glen cafe.

This was hardly Grethe's idea of a pleasant afternoon's entertainment. For one thing, cute kids in home-made frocks were not really to her taste; and worse than that, the children were due to arrive from the mainland any day now, and all Grethe could think about was Emil.

Signora Bertorelli nudged Grethe in the ribs.

'My son's boy, he come to me soon. Dame Joanna tell me so.'

'Yes?'

'And your *bambino*, your little Emil? He come to you soon?'

'Mrs Pantin says so.'

'He come.' Signora Bertorelli nodded wisely and patted Grethe's knee. 'He come. All our children come to us at the end of the month, that is what the welfare lady she say to me.'

Please, please be right, thought Grethe as she watched two small boys in embroidered shorts singing a German folksong. Two rows in front of her, Rachel Kotkin was rocking Esther on her knee, lost in the blissful world of new motherhood. Oh, please God, Grethe begged silently. I haven't asked you for much in the past and in any case you've never listened to me. Why should you? But please listen to me, just this once. Please let it work out for me and Emil.

She tried to think about something else and Harry Kerruish came into her mind. He'd been away 'at the fishing' for weeks now, and she missed him more than she'd thought she would. Funny how angry Miss Arnold had been about Harry. It wasn't as if there was anything to be ashamed of between them, only a closeness which had flourished in spite of their mutual hostilities and suspicions. Now he wasn't here, she missed his grudging warmth, his strength, his gruff admissions of respect.

'The news from London, it very bad,' cut in Signora Bertorelli.

'Yes.'

'My nephew, he tell me they bomb the pub across the road from our *ristorante* . . .'

'I'm sorry to hear that.'

'And Sophia Meroni, poor lady, first she lose her husband on the *Arandora Star*, now she hear her father is killed in the bombing. Terrible things, such terrible things I hear . . .'

Grethe almost wished the Home Office hadn't relented and allowed them access to newspapers and radios after all. She didn't need Maria Bertorelli to remind her what was happening back in London. Since the first week of September, German bombs had been raining down on the capital practically every night. With no letter from Claire in weeks, Grethe had no way of knowing what was happening in Streatham. Or what was happening to her Emil . . .

Oh please let him be all right, she prayed. Please, God, let him be safe. And let him be here, with me.

'Next, please.'

Evie Bannister got up from her seat in James McArthur's waiting room and carried the birdcage carefully across the room to the door of the consulting room.

'Ah, Miss Bannister, how nice to see you again.' James nodded a welcome.

'Mr McArthur. Miss Nadel,' added Evie as an afterthought, noticing that Elsa was sitting at the far side of the room, funnelling a thick, green liquid into a medicine bottle.

Elsa turned briefly, nodded. 'Good morning,' she said, then turned her back again. Miss Bannister was surprised. It wasn't like Elsa to be unfriendly – she seemed such a sensible and practical sort of young woman. She noticed that Mr McArthur didn't seem to be quite himself, either.

'Is everything all right?' she enquired.

'Yes, of course,' replied James quickly. She thought he looked uncomfortable, for all his assurances. 'Now, what can I do for you today?'

'It's Monty,' explained Miss Bannister, taking the cover off the birdcage. Inside sat a hunched, sad-looking mynah bird with its head under its wing. 'His feathers are falling out and he won't stop scratching.'

'Ah,' said James, opening the door of the cage and reaching inside. Monty awoke, let out a piercing whistle and wriggled as James's fingers curled around him. 'Now let's have a look at you, young fellow.'

Turning Monty onto his back, he lifted up the rather tatty wings and inspected the bird's ragged plumage.

'Mites,' he announced. 'That's what poor old Monty's got. No wonder he's so itchy.' He turned and looked at Elsa, as though unwilling to involve her. 'Miss Nadel?'

Elsa turned.

'Yes, Mr McArthur?'

'Please could you bring me some of that dusting-powder, the one you made up for me last week?'

'Yes. Yes, of course.'

Evie Bannister watched with interest as Elsa took a jar of powder out of one of the cupboards and came across to the examination table. It was obvious these two weren't getting on, she thought to herself. She wondered what they'd argued about. The war, perhaps. Yes, that would be it. When all was said and done, James was a patriotic young man and Elsa . . . well, Elsa was a German.

'Here you are,' said Elsa, her voice colourless as she held out the powder.

'Thank you.' James didn't even look at Elsa as he took it and began dusting Monty's feathers. 'There,' he declared as he put the bird back into his cage and closed the door. 'That should do the trick, but if it doesn't, bring him back.'

'Poor Monty,' cooed Miss Bannister, wiggling her finger through the bars at the not-very-interested bird. 'He's so out of sorts. And it's such a worry, getting the right food for him with all these shortages. Only last week Mrs Cammish's budgerigar choked because she couldn't get the proper seed for him.'

'Don't you worry, Miss Bannister, you're obviously feeding Monty perfectly well,' James reassured her as he covered the cage and helped her carry it to the surgery door. 'But any more problems, you come and see me.'

'I will. Goodbye for now, Mr McArthur . . . Miss Nadel . . .'

Evie called back to Elsa, but Elsa didn't turn to look at her. With a shrug she left and James closed the door behind her with a sigh of relief.

'That's the last one,' he said flatly.

'Good,' said Elsa, carrying on with counting out pills into a box.

'Elsa, we have to talk.' He stood over her but still she didn't look up at him.

'I . . . I'd rather not.'

'Okay, then I'll talk and you listen.'

'As you wish.'

'I can't cope with all of this, Elsa. I'm sorry. What happened was wrong. Terribly wrong.'

'Nothing happened.'

'It was a mistake, Elsa.'

He saw the stiffness in Elsa's body subside as the breath escaped from her in a long, low sigh.

'Yes.'

The burning shame in his belly drove him on.

'The thing is, Elsa, I think it would be best for both of us if you didn't help in the surgery any more.'

'*Gottenyu*, Reuben! Whatever are you doing?'

Sachs looked on in frank amusement at the spectacle of his friend Reuben sitting at the kitchen table in House forty-one, sorting through a pile of assorted embroidery threads.

'I am sewing clothes for the baby, what does it look like?'

Sachs laughed.

'Such a little mother you are becoming!' He sat down on the edge of the table, swinging his long legs. 'When is the next meeting of the husbands and wives?'

'One week, maybe two. Not long. They have promised we shall meet every month now.'

'I heard they are going to let others meet, too – those who are engaged to be married. Brothers and sisters, cousins.'

Reuben squinted as he threaded a length of scarlet silk through the eye of his needle.

'Who knows? And what is it to you? You don't even have a girl.'

'Ah.' Sachs tapped the side of his nose. 'But they aren't to know that, are they?'

'Meaning?'

'Meaning, perhaps your Rachel has a pretty friend? And if I had her photograph and told the Commandant she was my fiancée . . .'

Reuben spluttered with laughter.

'You are a reprobate, Sachs, do you know that?'

'What's wrong in a young man liking pretty girls? Tell me that, Kotkin. You know what the Rabbis say, that a man who is unmarried is without joy and without blessing.'

'This is true,' nodded Reuben sagely. His dark eyes twinkled. 'But it is not marriage I think in your mind!'

Sachs slid off the table and went to put the kettle on the boil.

'I should go with Green and fetch today's rations from the cookhouse. You will come and help?'

'In a moment. Just let me finish this.' Reuben pushed the tip of his needle through the soft fabric of the tiny dress. He had decided on a little garland of rosebuds across the gathered yoke.

'Ach, Kotkin, you're as much an artist as those fellows with their lino-cuts and their camp exhibitions,' commented Sachs. 'And more of an artist than that poor *shnuk* Ernst Müller,' he added on reflection.

Reuben nodded.

'Every day he sits and scribbles on his pieces of paper, every day, as if there's something in his head that won't come out.'

'Poor sap. I'm afraid he's lost his wits.'

'Perhaps.' Reuben finished off the tiny rosebud and bit off the end of the thread. 'I'm not so sure.'

'Surely you don't think he really is an artist? You've seen the mess he makes, he can't even draw a straight line!'

'True, but . . .'

A knocking on the kitchen door interrupted Reuben and Sachs's conversation.

'All right, all right, Green,' grunted Sachs. 'I'm coming. Keep your hair on.'

But it wasn't Samuel Green who opened the door and stepped into the kitchen.

'Reuben? It is you? It is really you?'

Reuben sat and stared at the newcomer, the needle falling from his fingers to the floor with a quiet tinkling sound. He paid it no heed. His eyes were fixed on the man's face.

'Isaac? No, it can't be!'

'You always were an unbeliever, Reuben Kotkin! Didn't I always say you wouldn't even believe the nose on your face if it wasn't stuck on?'

Reuben swallowed hard.

'Sachs . . . this is Isaac. My wife's cousin, Isaac Rubenstein.'

'*Shalom aleichem,*' nodded Isaac. Sachs replied with a shrug of his shoulders and a smile.

'*Aleichem shalom.*'

'Isaac – where have you been? What has happened to you? The last time I saw you, we were in Holland . . .'

'Patience, patience,' urged Isaac, easing his tall, bulky body onto one of the rickety wooden chairs which Sachs had managed to beg, borrow, steal and liberate for House forty-one.

'It never was one of Kotkin's virtues,' remarked Sachs. 'And now he has a family on the Island to think about, he's worse than ever!'

'This is true, Reuben? Rachel is safe and she has a child?'

'A little girl. Esther Sarah Kotkin. She is as beautiful as her mother.'

'And quite a lot more beautiful than her father,' added Sachs, 'which is just as well.'

'This is a blessing indeed,' declared Isaac. 'And to see you again is another blessing, Reuben.'

Isaac looked older, thought Reuben, quite a lot older than his twenty-nine years. The luxuriant black beard aged him, of course, but there was more to it than that. Something about the eyes, a depth and a darkness which belied his jovial demeanour.

'You are well, Isaac?'

'I am well, praise God. And I see that you are also well! You were thin as a stick of firewood when last I saw you, back in Holland.'

'How did you get away?'

'With difficulty. But I am here, as you see.'

'What happened? We were so afraid that you . . .'

Reuben recalled that terrible night when they had fled for the Dutch coast, leaving everything behind them. But Isaac, who had fled with them from Germany a year before, had refused to come with them. He would stay and take his chances, he had told them. He had had enough of running away.

'I was lucky,' confessed Isaac. 'Many were not.'

'Tell me how you escaped.'

'A Dutch family helped me – a Christian family, I still don't understand why they risked their own lives for mine, but I am profoundly grateful that they did. I remained one month in the cellar of their house and then, when it was too dangerous to stay, they helped me to escape to France.'

'And from there . . .?'

'There were ways and means. A fishing boat took me – it cost every penny I had, but what did I care about money? When I arrived in England, the police arrested me.'

Reuben nodded.

'That is what happened to Rachel and me. They split us up and put us in prison . . .' He looked across the table at Isaac. 'How did you find me?'

'I was taken first to prison, and then to a holding camp.' Isaac smiled. 'To Huyton Camp, near Liverpool.'

'Huyton!' exclaimed Sachs. 'That is where Reuben and I met.'

'Quite. And it is also where my wife's cousin the vandal scrawled his name on the washroom wall!'

'Of course!' gasped Reuben. He remembered now. 'Reuben Kotkin, AN INNOCENT MAN', that's what he'd written. 'You saw that . . . what I'd written?'

'As soon as I saw it I knew it was you.'

'How many Reuben Kotkins are there in Britain?' chimed in Sachs.

'And how many with that illiterate scrawl!' retorted Isaac. 'I knew it had to be my cousin, so off I went to the Camp Commandant. "Sir," I say, "my cousin's husband is here. I must see him." And the Commandant stares at me and asks me, "What is your cousin's husband's name?" "Kotkin," I say. "Reuben Samuel Kotkin." "He is not here," the Commandant tells me. "But he was," say I. "Well, he isn't here now!"'

Isaac pulled a face which expressed all the frustration in the entire world.

'So I ask the Commandant, I say, "Where is Reuben now?" "We have sent him to the Isle of Man," the Commandant replies. "So send me to the Isle of Man also," I beg him, and here I am as you see me now!'

Reuben shook his head slowly, trying to rid himself of the weird sense of disbelief.

'I can't believe this, Isaac! That you should be here, after all this time. Rachel will be so happy.'

'I had to find you, Reuben. How many of us will there be left when this terrible war is over? Tell me that. Believe me, Reuben, we must stick together.'

'Well, you are very welcome,' Sachs declared, taking the boiling kettle off the hob to make tea. 'What house have they put you in?'

'Number forty-three.'

Sachs wrinkled his nose.

'The musicians' house! You are a concert pianist perhaps, Isaac Rubinstein?'

Reuben chuckled.

'Only in his dreams. Cousin Isaac used to be a schoolteacher, isn't that so, Isaac?'

Isaac nodded his agreement.

'Ah, but always I had my dreams. I dreamed of being a farmer, of doing *hachshara*. I would go to live in Palestine and there would be peace forever for the Jews.'

'Peace!' Sachs poured water into the teapot and plonked it down on the table next to half a loaf of bread. 'I'm too busy wondering what we'll do if the Germans decide to invade Britain from Ireland instead of France.'

'It won't happen,' said Reuben firmly, only his clenched fists betraying the tension Sachs's words had awakened inside him.

'I pray that it will not,' replied Isaac.

'It will not.' He thought of all the men in the camp, all the women and children at Rushen Camp, all the stories of tragedy and triumph in the face of death. 'Too many have suffered already. It cannot.' Stroking the embroidered dress he was making for little Esther, he forced himself to smile. 'All will be well, you will see.'

'Ah, but when?' sighed Sachs.

'Tomorrow,' declared Isaac, pouring weak tea into three tin mugs. 'Things are always better tomorrow.'

'You all right, Grethe?'

Grethe nodded to Elsa.

'Never better. How about you?'

'Fine. Why shouldn't I be?'

'No reason.'

These meaningless exchanges had become increasingly frequent over the last few days as tension mounted in the camp and the women wondered if their children really were going to be brought to them on the Island, as the Home Office had promised.

Grethe couldn't understand for the life of her why any of this should make Elsa edgy. She hadn't even got a man, let alone a child. Perhaps her mood had something to do with the fact that she'd stopped working at the surgery and James

McArthur hadn't paid a visit to the *Bradda Vista* in almost a fortnight . . .

'What time is it?' asked Grethe.

Elsa glanced at her watch.

'Quarter to.'

'I'm going out.'

'They won't be arriving for ages. Someone will tell you when to go down to the station . . .'

'I know. But I have to get out. I need some air.'

Grethe put on her jacket and went downstairs. Cora was in the hallway, polishing the full-length mirror on the front of the hallstand.

'Hello, Grethe.'

'Hello.'

Cora looked up.

'He's coming – your little boy?'

'Mrs Pantin says she thinks so.'

'Only thinks so?'

'They haven't given her a list of names – she's not sure.'

'He'll come.' Cora shook a stray lock of hair out of her eyes. 'It'll be all right, you'll see.'

'I've been worrying myself silly, what with the bombing in London, and nothing from Claire . . .'

'You know what the post is like.' Cora went on polishing. 'I've made up a bed for him with the other children, on the second floor. It'll be so much better for him here,' she added. 'And you. You must miss him terribly.'

Grethe nodded dumbly. It wasn't like her to be short of something to say, but it wasn't every day that the children were brought to the Island from the mainland.

'I'm going to wait at the station,' she said.

'Are you sure? They won't be here for ages, and it's quite chilly and drizzly out there.'

'I'm sure. I have to be there – I have to see him when he gets off that train.'

★ ★ ★

271

'It's a long walk for the little ones,' commented Ellen Welbury, hoisting a very substantial toddler onto her hip and leading another small child by the hand.

Her fellow welfare workers nodded. It was a long journey for everyone. They'd begun yesterday afternoon, at Euston Station; travelled up to Liverpool by train and spent the night lying awake in a Liverpool hostel for evacuated children, listening to the threatening sounds of an air-raid on the docks.

Still, at last they'd made it to the Island, even if the children were so tired some of them were practically sleepwalking up the hill from Douglas Harbour to the railway station.

A tiny steam-train was waiting for them at the red-brick station. It was more like a toy train than a real one, thought Ellen as she ushered her charges into the carriages.

'Choo-choo,' squealed an excited little boy.

'Yes, dear, pretty choo-choo. Now sit still, there's a good boy and don't get your fingers shut in the door.'

'Where's my mummy?' piped up another voice.

'You'll see your mummy soon,' promised Ellen. On the platform, police constables were walking along the train, slamming the carriage doors shut and locking them.

'Oh, surely this is unnecessary,' called out one of the welfare workers.

'Sorry, madam, orders is orders.'

Little faces pressed up against the glass as the train began steaming out of Douglas Station and headed south towards Port Erin.

'Soon,' promised Ellen, as the young blond boy wriggled impatiently on her lap. 'Soon you'll see your mummy again, I promise.'

The platform at Port Erin station was packed with a heaving swell of bodies. It seemed that just about everyone in the village had come to the station to see the children arrive. Not just their own children either – even the prospect of seeing a friend reunited with her child was enough to cheer up women who had known so much of separation and despair.

'Here it comes – here it comes!'

Voices cried out, bodies pressing so close to the edge of the platform that camp officials and police officers had to push them back.

'Ladies, please. Think of the danger – stand well back.'

The little steam engine chugged slowly into the station, a plume of white smoke trailing out behind it. A shrill whistle announced its arrival and it came to a halt with a squeal of brakes. Instantly the crowd surged forward, hands scrabbling at carriage doors which refused to open.

'There – in there! Can you see? That's my little Nikki, I swear it's my little Nikki!'

'My daughter, oh my beautiful daughter . . .'

'Where is my boy?'

'Look how she's grown!'

'Why can't I open this door? Open this door and let me hold my child!'

Grethe Herzheim tried to hang back, but the crowd carried her forward. It was impossible not to be caught up in the scenes of chaotic happiness as one by one, the carriages were unlocked and the children came spilling out. Some looked sleepy, some bewildered, some overjoyed and a few were in tears. There were even two babes-in-arms, tiny children no more than a few months old. Grethe wondered how their mothers could possibly have allowed them to be left behind when they were interned. But then again, how could she have let them make her leave Emil?

Her eyes roamed the crowd for a sight of him, adrenaline making her palms damp and sweaty, and the drizzly air making her hair stick to her scalp. He must be here somewhere, he must be . . .

That blond boy, the one just getting out of the carriage with the welfare worker – could it be?

'Emil, my Emil!' she cried, pushing her way through the crowd to the front.

But as quickly as elation had filled her heart it was dashed away. For the boy ignored her completely and ran forward into the arms of Frau Metzner, who gathered him up and smothered him in kisses.

'Oh, Edrich, my little Edrich!'

Grethe turned away, the spectacle too painful for her to watch. She had been a fool, she knew that now. A fool to believe a word that Mrs Pantin and Reverend Newell had told her. A fool to believe other people's treacherous promises. It had all been a pack of lies.

Tears scored burning furrows down her cheeks. Emil wasn't on that train; he was still in London with the bombs and the danger. They'd stolen him from her and now they were hiding him from her, somewhere far away, where they thought she'd never find him.

But they were wrong. She'd find him all right. And when she did, she'd never let him out of her sight again.

Chapter 20

'This is a very serious matter, Fräulein Herzheim. Very serious indeed.'

Dame Joanna Cruickshank, Commandant of Rushen Interment Camp, addressed Grethe with the solemnity of a High Court Judge. Very stiff and proper in her navy blue dress and crisp white collar, she had no time for those who could not accommodate themselves to the rules. *Her* rules.

At her side, somewhat edgy, stood Betty Arnold, and welfare worker Mrs Pantin. Grethe regarded them all with at least the appearance of equanimity. Circumstances might defeat her, but authority never had and it never would.

'So you say,' replied Grethe coldly. The WPC escorting her snapped a reprimand.

'You will address the Commandant correctly, Herzheim.'

Grethe said nothing. Inside, she was an inferno of bitter resentment and grief. Dame Joanna returned her sullen gaze with a look somewhere between irritation and grudging sympathy. Opening the beige manila folder on her desk, she took out an envelope and pushed it across the desk.

'You wrote this?'

'What about it?'

'I asked you a question. Will you do me the courtesy of answering it?'

'Yes. I wrote it.'

The Commandant handed the envelope to Miss Arnold.

'Kindly read this. Out loud.'

Betty Arnold gave a nervous cough.

'It is addressed to the Editor, *Isle of Man Examiner*. "Dear Sir, I am writing to you to complain about the way I have been treated. Since I was interned, my son has been taken away from me and I do not even know where he is . . ."'

Dame Joanna put up her hand.

'That is enough.' She turned to Grethe. 'You do not deny that you attempted to write a letter to the local newspapers, detailing certain complaints against the authorities within this camp?'

'Why should I deny it?'

'And that you gave this letter to a visitor, requesting that she should post it once she was outside the camp?'

'What else could I do?'

'You could have addressed your comments to your house representative . . .'

'What! And you would have listened, would you? Listened and then ignored me, just like you did the last time?'

Mrs Pantin passed her hand over her weary brow. These situations were so difficult for all concerned.

'Grethe, I have been trying to help you. So has the chaplain. We all have.'

'And a fat lot of good it's done me!' Grethe's eyes glinted with anger. 'You promise me that my son will be brought to me, and what happens? I find out that you've been lying to me.'

'I'm sure the boy is being well cared for,' said Miss Arnold. If she intended her words to be soothing, she miscalculated badly.

'You have stolen my child from me and I want him back!'

'Please, Grethe, try to be reasonable. Understand the problems involved . . .'

'I haven't even heard from Claire Hodges in weeks. I demand you give me back my son!'

Dame Joanna's voice rose above the rest, cool and calm and authoritative.

'Fräulein Herzheim, you are scarcely in a position to

demand anything. And by causing this commotion, you merely damage whatever validity your cause may have.'

But Grethe was in no mood for conciliation.

'I was promised that my son would be brought to me. You lied to me. I have a right to my child!'

'While you are here, you enjoy only those rights which the Home Office chooses to grant you, Fräulein. And this hotheaded behaviour does you no service. There are proper ways and means of expressing your opinions.'

'I'll express them any way I damn well like.'

'Then I have no alternative to punish you for your repeated refusal to adhere to camp regulations. You realise, of course, that smuggling letters out of camp is a very serious offence?'

'I'll do whatever it takes.'

'And you realise that by approaching a visitor to this camp you involved her in your actions?'

'I . . . didn't think.'

It was true. Grethe hadn't thought through all the consequences. What happened to her, she didn't much care. But she hadn't meant to bring trouble for other people.

'Miss Herzheim, it is just as well that the person in question is a sensible and patriotic lady. It is she who handed your letter to me.' Dame Joanna leant back in her chair and contemplated the woman before her. 'Now to the matter of your punishment. This is by no means the first time I and Miss Arnold have had cause to reprimand you.

'As I told you, smuggling letters out of this camp is a very serious matter. In the current national emergency it might easily be construed as an act of treason. But I am aware of your difficult circumstances, and Mrs Pantin has spoken on your behalf.

'You will spend twenty-eight days in police custody. Perhaps a period of imprisonment will help you to see reason.'

'My, but she's growing!' exclaimed Cora as she watched Rachel changing little Esther's nappy. 'And to think she was such a tiny scrap when she was born.'

Rachel's face dimpled with pleasure.

'You would like to hold her?'

'I . . . well, I don't know if I should.'

Cora knew her reluctance to get too involved with Esther puzzled Rachel, but then Rachel didn't know that the last baby Cora had helped to care for had been Grace's poor little boy. Even though three years had elapsed since the tragedy of the child's death, every time Cora looked at Rachel's child she felt the old feelings returning – the suffocating grief, the anger, the suspicion.

But you couldn't hold on to the past forever, could you? And after all, there was still a chance that she might be a mother herself. Hadn't James once mentioned that he'd like to have lots and lots of children . . .?

'She likes it when you hold her,' said Rachel. 'She always goes off to sleep.'

'Oh – thank you, I'd love to.'

Cora took the child gingerly, as though she were made of porcelain.

'Hello, little one,' she smiled; and the child seemed to smile back, though Cora knew it was probably just wind. 'Oh look, she's holding onto my finger!'

'She likes you.'

'I can't think why! I never was much good with babies. That comes of being the youngest in the family, I suppose. There were never any babies around to practise on when I was a little girl. Grethe's much better – she's a natural.'

'Poor Grethe,' sighed Rachel. 'It isn't right, what they have done to her.'

'Well . . . I think she knew they would have to punish her, if she went on breaking the rules.'

'But to put her in prison for such a little thing!'

Esther began to whimper and Cora sat down on the edge of Rachel's bed, rocking her gently.

'I know. It does seem harsh.'

In fact, the whole house was still in shock after the news that Grethe was to be locked up in the cells at Port St Mary police station for a whole month, all for writing a letter. Some sniggered of course, said she'd feel at home in prison – a woman like that. But most were sympathetic, understanding how it must be for any mother, even a common prostitute, to be separated from her child.

'They won't treat her badly? While she is locked up?'

'I shouldn't think so. How is Elsa taking it? She seems very glum these days.'

'I don't know. She doesn't talk to me as much as she used to. I think there is something on her mind.'

'Grethe, perhaps? It must be lonely for her, being on her own.'

'Perhaps.' Rachel sounded unconvinced. She popped the lid onto the nappy bucket. 'She is not so friendly since she went to talk to the von Strondheim woman.'

'You think she sympathises with her? Surely not. Everyone knows Elsa's principles.'

Rachel nodded.

'I think perhaps . . . that she is scared of something.'

'Of the Nazis?'

'I don't know. But sometimes, when I look into her eyes, I can see that she is afraid.'

Since opening in the spring, Rushen Camp had developed its own life, independent of the villages around which it was based. Collinson's Cafe offered a social centre and a place to study, while the Marine Biological Station provided opportunities for supervised research projects. The nursery was thriving, and there was even a school for the older children, run by qualified teachers.

As the late warmth of September moved into the misty chills of October, the 'Service Exchange' brought a new buzz of activity to camp life. Internees were invited to swap their skills with others: knitting for hairdressing,

279

wood-carving for English lessons, and a craft shop was set up in Station Road, to sell items to the public.

Initially, Sarah Rosenberg had thought she had few skills to offer. Before the war she had done a series of menial jobs, whatever she could find. And it hadn't been easy for a Jewish girl to find work in Germany.

The best job she'd had was in a bookshop, where the elderly owner had treated her as well as if she had been his daughter. How it had shocked old Heimlich that day she had to go to work wearing a yellow star sewn to the sleeve of her jacket. So much so that he'd dismissed her on the spot.

What had happened next – the acts of subversion, her arrest, the weeks of torture – Sarah had tried to shut out of her mind. At least she had been one of the lucky ones. After a couple of months in Buchenwald they had let her go and she had fled to Holland. But the scars would never, ever heal. Her captors had made sure of that.

It wasn't until someone mentioned the little camp hospital that Sarah thought she might be able to do something of value. A benefactor had donated a house, just off the promenade, to be used as a surgery and hospital, and it was to be run by internee doctors and nurses. Sarah had no qualifications, but she had nursed typhus cases in Buchenwald. That was enough to convince the medical officer to take her on.

On a damp and blustery October morning, Sarah was busy cleaning a graze on a young girl's arm.

'How did you do this?' she asked casually.

The girl looked wary.

'I fell.'

'Were you pushed?'

'I told you, I fell, that's all.'

There was little point in exerting pressure, the girl obviously didn't want anyone to know that she'd been bullied. Most of the time the assorted inhabitants of Rushen Camp got on surprisingly well, but almost every day saw some petty dispute about food or whose turn it was to wash the dishes. And more disturbingly, there had been cases of fighting and bullying, with tension mounting as more women were released from the camp and those who remained resented their captivity more than they had ever done.

Dabbing the graze with a ball of cotton wall, Sarah handed the girl a square of dry lint.

'Hold this on it, fluffy side up. That's right. I'll just go and fetch some strapping to hold it in place.'

Sarah left the treatment room and walked into the dispensary, next door. She hesitated; then spoke.

'Hello, Elsa.'

Elsa nodded a silent greeting and went on writing out labels to stick on medicine bottles.

'Have we any inch-wide bandages?'

'Bottom drawer – over there, by the sink.'

'Thank you.' Sarah went over and opened the drawer, taking out a neatly rolled-up bandage. 'Things are a lot tidier around here since you decided to come and help out.'

'You think so?'

'Yes, definitely.'

Sarah wondered why she was making such an effort to talk to Elsa. After all, she hated everything the woman stood for: middle-class, educated Germany, which had welcomed Adolf Hitler with open arms and unquestioning obedience. Hadn't women like Elsa Nadel been doing their best to make her life a misery since she'd arrived in Port Erin?

Elsa finished writing out the labels and swung round on her chair.

'How are you, Sarah?'

'All right. I'd be better if those bitches from the *Erindale* stopped trying to cause trouble for me.'

Elsa avoided Sarah's gaze.

'I'm sorry to hear about that.'

'Yes. I'm sure. So – how is Rachel?'

'Well, but very impatient. She hopes she and Reuben will be released soon.'

'And so they should be – she deserves a little happiness,' replied Sarah. 'And how about you, Elsa, you are happy?'

'Happy? I get by.'

As the doorbell rang, Cora shut Bonzo in the living room and hurried downstairs from the rooms she shared with her grandfather. Thomas – knowing that James McArthur was about to pay a visit – had generously agreed to make himself scarce in return for the price of a few pints in the bar of the *Falcon's Nest*.

The bell rang again, and Cora called out:

'Coming.'

She glanced at herself in the hall mirror. The old lilac dress still looked good on her, and the lace collar she'd added gave it a touch of class. She just hoped James would like it.

Clicking off the light switch, she opened the door. James was standing on the doorstep, muffled up against the blustery October winds in cap, scarf and long raincoat.

'Come in, come in.' She stood back to let him in and closed the door behind him, switching on the light.

'I nearly couldn't come,' said James, as Cora took his coat and hung it on a peg by the door. 'I had to go out to Santon to see a horse with a twisted bowel. Then I got back to the house and Fergus had thrown up all over the hall carpet!'

'Oh dear – is he ill?'

'Not ill, just greedy. He stole one of Mrs O'Hara's pies.'

'Well, I'm very glad you could come.' Cora smiled up at him and he dotted a kiss on her cheek. It was only a light brush of the lips, hardly a great romantic clinch, but the night was young. 'Shall we go up?'

Cora had spent hours getting the sitting room looking exactly the way she wanted it to – the chintz chair-covers freshly washed and pressed, a bowl of dried flowers on the embroidered tablecloth and a fire blazing in the hearth.

'Sit down and put your feet up. I'll get you a drink.'

James sat in one of the armchairs beside the fire and watched Cora bustling around, pouring whisky into a tumbler, topped up with just the right amount of water. She knew him so well. Only she didn't really, did she?

Oh God, he thought to himself as the thudding pain of guilt hit him in the guts for the umpteenth time. What on earth did I think I was doing with Elsa Nadel? Ought I to tell Cora? Does it change anything, or everything?

'Thank you,' he smiled, taking the glass of whisky and tasting it.

'It's the way you like it?'

'Perfect.' He tried to swallow the lump that filled his throat. 'Just like you.'

She looked stunning. He knew she must have spent ages getting ready and if she knew what he'd almost gone and done with Elsa, he could only imagine what she'd think of him. What had possessed him to be so easily tempted?

Cora perched on the arm of his chair.

'Do you like the dress?'

'Suits you to a T. Is it new?'

'Just the collar.' Cora put her head on one side and scrutinised James. 'You're looking tired, you should let old Alastair Goodwin take more of the workload off you.'

'No I'm fine, really.'

He wished he was. He'd scarcely admitted it even to himself, but deep down he knew he'd been putting off spending an evening with Cora. In brief meetings, snatched conversations, it was easy to make out that everything was fine between them. But alone with her, sharing a whole evening together, that was something very different.

'I know what would liven you up,' announced Cora.

'Oh yes?'

'I'll put some records on the gramophone and we can have a dance.'

'I'm a bit tired, it's been a hell of a day . . .'

She stopped his protests with a smile and a shake of the head.

'Remember that disastrous dinner-dance you took me to? The one you had to leave in a hurry? We never did have that last dance . . .'

She took his hand and he got up out of the chair, leaving his stick leaning up against the side.

'What shall we have?'

'Anything, you choose.'

'How about . . . *They Can't Black-Out the Moon*?'

'Lovely.'

He slipped his arm about her waist, and the touch of her awoke all the feelings he'd been suppressing. The guilt, the confusion, the love. Real, warm love that he'd put off acknowledging for so long that it sneaked up on him and took him by surprise. As the music started, they began to move slowly round the room, Cora's face snuggled close against his shoulder.

From time to time she raised her head and smiled up at him, and he knew she wanted him to kiss her. He wanted it too, wanted it badly, but he kept seeing Elsa's face in his mind's eye, hearing her voice; remembering the sheer animal excitement he had felt at the taste and smell of her.

'Cora.'

'Mmm?'

'You look beautiful.' The words almost choked him. 'I . . .'

'What is it, James?'

'Nothing.'

Nothing and everything, he thought to himself as he danced with her to a smoochy love song. He wanted to tell her about Elsa, try and explain what had happened, but he just couldn't bring himself to do it – and what was there to confess if he did? That in his heart of hearts he wanted two different women? Cora could never accept that. He wasn't even sure he could accept it himself.

Chapter 21

At breakfast the next day, Rachel noticed that Maria Bertorelli was not her usual cheerful self. Her plump cheeks were pale and there were red circles round her eyes.

'What is the matter, Maria?' she enquired.

Maria's face crumpled like a paper bag, and she started to sob.

'It is my application, my application to be released.'

'The answer has come through?'

Signora Bertorelli nodded and blew her nose on the man's handkerchief she always kept pushed up the sleeve of her blouse.

'Miss Arnold, she call me to her office yesterday afternoon. She tell me the Release Board, they say no. They turn me down.'

'But why?'

Maria dabbed at her streaming eyes.

'It is my Tony. They say he is "unfriendly alien", not safe to be released.'

'Why do they think that?' All of this was confusing and worrying to Rachel, who cherished her own dreams of an early release.

'Because he say if they release him, he will not do war-work. He refuse to join Pioneer Corps – he and his friends, they all refuse.'

'Your Tony – he is a Fascist?' demanded Frau Kessler from the other end of the table.

'No, no, they make big mistake. My Tony, he is no *Fascisto*.

285

But he cannot help the British defeat his country – he is patriotic Italian, no?'

'The Pioneer Corps don't fight,' pointed out a girl sitting next to Frau Kessler. 'They clear bomb-sites, build things . . .'

'It is all the same to my Tony,' sighed Signora Bertorelli. 'And so he say no. And because my husband cannot be released, they say they keep me here, also. You understand?'

'I suppose so.' Rachel wondered if Reuben's reluctance to fight would hamper their chances of release – if their turn ever came round to be seen by a Release Board. The wheels of bureaucracy turned so very, very slowly.

'Can't you ask someone to put in a good word for you?' asked the girl. 'I heard of a woman at the Hydro who was graded A, but they gave her C and let her go because it turned out someone had been lying about her to the Tribunal.'

'That is right,' nodded Frau Feldmann. 'A friend of her old employer is a priest, and he wrote to the Home Office, explaining that she was of good character. He offered her work, too, as I recall . . .'

'Perhaps if you had a job to go to?' suggested Rachel.

'A job!' Maria raised her eyes to the ceiling. 'But there is our *ristorante* in Streatham, and only my poor sister-in-law and her aunt to take care of it. What will become of us? We shall be bankrupted when this war is over!'

'It does seem a little unfair,' admitted Frau Kessler. 'I heard they released a woman from the *Erindale* yesterday, and everyone knows their sympathies are with the Nazis.'

'Yes,' agreed the girl next to her. 'But that was an old lady. I'm sure she couldn't be a danger to anybody.'

'I wouldn't be so sure,' replied Frau Kessler. 'One does not have to be young to be a fifth-columnist.'

While this conversation had been going on, Elsa Nadel had entered the dining room. Rachel was shocked to see how haggard she looked.

'Hello, Elsa. It's not like you to be late for breakfast.'

'What if I am?' snapped Elsa. Every pair of eyes at the table turned on her in curiosity. This was not the Elsa Nadel they had come to know.

'Nothing,' said Rachel. 'Here, you can have mine if you like, I'm not very hungry.'

'I don't want anything to eat. Just tea will do.'

She poured herself a cup of tea, and Rachel noticed how the cup rattled against the saucer as she picked it up. What on earth was going on?

'Elsa,' began the girl at the end of the table.

'What?'

'You're house representative.'

Silence. Elsa just kept on staring at her cup and saucer.

'You go to meetings with the Commandant once a week.'

'So?'

'So perhaps you could put in a word for poor Maria? Her husband has been turned down for release, and now the Board are saying they won't release her either.'

'I don't see what you expect me to do about it.'

'Couldn't you put in a good word for her?'

'Why should they listen to me? I'm just an internee like you.'

'Yes, but . . . people respect you.'

Elsa laughed humourlessly.

'Oh they do, do they?' Well, they wouldn't if they knew what I was really like, she thought. 'Anyhow, why should I speak up for Maria?'

Rachel's jaw dropped. She'd never heard Elsa talk like this. It was as if all the horrible things Sarah had said about her were starting to come true.

'Because Maria is in trouble! Can't you see how upset she is? And because we have elected you to speak for us . . .'

Elsa banged her cup back onto its saucer with a clash of china on china.

'Oh you have, have you? Well, let me tell you something – all of you. I'm sick of your problems, I'm sick of this bloody place and as far as I'm concerned you can get yourself another

287

house representative, because I'm sick of the lot of you.'

After breakfast at the *Erindale*, Marianne von Strondheim gathered her troops around her in the common room. They were not, perhaps, quite as numerous as she might have hoped, but they were loyal – not like Elsa Nadel, whose rejection of her still stung like a half-healed wound.

Inge, Mathilde, Olga and the two Norwegian girls sat in a semicircle, acolytes at their mistress's feet. Marianne liked that. It made her feel secure in her influence.

'So what are we going to do next?' asked Frieda, a squat girl who had been picked up in a British raid on the Lofoten Islands, and had never quite recovered from the insult.

'We are going to continue making life as difficult as possible for those who oppose us,' replied Marianne severely.

'For the Jew-pigs?' suggested Inge with hopeful relish.

'Especially for the Jew-pigs. But for the British too. It is an outrage that they should imprison us with these *Untermenschen* and their squalling brats.'

'I threw a brick through the window of the *Breakwater*, like you told me to,' said Inge.

'And Irmgard and I gave that Sarah Rosenberg a scare,' added the other Norwegian girl.

'Good girls. Let's scare them all a little, show we don't mean to tolerate their insolence.'

'But we should be careful,' hazarded Mathilde.

'Careful?' Marianne met her gaze and Mathilde suddenly wished she hadn't spoken.

'We don't want to be caught.'

Marianne laughed scornfully.

'Not *scared* are you?'

Mathilde looked indignant.

'Of course I'm not!'

'Good. Because if you are not with us, Mathilde, you are against us – isn't that right, Inge?'

Inge nodded.

'All of us together, that's what we agreed. Don't turn chicken on me now, Mathilde.'

'As if I would! Haven't I done everything you asked me to do? Don't I hate the *Saujuden* just as much as you do?'

'So you *say*,' said Inge.

'What do you mean?'

'I mean, let's see you prove it, Mathilde. Let's see you prove how much you hate them.'

'What a good idea,' smiled Marianne. 'Inge, you're a very clever girl. Now, Mathilde, what test shall we give you?'

Mathilde was trembling inside, but put up a show of eagerness.

'Anything. I'll do anything.'

'I'm very pleased to hear it.'

Anything, thought Mathilde. God knows what that bitch Marianne will force me to do, but whatever it is – however cruel, however repellent – I have to do it, and more. Because if I don't, she's bound to guess the truth about me.

And then I'll be alone.

Grethe sat alone in the police cell. She had counted the tiles on the wall, the cracks in the plaster, read the scrawled messages a hundred times. And time was ticking away so slowly.

She had books to read, and the inevitable ball of wool and knitting needles, but all she could think about were the two people she cared about most in the world: Emil and Harry Kerruish. What she'd done could only make things worse for both of them.

The sound of a bolt being drawn back surprised her. It wasn't lunch-time yet. The door opened and a police constable peered in.

'Visitor for you, Grethe.'

He stepped back and the camp chaplain walked into the cell, taking off his hat. The door clanged shut behind him.

'How are you, Miss Herzheim?'

'I don't want to see you,' she said flatly. 'I've got nothing to say to you.'

'I understand that you're upset . . .' he began, but she cut him short.

'Upset? That's what you think, is it? I'm not upset, vicar, I'm bloody angry. You promised you'd bring my boy to me – you *lied* to me.'

'I'm sorry.' He spied the lone wooden chair in the corner. 'Mind if I sit down?' He didn't wait for her reply. 'I promised I'd help you, Grethe, and I meant it.'

'So how come I'm stuck in here and they've stolen my boy from me?'

Adrian Newell felt guilty. Grethe was right; he'd promised to help her and he'd let her down. He'd been over-optimistic, had underestimated the power of wartime bureaucracy.

'Look, Grethe, it wasn't the camp authorities who took Emil from you, it was the council in London.'

'What difference does that make?'

'It means it's harder for me to argue your case. But . . .'

'But what?'

'I think I know where they've sent him.'

The blood drained out of Grethe's face and she sat up straight on the hard prison bed.

'Where?'

He shook his head.

'I can't tell you.'

Grethe trembled with angry fear.

'What? You tell me you know where my boy is, then you won't tell me where?'

'It's not that easy. I'd be breaking a confidence.'

'Get out,' said Grethe quietly, her voice trembling. 'Get out and leave me alone.'

'No, Grethe, listen to me.' Newell leaned forward, his face close to hers. 'It's not much, and I shouldn't really be doing this, but . . . if you want me to, I think I can get a letter to your son.'

'So tell me, Sachs, how do I look?'

Sachs folded his arms and leant casually against the doorpost.

'Your Rachel will think she has married Ronald Colman, that is how you look!'

Reuben picked up his comb, sprinkled it with a little water, and combed back his hair, trying his best to make the dark waves lie flat.

'Give it up, Reuben. She loves you as you are.'

'I want to look my best for her – and Esther.'

'You have made yourself a new shirt, mended your trousers, even bartered yourself a pair of shoes from Finkel. Nu! What do you think – that your Rachel wants a new husband also? Relax!'

'It's all very well for you to say that, Sachs. You haven't been parted from your wife and daughter for four long weeks.'

'At least you *have* a wife and daughter. Even your Isaac has his cousin Rachel. All I have are my books, and few enough of them. You're sure you couldn't get me an introduction to one of Rachel's friends . . .?'

Reuben gestured in despair.

'Sachs, you are beyond me! Why don't you keep yourself busy, take a class, do some useful work . . .?'

Sachs aimed a desultory kick at the skirting-board.

'What's the use? I'm not a tailor like you, or a shoemaker like Sid Finkel.'

'You could teach a writing class . . . or learn something new.'

'All I want is to get out. I've had enough, Kotkin.'

'So have we all. But what can we do but be patient?'

'I don't know how you can say that! You with your wife and daughter, and only able to see them once a month. I tell you, Reuben, first chance I get I'll be out of here.'

'How? You said yourself you have no skills.'

'I'll volunteer for the Pioneer Corps. Or the Jewish Brigade.'

'You? The Army life?' Reuben chuckled. 'I never saw you as a soldier, Sachs. I'll bet you've never had to obey orders in your whole life. And you want to begin now?'

'I want to get out of here! If that's what it takes . . . And maybe you should do the same.'

Reuben shook his head.

'I could not.'

'You wouldn't have to fight. There would be uniforms, yes, but that is all.'

'I don't know . . . my father was a pacifist and his father before him. War is war, Sachs. I'm not sure I could.'

'And freedom is freedom. And that's what the British are fighting for, Reuben – your freedom and mine, and Rachel's and the baby's. Would you rather they let the Germans come to the Island and kill us all?'

'I will think about it,' said Reuben. 'I will think about what you say. But that I should be a soldier . . . there must be some other way.'

He brushed a few stray hairs off his trousers and put on his jacket. It was an old jacket, much repaired, but with his skill Reuben had made it look almost as good as new.

'You're sure I look all right?' he asked. Sachs swung a comedy punch at his head and he ducked.

'Get away with you, Kotkin! And leave us poor frustrated bachelors in peace.'

Reuben walked down the stairs and out into the street. Dozens of men, most of them wearing the best clothes they possessed, were gathering in the square. A buzz of excitement was clearly audible even before he stepped through the gate into the garden. Some of the men were carrying little presents they had made for their wives. One man had a picture he had painted; another, a wooden dog he had crafted from old pieces of skirting board purloined from his room.

Reuben fingered the package under his arm, and wondered if Rachel would like the dress he had made for Esther. He didn't even know if it was the right size! In the four weeks since he had seen her, the baby might have grown out of it. So many anxious thoughts whirling round his confused, excited brain . . .

Today's meeting was to be held in a big dance-hall in Onchan. Now that engaged people as well as married couples were allowed to meet, there were too many to fit inside Collinson's Cafe. Hopes and dreams were almost visible in the air, the atmosphere of this grey and windy autumn day electric with excitement, apprehension, fear.

'What you got there, Kotkin?' asked the man with the toy dog.

'A dress for my daughter, and a handkerchief for my wife.'

'I wish I had your skill.' The man glanced down at the dog. It had a lopsided smile and the wheels were far from perfectly round.

'It's a fine little dog,' Reuben assured him. 'Your Mitzi will love it.'

'I hope so. Sometimes I'm afraid she won't even remember her poor Pappi, it's so long since she saw me.' He nodded towards a couple of men over to his right. 'I see Vischer's taking his wife one of his precious lino-cuts. God knows what she'll do with it!'

Vischer's lino-cuts were the highlight of House forty-four. A successful sculptor before the war, he'd adapted his skills to the available materials by making use of the tatty old linoleum which lined the hallways of just about every boarding house in Hutchinson Square. And when he heard that a derelict old piano was being dismantled in a neighbouring house, he'd quickly snapped up two of the mahogany panels and taken up woodcarving too. Improvisation was the name of the game at Hutchinson Camp – implemented with such success that the camp already boasted its own illustrated newspaper and regular art exhibitions.

'Look,' said the man with the dog. 'There's that fellow from House thirty-two. If you ask me, he ought to be in an institution, not locked up with us.'

Reuben followed the line of his gaze and saw Ernst Müller, sitting on a folding chair by the railings. On impulse he walked over.

'Afternoon, Müller.'

Müller looked up. As usual, he had a wooden board across his knees, on which lay a sheet of paper.

'Hello, Kotkin.'

'What's that you're doing?' enquired Reuben, catching sight of something more ambitious than Müller's usual scribblings. 'Can I see?'

'Nothing.' Müller half covered the board with his arm, as a child might hide its work from prying eyes; then thought better of it and took his arm away. 'Just something . . . something that I thought I'd remembered.'

Reuben looked over Müller's shoulder at the drawing. Instead of inarticulate scribblings and meaningless shapes, the paper was filled with attempts at drawing the same figure: the figure of a tall, athletic woman with dark, bobbed hair. Underneath, Müller had written 'Max' again and again, in a long line across the bottom of the paper. For the first time, Reuben glimpsed real skill in the drawing.

'Who's that?' Reuben asked.

Müller shrugged.

'I wish I knew.'

'Is it your wife?'

Müller stared at the image, as though willing it to give up its secrets.

'My wife,' he repeated. 'No. I'm not sure.' He gave a sigh of irritation. 'I just don't know.' His fingertip traced the outline of the face, an outline it seemed to know so well. 'A part of me,' he murmured. 'A part of me – a part of Max.'

'Who is Max?'

Müller shook his head very slowly; a gesture of defeat. Then he looked up at Reuben.

'You are going to meet your wife this afternoon?'

Reuben nodded.

'My wife and my baby.'

'You're lucky.'

'Yes.'

More than ever when he spoke to Müller, Reuben knew that he really *was* lucky, no matter how often he might deny it.

'I wish I had a wife . . .'

Reuben laid a hand on his shoulder. Müller was a good few years older than him, but he felt like a father addressing his son.

'I'm sure you do have someone. Somewhere. This woman, perhaps. Try and remember who she is – I'm sure she must be important to you.'

Müller gazed down at the woman's picture, then lifted his pencil and drew a long line diagonally across the paper.

'No,' he said firmly. 'She was just a dream, it doesn't mean anything. If it was anything more than that, she'd have found me by now.'

Chapter 22

'Is Reuben well?' asked Cora, as Rachel brought Esther downstairs and laid her in Frau Metzner's pram.

Rachel smiled, a little sadly, at the remembrance of yesterday's meeting with the menfolk.

'He is well, but he misses us.' She arranged the cot-blanket so that Esther was snug and warm. 'Both of us.'

'Of course he does. It's such a pity you can't all be together.' Cora busied herself with a duster. She liked having a lot to do. It kept her from wondering why James and Elsa had exchanged hardly a word the last time he had visited the *Bradda Vista*.

'Reuben says they might release us if he volunteers to join the Aliens Pioneer Corps.'

Cora paused in her dusting.

'They might. Is that what he's planning to do?'

'I don't know. I don't think so – he is a pacifist, you see. And besides . . .'

'Besides, what?'

Rachel hung her head, ashamed.

'I don't want him to. He would have to go away, just when we have found each other again. I'm very selfish, I know.'

'Oh, I don't think so,' replied Cora, thinking of all the times she'd prayed that James's leg would get better – but not so much better that they would let him fight. 'I'm sure I'd feel just the same in your place.'

'Well, I must take Esther out for some fresh air. She is getting too pale with being indoors so much.'

'Mind you wrap that child up,' grunted Thomas, passing on his way to the kitchen. 'There's a raw wind blowin' off the sea, fair fit to chill her bones.'

'She's lovely and warm,' laughed Cora. 'So many blankets round her, you can hardly see the poor wee thing!'

Cora held the door open and Rachel wheeled the pram carefully down to the roadway, aided by Thomas, who lifted the wheels clear of the steps. Quite a transformation had come over her grandfather since the arrival of little Esther. There were other babies in the village, but none had taken his fancy like Esther Kotkin.

Mr Quine was right, thought Rachel as she pushed the pram along the road and out onto the promenade. The sky was iron-grey with scudding clouds, and lashing sea-spray filled the air with cold saltiness. Perhaps she ought to turn back? But she looked down at Esther's happy, wide-eyed face and decided to press on to the *Ben-my-Chree*.

It was on the corner of Station Road, at the top of the steep incline by the Falcon's Nest Hotel, that Rachel walked straight into trouble.

A group of women were jostling a girl, cat-calling and pushing her. Rachel recognised two of them as Inge and Mathilde, from the *Erindale*, and would have turned back immediately only she recognised the woman they were pushing, too – it was Sarah!

'Dare to ignore us in the street do you, Jew-pig?' Inge demanded, taking Sarah by the shoulders and shaking her.

'Get your hands off me!'

'Doesn't she squeal like a little piggy?' mocked a fat girl with mousy hair.

'Make her show us some respect,' demanded Mathilde eagerly.

'This is the only respect I'll ever show you,' retorted Sarah, spitting on the ground.

'Make her salute the Führer! Say "Sieg Heil", little piggy . . .'

Torn between concern for her child and concern for Sarah, Rachel stood stock-still and shouted:

'Sarah – oh, Sarah, are you all right?'

Suddenly all eyes were on her and the women were advancing towards her.

'Go, Rachel,' cried Sarah.

'Go, Rachel,' mimicked Inge, her face contorted with the ugliness of hatred.

'Go, Rachel,' chanted the others, moving closer.

Rachel backed away. She could see now that Sarah was all right, just a little shaken. All she cared about was getting her baby out of trouble.

They probably wouldn't harm her; not really harm her – all they wanted to do was frighten her. That's what Rachel told herself. But in her panic to get away she caught the heel of her shoe between two cracked paving-stones.

As she stumbled, the shock jolted the handle of the pram out of her hands and she fell heavily, landing on hands and knees half on and half off the roadway.

Everything happened so quickly and yet it seemed like slow motion. Afterwards, all Rachel could remember were a series of snapshot images: the faces of the women, white and open-mouthed; the helpless horror of two policewomen, rushing towards the scene of the commotion; the pram hurtling down the steep slope from pavement to promenade; the sight of her own hands, bloodied and scratched, tensing into claws of fear as she screamed and reached out . . .

'My baby, my baby!'

In seconds she was on her feet and running, scrambling, falling down the slope after the pram. It was hopeless of course – the pram was almost at the bottom of the slope. In a second's time, maybe two, it would hit the sea wall and turn over, throwing her beautiful, precious, fragile daughter towards the cruel and angry waves . . .

'No-o-o . . .!'

As she screamed in terror, certain that the worst must and

would happen, something miraculous happened. A figure appeared at the bottom of the hill, reaching out strong arms and catching the pram just as it was about to tip over.

Esther let out a loud wail of protest as the pram juddered to a sudden halt, one of its wheels bent slightly askew but otherwise undamaged.

'Esther, Esther, my baby . . .'

'Don't upset yourself, missus, your baby's all right.'

Rachel looked up into the face of Harry Kerruish. Tears were spilling down her face, but she didn't care. She didn't care one bit. All she knew was that her baby, her precious child, had been saved.

'Th-thank you,' she stuttered.

'That's all right, gel, don't you worry.' Harry's eyes drifted upwards to the top of the slope, where the policewomen were rounding up the troublemakers. 'Couldn't leave the bairn in trouble like that now, could I?'

'You're so kind. So kind. How can I thank you?'

Harry smiled. His heart went out to this poor girl, so young and so scared.

'No need for that, gel. No need at all. Now, you're all right are you?'

'Y-yes.'

'And the little un?'

Rachel nodded, and the tears came in a second flood; tears of relief this time. She sniffed and wiped her hand across her eyes. Harry reached into his pocket for the clean, folded handkerchief he always carried and handed it to her.

'There y'are, gel.'

She took it with a smile of thanks and blew loudly. He noticed that the knuckles of her right hand were white, her fingers wrapped tightly round the handle of the pram.

'There is just one thing you could do,' he hazarded. She looked up.

'Yes?'

'I've been away a long time at the fishin', see. Only got

back last night. I was wonderin' . . . have you seen Grethe Herzheim around?'

Rachel's brow furrowed.

'You do not know?'

'Know? Know what?' His stomach tightened in a sickening reflex as he wondered what it was that he didn't know.

'She . . . they took her away. To the police station in Port St Mary.'

'The police station? Why?'

'The Commandant said she must be locked up for a month, as a punishment.'

'Lord save us, no!'

Harry froze, his heart pounding, a cold sweat breaking out on his brow. A punishment? This was exactly what he'd feared ever since he first got friendly with Grethe. He only had himself to blame for doing this to her. He gripped Rachel's wrist.

'Why – why have they punished her, gel, did they say?'

'I'm not sure. Something about a letter . . .' She looked into Harry's face, a little scared by the intensity she saw behind the kind grey eyes. 'I . . . I should go now,' she said quietly.

His attention snapped back to the here and now, and he nodded.

'Aye, gel, you get on your way.' Out of the corner of his eye he saw the blue of a police uniform in the middle distance. 'It's for the best.'

Autumn moved on and October merged into November. Somewhere in the depths of Wales, a small blond boy stood by the kitchen window, squinting up at the leaden sky.

'I'm 'ungry.'

'Then you'd better stir yourself, boy. There's firewood to chop and pigs to muck out before you've earned your dinner. That's half the trouble with you city boys, you've no idea of the value of good, hard, physical work.'

301

'Mr Jones.'

'What?' The elderly farmer looked up from his newspaper.

'I want my Ma.'

Mr Jones glowered.

'Some children should be grateful that decent, kind-hearted people are willing to take them in.'

'But the lady said I could see my Ma. I want to go to my Ma!'

'Well, you can't. You're here now, and you'll do as you're told.'

'Please, Mr Jones.'

'What is it now?'

'It's rainin'.'

'Bit of rain won't do you no harm, boy. Now get out of my sight before I take my hand to your backside.'

Emil put on his mackintosh and gumboots and squelched out into the drizzle with a yardbrush and a pail. Days of almost continuous rain had turned the farmyard into a sea of mud, with the cobbled surface practically invisible under inches of black slime.

It wasn't that Mr and Mrs Jones were especially unkind – just that they'd never had any children of their own and didn't seem to understand. The farm wasn't that bad, either – Emil liked animals – but it was hard being so far from his Ma and Auntie Claire.

Heading across the yard towards the woodshed, Emil heard a shrill whistle. Turning, he saw two faces peeping out from the barn.

'Hoy! Emil.'

'Emil, boyo.'

It was Catsmeat Davies and Fatty Brownlow, two of the older boys he'd met at the local school. Emil didn't care much for Welsh school – people talked funny and took the mickey out of your name. Reluctantly he headed towards the barn.

'What you doin' here, then?' demanded Emil.

'It's a free country, boyo.'

'Not if Mr Jones catches you,' retorted Emil.

'Oh, and you'll tell him, will you?'

'Depends. I might.'

'Want to see something?' enquired Fatty Brownlow.

'What sort of somethin'?'

'A real piece off a real bomb.'

'Might.'

'Cost you two marbles or thruppence.'

Emil shrugged.

'I ain't got thruppence and you ain't havin' me marbles. Me Ma gave 'em me.'

'Hark at him!' sneered Catsmeat Davies. 'His *Ma*.'

'Where's your Da, Emil, where's your Da?' mocked Fatty.

Emil glared back, every bit as wounded as if they'd punched him in the eye, but determined not to show it.

'I ain't got one.'

'No,' agreed Catsmeat. 'He's got no Da, 'cause he's a little bastard aren't you, Emil? His Mam's a tart and he's a little German bastard.'

Emil lashed out with his small fist and made contact with Catsmeat's nose. To his immense surprise and satisfaction it went all red and squishy, and blood started dripping out of it. Catsmeat gave a howl and clapped his hand to it but the blood came oozing between his fingers.

'Ow! You little . . .'

'Don't you talk about my Ma like that!'

Emil wriggled out of Catsmeat's grasp and kicked Fatty Brownlow square on the shin. Fatty let out a curse and hopped around on one leg, slithering and stumbling in the mud. Emil took the opportunity to give him a good shove with the end of the yardbrush, sending him arse over tip into a pile of stinking straw.

Emil was so busy laughing that he didn't hear Farmer Jones come out of the house and clump his way across the rainy yard.

'What's this then, boy?' he thundered, and Emil froze, not

daring to look behind him. 'Well?'

'It's Emil, sir,' said Catsmeat. 'He hit me.'

'He started it, sir,' agreed Fatty Brownlow, picking himself up off the ground.

'No I didn't,' protested Emil. 'They said things about me Ma. An' they said I was a little German bastard.'

'Well you are,' retorted Catsmeat Davies. 'A snivelling little German bastard.'

'I don't care what anyone said or did not say,' growled Farmer Jones. 'I will not have unseemly brawling in my yard. Now, you and you get off my land before I call the police. And as for *you*, young man.'

He grabbed Emil by the collar of his shirt.

'Smarten yourself up and get inside. Parson Llewellyn's here with a letter from your mother.'

Harry Kerruish spent the next few days mending his nets and sitting watching the rain splash down out of a steel-grey sky.

Before the war, the hut on the quayside in Port Erin had served as an office and store-room for himself, Juan and young Petey Faragher. In the summers they'd run a pleasure-boat, taking holidaymakers on trips round the bay and sometimes to the Calf of Man. Nowadays, Harry liked to come to the hut just to sit and think. He had a lot to think about.

Before Dunkirk, he'd never thought much about the bad things; it had been enough just to get on with his life. But that hell on earth had brought it all home to him: pain, loss, his own mortality. His isolation, too. He'd no wife, no family, and he'd never been that close to Juan. And after Dunkirk . . . well, he'd no one to leave the business to. Not now. Sometimes he wondered what it was all for, why he bothered carrying on.

And then he'd think about Grethe, and it was like the glimmer of a distant sun, glimpsed through storm-clouds.

He'd never met a woman like Grethe Herzheim, and he knew he'd never meet another. But it was all wrong, their companionship had brought them nothing but trouble; and anyway, it was too late. Wasn't it?

One afternoon he was sitting gazing out of the tiny window at the distant sea when he heard footsteps approaching along the seafront. The rain was thundering and gusting down now, drumming angry fingers on the roof of the hut, sizzling like sausages in a pan. Even the seagulls were huddled in crevices in the cliffs, sheltering from the driving rain and capricious, gusting wind. Harry wondered who would voluntarily be out and about on a horrible day like this.

As the footsteps got nearer, a shadow fell across the hut and he looked up at the sound of a knock on the door.

'Harry. Harry, are you in there?'

He knew that voice! The fishing net slipped from his hands.

'Grethe?'

The door opened and a bedraggled figure stood in the doorway, silhouetted against the cold grey light of a November afternoon. Her bleached blonde hair hung in wet yellow rats'-tails that sent rivulets of water coursing down over her face, her neck, her shoulders. Her clothes were wet through and she was shivering. Without make-up, she looked vulnerable, intensely human.

'Hello, Harry.'

He got to his feet, unsteady and shocked. He'd known that Grethe was due to be released from the police cells, but he hadn't let that thought climb into his conscious mind. He couldn't. He hadn't dared to think about her because he knew that he would want to see her . . . and so it would start all over again.

He just stared at her, saying nothing. Wanting to say so much.

'Oh. It's like that is it?' asked Grethe quietly. 'I thought it might be.'

'Grethe . . . you're taking a big chance, coming here. What if someone sees you?'

'It's all right, I'll go away. I just wanted to say I was sorry.'

'Sorry for what?'

'For bringing you trouble you could do without, for getting you a bad reputation. Just . . . sorry.'

Harry prayed that the feeling inside him would go away and let him be. He didn't want to feel like this, had fought and fought it but still it came back.

'Oh, Grethe,' was all he could say. 'If anyone's sorry, it's me.'

'Well I've said my piece now, so I'd best go.'

She turned away but before she had taken one step away Harry was holding her by the shoulders, turning her round to face him again, bringing her inside the hut.

'Come inside, gel, we need to talk.'

'Harry, you know we can't. Not after all that trouble before . . .'

'Just sit down for a little while. Till the rain goes off.'

'A little while! It's been raining for days.'

Then stay for days, whispered a little voice inside Harry's head. I don't mind. Stay . . .

'You look frozen stiff, gel. Will you take a nip of potheen?'

Harry fetched his hip-flask out of the pocket of his old blue overalls, unscrewed the top and handed it to Grethe. She drank deeply. You couldn't help respecting a woman who could drink potheen like a man.

'Strong stuff,' she commented, handing back the flask and wiping her mouth. She pushed the wet hair off her face and Harry saw the dark roots. Seeing him looking at her, she laughed. 'I must look a proper sight after all that time locked up. Soon as I can I must get my hair done.'

Harry caught hold of her hand and held it fast. It was cold and clammy and as fragile as a child's.

'Some would say you'd look handsome with dark hair,' he said.

'Handsome!' Grethe laughed. He liked her deep, husky laugh. It held warmth and wickedness and honesty. 'I've never been called that before. I wasn't a bad looker when I was young though. Pretty even. But that was years ago.'

Harry caught himself looking right into Grethe's eyes and had to force himself to turn away, let go of her hand.

'Grethe gel, we should end this,' he said. 'Before it starts.'

'Yes.'

'We can't be seen together, it's too risky.'

'I know.'

Grethe hugged her wet coat around her.

'They still won't tell me where Emil is,' she said. 'Reverend Newell came to see me in the cells, said he could get a message to him from me. But I don't know if I can believe him. He said he'd get my boy brought to me, and look what happened.' She looked up at him. 'I did it for the boy, Harry. Writing that letter.'

'I know. It's not right, keeping a mother from her child. Not right at all.'

'It was trying to make them send him to me that got me put in the cells. But you're right, Harry, this is too risky. Not just for me – for you.'

'Don't you worry about me, Grethe. I'm old enough to look after myself.'

'You're a good man, Harry Kerruish. You don't need me making things difficult for you.'

The rain drummed still harder on the thin roof of the hut.

'It's turning to sleet now.' Grethe peered out at the gloomy November afternoon, the rain hitting the ground so hard that the droplets bounced back up and formed a fine white mist. 'But I'd better go.'

'You can't step out in that,' said Harry, holding her by the wrist.

'Please, Harry. You said it yourself, this can't happen. There could never be any future in it. Never.'

'I know what I said.' He coaxed her gently down onto the

bench next to him. 'Stay a bit longer, gel.'

'Harry . . .'

'Just a bit longer. Till the rain stops. Where's the harm in that?'

Elsa walked across the road towards the camp medical clinic. The rain was bucketing down out of a filthy grey sky and she was wearing only the thinnest of jackets, but she didn't care. She let the freezing rain cut through her, wishing it could scythe right down to her soul and end it all.

End the pain.

She pushed open the back door of the clinic. She could hear a couple of in-patients chatting and laughing to each other upstairs, but there was no one in the dispensary. That, at least, was something to be thankful for.

Elsa slid open a desk drawer and searched inside. It wasn't there . . . it wasn't there . . . Her fingers fumbled under a stack of papers and she let out a gasp of relief as they met cold, jangling metal. Dr Heinrich shouldn't really leave the keys there, but Elsa was glad she did.

On the wall above the sink was a small wooden cupboard with a red cross painted on it. Unlocking it, Elsa reached in for the bottle of brandy. They kept it for medicinal purposes. For people who were in shock . . .

Please, please, don't let anyone come. She sank down onto a chair and unscrewed the top of the bottle, raising the neck to her lips and taking a long, deep swig.

Reaching into her pocket, she took the letter and laid it on the desk. It was an official-looking letter, in a brown envelope stamped 'PASSED BY CENSOR'. She didn't need to take the letter out of the envelope to remember what it said.

Dear Miss Nadel,

With reference to your brother, Mr Maximilian Nadel, at this point in time sources of information remain confused and incomplete. However, we have reason to believe that he may have been a passenger on the *Arandora Star*, having voluntarily taken the place of another man.

There is no record of a Maximilian Nadel among the survivors . . .

She did not weep. She wanted to, but the tears wouldn't come. Ignorance was bliss, that was what they said, wasn't it? She should never have written to the Information Bureau in London. Never asked them to find out the truth about Max. And now she knew that truth, how could she possibly cope, knowing that he had died in some other man's place, and this other man – this stranger she hated with all her strength – must be alive instead?

'Max, oh Max,' she whispered to herself. 'I never thought you'd leave me. You were the other half of me – how can I go on with only half a life and half a heart?'

The brandy was strong. It burned as it trickled down her throat, but it wasn't strong enough. She wanted instant oblivion, not this lingering, unbearable ache of loss. But she would drink it all, every drop.

Maybe then, at last, she could forget who she was; forget that she had ever been Elsa Nadel.

Chapter 23

'Elsa? Fräulein Nadel, are you all right?'

Elsa jolted awake, the sound of a woman's voice in her ears and hands on her shoulders, shaking, shaking, shaking her into unwelcome consciousness.

'W-what?' Her eyes opened reluctantly, squinting in the pallid afternoon light. At her side stood Mrs Pantin. 'I . . . oh.' She put her hand to her temple. It throbbed with the dull remembrance of a quarter-bottle of brandy.

'Elsa, whatever has happened?' Mrs Pantin's gaze travelled from the half-empty brandy bottle, still sitting accusingly on the desk, to Elsa with her dishevelled hair and death-pale face.

'How long have I been . . .?'

'Goodness knows, my dear. An hour, perhaps more. I came in to find a patient's records for the Medical Officer.'

'And you found me. I'm sorry.'

Elsa sat back in her chair. Her whole body ached and her head swam with the after-effects of the brandy. There was a horrible taste in her mouth and she longed for a drink of water, but she felt incapable of movement, incapable of anything at all. It was like being hollow, with all the substance drained out of her.

Mrs Pantin drew up a chair and sat down.

'Whatever is it, Elsa, you can tell me.'

Elsa's head moved slowly from side to side, her eyes staring at some invisible, fixed point.

'I can't. I have to go to roll-call.'

She made as if to get up but Mrs Pantin gently held her back.

'I'll send a message that you are unwell.'

'Unwell.' Elsa gave a dry laugh. 'Drunk is what I am, but not drunk enough.' Her voice dropped almost to a whisper. 'Not drunk enough to forget.'

'Forget what? What's troubling you, Elsa? I might be able to help.'

'No one can help.'

'I could at least try.' Mrs Pantin searched her mind for the right key which might unlock Elsa's pain. 'I know it's hard to trust anyone, but you can trust me. Whatever it is.'

Elsa twisted a handkerchief in her long, thin fingers. Her eyes were dry; she was beyond weeping.

'It's Max.'

'You've had news of him?'

Elsa nodded and produced the crumpled letter from her pocket, handing it to Mrs Pantin.

'You read it. I can't. I know every word of it by heart.'

Mrs Pantin took the letter, unfolded it and read the two crisp, impersonal paragraphs which had ripped Elsa's life in two. She drew in her breath in a sharp gasp.

'Oh, Elsa . . .'

'You see now? You understand?'

'Yes, of course, but . . . they can't be sure. They don't say they're sure.'

'Would you believe that, if it was your brother? Would you allow yourself to hope they were wrong?'

'Well, I . . . there is always hope, Elsa.'

Elsa looked at her sharply.

'Hope in God? Faith? Is that what you're trying to tell me?'

'I'm not trying to do anything. Just to listen.'

Elsa passed her hand over her brow. It was cold, clammy, slimy with sweat.

'I've nothing to say – there's nothing left to say.' She took a long, deep breath, as though drawing strength into her body. 'Swear before your God that you won't tell anyone.'

Mrs Pantin looked at Elsa, moved by her pain, frustrated at the impossibility of reaching her.

'People are sure to find out sometime.'

'It's no one's concern but mine.'

'There are people who could help.'

'Swear.'

'Very well, I swear. Nothing you tell me will go any further. It's just between you and me.'

Grethe was cleaning the bathrooms at the *Bradda Vista* when Cora came to tell her that she had a visitor.

She sat back on her haunches and took off the rubber gloves which protected her precious nail enamel: almost the last vanity she had left.

'Who is it?'

'It's the chaplain.'

Grethe picked up the lavatory brush and started scrubbing vigorously at the bowl.

'Tell him I don't need his God-bothering.'

Cora cut a cake of soap in half and put the smaller half next to the sink.

'Tell him yourself. He's waiting for you in your room.'

With the utmost reluctance Grethe got to her feet and wiped her hands on her overall. She had no wish to listen to Adrian Newell's latest empty promise. Oh, he meant well enough, but meaning well wouldn't get her Emil back.

She clumped down the stairs to the first floor. The door of Room four was slightly ajar. She pushed it open.

'Well? You wanted to see me.'

Adrian Newell rose to his feet. He looked edgy, thought Grethe. No doubt he'd come to make more excuses.

'It's good news, Grethe,' he said, reaching into his pocket and taking out a small packet. 'I have a letter for you from Emil.'

Mouth agape, hands shaking, Grethe snatched the

envelope from him, tore it open, laughed aloud to see Emil's huge, wobbly writing: 'DERE MA, I AM WELL ARE YOU?'

And then, to Adrian Newell's complete astonishment, she flung her arms round him and hugged him for sheer joy.

It was market day, and the centre of Banbury was bustling with shoppers and farmers. Stalls were jumbled together in the square, their displays depleted by shortages, but managing a bright show on this dull November day.

'Get a move on, Grace, there's still the butcher's and the draper's to go to and you know your father hates it if his dinner's late.'

'All right, all right,' muttered Grace under her breath, heaving the heavy shopping basket over her arm and following her mother across the square.

This was worse than being a kid again, she thought to herself blackly. Much as she'd loathed living on the Isle of Man, she'd begun to miss the *Bradda Vista* – at least there, there was no interfering mother looking over her shoulder, reminding her how to iron William's shirts.

Passing a stall hung with dresses and blouses, Grace paused to take a look.

'These are quite nice,' she commented, fingering a pair of hand-sewn gloves in soft kid-leather.

'Pre-war quality, duck,' said the elderly stallholder, pausing in her knitting to launch into her sales patter. 'Can't get 'em anywhere now, you can't.'

'Really?' Grace stroked the soft leather. She had always liked the feel of luxury, always felt she deserved to have the best. William liked her to look nice, too. 'How much?'

'One pound ten. They're going to ration clothes soon you know.'

'You think so?'

'No doubt about it. You'll need coupons then.'

She fingered the purse in her bag. It seemed such a huge

amount for a pair of gloves, not far off the allowance the Army paid her out of William's wages. But they *were* lovely gloves, and she needed cheering up. If only William was a commissioned officer instead of just a sergeant, perhaps then she'd be able to afford to live properly.

'Grace. Grace.'

Grace turned to see her mother pushing her way towards her through the crowd, arms full of brown and blue paper parcels. Grace's expression turned to surly resentment.

'All right, Mother, I'm coming.'

She turned away from the stall, the dream gone.

'Must you dawdle, Grace? You know I'm at my wits' end, what with all this rationing and the terrible queues.'

'I wish you wouldn't go on.'

'I'm not going on, I'm just saying.' Iris inspected Grace for signs of any new purchases. 'And I hope you haven't been wasting William's money.'

'Why don't you just mind your own business?' snapped Grace, stalking off and leaving her mother open-mouthed.

Iris caught up with her outside the butcher's shop, flushed and irritable.

'That's enough of your cheek, my girl.'

'Leave me alone, can't you? I'm not a kid now, I'm a married woman.'

'Then act your age.'

Several women in the queue turned and had a good stare at the newcomers, then turned back to face the front again.

Grace didn't reply. She just joined the end of the queue and folded her arms, ashamed of the frayed sleeves of her winter coat. She hated this war, she hated her parents, she even – in black moments – hated William. Most of all, she hated this disgusting genteel poverty, this pretence of everything being 'all right'.

The queue moved forward slowly, towards the open door of the butcher's shop.

'Did you get that elastic?' asked Iris.

'No. Besides, you know they keep it under the counter for their regular customers.'

'All you have to do is be nice to Mrs Fletcher. It's not much to ask.'

A round woman in front of them in the queue turned round.

'They say he's got rabbits in.'

'What?'

'Mr Murdoch. He's got rabbits.'

'Oh. That'd be nice,' observed Iris to Grace, 'for your Dad's Sunday dinner.'

'Excuse me,' said someone behind Grace, tapping her on the shoulder. 'Has he got something special off the ration?'

Grace swung round to see a young woman, quite neatly dressed in a tight-waisted beige coat and a hat with a small veil. She was holding on tightly to a set of blue leather reins, at the end of which wriggled a lively little boy of three or four years old.

'Rabbits,' said Grace slowly and automatically, but her eyes were fixed on the child. Her stomach tried to turn a somersault. She couldn't get over how much he looked like . . .

'Bunny!' squealed the child happily, stretching out small stubby fingers.

'That's right, Sidney. Bunny-rabbits.'

'What a lovely little boy you have,' cooed Iris Pope, setting down her shopping bag so that she had two arms free to fuss over him. 'Sturdy little lad, isn't he?'

'His daddy fairly dotes on him. He's spoilt as anything.'

'And why not?' smiled Iris. Rummaging in her shopping bag, she produced an apple and held it out to the small boy. 'Say thank you, Sidney.'

Sidney hid in his mother's skirts, one plump hand emerging to clutch at the shiny red apple.

'Such a lovely child,' sighed Iris with a wry smile. Grace knew what her mother was thinking – she was thinking it too.

This child was the spitting image of her Billy, her little boy who'd have been just about the same age as Sidney . . . if he'd lived.

'Have you and your chap got any children?' enquired Sidney's mother.

Grace stole a brief glance at her mother, but Iris avoided her eyes.

'No,' she said.

'No children,' said Iris, out of the blue. 'But then she never really wanted them, did you, Grace?'

Knock. Knock-knock.

Rachel looked up as the door opened. It was Cora Quine.

'Hello, Rachel. I thought I'd see if you and the baby were all right.'

'We are quite well.' Rachel looked across at Esther, gurgling and kicking her legs in the cot Thomas had knocked together out of an old bedside cabinet. 'Quite well.'

At that moment a black furry blur slipped between her ankles and bounced into Rachel's room.

'Bonzo, no! Oh, Rachel, I'm sorry – I'll catch him and throw him out.'

'It is all right, he is quite friendly.'

'Oh, he's friendly enough, he's just a nuisance, aren't you, boy?'

Cora came in and closed the door softly behind her, keeping an eye on Bonzo as he sniffed his way round the room, exploring a whole new world of interesting smells.

'We haven't seen you outside very much lately,' began Cora.

'It is very cold. This windy weather is not good for the baby.'

'No, of course not. But if you wrapped her up warmly? Grethe was asking if you'd like her to take the baby out for a walk.'

'I'll take her. Perhaps later. If the sun comes out.'

'You should try to get some fresh air, you know. Both of you. It's not good to be cooped up all day.'

'You are throwing us out?'

'No! No, of course not. I just wondered . . . well, I wondered if anything was the matter.'

'Nothing is the matter. Nothing at all, please don't worry. We are safer in here.'

Cora bent down and scooped Bonzo up in her arms. His wet pink tongue flicked over her nose.

'Ugh! That's enough of your sloppy kisses, thank you very much.' She wiped her nose and tucked Bonzo under her arm. 'I'll leave you to it then. Don't want to get in the way.'

Rachel picked up Esther's rattle and waved it over her baby's face, clearly lost in her love for the child. Cora felt a flicker of worry, then dismissed it. After all, it was Rachel's baby, and Rachel had a perfect right to decide how best to care for it.

'I'll see you later then.'

'Of course.'

Cora closed the door and went downstairs. In the kitchen, James McArthur was sitting at the huge scrubbed table, sharing a mug of Bovril with Thomas. Archie was balanced across his knees, his orange tail swishing gently to and fro in the warmth from the gas range.

Something had changed in James; she wished she could work out what it was. One minute he seemed his old self, affectionate and warm – the next, distant, almost as if he was trying to push her away. She couldn't help wondering if it was something she'd done.

Cora breezed into the kitchen.

'How did the gardening go?'

James flexed his stiff leg gingerly.

'Think I overdid it a bit,' he admitted.

'Serves him right,' grunted Thomas. 'Diggin' an plantin' in his state.' He looked at Cora over the top of his Bovril. 'Any luck with Rachel?'

Cora shook her head.

'Poor kid must have been terrified by what happened with the pram. Since then she's hardly set foot outside on her own, let alone with the baby.'

'Them troublemakers want more'n a tellin'-off from the Commandant,' commented Thomas gruffly. 'I know what I'd do with them if I had my way.'

'It's a wonder the kiddie wasn't killed.' James shook his head in disbelief. 'Perhaps the shock will have knocked some sense into them.'

'Perhaps.' Cora made herself a drink and joined James and Thomas at the table. 'But we really must try and persuade Rachel to go out of the house.'

''Tisn't healthy for the bairn to be cooped up all day, nor its mother neither,' nodded Thomas.

'Rachel will be seeing Reuben soon, perhaps he'll be able to do something,' suggested James. Cora wished he would give her a smile, a touch, any little sign that everything was all right between them.

'What's needed,' she said, 'is a family camp. I'm sure it would calm everyone down. It's so upsetting for the women, being without their husbands.'

'The little 'uns miss their fathers an' all,' pointed out Thomas.

'And so many families have been split up. Brothers and sisters, even grandparents . . .'

James stroked the cat on his lap. It provided a welcome distraction, an excuse not to look too directly into Cora's eyes.

'How . . . er . . .?' he began, clumsy in his attempt to sound casual.

'Mmm?'

'I was wondering . . . How's Elsa Nadel?'

Cora paused, her cup halfway to her mouth. For a split second she felt a pang of jealousy. But that was silly. She had no reason at all to be jealous of Elsa. Why, James and Elsa didn't even work together any more, and this was the first time he'd asked after her in weeks. It was obvious the two of them had fallen out over something. She wondered what.

'I'm not sure really,' Cora admitted. She hadn't given Elsa a lot of thought lately. 'She seems very . . . preoccupied. I suppose she's anxious because she hasn't heard anything about her brother.'

'Yes, I expect that's it,' said James, fervently hoping that was all there was to it.

'Sachs, you are a terrible cheat!'

'I am not so!'

Sachs assumed an expression of wounded innocence which didn't fool Isaac for an instant.

'I took your pawn three moves back, and you have sneaked it back onto the board!'

'Ach, Isaac,' called Reuben, who was helping a group of men paste together long strips of newspaper to make paper chains. Whether they represented a celebration of Chanukah or Christmas, no one was quite sure – but you couldn't let the season pass by without some sort of recognition. 'Such a suspicious mind you have.' He grinned. 'But I am sure your suspicions are well founded. Sachs would cheat his own grandmother.'

'Lies, wicked lies,' protested Sachs.

'You will make a fine politician when this war is over,' grunted Isaac. 'Or a lawyer. But definitely not a chess player.'

The three men were playing chess in the Artists' Cafe, the one place in the camp where a man might keep himself warm and drink coffee while he huddled up against the stove.

'When do you suppose they'll issue us with more coal for the boiler?' mused Sachs, hugging his jacket around him for warmth. He was wearing every item of clothing he possessed, and still he was shivering. 'It is weeks since I had a hot bath.'

Isaac put up his hands.

'A bath? I don't care about a bath. I just want to be warm

again. This place, this island . . . never in my whole life have I lived anywhere with such a wind! It cuts right through me.'

'You'll never make a farmer, Isaac,' retorted Reuben, standing back from his handiwork and wiping paste-covered hands on a rag. 'You like your home comforts too much.'

Isaac shrugged.

'It is necessary to have a little faith, Reuben. To believe in one's ability to do anything.'

'Well, I wish faith would get a move on and get us out of this place,' replied Sachs with feeling.

'Still no luck with your application?'

Sachs blew on his numbed, reddened hands.

'Forms, more forms. "Fill in these forms," they say. And then they take the forms away and I hear nothing. Nothing! Anyone would think they didn't want me in the Pioneer Corps.'

Isaac nudged his queen forward three spaces.

'Check.' He looked up at Sachs. 'Perhaps they think you'll lose the war for them, single-handed.'

'The *chutzpah* of this man!' Sachs contemplated the board for a few seconds, picked up his knight and hopped neatly over Isaac's bishop. 'Checkmate. Another game?'

'With you, Sachs? A man would be safer playing with the devil.'

Reuben left the others hanging paper chains and came to sit down at the table. Sachs pushed his tin mug of coffee across to him.

'What about you, Kotkin? Have you and Rachel applied for release?'

Reuben sipped his coffee and shook his head.

'The Commandant says we have no grounds for release,' he explained. '*Nu*, we must stay where we are.'

'But you have a wife, a child. You are refugees . . .'

'True, but we are not essential war-workers, we are not Grade C internees, we have no one in England who will speak for us.'

'What about the Refugee Committee?'

'They do what they can – but there are others, far more deserving than we are. I am not a great scientist, or a great artist . . .'

'But you *are* a great tailor,' smiled Sachs. 'When I am rich and famous, I shall tell the world I buy all my suits from Reuben Kotkin, of Savile Row.'

They laughed together, but beneath the laughter each man nursed his own worries. For Sachs, it was the frustration of youth, caged and thwarted, hungry to get out and *do* something, anything. For Isaac it was the tension of expectancy, the impatience of having to wait and simply not knowing. For Reuben it was the ache of separation, the black despair which always hovered just beneath his cheerful exterior – the fear that he and Rachel might never be released.

'How is your Rachel?' asked Isaac.

'Well, from her last letter. But there are so few letters and they take so long to arrive. I want to *be* with her, Isaac, for Chanukah.'

'And you shall be. If not for Chanukah, then soon.'

'Ah, but when? I want to see my daughter grow up.'

'For a family man you are a most impatient mensch, Reuben Kotkin.'

'And you are an insufferable optimist!'

Isaac shook his head.

'A realist, Reuben. I know I shall be released – we all shall. Things are changing, since the *Arandora Star* and the *Dunera* the Government is beginning to understand that we are not all spies and traitors.'

'Well, I wish they would realise it a little more quickly,' said Sachs. 'I for one don't want to sit here like a rat in a trap, waiting for Hitler to come and kill us all.'

The thought made Reuben's heart turn over, not with fear for himself but for Rachel and the child. How could he hope to defend them, when he was miles away from them with barbed wire and soldiers in between?

'You think . . .?' he began.

Isaac put a fraternal arm round his shoulders.

'Take no notice of the young puppy, Reuben. Being cooped up in this place has given him an over-active imagination. For God's sake get your Rachel to find him a pretty girl to moon over before he drives us all to distraction.'

Grethe felt her way along the landing from the bathroom and back into the room she shared with Elsa. It was only ten-thirty, but 'lights out' was at nine-thirty sharp. With the black-out screens up, it was even darker inside the room than it was outside, where thick fog swirled in over the cliffs, obscuring the moon. It was a shivery cold night, the unheated air like liquid ice as she breathed it in.

Catching her nightdress on a nail, Grethe cursed as she felt the artificial silk tear. But what was one torn nightdress in the middle of a war? She heard the bedcovers rustle, and a soft sound that might be a greeting.

'Elsa? You awake, Elsa?' she whispered.

Silence. Then a word, more distinct this time.

'Max . . .'

Grethe shook her head. Talking in her sleep again – it was clear Elsa was driving herself crazy worrying about her twin brother. She could understand that: hadn't she shouted and screamed and wept herself hoarse trying to make them tell her where Emil was? Only that unexpected blissful letter, each word painfully spelled out in Emil's childish scribble, was keeping her from doing it all over again.

She padded across to the bed, taking off her high-heeled satin mules so as not to make too much sound on the bare linoleum. Best to let the girl sleep, the state she was in.

'Max . . . is that you, Max . . . don't go away . . .'

Grethe slipped off her dressing-gown and sat down on the edge of the bed. It creaked and squeaked on its rusty springs as she slid under the blankets. God but it was cold, hellishly cold. You could hear the wind rattling the sash windows in

323

their frames, screeching and howling above the crash and roar of the surf.

Her feet were cold, too. She wriggled them down, half wishing she'd put on that pair of huge woolly socks Rachel had knitted for her; vanity always was her downfall.

Lying half on her side, half on her belly, Elsa stirred in her sleep, flinging her arm over the bolster. Grethe heard her fingernails rasping on the cotton ticking as she clenched her fingers tight.

'Don't leave me. Don't go away . . .'

Grethe lay down beside her, feeling the rigidity in Elsa's body; hard and cold as wood. Poor kid. What must be eating her up inside for her to be like this? She'd heard the rumours too – persistent, malicious rumours that Elsa had been found drunk. Could she believe that of Elsa? It wasn't like her, Elsa had always been so calm, the one who kept everyone else on an even keel.

'It's all right, I'm here,' Grethe heard herself say. Suddenly she was the one doing the reassuring. 'I'm here.'

Elsa let out a little sigh that ended in a sob of release.

'Here. Here. Safe . . .'

'Safe as houses, *liebchen*. Safe as houses.'

Relieved by the more measured sound of Elsa's breathing, Grethe stretched out alongside, her hip just touching Elsa's flank. Who would have thought that two so different women could have been brought together, into this artificial intimacy? In the months since they had met at Streatham South Police Station, Grethe had come to value the curious friendship which had grown between them. Recently it had seemed to be slipping away again, the war pushing them apart as capriciously as it had forced them together.

But now, lying beside Elsa in the enfolding darkness, Grethe made a silent vow not to let that happen. Somebody had to help Elsa, whether she liked it or not. Somebody had to keep on telling her that things could – and would – get better.

She turned her back on Elsa, curling her knees up to her chest as she thought about Harry Kerruish; the good, kind, honest man who had freely offered her his friendship and respect even though he put himself in danger of punishment every time he passed the time of day with her.

Harry. He too had come to mean a lot to Grethe. She smiled to herself in the darkness and, hugging the blanket about her chilled shoulders, she allowed the warm glow of hope to enter her heart.

Chapter 24

The storm raged on into the next day, brownish-pink clouds scudding across a huge sky as a gusting wind bent trees and tugged at loose slates and chimneypots.

At Hutchinson Camp the square was empty, except for the dried-up corpses of last year's leaves. The artists were indoors, devising wonderful new projects, the rabbis were at prayer, and the soldiers who guarded them were huddled into the turned-up collars of their greatcoats, their noses crimson with cold.

'*Gottenyu*,' muttered Reuben Kotkin, opening the front door of House forty-one and peering out into the wild December morning.

Wind gusted in, buffeting the newspaper chains slung across the hallway. The air stung his face and he tasted salt on his lips. In the distance, beyond the jumbled rooftops of the town, white horses were galloping over the tops of a thousand angry waves.

'For God's sake shut the door,' grunted Sachs, winding a red woollen scarf around his neck. He had bartered two of his philosophy books and a fine edition of Goethe just to get that scarf; but being frozen to the marrow could make you do the most insane things.

'The sleet has stopped.' Reuben turned to look at Sachs, his body so muffled in scarves and jumpers and a huge naval overcoat that his head seemed absurdly small. 'Thinking of going out?'

Sachs threw up his hands in horror.

'God forbid!'

'I thought I might go over to the Artists' Cafe.'

'So go. Bring me back five cream-cheese bagels and a beautiful girl.'

'Will you settle for a beetroot sandwich and a game of chess with Isaac?'

Sachs gave a shrug of resignation.

'A man must make do with what he can get.'

Reuben stuck his nose outside the door again. It was certainly wild out there, but he was sick of sitting inside mending other men's suits and shirts. He would have written again to Rachel, but they were only allowed to write three letters a month and he could have written that many in a day.

'I'll see you later.' Pulling his hat down over his ears, he set off across the square towards the cafe. His coat tails billowed out behind him, flapping like the black wings of some bird of prey.

Turning past House thirty-two, he glanced to his left. There was a figure sitting in the porch at the top of the front steps; a man with a beard and wild, reddish-brown hair.

It was Müller – but Müller as Reuben had not seen him before. This time he was not scribbling aimlessly on a piece of paper, or staring into the distance. There was a wooden board balanced across his knees, and he was working away at something with purpose and intensity.

Reuben paused, almost changing course to walk over and talk to Müller; but something stopped him. Something told him that whatever it was that Ernst Müller was up to, he oughtn't to be disturbed. Turning deliberately aside, he walked on towards the Artists' Cafe.

Müller sat at the top of the steps, his back sheltered by the stone porch of the guesthouse. Even if he had had to stand in the middle of the storm he would have done it, the urge was so strong.

This was what he had been longing for, searching for

somewhere in the darkest recesses of his injured mind; the memory of a skill which he had once had, and which must surely be there still, if only he knew where to find it.

The board across his knees had been nailed and glued together from two lengths of mahogany taken from an old piano. The homemade paper, he had been given by a Czech artist who had taken pity on the wild, shambling figure who was so convinced, against all the evidence, that he was an artist too.

He held the pencil wonderingly, as if discovering the feel and the balance and the power of it, all at once. A tremble of excitement ran through his body but his fingers remained rock-steady, for the first time since he had come to this place.

Raising his face to the sky, he let the storm rage and tear around him. Sleet was hardening into hail now, but Müller didn't care. He was getting somewhere at last, forcing his mind to go blank and letting his body remember instead.

Slowly but confidently, he made the first pencil-stroke. It was perfect, precise, just the way he'd intended it to be. Overcome by excitement, he began to draw again; another pencil stroke, and then another, more confidently now, his hand guiding him where conscious thought had been unable to take him.

Hailstones bounced around him, stinging his bare hands and face, but he could hardly have cared less. He was creating a picture of the storm – a picture of violent beauty, like the tortured beauty of his troubled mind.

For these moments at least, it didn't matter that he still didn't know who he really was, couldn't remember anything but fragmented images from his past life. From somewhere deep inside him – somewhere that was not Ernst Müller but Max – he was becoming what he had known instinctively that he must be.

An artist.

★ ★ ★

Grethe was sitting on a rock beside the Meayll Circle when Harry found her.

'So here y'are, gel, I was wondering where you was hiding yourself.'

She watched him walk up the hill towards the chambered cairn, his broad shoulders hunched with the effort of climbing the steep incline.

'I thought perhaps I should keep out of sight.'

'Aye. Aye, you're right at that.' Harry clambered over the stile and dropped down onto the rough grass. 'You're keepin' well?'

'Quite well. And you?'

'Oh, middlin', middlin' fair.'

All the better for seeing you, he thought to himself, but he didn't say it though he was burning to. Of late Harry had felt a new awkwardness between them. He sensed that Grethe could feel it too. It was the awkwardness of a man and a woman who have gone beyond the warmth of first acquaintance and are not yet sure how much further they dare take their friendship.

He thrust his hand in his pocket.

'You'll take a nip o' whisky? To keep out the cold?'

'No, no thank you.'

'Now, gel, why don't you tell me what's troublin' you?'

Grethe looked into his warm grey eyes and all the things she'd meant to say dried up in her throat.

'I . . . wanted to ask you something.'

'Ask away, gel.'

She uncurled her gloved hand and held out a tiny, tissue-wrapped package.

'I want you to sell something for me.'

'*Sell* something?' He regarded her quizzically. 'You in some sort of trouble, gel?'

'No, no, not that.' She shook her head. 'Not trouble exactly. But I don't have any money – I couldn't bring much with me and . . . well . . . I never was much good at saving. If

330

I needed money . . .' For the first time she found his uncritical gaze physically painful, and her eyes dropped down. 'I'd go out and earn it.'

She took the tiny paper package and placed it in Harry's hand, folding his fingers over it.

'Please, Harry.'

'What is it?'

'It's a gold locket my mother gave me. It's all I have.'

'Your mother! You can't sell this.'

'I have to.'

'But I don't understand, Grethe. What do you need the money for?'

'It's Christmas soon. I want to buy a present . . .'

'For Rachel? Elsa?'

'For Emil. I had a letter . . .'

Harry passed his hand across his brow. His outrush of breath turned to white smoke in the frosty December air.

'But, Grethe gel, you don't even know exactly where the lad is.'

'Adrian Newell says he'll get it to him somehow.' She got to her feet and took two steps closer, until her face was just inches from Harry's. It wasn't a young face, he thought to himself, and the harsh December light wasn't kind to it. They were neither of them youngsters, life had marked them both. But Grethe was a handsome woman for all that, none handsomer. There was a strength in her he wanted to reach out and embrace. 'And I'll make them tell me where he is.'

'Don't get your hopes up, Grethe.'

'I have to try, Harry, don't you see? I'm his mother. Oh, I may not be a very good one, but I love him. Even whores can love their kids.'

Her upturned face, her parted lips, invited kisses and it was a battle to force himself not to answer the yearning.

'He's a lucky boy, Grethe.'

'You'll do it for me, then? You'll sell the locket?'

Harry stared for a second at the little package, then slipped

331

it carefully into the inside pocket of his old jacket.

'Let's just say you needn't worry about the money.'

She followed the changing expressions on his face.

'No charity, Harry. I won't take charity.'

'Lord but you're a suspicious woman, Grethe.'

'I have to be.'

'Not with me you don't. I know it's hard, gel, but try to trust me.'

She met his gaze and smiled, a beautiful open smile that made her eyes sparkle.

'I do, Harry. I do trust you. What a fool I must be.' And very gently, very lightly, she planted a kiss on his weatherworn cheek.

''Course . . .'

'Hmm?'

''Course, in the old days . . .'

James McArthur hardly knew whether to laugh or cry. Every single time he came up to the Kneen farm, he was subjected to Cyril Kneen's encyclopedic knowledge of Manx folk-medicine: that and the tale of how well Fenella was doing in the ATS, even though everyone knew he'd never wanted her to go.

'. . . in the old days, if you'd a cow that was bewitched . . .'

'She's not bewitched, Cyril. She's a bad case of mastitis. Now if you'll just stand back and let me get a proper look . . .'

'. . . if you'd a cow that was bewitched, you'd use the egg charm.'

James looked up. He hadn't heard that one before.

'The egg charm? What's that?'

Pleased to have hit upon something to impress the 'vet'nary', Cyril leant back against the cow-byre, arms folded.

'You go to one as has the power, and get a bunch of herbs. Then you get nine eggs from a way off, so they're clean of *buitcheragh*.' He watched placidly as James opened his medical bag and got to work on the cow. 'You all right there, Misther?'

'Right as rain,' muttered James, rummaging for the right jar. Since Elsa had stopped helping out at the surgery things had become disorganised again.

'When it comes to midnight, see, you must be fastening up all the doors an' boiling three of the eggs with a third of the herbs, for exactly three minutes.'

'And then what?' James fished out the jar he'd been looking for. It contained a salve which Elsa had prepared, using elderflowers, wormwood and groundsel she'd collected herself. The top hadn't been screwed on properly and the contents had oozed over the inside of his bag.

'You do that for three nights running, an' the cow will be cured.'

'Sounds like a waste of good eggs to me,' commented James. 'Not to say messy.'

'An, then there was old Crellin, the horse charmer.'

Saints preserve us, thought James as he wiped the sticky jar on his clean handkerchief. But perhaps Cyril had a point. *Nothing* could be messier than the inside of this medical bag.

'Did I ever tell you about Crellin?'

'No, I don't think you did,' James said faintly.

'Fine man, Crellin. Didn't matter how wild a stallion you had, he'd just speak to it in the Gaelic an' it'd follow him like a lamb. Then there was the wise woman, Nan Wade. Ter'ble good she was at mixing the herbs, she'd a real skill on her.'

'Hmm?' James wished Cyril would concentrate on holding the cow still.

'Aw, 'twas a real gift. Cured all sorts she did with her potions – a bit like that Miss Nadel you had helping you when you last came up here.'

James felt the tiny hairs on the back of his neck bristling.

'Is that so?' His mouth felt dry.

'She's keepin' well, is she?'

'As far as I know.'

'She's not helpin' you now then?'

'No.'

Cyril squinted into the wintry sunlight.

'Fine-lookin' woman that.'

'I . . . can't say I've noticed. Pass me that bucket of hot water, would you?'

'Mind you, what a man needs is a steady girl, someone with her head screwed on like my Fenella. That Miss Nadel's too clever for my taste . . .'

James finished washing down the cow's udder and dried it off.

'I'm sure you're right.'

'Will we be hearin' weddin'-bells then?'

'What?' James looked up, startled.

'You and Miss Quine. Been walkin' out a good long time now, haven't you? If there's one thing I've always said, it's that Cora Quine would make someone a fine wife.'

It was just before noon when Cora, Grethe and Elsa emerged from Hudson's Bazaar and stepped into the crowd of shoppers.

Strand Street was Douglas's main shopping street, running roughly parallel to the Loch Promenade. If the shops weren't quite as well stocked as they had been before the war, they made up for it with eye-catching Christmas displays. Norton's 'furnishing drapers and outfitters' sported an array of coloured advertising posters, and Percy Towns's jewellery shop sparkled with paper chains and tinsel in between the pawned gold and silver trinkets.

Grethe quickly scanned the window of the jeweller's for a sight of her gold locket, but she couldn't spot it. She was glad, certain of the second thoughts she would feel if she saw it lying there with a price-tag on it.

'It was good of the Commandant to let us come to Douglas,' said Grethe brightly. 'Wasn't it, Elsa?'

Elsa was miles away. Grethe nudged her.

'I said, wasn't it?'

'Wasn't what?'

'Oh, never mind.' Not for the first time, Grethe wondered

what was the matter with Elsa. She looked down at her groaning shopping basket, filled to the brim with small gifts. 'That must be almost everything.'

'Not quite,' replied Cora. 'Not if you want to make sure that everybody at the *Bradda Vista* gets something. We'd better go to Woolworth's.'

'How much money is there left from the collection, Elsa?' Elsa opened the purse and counted.

'Eight and six.'

'Do you think that will be enough?'

'How should I know?' snapped Elsa.

Grethe felt the quickening of annoyance inside her.

'It's nearly Christmas, Elsa! You could at least try . . .'

'I don't see why. Frau Kessler's the house representative now. She should be doing this, not me.'

Grethe and Cora exchanged glances. Cora too was baffled by the change in Elsa. These days she scowled more than she smiled, spent hours on her own, and snapped at people for no apparent reason. Something had to be done – but what? Perhaps if James could be persuaded to talk to her, sort out whatever silly argument they'd had . . .

'Come on,' said Cora. 'Woolworth's. Then we can go and have a bite to eat before we go back.'

Grethe followed Cora and Elsa through the big swing doors. Emil had always loved going to Woolworth's, rummaging in the trays of nicknacks and pressing his nose against the glass cases. 'Nothing over sixpence' – that slogan had drawn him like an irresistible magnet. How she'd scolded him for spending his pocket money on rubbish; and how she wished he was here now. If he was only with her she'd never scold him again.

She fingered the small parcel in her coat pocket. It wasn't much – just a cheap watch, not the expensive one she would have bought him if they'd been back in Streatham. But she'd promised him a watch this Christmas and she'd been determined to buy him one if it cost her the clothes on her back. Now all she had to do was pray that Adrian Newell could get it to him . . .

'Will these do?' Cora pointed to a display of cheap printed cotton handkerchiefs.

'Whatever,' said Elsa, turning away.

'They'll do,' said Grethe firmly. 'It's the thought that counts,' she added with humour, as she sorted through the patterned hankies for the least garish.

'Besides, everyone needs to blow their nose sometime.'

'I think Frau Feldmann would rather die than blow her nose on that. Her husband's a film director, you know. Worked with Leni Riefenstahl before the war.' Grethe looked round. 'Where's Elsa?'

Cora scanned the heaving mass of shoppers.

'She must have wandered off somewhere. We'd better find her.'

'She'll be all right, she can look after herself.'

'Yes, but I'm responsible for both of you. We were supposed to come here under police guard you know. Besides, she's not been herself lately.'

'Perhaps she's gone outside for some fresh air.'

'Fresh? It's freezing out there.'

Leaving the handkerchiefs behind, Cora pushed her way between the shoppers, easing her way past a display of china dogs and a stack of alarm clocks. Grethe followed in her wake, arms full of bags and parcels, the little package for Emil reassuringly heavy in her pocket.

'It's hopeless – she could be anywhere.' Cora stopped near the doors and turned to scan the crowded store.

'Perhaps she's . . . oh look, there she is. Outside. Look.'

Cora turned and looked out through the glass doors, criss-crossed into diamonds with brown sticky tape.

Grethe was right. There Elsa was. Outside in the street, talking to James McArthur. And neither of them looked very happy . . .

* * *

Elsa couldn't stand it any longer. It was all so stupid. Who cared less whether or not Frau Feldmann got a handkerchief for Christmas? Come to that, who cared about Christmas at all?

She was sick of it all. Sick of Cora's well-meaning smiles, sick of Grethe and Rachel's continual questions. Sick.

The air in the shop was suffocating; not hot, just airless and choking, like a pillow trying to stifle her. She could hardly breathe. And all this noise – this chatter, like monkeys in a cage, screeching and gabbling nonsense all around her. She needed to get out.

Turning away from Grethe and Cora, Elsa pushed and shoved her way through the milling throng of shoppers. She trod on a few toes but hardly noticed the muttered curses. Getting outside, that was all she cared about.

Pushing open the door, she stepped outside and just stood there, dragging great gulps of icy air into her lungs. She could feel her heart racing, thumping ridiculously fast, an irrational sensation of panic tightening every muscle in her body, making her stomach contract so that she wondered if she was about to throw up.

Deep breaths, that was it. Deep breaths, try to control it, ride it out. She closed her eyes and listened to the seagulls, screeching and laughing as they wheeled over the rooftops and the bay. Don't let the blackness win.

'Elsa?'

She froze, her heart stopping for what seemed like whole long minutes.

'Elsa – are you ill?'

Her eyes snapped open. She didn't want to believe it was him, she'd been avoiding him for weeks now, but it *was* him, and in her heart of hearts she was perhaps just a little glad.

'Ja . . . Mr McArthur . . .'

'You're as white as a sheet. Is there anything I can do?'

James's concern hurt her even more than his rejection. He was every bit as kind, as professional, as detached as he had been before that disastrous morning in his surgery.

'I'm fine. Just leave me alone.'

His hand touched hers and she trembled; with fear this time, the fear of what she did not want to feel.

'You look ill.'

'I told you, I'm fine.' Her voice faltered. 'And anyway, what do you care?'

'You know I care.'

'Oh yes, you *care*. Like you'd care for a sick dog.'

'No, no, it's not like that. You don't understand.'

'Don't I?' Her eyes challenged his, defying him to make some declaration of undying love which, of course, he never would.

He looked away, profoundly uncomfortable. He'd been trying to talk to her for weeks, but now that he had the chance it was all going horribly wrong.

'What are you doing here in Douglas?'

'It's all right, James, I haven't escaped or anything,' she said archly.

'I didn't think you had.'

'I had to come here with Grethe and your precious Cora. To buy Christmas presents. As if I cared about any of it . . .'

'Look, Elsa, I wanted to . . .'

'It's all right, don't bother.'

Another voice sounded behind her.

'Elsa, you're here! We've been looking all over for you.'

She answered without looking round.

'Well, you've found me now, haven't you?'

Cora and Grethe emerged from the shop. Cora looked from Elsa to James and then back again, trying to fathom whatever it was that had passed between them. Whatever had made Elsa's eyes so very bright. Too bright. And James looked flustered, evasive – as though there was something he wanted to hide.

'Hello, James.'

James greeted Cora with relief.

'Hello, Cora.'

'Is something wrong?'

'No, of course not. We were just . . .' He dried up.

'Just what?'

'Talking. Just talking.'

Cora hadn't known James like this before. He was always so straightforward. And he was a terrible liar, thought Cora. But why should he *need* to lie?

James's eyes met Cora's and he felt an unexpectedly strong surge of love. He really did love her, he was certain of that now. But did he love her enough? Did he love her enough to put Elsa Nadel out of his mind for ever?

Chapter 25

'She's so beautiful, your little Esther.'

Signora Bertorelli dandled the child on her knee, beaming with the simple pleasure of imagining herself a young mother again. Rachel Kotkin folded up the last of the clean terry nappies and straightened her aching back.

'Beautiful and heavy,' she laughed. 'She grows so fast, hardly any of her clothes fit any more.'

'I knit you more,' said Maria Bertorelli, making funny faces at little Esther who stared back, fascinated.

'Oh, Maria, you've already done enough . . .'

'You give me old clothes, I unravel and knit you more. Yes?'

'If you're sure you don't mind.'

'Mind? For my beautiful little princess?'

'You will spoil her!'

'Quite right too,' cut in Grethe, who was sitting at a table by the big bay window of the common room, wrapping little gifts in cut-up paper bags. It wasn't very Christmassy, but they were lucky to have any wrapping at all, what with the paper shortage. 'Kids *should* be spoilt at Christmas.'

'For us it is Chanukah,' said Rachel.

Signora Bertorelli chuckled as she dangled a pretty ribbon over Esther's face and the child reached out to grab it with plump, rose-pink fingers.

'Chanukah, Christmas, what does it matter? It is time for giving, time for love.'

'A time for families,' sighed Rachel. 'I wish I could be with Reuben.'

341

'Soon, you will see him soon. You have present for him?'

Rachel opened her work-bag and took out a tissue-paper parcel, which she unwrapped slowly and carefully, peeling back the precious tissue as though it was fragile as gold leaf.

'So that's what you've been hiding from us!' Grethe got up and walked across to take a look.

'It is a shirt.' Rachel held it up. 'A shirt for Reuben.'

'Very fine shirt, very fine.' Signora Bertorelli ran her fingers over the intricately worked stitching.

'It is an old Russian design,' explained Rachel. 'Cora's friend Miss Bannister gave me the embroidery silks.'

Grethe whistled her approval.

'Wish I could sew like that. I was never much good at anything.'

'Nonsense! You sing like an angel, doesn't she, Maria?'

Maria nodded her agreement.

'*Bellissima.*'

Grethe laughed.

'I'm only singing a song in the Christmas revue, Rachel.'

'You'll be the star of the show.'

'If you say so. But I think Broadway will have to wait.'

Grethe had only reluctantly agreed to take part in the joint Christmas/Chanukah revue. It was years since she'd sung in public – that part of her life, those ambitions, had died and been buried a long time ago. Besides, there were so many other, far more important things to think about. Then she'd remembered how much Emil had loved her to sing for him when he was little, and that thought had changed her mind.

'What about you, Maria? Have you made a present for your Tony?'

Maria's plump cheeks creased into a smile.

'Cora, she promise me a little fruit, a little fat, an egg . . . my Tony, he love to eat cake.'

'Don't we all,' commented Grethe. The whole world liked to eat Maria Bertorelli's cakes – with the possible exception of Cora's grandfather Thomas, who became unaccountably flustered whenever Maria was in the same room.

'When he released, and we go back to Streatham, I feed him up. He too thin. I make him good and fat again . . .'

At that moment, the distant jangle of the doorbell interrupted the conversation.

'I'll go,' said Grethe, heading off into the hallway. With the blackout curtain drawn back, she could see the silhouette of a figure standing on the doorstep. It didn't look tall enough for James McArthur, not broad enough for Harry. And George always took the post round to the back door so that Cora would invite him in and feed him Mrs Bertorelli's homemade bread.

Twisting back the latch, she opened the door. A woman was standing on the doorstep, surrounded by a pile of suitcases and boxes. Grethe didn't recognise her. She was in her mid-twenties, nicely if fussily dressed in a green coat with a fur collar; and hair the colour of clarified honey. Attractive, in a cold sort of way, thought Grethe to herself.

'Good morning,' she began.

The woman stared at her as though she had grown an extra head.

'Who are you?'

'Grethe Herzheim,' replied Grethe, slightly taken aback.

'You're one of . . .?'

'One of the internees, yes.'

'I see.'

Grethe couldn't tell whether the young woman's expression was one of apprehension, disdain or both.

'Can I help you?' she volunteered, purposefully not standing back to let the woman in. There was something about her that she just plain didn't like.

'Is Miss Quine at home?'

'Yes.'

'Then you can find someone to carry my bags, and tell Miss Quine I'm here.'

Carry your bags? thought Grethe. Who do you think I am?

343

'Yes, but who . . .?'

The young woman slipped off her leather gloves. Good leather gloves, noted Grethe. This girl might not have any manners, but she certainly had a taste for quality.

'My name is Grace Quine. I expect Miss Quine has told you about me. My husband and I own this place.'

Grace stepped into the hallway of the *Bradda Vista* with a sinking feeling somewhere between claustrophobia and distaste.

The place had changed – and not for the better. It even smelt different, imbued with funny foreign smells as well as the more familiar scents of boiled cabbage and floor polish.

She wouldn't have come back here, not for the world, if only things hadn't become so unbearable in Banbury. Since William had been posted overseas with his unit, all her parents' worst qualities had come to the fore. It had been William, William, William, morning, noon and night. William this, William that. What a good, reliable, hardworking husband William was. What a catch. How lucky she'd been that he'd never threatened to leave her, despite what had happened to little Billy . . .

Her mother's hurtful remarks had been the last straw – the snide little digs that cut far deeper than Grace ever showed. She knew what some people thought of her since Billy's death, knew the things they whispered about her behind her back, but why should she have to justify herself to them? Why couldn't they just leave her alone to bury the memory as she had buried her child?

She felt all the eyes on her as she walked along the corridor past the common room. Foreign eyes. Eyes that might belong to spies or traitors or worse. She heard the chattering voices – what was it they were talking, German? She was sure she could hear other accents too, Italian, Scandinavian. There were nasty cheap little Christmas decorations festooned all over the place, children running about on an upstairs landing, and a nine-branched candlestick on the mantelshelf over the fireplace.

'Miss Quine is in the kitchen,' said Grethe.

'Have my bags taken up to my room.'

'Your room?' enquired Grethe between clenched teeth.

'On the first floor, the large front room.'

'I . . .'

'What is the matter?' demanded Grace impatiently. Were they all imbeciles as well as traitors? she wondered.

'I'm afraid that room is occupied.'

'Occupied! Impossible.'

'An internee lady . . . with a child.'

Grace's lips pursed tight with displeasure. Grethe almost cheered.

'Then tell them to move to another room. They'll have to share.'

'I don't think that's possible.'

This time Grace's expression was easier to read. It registered utter contempt.

'I am the owner of this hotel, if I say something is possible, it is.'

Grethe shrugged.

'I don't care if you're the Queen of bloody Sheba. I'm not telling anyone to move. You'll have to do it yourself.'

'You can't talk to me like that,' gasped Grace as Grethe turned on her heel and stalked off down the hallway back to the common room.

'Grace!' exclaimed Cora, emerging from the kitchen at the sound of raised voices.

Grace swung round.

'Hello, Cora.'

'You might have told me you were coming.'

'I . . . didn't decide until a couple of days ago.'

'I see.' Cora's eyes searched Grace's face for any sign of sisterly warmth. She couldn't find any. 'So how long will you be staying?'

'For Christmas, maybe longer. I don't know.'

'Well, I hope you've brought your ration book. The shopkeepers do their best to give us a little extra, but it's quite a struggle sometimes, feeding all these mouths.' She paused. 'Grandad Quine will be pleased to see you.'

'You think so?'

'Yes, of course. Just one thing – I don't think you should be ordering my ladies about like this.'

'Your *ladies*? Cora, I think you are making a very big mistake allowing these women to behave like that.'

Cora shrugged, wiping wet hands on a tea-towel. She looked a complete mess, thought Grace, with her hair scraped back and that horrible shapeless overall. It was no wonder no man would marry her.

'They've done nothing wrong, I don't see why they should be badly treated. Besides, it's my decision how I run this place.'

'Well I'm here now,' said Grace, taking off her hat and jabbing the pin through the crown.

'So?' Cora folded her arms and returned Grace's belligerent stare with a calm, steady gaze.

'So I shall be able to guide you in the running of this place.'

'No, I don't think so, Grace.'

'What do you mean, you "don't think so"?'

'You made it quite clear, when you dumped this place on me, that it was going to be my responsibility. You wanted nothing to do with it, remember?'

'That was then . . . things have changed.'

'What things?'

'William – he's been posted overseas.'

Cora felt a twist of panic in her guts for her brother's sake, if not her sister-in-law's. In recent years she and William hadn't always seen eye to eye, but as children they'd been very close. Until Grace came along and everything changed.

'You could have let me know.'

'Sorry.'

'Do you know where he is?'

'No. I haven't heard from him since his embarkation leave.'

Cora groaned, half in exasperation, half in despair. Why did Grace have to turn up again, just when she was getting things straight, making the best of a job she'd never wanted?

'Come into the kitchen,' she said. 'I'll make a pot of tea and then we can decide where we're going to put you.'

As they were sitting down to wait for the kettle to boil, there was a knock at the kitchen door.

'Come in,' called Cora.

The door opened and a familiar figure walked in. It was Rachel, the baby asleep in her arms.

'Please, Cora,' she began, then stopped as she saw Grace sitting at the table.

'It's all right, Rachel, go on. This is Mrs Quine, my brother's wife. She used to run this hotel before the war,' she added pointedly.

'I wondered – could we save up our rations and have a little party for the Czech girl at Christmas? She is getting married by proxy, and we wanted to do something to help her celebrate. It is a lonely time for her, with her man so far away.'

'I don't see any reason why not. Talk to me about it later. I'll have a word with Mrs Bertorelli.'

Cora turned to Grace, saw the way that she was looking at Rachel's baby; her eyes fixed on the now-wakeful child, kicking and smiling in her mother's arms. Her stomach turned over in a split second of blind, irrational panic.

'This is Rachel,' she said. 'Rachel Kotkin. Her baby was born here, back in July.'

Rachel stepped closer, holding out the child so that Grace could see her more closely.

'Her name is Esther,' she said. 'It means "hope".'

Grace extended a slender, well-manicured right hand to touch the child; but stopped, her fingers not quite brushing the baby's face.

347

'Could I hold her?' she asked, much to Cora's surprise. Since the day of Billy's death, Grace hadn't shown the faintest interest in babies – or in Billy's memory, for that matter.

Rachel drew back, hugging the child more closely against her bosom. Her expression changed from friendliness to apprehension.

'I . . . I have to be very careful with her . . .' she stammered, her mind still touched by images of the street attack which had so nearly cost her and Reuben their precious daughter.

'Quite right too,' said Cora, her eyes never leaving Grace's expressionless face. 'Quite right too.'

Hutchinson Camp too was doing its best to enter the spirit of the festive season. The camp newspaper was full of seasonal poems and pictures, someone had designed a camp Christmas card, and some bright spark had even decided to put on a concert.

Reuben and Isaac were reluctant recruits to the theatrical company – Sachs not quite so reluctant.

'I despair of you, Sachs,' said Isaac, banging nails into an improvised proscenium arch. 'You are a shameless exhibitionist.'

Sachs executed an exaggerated bow.

'My public love me,' he grinned.

'My boy, your public would throw eggs and tomatoes at you, had they any to throw.' Isaac gave the nail a final tap and leaned back to take a look at his handiwork. 'Not bad for a schoolteacher,' he declared.

'So, you are thinking of another new career, are you?' enquired Sachs, swinging his long legs over the edge of the stage and jumping down. 'But I must tell you, Isaac, a carpenter, *nebech*, you are not!'

'I thought you were going to be a farmer,' commented Reuben, busy weighting the stage curtains by sewing small pebbles into the hem.

'And so I am. Sooner than you think.'

Reuben bit off a length of cotton and looked up.

'You have heard something? About your application?'

'I had a letter from the Jewish Refugee Committee yesterday. They think they have found a farmer who will take me for *hachshara*. A good man, the distant cousin of a friend I knew when I trained to be a teacher.'

'That is good news,' said Reuben, rather more quietly than he would have liked. He wanted to sound happy for Isaac, not grudging. But it was so difficult not to feel a little resentment each time someone he knew was released.

'Isaac – a farmer?' laughed Sachs. 'He will plant the horses and try to ride the cabbages.'

'Oh? And you, of course, know all there is to know about farming?'

'Of course!'

'How about you, Reuben?'

'No, Rachel and I have heard nothing. Not yet. We have not even been given the date for a tribunal.'

Isaac clapped him on the shoulder.

'All will be well, cousin. You will see. What is it the prophet says? "Not by strength, not by power, but by My Spirit, sayeth the Lord of Hosts." Patience is a virtue, Reuben.'

'That is easy for you to say, they are letting you out!'

'What about Sachs? How much longer will he be troubling us all?'

Sachs pushed back his shock of wavy hair.

'Not much longer, God willing. The forms have been sent off, now I must just wait.'

'Waiting,' sighed Reuben. 'That is all I ever seem to do. I am waiting my whole life away.'

'Don't just sit there, Kotkin, help me get this onto the stage.' Isaac indicated a heavy table, spotted here and there with blobs of coloured paint from over-enthusiastic scene painting. Together they dragged it up onto the stage. Isaac's gaze swept from one side of the stage to the other, taking in the backdrop: a wild landscape of rolling hills, tumbling sky and an angry, grey sea. 'Interesting scenery that – whoever painted that has a real talent. A little raw, but talent.'

'Yes,' said Reuben, setting down his end of the table and standing back to look at the scenery. 'It was painted by Ernst Müller.'

It was Christmas Eve; a cold, drizzly evening with the rain falling softly into an oily, deceptively calm sea. Standing on a table in the parlour of the *Bradda Vista*, Grethe Herzheim sang to a hushed audience.

A few tears were wept and wiped away as she sang the last notes of the love song, her husky contralto fading away into thunderous applause.

'Bravo,' someone called from the back. '*Encore!*'

Grethe shook her head, blushing as she jumped down into the throng. Blushing! Who would have thought that Grethe Herzheim was still capable of colouring up like a schoolgirl?

'Grethe, that was beautiful, such a beautiful song,' said Rachel breathlessly, her eyes just a little wet with tears.

'To sing for us in Yiddish . . .' smiled Lena. 'You bring us all together.'

'You must sing again,' urged Maria Bertorelli.

'No, no, later perhaps.' Grethe brushed aside all the compliments, pleased that she had given pleasure, that she could still hold an audience spellbound; but uncomfortable with so much praise. 'It's time for dancing – what will Helga think if we don't dance at her wedding?'

'Yes, yes, but first the toast,' urged Cora, topping up a dozen glasses with watery fruit punch. The bride smiled through a few misty tears. It was a strange wedding day for her, with no bridegroom, just a veil made out of one of Bessie Teare's old tablecloths.

'You are kind, all very kind.'

As they all raised their glasses to their lips, Cora thought of Grace, stubbornly shut away in her attic room and refusing to have anything to do with 'those women' and their festivities.

'Shall we switch on the radio for the news?' someone asked, to a chorus of disapproval. No one wanted to hear the news tonight, not at Christmas time.

'I not want to hear what the bombs do to my beautiful *ristorante*,' protested Maria Bertorelli.

Someone turned the dial to the Light Programme. Dance music filled the room; happy music that couldn't help but transport you to another time and another place, a place of love and carefree laughter.

Frau Kessler dragged Helga into the middle of the common room and bowed.

'May I have the pleasure of this dance?'

'Irmgard, I couldn't!'

Helga laughed and cried all at once as Irmgard Kessler swept her into the rhythm of the dance, her white veil billowing and swirling behind her. Other ill-assorted couples joined in, tripping over each other's feet as the happiness of the dance tune carried them with it.

Thomas Quine and Mrs Bertorelli eyed each other from opposite ends of the buffet table, laden with cheesy potato puffs, prune jellies and parsnip sandwiches.

'You a very fine man,' she said, with a twinkle in her eye.

'I'm a respectable widower.'

'We kiss? Under the mistletoe?'

'Steady on, gel!'

'Just one kiss? A kiss for Christmas?'

Cora giggled.

'Care to dance?' she asked James.

He hesitated for just one moment, then his face relaxed into a smile. 'Why not?'

His arm slipped round her waist. She danced so well and they moved so easily together. If only life were as easy as dancing.

'Mind your leg,' said Cora.

'To hell with my leg.' James tossed his stick onto a nearby

chair. 'There! I don't really need it anyway.'

'You're sure?'

'Sure. You look beautiful,' he said, and he pressed his lips into the golden softness of her hair.

'Don't tease.'

'I'm not teasing. You *are* beautiful.'

'Oh, James . . . to you, perhaps.' She blushed with pleasure, happy that he seemed happy again; happier still to be dancing cheek to cheek.

'To me.' He kissed her hair again, breathing in the soft, sweet scent of her. It hurt to feel the sheer power of the goodness in her. She deserved better than him. 'To any man with any sense.'

She leant her face against his chest, profoundly content at this moment. The war was going badly, Grace had come home to drive her crazy, but at this moment she was the happiest woman alive. All she wanted was to dance, and to keep on dancing forever, in James's arms.

James, too, felt the release of simple pleasure – the pleasure of just being with Cora, and not having to think. Tonight they were together, and that was all that mattered.

The music faded to an end and the announcer's voice droned into the room. Dancers parted, some laughing and panting for breath, others quiet and self-absorbed. James and Cora stood still for a few moments, just looking at each other.

'I should really be going,' said James. 'It's getting late.'

'Please stay – a little longer.'

'Well, just a wee while then.'

Their hands fell apart slowly, reluctant to let go.

'I'd better go and check that Grace is all right,' said Cora.

'Must you?'

'She's all on her own up there. But I'll be back very soon.'

James watched her go, picked up his stick, leant on it. Perhaps he had been a bit over-enthusiastic; his leg ached, the way it did when the weather turned damp.

He turned to take a drink from the table and saw Elsa,

standing in the doorway, a glass in her hand. Before she had a chance to turn tail and walk away he crossed the room and took hold of her gently by the arm, leading her out into the empty hallway.

'Elsa, where have you been hiding yourself? We need to talk.'

'I don't have anything to say.'

'But I do. I want to explain.'

'I think you've done enough explaining already.'

'No.' He shook his head vigorously. 'No, you have to listen to me. What happened at the surgery . . .'

'You mean, what didn't happen.' There had been such bitterness in her voice the last time they spoke, now there was only a kind of flat cynicism.

'I made a mistake, so did you. Things got . . . out of hand.'

'You made me feel . . . made me believe you wanted me.'

'Oh, Elsa, please don't do this to me. Don't do it to yourself, you're just torturing yourself.'

'No, James, it's you who tortured me. You led me on and then . . .'

She turned away but he tightened his grip on her arm and tried to force her to swing round and look at him. Her eyes were dry but hard and bright as diamonds.

'Don't touch me. Take your hands off me.'

Meekly he let go of her.

'I'm sorry. I didn't mean to hurt you. I never meant to hurt you.'

'Sorry? You think sorry makes everything all right?'

Her words stirred his anger.

'It takes two, Elsa. Don't you think you should remember that?'

'Oh, that's it, is it? You feel guilty, so you want to blame it all on me?'

James put his hand to his head. All the quiet happiness he'd been feeling was being pushed out of the way by guilt and hurt.

'I was stupid, I'm sorry. I must have given you the wrong idea about me.'

Elsa looked him straight in the eye.

'Yes.'

'I care, I really do. We can be friends. Good friends.'

'Oh really?' Elsa's gaze was steady and, he thought, softening. Then, out of the blue, she raised her glass and flung the contents in his face; smashing her glass on the floor. 'Well, that's what I think of your friendship, James McArthur.'

Standing at the top of the stairs, Cora heard and saw very little of what had happened. But as she came down the last flight, she saw something at once baffling and disturbing. She saw Elsa Nadel throw a glass of fruit punch in James's face.

All the old suspicions flooded back. James and Elsa . . . what bad blood was there between them, and why? What could James have done to Elsa to make her hate him so much?

She ran down the last few steps. James was standing on his own at the bottom of the stairs, wiping his face with a folded handkerchief.

'James? James, why did she do that?'

He shook his head slowly, momentarily struck dumb.

'I don't know.'

Cora stared at him in disbelief.

'Oh, come on, James, you must have some idea.'

'N-no. No idea.'

She was anxious and angry now; it was so obvious he was lying to her.

'Well, if you won't tell me, James, I'll find out for myself.'

Cora left him standing there, and hurried after Elsa. She found her standing by the kitchen sink, her whole body trembling.

'Elsa – what's got into you?'

'Go away. Please.'

'But what's the matter? Why did you do that?'

Elsa turned round slowly to face Cora.

'I think that's my business.'

'No, Elsa, it's my business if you insult a guest in my house.'

'Then perhaps you'd better ask your precious James.'

'He says he doesn't know.'

'Really?'

Cora took a step forward.

'Look, Elsa, I'm worried about you. *Really* worried. You used to be so different, so . . . in control. And now this. It just isn't like you.'

'Not like me?' Elsa laughed flatly. 'What would you know, Cora Quine? What the hell would you and your kind ever know about me?'

Grethe was upstairs in Rachel's room, taking her turn at looking after Esther, when she heard the knock on the door.

'*Komm.*'

The door opened and she gave a gasp of surprise.

'Harry! You can't come in here.'

He came inside and closed the door quietly behind him.

'If they find out, Harry . . .'

'Well, I shan't tell 'em, gel, and I don't suppose you will, neither. Besides, I'm here to see my niece, what's wrong with that?'

Grethe laid Esther down in her cot and regarded Harry with a smile of understanding.

'You're a stubborn old devil, Harry Kerruish.'

'No more'n you are.' He sat down on the edge of Rachel's bed. 'You sang beautiful down there, gel. Grand it was.'

She felt herself colouring up and looked away. Had he guessed that she'd been singing just for him?

'Thanks.'

'How've you been keepin', then?'

'Well enough.' I missed you like crazy, you old devil, she whispered in the silence of her thoughts, sitting down on a chair opposite Harry.

'I was wonderin' – did you manage to get that present for your boy?'

She nodded.

'I didn't get a chance to thank you properly,' she said. 'For selling the locket for me.'

'You were happy, that's all the thanks I want.'

'I bought Emil a watch. It wasn't a very good watch, not like the one I would have bought him if . . . Anyway, I bought it and I wrapped it up and sent it with a letter.'

'Did Newell tell you where he is?'

'No. But he promised he would make sure the watch got to him.' She raised her eyes to look into Harry's face. 'Do you think he'll have it for Christmas?'

'If he doesn't, the lad'll understand.'

'How can you be so sure?'

'Because he's a good lad. He's *your* lad.'

He thrust his hand into the pocket of his old corduroy trousers.

'I want you to have this.' He held out a tiny package, wrapped up in a twist of brown paper.

She took it from him wonderingly, as excited as any child.

'What is it?'

'Open it and see.'

She fumbled with the paper, her fingers grown clumsy with expectation.

'Oh, Harry. Oh, Harry, no.'

The paper yielded, and the tiny golden thing tumbled into the palm of her hand, the chain like a miniature waterfall of gold. She looked up.

'Harry, you promised. You promised you would sell it. No charity you said . . .'

'Steady on, gel.' He reached out and took her free hand, enclosing it tightly with his own. 'You wanted me to sell it?'

'You know I did.' Anger mingled with another, less definable emotion, making a lump rise in her throat.

'You wanted me to, so I sold it.' He sat back, hands on

356

knees. 'Then I bought it back. As a present – for you.'

'Harry . . .'

'It's Christmas. It's a Christmas present, I wanted you to have it back. 'Tisn't right that you should part with something your mother gave you. An' besides, I've no one else to spend my money on.'

'You're a stubborn, pig-headed fool.'

'You're not tellin' me anything I haven't heard before, gel.' He felt in his capacious pocket a second time. 'I got you a little somethin' else besides.'

'What?'

''Tisn't much. Just a brooch I saw when I was in Castletown – I thought you might like it.' He looked into her astonished face and wished he had the words to tell her all he felt. 'The blue stone . . . it matches your eyes.'

Grethe Herzheim thought she had left love a long way behind, somewhere in the dim and distant past when she had been a naive seventeen-year-old nightclub singer who believed all men could be trusted and all love lasted for ever. She certainly didn't expect to find it in a prison camp with a middle-aged fisherman.

So why were the tears spilling down her cheeks? And why did her heart beat so fast when he held her close against him, rocking her in his strong arms as he kissed away her fears?

Christmas Eve was not a good time for Mathilde, sitting with Inge and Marianne in the dining room at the *Erindale*. Marianne had spent most of the day making spiteful comments about the Jews and their Chanukah celebrations, or giving her sarcastic impressions of the concert the women had staged at the *Bradda Vista*.

Of course, Mathilde had agreed with everything Marianne said, just like she always did. But then again, what choice did she have? She gazed into the bottom of her teacup, trying to push back the inexorable tide of memory.

She was a child again; the child of a Jewish mother and an

357

Aryan father. In those days, before Hitler, it had been safe for people like them; and Mathilde and her two brothers had all been brought up in the Jewish tradition. One of her earliest memories was of Chanukah, the 'feast of lights'. Every day for eight days, a candle would be lit and placed in the nine-branched *menorah*, with the ninth candle standing proud above the rest. There would be parties, games, presents. She remembered her father's smiling face as they played the traditional Chanukah game with the *draydl* spinning top.

Such happy times, before the badness came and suddenly the family had to stop being Jewish and pretend to be German. It had been easy for Father and Mathilde, of course, with Father being German and Mathilde a natural blue-eyed blonde. Not so easy for dark-haired, dark-eyed Sophia and Karin; or for Mother, so beautiful and so sad on the day she sent them away to Austria, for their own safety.

Mathilde hadn't seen her mother or her sisters since that day. She wondered what had happened to them, knowing that in saving herself she was in effect betraying them all.

And so it was that she had become Mathilde the good Aryan girl; Mathilde who hated Jews so much that she delighted in tormenting and persecuting the *Untermenschen*.

She looked from stern, sour-faced Marianne to Inge's laughing face and her heart sank. How on earth had she come to this? It wasn't the Jews she hated, it was them. But it was too late to speak the truth now. Somehow she would have to see this through.

Chapter 26

'It's ages since we did this,' panted Cora as she slithered down the slippery slope.

'Aye, too long. Not since last spring.'

Cora glanced back at James. It was quite a steep path down from the top of the glen to the bottom, and the January rain had left it muddy and treacherous.

'You're sure you can manage?'

'Quite sure.'

'Your leg must be feeling better then.'

'A lot better since I ditched the stick. I told you it would mend, didn't I?'

James was holding on quite tightly to the rough handrail as he edged his way down, but he certainly did seem steadier on his feet, more confident without the walking stick. Cora felt a twinge of resentment. Injured, James would always be here; safe and sound on the Island, out of the range of the war. If he got better, really better, who could say how much longer he would stay?

'You did, James.' Reaching a convenient stopping-place before a flight of steps cut into the earth, Cora perched herself on the rustic wooden balustrade and breathed in the scents of bare earth and wet leaves. 'It's so peaceful here.'

'Except when the Home Guard are using the place for one of their training exercises!'

Cora laughed.

'George said they were here one night last week. Juan and Chalse had to pretend to be escaped prisoners of war and the others had to hunt them down. Only Chalse sprained his ankle and fell in the river, and they spent all night carrying him back to Port Erin.'

She surveyed the sodden browns and greens of the tree-canopy above and all around them. Water drip-drip-dripped from the waterlogged leaves onto the rich brown earth, but rain didn't bother Cora. She had something on her mind.

Was this the time or the place? She stole a glance at James. He looked happy, relaxed. And over the past few weeks they seemed to have regained much of their old closeness. Why risk losing that? Why not leave things be? But the same thought kept on nagging away at her, and she couldn't let it go. She *had* to know.

'I wanted to ask you something,' she began.

'Oh?' He turned interested eyes in her direction. 'Go on then.'

'It's been bothering me ever since the Christmas party. No, longer than that.'

'What has?'

'You and Elsa.'

There was an almost audible sound of indrawn breath as James flinched.

'How do you mean, me and Elsa?'

'Whatever it was that you argued about, it must have been something pretty serious.'

'What makes you say that?'

Cora felt the anxiety in him, the edginess; saw the way he avoided looking directly at her. It angered her.

'For heaven's sake, James, she threw her drink all over you! And she's been like a lost soul ever since she stopped working with you at the surgery.'

'She's very anxious . . . about finding her brother.'

'I think it's more than that. I'm worried about her, James.'

There was a long pause, during which James counted the raindrops as they fell to the ground at his feet.

'Yes,' he said finally. 'So am I.'

Cora could feel her heart thumping in her chest. Now that she was about to find out what this was all about, she wasn't sure she wanted to any more.

'What's been going on, James? Why won't you tell me?'

Cora took his hand in hers and James turned to look at her again. It surprised him again how much love he felt for her, how it welled up inside him, warm and strong. Desire too, though it was different from what he felt for Elsa Nadel. No less strong, just different. He knew he had been a complete idiot.

'It's best if you ask Elsa.'

'I did. She practically spat in my face. So I think you'd better tell me, for everybody's sake.' Especially for mine, she thought. However bad the truth is, it can't be as bad as not knowing.

'Walk with me?' James indicated the flight of earth and stone steps leading down towards the glittering stream.

'Okay.'

Side by side, they descended into the whispering twilight of the wintry glen.

'It was my fault,' he began.

'What was?'

'I should have kept my distance, told her from the start that I wasn't interested in her.'

Cora felt a slight tightening of her stomach muscles, the faint sickliness of a realisation she had been pushing to the back of her mind.

'Elsa . . . she had a crush on you?'

'Yes. I suppose you'd call it that.'

'But how is that your fault?'

James felt as though he were standing on the edge of a precipice. He could lie of course, make out that it had all been on Elsa's side; but lying wasn't his style.

'I wanted her too, Cora.'

Cora stopped dead in her tracks. The silence was deafening, only the cold clarity of a solitary blackbird's song cutting

361

through like a sharpened skate on thin ice. Suddenly she felt very cold, very alone.

'What did you say?'

This time he raised his voice. What was the point in whispering? He'd said it and he couldn't unsay it.

'I . . . was physically attracted to Elsa. I know how that must sound – and you've no idea how bad it makes me feel – but it's true. There was something there . . .'

'Was?'

'Was. It's over now – not that it ever amounted to anything.'

'I see.'

'No, Cora, you don't see. You can't see. I can hardly understand it myself.'

Cora cleared her throat, determined to be adult about this, finding it so very hard not to let emotions take her over.

'What happened? I want to know.' She gripped both his hands tightly. 'I need to know.'

He nodded.

'You've every right.' He leant against the balustrade, his leg suddenly cold and aching. 'We always got on well, right from the start. She's an intelligent woman, educated . . .'

Cora greeted this with sarcastic laughter.

'You're telling me all you wanted was her mind? Come off it, James. I wasn't born yesterday.'

'No, of course not. But somehow we just got on so well, we could sit and talk for hours. We'd both had our troubles . . . she seemed to understand. It never occurred to me that she might feel . . . that way . . .'

'And you?'

'I tried to block it out, but yes, I was attracted to her. But there was no more to it than that. It was you I really wanted all along. Don't you understand?'

Cora shook her head.

'Quite honestly, no, I don't think I do.'

'I should have realised what might happen.'

'So should I,' replied Cora with a flash of anger. She tried

362

to calm herself. 'So what did happen?'

'One day, before morning surgery, she came in very upset. She was in tears, I wanted to do something to help her . . .' He faltered, in his mind reliving it all over again. 'You don't want to hear this, Cora.'

'Go on, James. Please.'

'She . . . made a pass at me.'

Cora felt almost relieved.

'Is that all? She threw herself at you and you gave her the brush-off?'

'Not quite. You see – I was very tempted, Cora, it's no good pretending otherwise. She was crying and I put my arm round her. It felt good. One thing led to another and we ended up kissing.'

'And . . .?' Don't lie to me, James, don't lie to me, pleaded a silent voice inside her head.

'And . . . nothing.' He looked deep into Cora's eyes, forcing himself not to look away. She was right. Now that he had come this far he had to tell her everything. 'But there could have been.'

The thudding pain of his words took Cora's breath away.

'You wanted to make love to Elsa Nadel?'

He took a deep breath.

'For a moment I did, yes. I almost lost control. And then, when I came to my senses and told her I wasn't interested, she took it very badly. She was in a terrible state. I can't blame her.'

'No.' Neither can I, thought Cora.

'It happened once, Cora. Once only. The day after, we agreed it would be best if we stopped working together.'

Cora shook her head, more sad than angry.

'You led her on, then you rejected her? That's pretty low, James.'

'I told you it was my fault.'

Cora's fingers felt cold and stiff. She let go of James's hands. 'Why did you?'

'What?'

'Why did you reject her?'

'Because it was all wrong. It was crazy of me.'

'Why, James? Why was it crazy? I mean, it's not as if you were thinking of me, is it?' She challenged him with her eyes, daring him to tell her the truth. 'Or were you just afraid someone might find you out?'

'It was crazy because I don't love Elsa Nadel.' He swallowed, trying to get rid of the choking dryness in his throat. 'I love you, Cora. I always have done.'

'Don't do this to me, James.' She turned and started walking quite quickly away, down the steps towards the river.

'Cora, wait.' He hurried after her, stumbling and cursing at the residual stiffness in his leg. 'Listen.'

She half turned, looking at him over her shoulder. This was more than she could bear.

'It won't do, James.'

'What won't?'

'You can't do this, telling me you wanted this other woman and then telling me you love me.'

He heard the catch in her voice, knew this must be killing her; and all he wanted to do was sweep her up in his arms and kiss and hug her pain away.

'I've been a bloody fool, Cora.'

'So have I.' She gazed down into the sparkling water, watching it rush and bubble over half-submerged, mossy stones. It was a lot easier being a stone. She was sick of having to think. Sick of being strong, and decisive, and dutiful, and loyal. 'You know, I used to think we might have a future together. Pretty stupid, wasn't I?'

'Please.' He joined her on the riverbank, not attempting to touch her, wanting only to be close to her.

'When did this happen?'

'September.'

'And all this time . . .?'

'I know. You can't make me feel worse than I already do.'

364

Pity, thought Cora. But in her heart of hearts she knew she could not sustain the force of her anger.

'James.'

'Hmm?'

'Why tell me now?'

'You wanted me to. And the guilt's been with me for so long . . .'

'No, not about Elsa. About us. Why choose now to tell me that you love me?'

'I think it was the guilt that made me realise how much you mean to me. And what a fool I've been to risk losing you.'

She turned to look at him. Her eyes were soft and bright, her lips red and moist against her creamy complexion.

'Is that a lie too? Or do you really love me?'

'I'll swear it if you want me to.'

The curious surge of disappointment surprised Cora. After all, this was what she had longed to hear for the last four years – wasn't it? She felt at once upset, elated, angry, unsettled.

'Cora, I want to prove to you how much I love you.'

'There's no need.'

'I want you for always.'

'James, I . . .'

'I'm asking you to marry me, Cora.' He drew her to him. 'Forgive me and be my wife. No one could love you more.'

She drew away, gently and not without regret.

'I don't know, James. After what you've just told me . . . No, it's too sudden.'

'You don't have to give me an answer now.'

'I need time. Time to think about this.'

'Take all the time you need. I won't change my mind.'

Time. Cora looked into James's eyes and felt the true pain of love. Did she love him? Without a shadow of a doubt. Could she forgive him? She knew that she would. But there was more to it than that. More to marriage than love. And more to life than settling down and getting married.

This was one decision she wasn't going to make in a hurry.

'Elsa.'

Elsa froze on the seventh tread of the staircase. She did not look round.

Standing at the bottom of the staircase, in the hallway of the *Bradda Vista*, Cora wondered if she was doing the right thing in approaching Elsa. Maybe it would have been better just to have let sleeping dogs lie. But things burned to be brought into the open, and Cora Quine wasn't a woman to leave them unsaid.

'Elsa – can we talk for a moment?'

With obvious reluctance, Elsa turned and came down the stairs, stopping on the first step so that she retained a significant height advantage over Cora.

'What did you want to see me about?'

'It's . . . private. Perhaps we could talk in the kitchen? There's no one there at the moment.'

'I don't see . . .'

'Please, Elsa.'

Sensing the determination in Cora's voice, Elsa followed her along the passageway and into the kitchen.

'Close the door, would you, Elsa?'

Elsa pushed the door to with a click.

'Well?'

'I know, Elsa. I know everything.'

Elsa felt cold fingers running over her body. Surely Cora couldn't know about Max? She'd told no one, hugged her grief to her like a worn-out overcoat, so jealous of the love she had had for Max that she could never share it.

'I don't know what you mean.'

'About James. He told me all about what happened.'

'Oh.' There was a palpable sense of relief in Elsa's voice, which startled Cora.

'You know, about what went on between you in the surgery.'

'What about it?'

366

Cora fought down her anger. Hadn't this woman come close to wrecking everything she had with James? Hadn't she offered herself to him, knowing he was involved with Cora? But there seemed little point in starting a screaming match.

'So I wanted to tell you that it's all right. I was furious at first, but I know how lonely you are and . . .' Cora's voice tailed off. 'Look, I just wanted to say that I understand.'

'Understand?' Elsa's expression changed from blank incomprehension to sudden, open hostility. 'How dare you patronise me! You do-gooders think you know everything, don't you? You and James McArthur deserve each other.'

The following morning, Grace Quine stepped out of the front door of the *Bradda Vista* at eight-thirty precisely. It wouldn't do to be late, not even for an appointment at the veterinary surgery.

At the end of her arm swung an old wicker picnic basket, secured with buckled leather straps. It swung rather more than it might have done because it contained the loudly protesting Archie. There were three things that Archie particularly disliked: baskets, vets and Grace Quine.

Cora had offered to take Archie to the surgery, but Grace had been adamant. She was back, Archie was her husband's cat, not Cora's, and it was high time she was allowed to take some active part in running the *Bradda Vista*.

As she walked through the side-streets of Port Erin, Grace began to wonder if this was a good idea. Archie was yowling fit to wake the dead, and her wrist ached already from trying to keep the basket still.

'Shut up,' she hissed. 'Shut up, you wretched animal.'

George the postman came creaking up the road on his ancient bicycle.

'Mornin', missus, terrible windy last night.'

Grace sniffed.

'It's always freezing in this place.'

'Aye, well 'tis blowy on the west of the Island.' George

367

peered over his handlebars at the swaying wicker basket. 'What you got in there then, missus?'

'What does it look like?' she snapped. 'It's Archie. He's been in another fight.'

'Don't seem much wrong with him,' observed George.

'He's got a lump on his head.'

'Ah,' said George with some satisfaction, as though he was sole custodian of all knowledge about lumps on the head. 'That'll be an infection. When I was a lad my Nan had this old tom-cat, black as the Devil himself it was, and twice as fierce. Anyways, it goes an' gets into a fight an' gets this powerful big swellin' on its head. Anyways . . .'

'I really must be going,' interjected Grace. 'I'll be late.'

'Anyways,' continued George, undeterred, 'there was none of this fancy medicine an' such. So what does she do? She heats up the old kitchen range and pops him in the oven for a while. Burst the boil lovely, it did.'

'Lovely,' echoed Grace, wrinkling her nose. Disgusting, she declared in the privacy of her thoughts. 'But I'm sure Mr McArthur will be able to put him right.'

'Aye, no doubt he will,' nodded George. 'For them as can afford vets,' he added, with a countryman's disdain for unnecessary expenditure. 'But I tell you, if you pop him in the gas oven . . .'

'Thank you, George, I think I'd sooner get an *expert* opinion,' replied Grace and, bidding the postman a brisk 'good morning', she crossed the road and walked towards the surgery.

'Next.'

James was surprised to see Grace Quine sitting in his waiting-room as he popped his head round the surgery door. In the course of their slight acquaintance, Grace had never shown the slightest interest in animals – except as potential fur collars for her winter coat.

'Come in, Mrs Quine . . . Grace.'

Even though he had met her at various Quine family gatherings, James had never felt particularly at ease with her. Cold, that was what a lot of people called her; cold and heartless. But James saw her differently, suspecting that something dark and dangerously emotional might lurk beneath that frosty exterior. Not that that made her any more likeable, he thought to himself as she bustled into the surgery. He winced as she plonked the picnic basket down on the examination table, eliciting a growl of protest from its unwilling occupant.

'Good morning, James.' She sounded no less uncomfortable with first-name terms; James wondered vaguely why they bothered.

'How are you?'

'I'd be a lot better if it wasn't so unbearably cold. I haven't thawed out since I got back to the Island,' she added bitterly.

'Aye, well, you've picked just about the windiest spot on the Island – Port Erin's famous for it.'

'*I* didn't pick anything,' snapped Grace. 'It's William's lot who come from this godforsaken hole.'

'Well then.' James made an adroit change of subject. 'Who've you got in there?'

Grace fiddled with the buckles holding the basket lid.

'It's Archie. You'd better take a look at him.'

Reaching under the half-open lid, she tried to grab him by the scruff of the neck, but Archie was too quick for her. With a squeal of rage she sprang back, nursing a scratched hand.

'Little bastard.'

'You're all right, are you?' James took a cursory look at Grace's hand. 'Just a wee scratch, I'll pop some iodine on that before you go. Now, let's take a look at you, old feller.'

With a vet's practised dexterity, he whipped open the lid at precisely the moment that his other hand dived in to grab hold of Archie, immobilising him and hauling him onto the table.

'Been in the wars again, have you, boy?' He couldn't quite

suppress a smile at the sight of poor Archie, his head lopsided from the huge swelling on his right cheek.

'He will fight with the local cats. I can't see why; he gets fed.'

'It's instinct, I'm afraid. Poor old feller, that must hurt.' He palpated the swelling gently and looked up. 'It's an abscess. He's taken a swipe from some tom-cat's claw and it's got itself infected. I shall have to lance it so it can drain properly.'

Grace only half watched as James prepared the gleaming metal lancet, shaving off a little of Archie's fur to get at the abscess more easily. She was far more interested in James himself. How, she asked herself, could a mousy creature like Cora interest a man like James McArthur?

Resentment ate away at her. It wasn't that she particularly wanted James McArthur for herself, though it might be amusing to steal him from Cora, just for the hell of it. No, it was the injustice of it all. How come her sister-in-law, who had never had a single remarkable thing about her, could find herself an eligible bachelor; whilst she – the pretty one, the one who'd had everything in front of her – should be locked into a loveless, sterile marriage with William Quine?

They'd all said she'd make a beautiful dancer, all of them. She'd have done it, too, if it hadn't been for William. Then the pain hit her again, the pain that sneaked back to torment her just when she thought she had put it out of her mind. Killed it, like they'd said she'd killed her baby.

It wasn't fair. None of it was fair. And she wasn't going to stand for it, wasn't going to let Cora have everything her own way. She'd show her who was mistress of the *Bradda Vista*.

370

Chapter 27

Elsa knew she shouldn't be here. But lately, Mrs Pantin had been watching her like a hawk; there was no chance of taking anything from the camp hospital without being seen.

Which was why she had sneaked into James McArthur's surgery. It was risky of course, but what did that matter? Besides, no one was here, there was never anyone here on a Thursday afternoon.

She slipped through the surgery door into the dispensary. It was careless of James, not locking it. More careless still not to have remembered that Elsa still had a key to the drugs cupboard. But she was glad he hadn't. He owed her this.

Little had changed in the dispensary. Obviously James was every bit as untidy as he had been when they worked together. His favourite Fair-Isle pullover hung over the back of a chair, one sleeve trailing on the floor. Once, she would have picked it up and folded it. Not any more.

The key turned smoothly in the lock and it was the work of seconds to empty half the contents of a drum of pills into the bottle she had brought with her. Lid back on the drum, drum back on the shelf, label to the front. Done.

Just as she was dropping the key into her coat pocket, she heard the front door of the house open. Damn. Then a tuneless, strident voice picked up the strains of a sentimental old Irish song: 'I'll take you home again, Kath-*leeeen*.' Elsa knew that voice. It belonged to James's daily help – and if Dolores O'Hara found her in here, she would be hard-pressed to think of an excuse.

Hastily she slipped the bottle of pills into her pocket, unbolted the back door of the dispensary and looked outside. There was no one about except Fergus, dozing in his kennel with one eye open. He gave a little whine of greeting as she closed the door behind her.

'Good boy, Fergus,' she said softly. And he seemed to know that he had to keep quiet, because he laid his big shaggy head on his paws and followed her with big, expressive eyes as she hurried to the back gate.

Soon, there would be no more pain, no more memories, no more excuses.

'You should never have let her have that rug in her room,' Grace grumbled. 'She was obviously going to ruin it.'

'The baby was sick on it, these things happen.'

'It's ruined.'

'It's my rug and anyway, it'll clean up.'

'I still say . . .'

Cora took a deep breath and counted to ten. Grace had a lot of things to say.

'She was cold, Grace. And you've done nothing but complain about the cold ever since you got back here.'

'Well, if you lit the boiler . . .'

'Oh, and how am I supposed to do that? Where am I going to get the coal from? There's a war on, Grace, or have you forgotten that?'

The two women glared at each other across the kitchen table, open hostility mellowing – for the moment at least – into an uneasy truce. Grandad Quine didn't even bother looking up. He was beginning to wish he'd stayed in his room, even if it was warmer down here in the kitchen.

'I could hardly forget that, could I?' replied Grace, picking her gloves off the table in a murderous swipe, and easing the right one on over her scratched and bandaged hand. She was sure that cat was smirking at her, watching her from his basket by the gas range. 'Well, are we going?'

'Really, there's no need. I can go on my own.'

'This is William's guesthouse, I'm here to make sure it's properly looked after.'

'Yes, Grace,' muttered Cora between clenched teeth. 'But I don't think it takes two of us to buy a door handle.'

'Then *you* stay here,' suggested Grace, with disarming sweetness. 'I'm sure I can manage on my own.'

No fear, thought Cora, following Grace out of the back door into the freezing, salt-laden January air.

They walked side by side down to the hardware shop, together and yet not together, each wishing the other a million miles away.

'How's your hand?'

Grace flexed the fingers of her right hand and shrugged.

'I'm lucky I didn't get blood poisoning, vicious brute.'

'I expect being in pain put him in a temper,' observed Cora.

'He never used to be so touchy, not before.'

'Before what?'

'Before – when William and I were here.'

'Really?' The criticism stung, and Cora came back with: 'Didn't he sink his teeth into your leg, the Christmas before last? You remember, when you had the postmaster and his wife round for mince pies . . .'

'This door handle.' Grace produced it from the depths of her handbag.

'What about it?'

'I want to know how it got broken.'

'How should I know?'

'You ought to. You're supposed to be in charge, or that's what you're so fond of telling me.'

'I've got better things to do than go round counting door handles.'

'"Take care of the pennies and the pounds will take care of themselves", that's what William always says,' commented Grace smugly.

'Really? And does he know you've just bought yourself a new winter coat? And I bet that pair of gloves didn't come cheap.'

'Mind your own business!'

'That's exactly what I am doing. And I wish you'd mind yours.'

'It *is* mine.'

'The *Bradda Vista* belongs to William, not to you.'

'I'm his wife. What's his is mine.'

'Oh, so you're planning on doing your share of the hard work now, are you?'

'I would, if you'd let me.'

Cora spun round to look at Grace.

'Look here, Grace, I don't know what you're up to, but you were the one who dumped the *Bradda Vista* on me, remember? I've turned my whole life upside down for this place. You couldn't have run away from it faster if it had been on fire.'

'I'm back now.'

'Why, Grace? Because you were bored? And you expect to just walk straight back in and take over?'

'I'm only doing what I think is right. Offering you the benefit of some sensible advice.'

'Oh really? And you think you could run the *Bradda Vista* better than I can?'

The temptation was just too great for Grace to resist.

'Of course. You've done your best, but you don't know anything. With William, I have had several years' experience of the hotel trade.'

'Oh yes, I was forgetting all those nights you sat filing your nails while he did the dirty work.'

'Cora – you're such a little bitch.'

Cora shook her head.

'Not a bitch, Grace, just a realist.' She looked back over her shoulder at the distant shape of the *Bradda Vista*. How she'd hated the whole idea of going back there at first, and how strange it was to feel it now, pulling at her heart-strings. 'Are you telling me you want to run the guesthouse?'

Grace hesitated for a fraction of a second, but her natural impulsiveness took over.

'Yes.'

'Without any help from me?'

'I don't need your help.'

'Good. That's fine by me.' It wasn't, but she couldn't go back now. 'From now on, Grace, you're on your own.'

The unheated dance-hall at Derby Castle was hardly a romantic setting, and Rachel Kotkin felt tired and weepy.

'Come on, *bubeleh*.' Reuben stroked the hand that cradled Esther's sleeping head, and Rachel raised her dark eyes to his. 'The winter won't last for ever.'

'While we are here, in this place, it is winter always. Now even cousin Isaac is going. Why do they free everyone except us?'

'It will be us soon,' Reuben reassured her, though in his heart of hearts he was beginning to wonder if she might not be right.

'Pretty kid you got there,' cut in a grey-haired Lance Corporal who had been allocated the 'cushy' job of guarding the internees.

He reached out to touch Esther but Rachel shrank away, her eyes fixed on the bayonet at his waist, the rifle slung over his shoulder. Startled by the sudden movement, Esther began to cry.

'I got five o' me own at 'ome,' observed the soldier, clearly oblivious to Rachel's terrified reaction. 'Two girls an' three boys, an' another on the way.'

'Please, sir.' Reuben touched the soldier's arm. 'My wife . . . she is very afraid.'

'Afraid?' He looked puzzled.

'Of soldiers. They turned us out of our home in Germany. They almost killed us when we escaped from Holland.'

'It ain't like that 'ere, son. We're civilised, not like bloody Fritz.'

'That's right,' cut in a fierce-looking Sergeant. 'This man insulting the King is he, Corporal?'

'No, no, of course not,' sighed Reuben. He looked across at his wife. She looked like a frightened rabbit, the way she had done on the deck of the lifeboat. 'Here, give her to me. Come to *Pappi*, Esther.'

He took the child in his arms and she clutched at him with fat little fingers, her cries turning to laughter as he dandled her on his knee. As the two guards wandered off to another group of internees, Rachel leaned across the table.

'Oh, Reuben, how could you?'

'How could I what?'

'How could you insult that soldier?'

'I didn't mean to, I was only trying to protect you and Esther.'

'I know. I know.' Rachel stroked Esther's silky mop of black hair. 'But if we make these people our enemies, soon the whole world will be against us. And then how shall we ever be free?'

Sarah Rosenberg knotted her headscarf tightly underneath her chin, and pulled up the collar of her coat. It was a thin coat, made from the poorest woollen cloth, but it was all she could afford. The camp authorities sometimes arranged clothes allocations for destitute internees, but Sarah had no intention of admitting to destitution. Despite everything she had gone through, Sarah Rosenberg still had her pride.

It was precisely because of her pride that Sarah had wanted to join in the Service Exchange scheme, offering what skills she had in return for payment. At first it was only three pence a day for domestic work, paid in cardboard tokens cut from cornflake packets; then it rose to sixpence. Not much if you were rich – a fortune to Sarah Rosenberg.

Sarah now did two types of work: crocheting string bags

for sixpence a dozen, and helping out at the nursery. Without children of her own, she loved to be with them; to feel the exuberance and energy sparking from them, the warmth of their love.

On a January day like this, though, even the most dedicated nursery school teacher might think twice about going out. Rain was lashing down, the cloud level so low that it obscured the top half of Bradda Head.

She squelched out into the street. It had been raining for three days now, and it felt as if it had been raining everywhere in the whole world, since for ever. Head down, she strode out into the curtain of wetness, bracing herself against the wind that roared and gusted past her ears.

Turning down a narrow passageway between hotels, she saw them – at first just as blurs behind a curtain of rain, then as distinct figures. There were three of them, and she sensed instinctively who they were, even before she could make out their faces.

Marianne von Strondheim, Mathilde, and Inge. Waiting for her, just as she had known they would be, one day.

'Jew-pig, Jew-pig,' their voices hissed above the sizzling of the rain on the wet pavement. Sarah thought of turning tail and running, but looking back over her shoulder she saw another figure at the other end of the alleyway. A look-out. Whatever else the Nazi women might be, they were certainly organised in their brutality.

'Waiting for someone?' she asked, as coolly as she could manage.

'For you,' replied Marianne simply. 'Isn't that so, girls?'

'Waiting to teach you a lesson,' smirked Inge. 'Teach you that it's not right for stinking Jew-pigs to look after good Aryan children.'

Mathilde seemed quieter than the rest, restless.

'Marianne, this is dangerous.'

Marianne turned on her.

'Shut it, Mathilde, are you with us or against us?'

377

'With . . . of course.'

Marianne's face relaxed into a smile of sublime cruelty.

'Get her.'

The first blow struck Sarah's arm, raised to protect her from the stick, thin and flexible like a schoolmaster's cane. That stung, but she did not cry out. That would have been a waste of time and energy. All that mattered was getting out of this, and the instinct to survive was strong.

Then Inge grabbed her headscarf and tore it off. Hands seized great lumps of her hair and twisted it, jerking her head backwards. Her fingers scrabbled to free herself, but she was a prisoner of the pain.

Blows rained on her now, and she closed her eyes for a few moments, unable to bear the sight of the cruel faces, the eyes bright with pleasure at her suffering and humiliation. She had seen expressions like that before, in Germany; on the faces of the concentration camp guards.

'I think she's had enough.'

'Don't be stupid, Mathilde, we've hardly started. Come on, girls, let's have a little fun.'

'Do you want us to stop, Jew-pig?' taunted Inge.

'Go on, Jew-pig. Say "please".'

But Sarah wasn't going to plead with anyone, even though her head was spinning and blood was streaming from her split lip, mingling with the rainwater which trickled down her chin and neck.

They started throwing her about, pushing and shoving her like some kind of children's toy; flinging her between themselves, getting in the odd punch or kick.

'Let's *do* her. I want to really *do* her.' It was Inge's voice, heavy with excitement.

Mathilde's now: 'You're crazy!'

'Shut up, both of you. I want to hear her beg for mercy.'

It went on. It seemed to go on for ever, a red mist clouding Sarah's eyes as a cut opened on her forehead. But she said nothing. And she certainly didn't beg. They'd made a mistake if they thought she couldn't take this. She'd already taken far more than they could imagine in their darkest nightmares.

They threw her again. This time she stumbled and fell, like a sack of potatoes. There wasn't much point in fighting back, it would only make things worse. Then hands caught her. She waited for the pain but it didn't come, though the hands held her fast.

A voice whispered in her ear, pushing its way into her brain across the whirling dance-floor of her thoughts. Mathilde's voice. Mathilde was whispering to her. What was she saying?

'Next time I catch you, push me. I'll slip.'

Then she flung Sarah away from her. She landed on hands and knees on the wet and broken flagstones, and a sliver of shattered stone drove up through the flesh of her palm. She didn't feel the pain, only an incredibly calm anger. When Inge dragged her to her feet and shook her, throwing her towards Mathilde, she knew just what to do.

One hard shove in the guts, and Mathilde went flying – easily, too easily; Sarah knew that. She fell sideways, stumbling on the slippery roadway. And Sarah saw her chance. Running, slithering, fleeing, she broke through the gap and made for the end of the alleyway. For freedom – at least for a while.

Dripping wet and with grazed knees and palms, Mathilde hauled herself to her feet. She was pleased inside, pleased that Sarah had got away, but frightened too. And as she looked into Marianne's eyes she knew that she was right to be afraid.

'I'm so glad that you agreed to be one of our judges, Mr McArthur. It's a real honour.'

James smiled. Sometimes Miss Arnold, Dame Joanna's assistant, could be over-enthusiastic in her praise.

'The pleasure's all mine. And,' he added, surveying the rows of neatly laid-out stalls in the church hall, 'I'm not sure I'm really qualified to judge this sort of thing.'

'Nonsense,' cut in Bessie Teare. 'I've always thought you had an excellent eye for detail. Don't believe a word he says, Miss Arnold, he's far too modest for his own good.'

James and Bessie had come across to Port St Mary, where some of the internee women had organised a winter craft show.

'Come along, James, let's take a look at this lovely shell-craft.'

'Shell-craft!' James looked blank. 'I don't know anything about shell-craft.'

'You know what you like, and that's enough.' Bessie fingered a small, handmade box covered with patterns made from shells, but all the time she was watching James out of the corner of her eye. 'James . . .'

'Yes?'

'Are you quite all right? You look very pale.'

'Well . . .' It was really no use pretending that he felt A1. James had been feeling queasy since the morning, and now – all of a sudden – he felt much, much worse. 'To be honest I'm feeling a bit off-colour.'

'I thought as much. You've been overdoing it.'

'Oh, I don't think it's that . . .'

'I must ask Mrs O'Hara to keep a closer eye on you. I bet you've not been looking after yourself properly. You may be living on your own, James, but that's no excuse not to eat proper square meals.'

James put his hand to his stomach. The mere thought of any sort of meal, square or otherwise, made him feel queasier than ever. There was more, too: a pain in his guts, and a pounding headache which made him dizzy with its relentless thudding.

'Miss Teare . . . Bessie . . .'

'My dear James, whatever is the matter?'

'I . . . think I'd better sit down.'

'Yes. Yes of course, James. Just you wait here and I'll fetch you one of those folding chairs.'

But before Bessie had a chance to slide a chair underneath him James had slumped to the ground, his hand clasped to his belly and his face the colour of glazier's putty.

Chapter 28

James McArthur wasn't feeling well. Not well at all.

Dr Jefferson took off his stethoscope and stuffed it back into his Gladstone bag.

'You can put your pyjama jacket back on now, James. You're not going to die.'

'What's the matter with me, doc?'

'Food poisoning. Quite a nasty dose.'

'I suppose it must have been that pork pie.' James winced as he wriggled down under the sheets and tried to get warm. His stomach ached with vomiting and he was shivery and dizzy. 'Or that bit of home-cured ham Cyril Kneen gave me. It did look a wee bit past its best.'

The doctor shook his head.

'A medical man like yourself, James, you should be ashamed of yourself. You don't eat properly; there's food that's been in that pantry of yours for weeks.'

'You know how it is, doc.'

Dr Jefferson allowed himself a disapproving smile.

'Aye, James, I do. I well remember how it was when I was a young bachelor coming home to a cold and empty house.' He took off his half-moon glasses and gave his patient a searching look. 'Are you ready for your visitor now then?'

'Visitor?' James cast a critical eye around the sick-room. Mrs O'Hara had done what she could to tidy up the place but it still looked like a bomb had hit it. 'It's not George, is it? Or Bessie Teare? I know she means well, but I don't think I'm quite ready for all that beef tea.'

'It's Miss Quine. Your friend Cora.' The doctor rummaged in his bag and took out a small bottle. 'Two drops in warm water, four times daily. And don't try eating anything till you're stronger. Give that stomach of yours a rest! Now, shall I ask her to come up, or shall I say you're sleeping?'

'No, don't do that,' replied James hastily. He might be feeling several degrees below par, but that didn't mean he wanted to chase Cora away. There were so many things that remained unsaid between them. 'Show her up – I just wish I had a chance to tidy myself up a bit.'

'Don't fret yourself about nonsense. She's got her head screwed on, that one, which is more than I can say about you, James.'

Dr Jefferson opened the bedroom door and called down the stairs.

'You may come up now, Miss Quine.'

'Thank you, doctor.' She hurried up the stairs. 'How is he? I was so worried when I heard.'

'Come in and see for yourself.'

He held open the door and Cora stepped inside. The sight shocked her.

'James!'

His face was a funny shade of greenish-grey, the sort of colour you read about in books but never see in real life. All the reds and pinks and healthy browns seemed to have drained away, leaving pallid, sunken cheeks and cracked, bloodless lips.

'Hello, Cora.' He hesitated. 'I thought you might not come.'

It was true that she'd thought long and hard before coming. But Cora had known in her heart that she couldn't stay away.

'You look dreadful! What have you been doing to yourself?'

'Went and ate a dicky pork pie, didn't I?' said James sheepishly. 'Got myself a dose of food poisoning.'

'Don't you worry yourself, Miss Quine,' reassured Dr Jefferson, picking up his bag and jamming his hat back on his head. 'He'll live.' Looking from one to the other, he winked. 'There's nothing wrong with this young man that the love of a good woman couldn't cure.'

Cora hardly knew where to look. She busied herself pouring James a glass of barley water from the jug on his bedside table.

'That's right, my dear, make sure he gets plenty of fluids down him.' Dr Jefferson opened the door. 'I'll be sending you my bill, young man, so you'd best hurry up and get better.'

When he had gone, the silence in the room seemed to close in, the tension between Cora and James almost visible in the still air.

'I would have come yesterday,' said Cora, pulling up a chair. 'But you were so ill I thought I'd best leave you in peace.'

'I wasn't a pretty sight,' admitted James.

'You really think I'd worry about what you look like?'

'I don't know what to think. After – you know – what we talked about.'

Cora looked down at her knees.

'Let's not talk about that now.'

'We need to talk.'

'But not now. You promised you wouldn't,' she reminded him.

'I'm sorry. You know how it is when something's eating away at you – you just can't think about any damn thing else.' He shifted in the bed, feeling cold and shivery, hoping Cora wouldn't think he was playing it for sympathy.

'Are you all right?'

'Yes, fine, just a bit cold.'

'I could make you a hot drink – or a hot water bottle?'

'No, really, I'm fine. Mrs O'Hara said she'd pop round at lunch-time.'

'I'd like to help, that's all.'

'You do.' James's right hand crept out from under the blankets and reached out to hers. It stopped just short of touching her. 'Just by being here. It's good to see you.'

'Well, you'd better hurry up and get better,' said Cora, her fingers lightly brushing James's then drawing away. It was too soon. Too soon to forget. 'Uncle Harry says Fergus is eating him out of house and home.' She laughed. 'He stole one of Harry's old vests, took it right off the washing line and ate it!'

James groaned in mock despair.

'That dog is a born fifth columnist. I think I'll have him parachuted behind enemy lines.' He took a sip of barley water. 'So, tell me all the latest gossip.'

'Let's see. They're enrolling for the Manx Squadron of the ATC . . . There's going to be some sort of ARP exercise on the Island next month . . . There's a bit of a flap on at the camp hospital because some stuff has gone missing . . . Fenella's got herself promoted to corporal, I always knew she would . . . and Bessie's cousin's girl . . .'

'The one in the WRENs?'

'That's the one. Jennie, I think she's called. Anyway, she was injured in a bombing raid on her naval base.'

'Poor girl.'

'Oh, and everyone's saying the Home Office is going to set up a mixed internment camp at Port St Mary – you know, for the husbands and wives and the women with children.'

'So how are things at the *Bradda Vista*?'

Cora raised her eyes to heaven.

'I think I've done something very stupid.'

'What do you mean?'

'Grace and I had an argument, and I really lost my temper.'

James shrugged, then winced. Every muscle in his body ached.

'That's hardly surprising. I mean, Grace isn't the easiest person in the world to get on with.'

'No, but . . . well, she told me she thought I was doing a rotten job of running the *Bradda Vista* and she could do better.'

'Ah. The penny drops. You didn't tell her to go right ahead and prove it, did you?'

'I'm a fool, aren't I?'

James smiled.

'I'd say she's a bigger one,' he replied. 'Buck up, if it all goes wrong you'll be there to pick up the pieces – and if she comes up trumps and does a good job, you'll be free, won't you? Isn't that what you've wanted all along?'

'Yes. I suppose so. I don't know.' She looked at James and burst out laughing. 'Oh, James, how could I?'

'It's no more than she deserves.' James set down his glass on the bedside table. 'I'm sorry this place is such a tip.'

Cora surveyed the general clutter, the heap of unwashed clothes on the floor, the pair of braces dangling half in and half out of the wardrobe, the model aeroplanes arranged in a line along the top of the bookshelves. It reminded her of William's room when they'd been kids – in the days when they were inseparable.

'You're not fit to tie your own shoelaces, James McArthur,' she declared. She knew she loved him, that she could so easily be the woman to pick him up, dust him off, care for him the way he needed to be cared for. Yet there were things she wanted to do – places she wanted to go, a great big unknown out there, just waiting to be explored . . .

'You think I need some help?'

'Oh definitely.'

The laughing stopped as his hand reached out again, stroking her outstretched fingers. He needed her; and for the first time he was admitting it. But did she need him – and could she allow herself to let go of the pain she felt whenever she thought of him kissing Elsa Nadel?

Elsa waited for Grethe to leave the room then bolted the door. She turned back the blankets on the bed and lifted up the corner of the mattress.

Underneath lay forty-three little yellow pills, wrapped up

in a twist of blue paper from an old sugar bag. She knew there were exactly forty-three because she had counted them again and again, whenever she was alone.

She had heard about James from Cora – she hadn't wanted to hear any of it, but Cora was full of it all. Poor James this, and poor James that. Huh. It was funny really, ironic if you thought about it: for one mad moment when she'd stolen the pills, Elsa had thought how satisfying it would be to poison James. As things had worked out, she hadn't needed to – he'd gone and poisoned himself.

Elsa took out the twist of paper, sat down on the edge of the bed and unwrapped it. One, two, three . . . they were all there, little round yellow things, so colourful and so innocuous. It would be easy enough to swallow the lot, and then all her troubles would be over. Of course, that would be a coward's way out but she'd ceased to care about pride or self-respect. And besides, what other way out would be so sure and so swift as these little yellow pills?

Wrapping them up again, she pushed them back under the mattress and stood up. Outwardly she was calm, but inside she felt restless, as wild and tormented as the wind that buffeted and rattled the glass panes in the window frames.

Downstairs there was an argument going on – four or five voices raised in heated debate about something that didn't matter. At one time Elsa would have gone straight down and sorted it out, but now she could see how futile it had been to get so involved. They didn't care about her, for all their smiles and fine words they didn't give a damn; so why should she care about them? Why should she share her secret grief with them?

The wind rattled the glass again, so powerful that it made the panes bulge inwards before letting up for a few seconds, jiggling and rattling the loose window frame. There were still feathers of ice on the glass from last night – in this bitter wintry weather it was hardly ever warm in the *Bradda Vista*, especially since Grace Quine had taken over.

Walking across to the window, Elsa put her hands on the sill and looked out. In the distance, sea birds fought to stay in flight in a tumbling grey sky, rising and falling over a boiling, spitting sea. The distant crash of the breakers seemed to insinuate itself into her mind like a whispering voice.

'The sea, Elsa. Max loved the sea and it was the sea that took him away . . .'

Yes. The great grey, fathomless ocean. Why hadn't she thought of it before? The sea was calling to her and she had refused to listen to it until now.

If she listened to its call, the sea might reunite them still.

It might be a wild and inhospitable February day, but the inhabitants of House forty-one were celebrating.

'*Gai gezunterhayt*, Isaac.' Reuben patted him on the back. 'Go in health, you have waited too long.'

Isaac accepted his friend's congratulations with a philosophical, slightly wistful nod.

'You are a good man, Reuben Kotkin, the truest *mensch*. It is not right that they should release me and leave you and Rachel here.'

Reuben topped up Isaac's coffee cup from the pot on the stove. Champagne it wasn't, but they had been saving up for weeks to give the latest batch of released internees a proper send-off.

'It will be our turn soon.'

'You are a married man, and I am just a schoolteacher. Why is it that they release me to do farm work and leave you locked up?' Isaac drained his cup, wiping the back of his hand across his face. '*Ay*, there is no reason to this war, no reason at all.'

'God willing it will soon be over,' cut in Abraham Fischbein, helping himself from the tray of sandwiches donated by the Artists' Cafe. 'Let me tell you, *boychik*, when you take your Rachel and that pretty daughter of yours to the tribunal, they will see how foolish they are that they should lock up a fine tailor.'

'Of course,' joked Isaac, 'it is my firm opinion that you are only kept here because you haven't yet finished the camp commandant's new pair of trousers!'

Reuben joined in the hilarity as best he could. He was a serious man by nature, and if he was scrupulously honest with himself he found it difficult to be wholly happy for Rachel's cousin Isaac. Oh, he was glad for him, of course he was. Isaac was a fine man and should never have been locked up in the first place; but then, should he and Rachel? The camp was going to be a lonelier place for Reuben Kotkin once Isaac was gone.

'Have you heard, Kotkin?' asked Fischbein, with a mouth full of food.

'Heard what?'

'They say there is to be a camp for husbands and wives.'

'*Ach*, Fischbein, you know they have been talking about it for months now, ever since the camps opened. Why should it happen now?'

'But Kotkin, they say—'

'Who says?'

'*They* say this time it is really going to happen. There will be a camp at Port St Mary, and all the husbands and wives and children will be able to live together.'

'If you say so,' shrugged Reuben.

He had long since trained himself out of excessive enthusiasm, frightened that too much optimism would lead to yet another disappointment. Odd really; he had always been the optimistic one and Rachel the one who feared the worst; but these days their positions seemed reversed. Ever since Rachel had had the baby, she had gained visibly in strength and determination, and Reuben had found himself not only loving and respecting her, but admiring her too.

'It will happen,' Fischbein nodded vigorously. 'It will happen, you mark my words.'

'Not that it will be of any interest to Reuben,' replied Isaac. 'Reuben is going to be released soon, aren't you, my boy?'

It was a poor sort of celebration, thought Reuben; but it was the best that wartime and poverty could afford. When all was said and done they were lucky to be alive, and even the chronic moaners in the camp realised that, deep down. The Manx Regiment were in the Far East, bombs were raining down on London and no amount of cheery BBC propaganda could hide the pain the British were suffering at the deaths of their sons and daughters. Now he too had a daughter, Reuben was beginning to understand how that must feel.

'Sachs,' he began, but Sachs wasn't there. He wondered why. Whenever there was a party, a practical joke, any sort of gathering, Sachs would be there in the thick of it, driving everyone mad. But this morning Sachs had seemed down in the dumps, not himself at all.

Reuben glanced around. At first he couldn't see Sachs and thought he wasn't in the room, then he spotted him, huddled on a chair by the blacked-out window, hands cradling a tea-cup with no handle. On the window-ledge beside him lay an untouched slice of cake. He looked more like Ernst Müller than Drexel Sachs.

'Sachs, why don't you come and join us? Isaac must soon go to pack his suitcase.'

Sachs shook his head.

'Wish him well from me, Kotkin.'

'Why not wish him well yourself? Is there something wrong?'

'Nothing you should bother yourself with.'

If this was designed to drive Reuben away, it had the reverse effect. Pushing the plate out of the way, he perched himself on the window-ledge.

'If it bothers you it bothers me.'

'You're a stubborn man, Reuben Kotkin.' A flicker of a smile twitched Sachs's lips, then he signed. 'If you must know, *shtarker*, I have had some bad news.'

'What news?'

'They have turned me down for the Pioneer Corps. They

say I have something wrong with my heart – a murmur they called it.'

'Your heart!'

Sachs waved away his concern.

'Oh, I am well enough, but they say I am just a poor *nebech*, nothing but a weakling. And so they say I must stay here.'

'Oh, Sachs, why did you not tell me before?'

'You have the power to get me out of here? Into the Pioneers?'

'You know I don't. I can't even get myself out.'

'Then what was the point in telling you?'

'True.' Reuben broke off a piece of bread and stuffed it into his mouth, chewing thoughtfully. 'So you'll just have to stay here with the rest of us and make the best of it.'

'It wouldn't be so bad,' sighed Sachs, 'if I had someone.' His eyes met Reuben's. 'You know – someone special. You have Rachel, Isaac has his pig farm to go to, but what have I got?'

'You have us.'

Sachs laughed.

'Indeed I have, Reuben. Take no notice of me – I'm just hankering after a decent cup of coffee and a pretty girl on my arm.'

The light of battle was in Grace Quine's eyes.

Rolling up her sleeves, she knotted a turban over her neatly styled hair. It was the prettiest, most stylish of flowered turbans. Well, she might be taking her new housekeeping duties seriously, but that was no reason to look dowdy.

Cora was out of the way, and that made Grace feel positively triumphant. If Cora chose to spend her time playing nurse to James McArthur, that suited Grace very well indeed. If Cora was not around, Cora could not be tempted to interfere.

Organisation, that was what the *Bradda Vista* needed. Grandad Quine had been doubtful when she outlined her plans to him, but then what did Thomas Quine know about running a boarding house? William was going to be so impressed when he came home on leave. She'd show him that he couldn't treat her like a child.

Reaching the first-floor landing, she walked straight into Grethe and Elsa's room. She didn't bother knocking – why should she? These women were effectively criminals and Grace saw no reason to treat them indulgently. They might be up to all sorts of things when her back was turned.

Grethe was alone in the room, writing a letter, when the door burst open.

'Miss Herzheim?'

Grethe pushed back her chair and stood up.

'You could knock before you barge in. I might have been undressed.'

Grace ignored this trifling objection.

'This room is a disgrace.'

Grethe bristled with quiet rage.

'What's it got to do with you?'

Grace raised one eyebrow. She was several inches shorter than Grethe but that didn't seem to worry her.

'It's got everything to do with me. I own this guesthouse, and while you are here you will abide by my rules.'

'Oh, and what will you do if I don't? Throw me out? Send me back home?' Grethe smiled. 'Perhaps I should misbehave more often.'

Grace turned away, this time visibly irritated.

'I might have expected that a woman like you wouldn't know how to behave,' she snapped.

'Really?' replied Grethe. 'What's your excuse?'

Grace slammed the door behind her on the way out, annoyed that a common prostitute could have got the better of her. Next time she'd be prepared for that slut's acid tongue.

But for now, there were other things to attend to. The food, for example.

She was just in time to find Maria Bertorelli in the kitchen, sleeves rolled up to the elbows, strong red hands kneading a huge white ball of bread dough.

'Ah, Mrs Bertorelli. I want a word with you.'

The Italian woman swung round, startled by the harshness of Grace's tone.

'You wish something, Signora Quine? I very busy.'

'So I see.' Grace inspected the ball of dough. 'You are making white bread?'

Maria looked completely baffled.

'Si. Si, Signora. The bread, it is white.'

'In future you will use the brown National Flour for the internees, and white for myself and Mr Quine. He and I prefer white bread, it's more refined.'

'I . . . not understand.'

No, of course you don't, you stupid woman, thought Grace. But she realised that she must make allowances for these people with their simple peasant outlook and limited command of English.

'The brown bread is quite good enough for the internees, and it is cheaper. I have costs to think about, Mrs Bertorelli.'

'You say I must make different bread for internees?'

'Yes. And you will cut down on the amount of meat you use in the evening meals. Some of you,' she looked Maria Bertorelli's considerable bulk up and down, 'some of you are getting quite fat.'

Maria stared at Grace, open-mouthed.

'Why you say these things?' she demanded indignantly. 'Why you do this to us? Miss Cora, she treat us well, everybody like her. Why you do this . . .?'

A tear escaped from her eye and she wiped it away, leaving a smudge of flour across her red cheek. Grace clenched her teeth in exasperation. Why did these silly women have to be so emotional and so hostile? Grace had a good mind to have this one replaced. She didn't like the funny Italian food she cooked anyway.

If Maria had wanted to infuriate Grace deliberately, she could not have done so more effectively.

'Cora is no longer in charge of this house. *I* am,' said Grace, icily polite. 'And since you are being paid for your domestic duties, you will do exactly as I say.'

Maria Bertorelli took a last, loving look at her baking. Her hands were covered in little white threads of sticky bread dough, which she wiped off on a tea-towel.

'Signora Quine, I am not slave, not slave, you understand?' She dropped the tea-towel on the scrubbed pine table-top. 'I not work for you any more, I not take your money.'

Grace watched Mrs Bertorelli rush, weeping, from the kitchen. It was annoying, of course, that she should have left right in the middle of her baking – but it would be the easiest thing in the world to replace her with someone younger, more efficient, more economical. The *Bradda Vista* was full of cooks, simply longing to be paid for their work.

The house would take a little time to sort out, of course. But all in all, Grace decided, things were really going quite well.

Chapter 29

'What day is it today?'

The man they called Ernst Müller stood in the middle of the exhibition room and turned slowly round, his eyes travelling across every one of the paintings, woodcuts and sculptures on display.

The young British officer turned from a group of earnest Czech sculptors to look at the thin-faced man with the grey, staring eyes. To be fair, Müller didn't look quite as wild as he had done when he'd first arrived in the camp. One of the barbers had been at his hair, exposing more of the long, deep scar running up the left side of his face from jawbone to scalp; and that Kotkin fellow had tailored him a makeshift suit of clothes. But Ernst Müller was still a man most people avoided. He was too intense, too confused, too tragic: a too-vivid reminder of what any one of them might have become if they'd been on the *Arandora Star*.

'What did you say?'

'Today. What day is it?'

Captain Jeremy Hollingsworth shuffled his feet.

'Wednesday. The fifteenth.'

'Of?'

'February.'

Müller nodded sagely, as though confirming something to his silent inner self.

'I know it is a special day. If only I could remember why.' He raised those sad grey eyes which always turned the young captain's blood to ice. 'Max would remember.'

Captain Hollingsworth patted him on the shoulder. He didn't know what else to do – like everyone else, he tended to treat Ernst Müller with the sort of patronising kindness you'd reserve for an old dog. Really it wasn't right that the man was still behind the wire, though what else they could do with him, he didn't know.

'There's no such person as Max,' he said gently.

'No?'

'You know there isn't. The doctor told you so, didn't he? You're Ernst Müller.' Desperate to change the subject, the young captain glanced down at the painting clutched in Max's hands. 'Is that one of yours for the exhibition?'

The clouds in Müller's eyes seemed to disperse. He nodded.

'You think it is good enough?'

'Let me see.'

This, at least, was something that Jeremy Hollingsworth could deal with. He had been at art school in the summer of 1939, as convinced as all his friends were that there would be no war. If only he had been right, perhaps he would still have his right arm instead of a sleeve hanging loose from the elbow, his hand shot clean off in the retreat from northern France.

Müller's hands released the picture slowly and painfully, like a mother letting go of her newborn child. The captain balanced it adroitly between left hand and knee. It took his breath away.

'It's brilliant. Quite brilliant.' His eyes scanned the wild sea, the oranges and purples and sick yellows of the stormy sky. It was half naturalistic, half abstract; if you looked into the waves, you could almost make out other pictures, faces . . .

'There are others – that one there, the one by the door. And that small one . . .'

Now that he had seen Müller's work, it was easy to pick out his other paintings from the dozens crowded onto the whitewashed wall. They were both brilliant and disturbing, as though they were the contents of Müller's damaged mind, spewed with pain onto paper, canvas, wooden panels, anything he could get his hands on.

'You know, Müller, I could swear I've seen some of your work before – or something quite similar. Were you an artist before the war?'

Müller reacted like a small child confronted with something dark and frightening, wrapping his arms around himself, hugging his fear to him.

'I don't know.' The grey eyes flicked from the picture in Hollingsworth's hand to his face and back again. 'Max knows. Max knows.'

Max. Why was Müller obsessed with this non-existent Max? He even scrawled the name across the bottom of his paintings, in great black slashes of paint. Something was niggling at the back of Hollingsworth's mind, but he gave up trying to remember. There were other things, more urgent than Ernst Müller's wild fantasies.

Ernst was trying to remember, too. He looked deep into the waves and the pictures resolved themselves instantly. He knew they were there, because he had put them there – swirling, blurred pictures of faces. The same face over and over again. A woman's face, the one he kept seeing in his dreams. He was sure that she was important to him, yet the butterfly of memory kept fluttering just out of reach. What was her name? Alice, Elisabeth, Esther . . .?

Max would know. But Max wasn't saying.

Thomas Quine pushed the remnants of a burnt rissole round and round his plate. Bonzo sat dejectedly at his feet, whiskers drooping, round eyes fixed on his master.

'Eat your own, boy; you don't want none of this,' grunted Thomas, dropping his fork with a clatter.

Cora eyed him from the other end of the table.

'Not eating up, Grandad?'

Thomas gave a loud belch and rubbed his stomach through his waistcoat.

'Got any bicarb, gel? This stuff fair sits on your stomach.'

Cora sighed. She felt guilty. After all, this was her doing.

'I'll get you some.' She gathered up the half-empty plates. Bonzo gave them a quick sniff and backed off with a sneeze of disgust. 'George's pigs will have to have this lot.'

'You got it in for them pigs, or what?' joshed Thomas, pouring himself a nip of medicinal brandy to take the taste away.

Cora scraped the charred leavings into the pig bin.

'Shall I cook you something else?'

'I couldn't.' His stomach rumbled ominously. 'I thought Grace said that Romanian girl could cook.'

Cora managed a grim half-smile.

'Grace said *anybody* could cook,' she corrected him. 'And I think Nadia rather likes the idea of earning sixpence a day.'

Thomas shook his head.

'I'm too old to stand all this,' he announced. 'Can't you two sort this nonsense out?'

'Oh, Grandad, I'm sorry.' Cora wiped her hands and sat down beside him. 'Really I am. But Grace is right – this place belongs to her and William, and if she insists on running it, what can I do but let her?'

'You could talk some sense into her.'

'I've tried.' Cora brought a bottle of Milk of Magnesia over to the table. 'Now I'm just going to let her get on with it. There's nothing else I can do.'

Thomas swallowed the slimy white liquid and wiped the chalky residue off his mouth.

'She's makin' a powerful mess of things, you know that?'

Cora did know; and it hurt. She hadn't spent a year building this place up just for Grace to ruin everything. But she had to let go.

'That's her problem. She'll have to sort it out herself.'

'You're as stubborn as she is, you know that, gel?'

'Stubborn, pigheaded, you can call it what you like,

Grandad. But I've done arguing with her. If she wants my advice she'll have to ask for it.'

Advice was the last thing on Grace's mind. Everyone wanted to give her advice, and she was sick of it. Why did people insist on trying to live her life for her? As she stomped up the stairs to the first floor, she tweaked her hair into place and tried to ignore Rachel Kotkin, standing outside her room trying to attract Grace's attention, the baby on her hip.

'Please, if I could speak with you . . .'

'Later.' Grace waved her away irritably.

'I only wanted to ask . . .'

'Later. I'm busy. Can't you talk to Frau Kessler about it?'

Without waiting for Rachel's reply, Grace bustled past and pushed open the door of Cora and Thomas's apartment. She didn't bother knocking – she didn't see why she should.

Cora was standing over that smelly little gas-ring she'd had installed, warming something in a saucepan. Grace wrinkled her nose.

'Ugh, what's that horrible smell?'

'Rissoles,' said Thomas.

'They smell disgusting – all burnt. You surprise me, Cora, I thought you were such a perfect little housewife.'

Cora's back stiffened as she took a deep breath and held it, determined not to let her annoyance spill over into a lack of control. Lose her temper, and Grace would have won. She turned round with the calmest of smiles.

'Actually, Nadia cooked them.'

Grace professed a lack of interest.

'Oh well, if you will eat the same food as the internees.'

'You don't think they should eat properly?'

'I think they should eat what they're given and shut up.'

'Oh, and what does Dame Joanna think about that – and Mrs Pantin?'

Cora couldn't help feeling a sneaky thrill of satisfaction. She knew she had hit one of Grace's sore spots.

'Don't you talk to me about that Pantin woman. She's an

interfering do-gooder who likes poking her nose into other people's business.'

'I'm sure she means well.'

'Means well!' Grace took the lid off the teapot and peered inside. It was empty. 'These German women go whining to her and she listens to every word they say.'

'She has to. It's her job, she's a welfare worker.'

'And that chaplain's no better, telling me the house representative has been complaining about "ill-treatment". These pacifists don't know what they're talking about. Make me some tea will you, Cora?'

'You know where the kettle is,' replied Cora sweetly. 'Why don't you make it yourself?'

Thomas looked from his granddaughter to his grandson's wife and felt like knocking their heads together.

'I'm off,' he announced, picking up his cap and jamming it on his head.

'But it's cold out there,' said Cora, surprised.

'It'll be a darn sight warmer than it is in here.'

Grace watched the door close behind Thomas and turned back to Cora.

'Now look what you've done.'

'What *I've* done?' Cora ladled a dollop of porridge out of the saucepan and into a bowl, then dragged the kettle onto the gas-ring and sat down at the table.

Grace drummed her fingers impatiently on the table-top.

'It won't do, you know.'

'What won't?'

'You've been far too slack with these women. And you haven't made a pennyworth of profit.'

'Profit?' Cora stared at Grace, her spoon poised halfway between dish and open mouth.

'This is a guesthouse, not a charity.'

'You can't make a profit when you're trying to feed a grown woman on a guinea a week.'

'You can if you stop molly-coddling them. All these fresh

eggs, butcher's meat, I even saw them eating cake, for goodness' sake!'

'That was a birthday cake for one of the Italians. She saved up her rations and paid for it out of her own money.'

'Really? Then she should be paying for her keep, not enjoying a free holiday at our expense.' Grace glanced across at the gas-ring. 'Will that tea be ready soon? Only I have to check up on the second-floor toilets. If you don't keep an eye open, they don't clean them properly, you know.'

'And they won't if they think you're standing over them,' countered Cora.

'Well, if that's what you think, it's probably just as well I've taken charge,' replied Grace. 'Oh, by the way,' she added, 'did I tell you William's coming home? I had a letter from him yesterday. He has fourteen days' leave coming up.'

She enjoyed the look of astonishment on Cora's face. Grace liked to keep people on their toes, and it gave her a particular satisfaction to wrong-foot Cora; organised, respectable, popular Cora who was always right. Not this time though.

To her surprise, Grace found that she was actually looking forward to seeing William again. He was going to be so surprised and so proud when he saw what she'd done with the *Bradda Vista*.

Sarah Rosenberg was in pain. Not the stabbing pain she had experienced at first, but the dull, continuous ache which came from injuries only half-healed. The physical scars would fade with time, but other, deeper injuries might never heal.

The street attack had left its mark on Sarah. With cracked ribs, a gashed forehead and a sprained wrist, she might seem to have escaped relatively lightly; but every time she closed her eyes she could see the laughing, spiteful faces. Sometimes it seemed like the whole world was filled with hatred.

She walked alone along the blustery cliff-top, self-contained and self-sufficient. Sarah had found her own way of coping now: she trusted no one, relied upon no one save herself, not even Rachel, though in happier times they might have been close. It was better this way. This way, no one had the power to hurt her, and in time she might achieve her own kind of happiness.

February really was a wild month, the wind rippling across the cliff-tops and whipping the sea up into foam-crested peaks. But Sarah quite liked this weather. She found the rawness of it exhilarating, and since few other people – locals or internees – ventured outside unless they absolutely had to, it gave her an opportunity to be on her own.

Descending the zig-zag path down the cliffside, Sarah had her work cut out simply to cling to the handrail and not be plucked off by a gust of wind. Her still-bandaged ribcage ached with every breath, and her weakened right hand found it difficult to grip the slippery metal rail.

Down on the beach, the weather was quieter; the sheltering bowl of the cliffs created an artificial calmness belied by the thundering sea. The tide was a little way out and the sand was soft and wet, ribbed into wavy patterns by the retreating sea and decorated here and there with clumps of seaweed, shells and splintered spars of driftwood. Sarah walked along, letting the wind tug at her hair and the spray lash her face, making the skin pink and tingly. At each step, her feet left water-filled depressions in the sand.

There was someone else on the beach. That fact alone was worthy of note. On a day like today, the world preferred to take itself indoors. But the solitary figure of a woman was walking at the other end of the beach. Sarah walked a little more quickly towards her, interested to see who it was, though instinctively cautious – it might be someone she'd rather not meet.

As she got nearer, she noticed two things about the woman. First, she was all dressed up. Not wrapped up against the weather, but actually dressed up in her best clothes, as if she was going somewhere special. A long grey coat with a fur collar, small feathered hat pinned to her short brown hair, high-heeled shoes . . .

Sarah stopped dead in her tracks for a few seconds. She had just recognised the woman – it was Elsa Nadel, one of the Germans from Rachel's house. The one who had been kind to Rachel when she was alone and afraid. Instinct told Sarah to keep away; hadn't this woman been seen talking to Marianne von Strondheim? But another, deeper instinct clicked into play. For the second thing that Sarah had noticed was that Elsa Nadel wasn't just walking towards the sea, she was walking into it.

She looked around. There was no one else in sight – no policewoman, no fisherman, no one at all. No one but Sarah Rosenberg and the woman walking slowly and deliberately into the water.

'Elsa! Elsa Nadel!'

Ankle-deep, then wading in deeper to the knee, to the thigh, the hip . . . the woman looked neither back nor around her. She just kept on staring ahead of her, as though hurrying towards something – or someone – that Sarah could not see.

'Elsa, oh my God, Elsa, what are you doing?'

Sarah started running. Every step was an agony, each indrawn breath making her muscles spasm as her cracked and bruised ribs struggled to obey her. Adrenaline made her heart pound and a cold sweat started to prickle on her skin.

'Elsa, come back. Listen to me, come back!'

Whether or not Elsa was listening, she made no sign that she had heard. She kept on wading into the water, more slowly now because the waves were powerful and the water resisted, pushing against her waterlogged clothes as she forced herself into the sea.

Sarah cried out, all the breath leaving her body as she ran into the water and the icy chill hit her. Suddenly she was afraid – not just for Elsa but for herself. She hadn't felt such intensity of emotion for a very long time, not since she and her mother and two brothers had been taken away to Buchenwald.

Suddenly, and very powerfully, she knew that she did not want to die.

'Elsa . . . are you crazy?'

Perhaps it was she who was crazy, thought Sarah as she splashed and floundered closer to the German woman she had never trusted, never liked. Why should she endanger her own precious life to save this woman? Why not just stand back and let her drown if that was what she wanted?

Elsa was out of her depth now. Sarah saw her splash and struggle for a few seconds, her body fighting to overcome the urge to oblivion, then . . . nothing. Elsa was lying face-down on the water, limp, like so much flotsam.

No, no, no, this couldn't happen. She couldn't allow it to happen. Elsa, you bitch, she muttered under her breath, anger pushing her on. You German bitch, don't die on me. Don't you bloody well die before I get to you.

Almost there, almost within reach. Sarah fought the waves as they pulled her off her feet, and lunged forward for the inert, waterlogged body of Elsa Nadel. But the strong undercurrents pulled her off-balance and washed Elsa further away, just beyond the grasp of her outstretched hand.

I won't let you do this, I won't let you, she kept repeating in her head. Whatever it is you're trying to escape from, I won't let you. I didn't escape from my pain, why should you?

Now . . . almost. She had a mouth full of seawater. Coughing and spluttering, Sarah shook the wet hair from her stinging eyes. She was dangerously cold, knew she had to get both of them out of this deadly sea before numbness and exhaustion took over.

Now.

Her fingers grabbed hold of the collar of Elsa's coat. Sarah let out a cry as pain shot through her wrist and chest. Why was she doing this? She couldn't answer, only feel the elation of knowing that she had Elsa in her grasp.

With the greatest difficulty, she succeeded in lifting Elsa's head out of the water. The eyes were closed, the open mouth dripping water, but as Sarah turned her over and began half swimming, half scrambling back towards the shore, the seemingly lifeless body let out a low, choking groan.

'Elsa, that's it, come back to me, Elsa, I'm not letting you go this easily.'

'No. No . . . Max, let me go to Max . . .'

The salt-reddened eyes opened, and Elsa began struggling, gasping, hands fighting feebly to push Sarah away. Sarah almost wept for the pain of trying to breathe and hold Elsa still.

'I swear if you don't stop struggling I'll hit you,' coughed Sarah, a wave breaking over her and very nearly tearing Elsa out of her grasp.

'Don't make me . . . don't make me live. Max is waiting . . .'

'Shut up, lie still, stop fighting me.'

'Max . . .' The voice tailed off into a sob of defeat, and the fight was over, all the strength and resistance suddenly draining from Elsa's body.

And Sarah began the long, painful process of dragging her back towards the shore. Towards life.

Cora looked down at the figure in the bed.

'I think you'd better tell me exactly what happened.'

She looked from Elsa to Sarah and back again, sensing a complicity between them. Cora had known that something very odd was going on, the moment that Sarah Rosenberg and Elsa Nadel appeared on the doorstep of the *Bradda Vista*, soaked to the skin and half dead with cold.

'Elsa . . . had an accident,' said Sarah, and promptly clammed up.

'I was walking on the beach,' said Elsa, her face even whiter than the pillow on which she lay, a fresh bruise showing crimson on her temple. 'A wave washed me into the sea.' Her eyes met Sarah's. 'Sarah rescued me.'

Cora shook her head.

'You really expect me to believe that, do you? Because if

you do, you must think I'm naive or stupid or both.' She sat down on the edge of the bed. 'Why don't you tell me what really happened?'

'I've told you,' said Sarah.

Elsa remained silent, but there were tears at the corners of her eyes. Cora felt shocked; she had never seen Elsa cry before, had hardly seen her show any trace of emotion except anger over the last few months.

'I can't . . .'

Cora thought hard. Should she let it drop, accept Elsa's explanation even though it was patently untrue?

'It is something to do with your brother?' she hazarded, unprepared for the reaction her words provoked. Elsa's white face dissolved into a mask of tears, her whole body shaking, her fingers clenching and unclenching convulsively, raking the quilted bedspread.

'Max is dead.' Elsa's voice was very small; a child's voice, vulnerable and scarcely audible.

Cora felt a cold shiver run down her spine, erecting the tiny blonde hairs on the back of her neck.

'Dead? But Elsa . . . he can't be, we would have known . . .'

Elsa's red-rimmed eyes were fixed on some indeterminate point in the middle distance.

'Max is dead.' This time her voice was clearer, firmer; as though she had just come to the realisation that what she said was true. 'He's left me.'

Sarah came forward, a thick grey blanket wrapped round her, her hair hanging in black rats'-tails. Her eyes seemed huge and round in her small, oval face.

'How do you know this thing, Elsa? Is it true?'

Elsa met her gaze.

'They sent me a letter. The Information Bureau. They said he was on the *Arandora Star*.' Her voice faltered as she choked back a sob. 'That he had taken another man's place.' The tears flowed freely, silently streaming down her face. 'He should have been safe.'

'Oh, Elsa.' Cora wished she knew what to do, but there was such a barrier of awkwardness and grief between them. She would have liked to put her arm round Elsa, touch her hand, find some way of making contact, but she seemed chilled right down to her soul. 'Oh, Elsa, how long have you known this?'

'A few months.'

Of course. It all clicked into place now – the mood swings, the sudden apathy, the fallings-out with Grethe and Rachel. Perhaps even the comfort that Elsa had sought with James McArthur . . .

'But, Elsa, why didn't you tell anyone?'

'Why should I?' Elsa stopped avoiding Cora's gaze and met it, full-on. 'Why should I share my pain with you? He was my brother, mine.' She rested her forehead on her hand, as though the weight of her head had grown too heavy for her shoulders. 'Today . . . today is . . .'

A gasp of remembrance escaped from Cora's lips. How could she have been so stupid?

'Today is your birthday, isn't it?'

Elsa shook her head.

'*Our* birthday. Mine and Max's. The sea took him and I wanted it to take me too. But the sea doesn't want me. It's so hard . . .'

'I know.' Cora tried to imagine how Elsa must feel, how she must have felt over these past months; but all she could feel was her own guilt at not understanding sooner, not guessing what was wrong.

Sarah hesitated before she spoke – what concern was it of hers? Every concern, whispered a voice inside her head. This woman threw her life away, and you have given it back to her, whether she wants it or not.

'I won't say I ever warmed to you, Elsa Nadel,' she said. 'But I never took you for a coward.'

Elsa looked at her in surprise.

'I don't understand.'

'Dying is easy, Elsa. It's staying behind that's hard, going on living when all you want is to give up.

'Don't you think it's time you stopped feeling sorry for yourself?'

Chapter 30

Sarah waited, shifting uneasily on the hard wooden bench. The woman police sergeant sitting next to her touched her on the arm.

'Cup of tea?'

Sarah shook her head.

'No, thank you.'

'Please yourself. But I'll have one if you're brewing up, PC Cammish.'

Sarah's eyes roamed restlessly around the dull yellow walls, decorated here and there with official notices and signs: 'Prevention of Damage by Rabbits Act, 1940'; 'Isle of Man (War Legislation) Act, 1940'; 'Careless talk costs lives'; 'Defence Lighting Restriction (No 4) Order' . . .

She had not wanted any of this, but the decision had been taken out of her hands; and so here she was at the police station, feeling as though *she* was the accused, not the women she could hear talking in the inner room.

Thoughts whirled through her brain. These past days had been strange, to say the least. She had only just begun to recover from the vicious street attack when Elsa Nadel had taken it into her head to kill herself.

Not that that was the official story. Everyone knew what had been in Elsa's mind that February afternoon, but Dr Jefferson had been told that it was an 'accident', and he'd seemed to accept the explanation, even if he didn't believe it. Better to accept a white lie than have poor Elsa whisked off to Ballamona mental hospital. In her heart of hearts Sarah

Rosenberg felt a sneaking sympathy for Elsa Nadel.

The door to the Inspector's office opened and a constable stuck his head out.

'You can bring her in now.'

'Come along, we haven't got all day.'

Sarah followed the sergeant into the Inspector's office. He was a grey-haired man in his fifties, very important-looking in his uniform with its shiny buttons.

'Miss Sarah Rosenberg?'

'Yes.' Sarah caught the look in the sergeant's eye. 'Yes, sir.'

He shuffled a pile of papers on his desk.

'You understand that we require you to identify the women who attacked you in Port Erin on the afternoon of the fourteenth?'

Sarah nodded.

'We are going to take you into a room where you will see a number of suspects. You will tell me if these are the women who attacked you. You understand?'

'Yes. Yes, I do.'

'You think you can do that? These are very serious charges.'

She found his tone of voice irritating. He wasn't hostile, but it was like being a child again.

'Inspector, I would never forget their faces. *Never*.'

'Good. You may proceed, Sergeant.'

The sergeant led Sarah along a dimly lit corridor, past a row of cells which recalled the cold, friendless days in Holloway. Sarah felt chilled to the bone.

'Through here.' She held open the door. 'Take your time. You must be *sure*.'

This is a farce, thought Sarah as she stepped into the room. There they were: Marianne von Strondheim, Inge, Frieda, Mathilde, and three others she didn't recognise, brought in to make up the numbers.

Marianne had a thin-lipped smile on her face; the sort of intimidating smile which said: 'You won't do anything to me,

412

will you? You won't tell on me, because you're frightened of what might happen to you, aren't you, Jew-pig?' Sarah forced herself to look straight into Marianne's ice-blue eyes.

'That one,' she said. Marianne's face darkened into rage.

'She's lying, the dirty Jewish bitch is lying, can't you see that?'

'Be quiet,' said the sergeant. 'I'd say you were in enough trouble already, wouldn't you?'

'And that one.' Sarah moved on to Frieda, then Inge. 'And her.'

'She can't prove anything,' hissed Marianne.

Mathilde was next. Sarah felt a turmoil of uncertainty descending on her, tightening her stomach muscles, making her feel sick with apprehension.

It was impossible to look into Mathilde's face and not feel a twinge of sympathy. Sarah opened her mouth to condemn her, but no sound came out. Guilty feelings were gnawing away at her as she remembered the afternoon of the attack, and what Mathilde had done to save her. Why had she done that? Why had she opened herself up to Marianne von Strondheim's vicious resentment by letting Sarah go? If only she could understand the reasons behind Mathilde's change of heart . . .

She looked at Mathilde. There was an old, yellowing bruise on the side of her face, and the scar of a cut, now almost mended. Her eyes were filled with fear.

The sergeant laid a hand on her arm.

'That one?'

Sarah turned away.

'No, not that one. She had nothing to do with it.'

The moment she had spoken Mathilde's reprieve, Sarah wondered if perhaps she had done precisely the wrong thing. Mathilde's face registered no relief, no gratitude.

She just looked scared out of her wits.

It wasn't like Sachs to be depressed, but he didn't seem able to shake off the black cloud which had hovered over his head every since the news of his rejection by the Pioneer Corps.

He didn't look ill, he didn't feel ill. The doctor at the camp had even told him that there was no need for him ever to be ill, not if he took things easy. But Sachs didn't like taking things easy. He was young, restless and impatient. And bored. He had never been so bored in his entire life.

He wandered down the street towards the perimeter fence of barbed wire, slung between a double row of stout wooden posts. Was he ever going to see the outside world again? OK, so it was just as grey and misty on the other side of the wire, and with the war going so indifferently for Britain that outside world was an uncertain place; but out there lay freedom. And freedom was what Sachs craved more than anything else, even if it was only the freedom to make mistakes.

The sound of footsteps made him glance behind him, and he slowed down to enable Ernst Müller to catch up with him.

'Hello, Ernst.'

Ernst looked him up and down, head on one side, the low, filtering sunlight casting a dark hollow where the deep scar scored the side of his face.

'You are sad.'

Slightly taken aback, Sachs shuffled his feet.

'Oh, I'm fine.'

Müller shook his head.

'No, you are sad. I have been watching you.'

Sachs allowed himself a wistful smile. Just about everyone in Hutchinson Camp had been giving him advice – he supposed it was inevitable that even Müller would join in eventually.

'Just a little sad, perhaps.'

'You are young, you have everything.' Müller's voice was earnest, full of a conviction Sachs hadn't heard before.

'I hadn't noticed.'

'You have your past and your future. Yesterday and tomorrow.' Müller passed his hand over his hair, searching his muddled thoughts for what he wanted so badly to say. 'I

414

have only today – do you understand? I remember so little about what happened before, about what I was.'

'You'll remember, in time.'

'Sometimes I feel it is all there, if I could just reach out and touch it.' His face arranged itself slowly into a lopsided smile, the left side of his mouth dragged down by the deep scar. 'But I have much still. I have these.' He held out his hands, gazing at them as he turned them over and over again.

'You have a great talent.' That, at least, was true. Sachs was no expert but he knew that Müller's work held something remarkable, a chaos touched by genius.

'I do what I can. And I am beginning to be happy.' Müller's fingers scrunched up the sleeve of Sachs's jacket. 'You should be happy too. I drew this for you.'

Müller felt in the pocket of his baggy trousers and took out a scrap of paper. It carried a small, but unmistakeable pen-sketch of Sachs, bright-eyed and smiling.

'Remember,' nodded Müller, 'this is how you must be.' And patting Sachs lightly on the arm, he turned and began to walk back towards House thirty-two.

'I always think Milner's Tower looks its best this time of the year,' commented Cora, pausing to rest for a moment, leaning against the drystone wall which bordered the path along the side of Bradda Head. She leant back, looking up to the crest of the hill where the yellowish-gold of the tower stood out against a turquoise-blue sky. 'The March sun brings out the colour of the stone.'

Looking back over her shoulder, she gazed at the play of sunlight on the sea. She had always loved watching its shifting patterns; but now, she had the strangest need to know what lay beyond the deep-blue smudge of the horizon.

'It's a funny-looking building when you look at it close up,' said James, glad of a chance to get his breath back. 'Makes you wonder why they went to all the trouble of building it up here. Do you think it really is based on one of Milner's safe-keys?'

'Who knows? When I was little, I was scared of it. William used to say the ghosts of dead sailors lived in it. I believed him!' She chuckled. 'In those days I'd believe anything he told me.' She threw a glance at James. 'Are you all right to go on a bit further?'

'Fine.' James straightened his tall, angular body. 'Just a bit out of breath. It's been a while since I was able to climb all the way up here, I think my muscles have gone flabby or something.'

'And the leg . . .?' ventured Cora.

'That's fine too. In fact . . . that's something I wanted to talk to you about.'

He picked his way carefully over the scree, choosing the steepest of the paths as if he felt he had something to prove. Cora followed close behind, occasionally missing her footing and slithering down a few inches as the loose stones slid over each other. James reached out.

'Take my hand, I won't let you fall.'

She smiled and shook her head.

'It's all right, I can manage.'

At the top of the hill, James paused and turned to her.

'I saw the doc yesterday, up at Noble's.'

'Oh.' Cora waited, not sure what she wanted to hear.

'The thing is . . . well, he says my leg's better. At any rate, as better as it's going to be.'

'That's . . .' Cora had to fight the sinking feeling in her stomach. 'That's wonderful, James, just wonderful.' She put her arms round his neck and kissed him on the cheek. 'I'm so pleased you're well again, really I am.' And she truly was happy for him, though there was sadness in her happiness.

'Steady on, it's not quite A1 and it never will be.' He flexed it gingerly, noting the stubborn stiffness in the knee joint, the slight pain when he tried to straighten it out. 'The doc says I'm no good for front-line service.'

Cora was caught between relief and guilt. Whatever else was going to happen between them, whatever their future might be, she wanted James to be safe. And yet she knew that more than anything, he wanted to fight for his country.

'Does that mean . . .?'

'It means they'll let me join up but I can't fight. I'm . . . I've decided to accept a commission in the Veterinary Corps. It's not what I wanted but . . .'

'But it's better than nothing?' She met his gaze. 'Better than staying here?'

'You know it's not like that, Cora. I love this place. I love you too, I don't want to leave you. But it's been hard for me, being here while my brothers are both fighting overseas.'

'I know. I understand.' Cora took his hands in hers, confused by the welter of feelings inside her. Their separation was inevitable now, and yet she felt closer to James than she had ever done. She paused. 'When will you be going?'

'I don't know yet, but soon. A few weeks maybe.'

He drew her towards him, the wind ruffling her soft golden brown curls. His warm encircling arms made her feel safe and loved.

'There's something else we need to talk about. You've been avoiding talking about it ever since I asked you.'

Cora drew away, the bond broken.

'If this is about getting married . . .'

'Of course it's about getting married!' He searched her face, trying to understand. 'Cora, I love you. You're free of that damned hotel now, what's stopping us just going ahead and doing it right now?'

She shook her head. She hated hurting him, but it was all so sudden. And so irrevocable.

'Hold on, James, why the hurry? Why does it have to be now?'

'Because I'll be going away soon.'

'This is a terrible time for anyone to think about getting married,' parried Cora. 'There's a war on, we could be invaded tomorrow.'

How could she explain that there was more to it than that

417

– that over the last year she had grown, discovered strength, confidence, a new zest for life? Her own life. A life she was afraid to share.

James looked crestfallen.

'Does that mean you don't love me?'

Cora shook her head. That was the last thing she wanted him to believe.

'No, James. It means I'm just not sure if I want to marry you.'

'That corner's disgusting, you'll have to do it again.'

Arms folded, eyes bright with annoyance, Grace Quine was supervising the cleaning of the kitchen at the *Bradda Vista*.

Nadia, on her knees with a scrubbing brush, sat up on her haunches, rubbing the small of her back.

'I do the best I can, you see that I do. An hour I have washed and scrubbed this floor . . .'

'Well, it's still filthy. I want to be able to see my face in it. And as for you,' she cast a critical eye on Nadia's friend Sonja, who was busy washing down the kitchen cupboards, 'you'd better take a knife to that grease. Bone idle, that's what you are.'

'I am not lazy,' declared Sonja, throwing her cloth into the pail of soapy water. 'And I will not do this any more. You cannot make me do this! Everything I do is wrong. All day long you shout, you complain . . .'

'. . . It is not right, it is not right!'

Grace sighed, tapping an impatient foot.

'I pay you for this work, out of my own pocket – and I'm here to make sure you do it properly.' She ran a finger along the top of the cupboard. It came away with the faintest smear of oily brown. 'You see? Filthy! You foreigners seem to thrive on filth.'

Elsa Nadel was on her way to the common room when she heard the commotion in the kitchen. Voices raised, someone sobbing, a couple of thuds and a clatter . . .

She turned away. It was none of her business. Then, on impulse, she turned back and walked back down the corridor to the kitchen door.

'. . . and I won't do it any more, I won't.'

'Why don't you just stop whining and get on with your work?'

'. . . I'm going to write to the Commandant and tell her . . .'

Elsa pushed open the door. The floor was awash with soapy water, a metal bucket upended in a huge puddle and Grace Quine standing in the middle of it all, her shoes and stockings soaked to the ankle and her skirts hoisted above the knee. Her face was red with fury.

'You stupid girls! You stupid, ignorant girls.'

Elsa stepped inside, avoiding the worst of the water.

'What is going on?' she enquired calmly.

'Since when was this any of your business?' demanded Grace, wading out towards the edge of the puddle.

'It is her,' spat Nadia. 'She makes us do our work over and over again . . .'

'She is shouting, always she is shouting . . . Everything we do, she say it is wrong.'

'Is it my fault if you haven't got the sense you were born with?'

Elsa raised her hand.

'Please,' she said quietly. 'I hardly think shouting will serve any purpose, do you, Mrs Quine?'

Grace gave her a murderous look, but said nothing. Elsa picked up the kitchen mop and righted the bucket.

'Let's get this cleaned up, shall we? Nadia, would you please open the door so the water can run outside?'

Grace looked on with annoyance as Elsa organised her two fellow internees with calm, quiet efficiency. This woman was trouble, that was perfectly clear to see – an interfering, over-educated harpie who meddled in other people's business because she couldn't get herself a man. She would have to think about having Elsa transferred, so that she could become somebody else's minor irritation.

But Thomas Quine, watching Elsa through the window from the bottom of his cabbage patch, raised a silent cheer.

Grethe didn't often come to Port St Mary. On this particular day, she had taken the precaution of getting permission to come and see an old friend from Streatham, who was interned at the Ballaqueeney.

Half an hour took care of that duty, and Grethe slipped away along the shoreline towards the outskirts of the village. She shouldn't be doing this, but rules were made to be broken and it seemed an age since she'd seen Harry.

At last finding the small, whitewashed cottage, Grethe raised her hand and knocked at the door. The sound echoed, impossibly loud in the silence. She waited. Knocked again. Perhaps this wasn't the right cottage, perhaps she'd got it all wrong and he didn't want to see her at all.

'Grethe!' The door opened and Harry was standing just inside, an untidy figure in open-necked shirt and corduroys. 'You'd better come inside quick, don't want you gettin' yourself in trouble.'

'You're sure you want me to . . .?'

Harry gave an impatient grunt and beckoned her inside.

'Told you before, gel, I say what I mean. Now come in, will you?'

She followed him along the stone-flagged passageway. The house was clean but bare, a bachelor's house without ornament or comfort.

'Come in the kitchen, I've just lit the fire.'

Harry's kitchen looked as though it had remained unchanged for the best part of a century. The wooden beams made the ceiling so low that Grethe had to stoop, and the walls were a jumble of pots and pans, strings of onions, dried herbs, lengths of old tarry rope.

''Tisn't much of a place for a lady,' observed Harry. 'It

never had a woman's touch. But 'tis middlin' warm. Shall I be takin' your coat?'

Grethe caught his arm.

'Did I do the right thing? Coming here?'

His soft blue eyes crinkled.

'For a sensible woman you talk a lot of nonsense, Grethe. Now sit you down.' His hand touched hers as he took her jacket from her, and he let the touch linger. ''Tis good to see you again.' Better than you can ever know, he thought to himself.

She sat down on an old wooden settle and watched him busying himself, stoking up the fire. Its leaping gold and orange flames filled the kitchen with a warm, welcoming fug, a protecting blanket against the hostility of the world outside.

'Tell me how you've been, Harry.'

'Ach, well enough. And yourself?' He looked her over. 'You're all right?'

'As well as anyone can be on a diet of soup and potatoes. That Grace Quine is a skinflint. She'd have us on bread and water if she dared. Elsa's better than she was, though,' she added.

'Elsa Nadel? I heard she tried to do away with herself.'

'And so she did, poor girl. Tried walking into the sea off Port Erin – if it hadn't been for Sarah Rosenberg dragging her out again, we'd have lost her. But it's like she's woken up and knows she's got a second chance. Which is more than some of us get.'

'Aye, she's a lucky one. 'Tis not often the sea lets you go, once she's claimed you. She drags you under and sucks the life out of you.' A shadow of pain crossed his face.

Grethe looked up, struck by the bitterness in Harry's voice.

'Is something wrong, Harry? Is it something to do with what happened at Dunkirk?'

'It's all right, gel. Nothin' to bother yourself with.'

The fire was warm, the cottage kitchen cosy and welcoming.

But Grethe's thoughts went out to her little Emil, so far away in a stranger's house, forgetting all about his Mutti. Did he have a warm fire to sit by, someone to love him? Was he missing her the way she missed him? One letter was all she had had from him. It was so very little . . .

She looked up at Harry. Something about him worried her. She wanted him close. He had been so strong for her for so long; now she longed to share the secret sadness in his heart.

'Harry . . .'

'Aye, gel?'

'Come and sit by me.' She patted the other end of the wooden settle. 'Here, next to me.'

His solid bulk felt reassuring next to her. They sat in silence for a few minutes, each lost in thought.

'There *is* something, isn't there, Harry? Something that hurts you very much?'

This time, Harry did not answer. He could not. He could never lie to Grethe. In the silence her hand sought out his, her fingers curling around his, squeezing them tight.

'Won't you tell me, Harry? I thought you trusted me.'

His fingers responded, completing the clasp.

'You're right, it was Dunkirk. I can't get it out of my mind.'

'It must have been terrible. But you came back safe . . .'

'Aye, gel. I did, but what about the rest?' He paused, condemned to relive every second of the horror in his mind's eye. 'There were four of us crewing the *Mary Jane*: me, Davey, the Irish lad Padraig O'Keefe, and Petey Faragher, my apprentice boy. Petey was only seventeen, I should never have let him come, his mother begged me to make him stay home . . .

'It was bad, Grethe, terrible bad. Bombs and bullets everywhere, dead men floating in the sea and the sea was all red with their blood. We got almost twenty of the poor buggers on board, loaded to the waterline we was, and close to shore – too close for safety.

'Padraig spoke to me. It was the last thing he ever said. "Harry," he says, "we have to take on more – we can't leave them here like this to die." And he's hauling this Tommy on board when a bullet gets him, hits him in the head.' He gazed deep into the flickering fire. 'Blew half his skull away. And all the time the guns is goin' and the bombs is fallin' and the water's boiling with all this red foam . . .'

'Oh, Harry, Harry, it's all right. Don't talk about it if it hurts so much.'

Instinctively Grethe put her arm round his shoulders, the way she would do if it was Emil, terrified by some bad dream. Slowly she stroked the thinning hair away from his forehead. It was damp and cold with sweat.

'The noise, Grethe, you wouldn't believe it. The smell of panic. And those frightened faces, pleadin' with us to help them. Padraig was lying stone-dead on the deck and I knew I should turn the boat round right there and then, get away from the shore. Only there's these two soldiers – young lads, hardly older than Petey – tryin' to scramble up the side, and Petey's callin' out to them: "Come on, come on, you can make it."

'That was when the mortar shell exploded in the water, just a few yards from the *Mary Jane*. It threw the boat sideways, I thought we was goin' to capsize; there was bodies slidin' and fallin' everywhere, people shouting out.

'Out of the corner of my eye I sees Petey, he's slidin' t'wards the rail, I reach out to grab him but he hits his head on the corner of the wheelhouse and falls sideways. The next thing I know, he's fallin' into the sea.

'There was blood comin' from his head, Grethe. There was men drownin', men fallin', men tramplin' his body underfoot. He was gone, gel. Gone, like he'd never existed.'

Harry put his head in his hands. Grethe held him close, wishing that the warmth from her own body could enter his, take away the pain.

'It was my fault,' he said. 'My fault the boy is dead.'

'No, Harry, it wasn't. You couldn't stop him – he was a brave boy. He wanted to do what was right.'

'Not just a brave boy,' said Harry quietly. He clung tightly to Grethe's hand, his fingers crushing hers so tightly that the grip was painful. 'My boy.' He swallowed, but the lump in his throat refused to go away. 'If only I hadn't been such a coward, he'd have known that.'

'Your boy . . .?'

'Petey was my son. His mother and I got close, years ago. She was married, she didn't want to leave the nice life she had with Evan Faragher. And she wouldn't have it known who his real father was, not for anythin'. I let Petey die before I'd even told him I was his dad. What kind of father does that make me, Grethe? What kind of man?'

'A good man.'

'At least your boy's safe. Petey's gone . . .'

'I know. I know.'

Grethe was profoundly shaken. She had held back for so long, afraid of her own vulnerability; but now, with all their secrets spoken and their sorrow shared, there seemed no rhyme or reason not to be honest.

'You're the finest man I ever knew, Harry Kerruish.'

'How can you say that, Grethe? You're a mother, you must understand how it feels. I failed him . . .'

'Hush.' She quietened him as she would quieten a child, stroking and kissing his face, rocking him in her arms. 'I love you.'

The words were whispered, barely audible. Tears flooded her eyes. It was so long since she had wept that she had forgotten the taste of her own tears.

'Don't say it, gel. Don't . . .'

'What if this is the only chance I have to tell you? What then?'

Their eyes met. Met as though they were truly meeting and seeing each other for the very first time. Why didn't I realise it before? thought Grethe. Or have I just been suppressing the truth, afraid of what it could do to us both?

'We said we wouldn't let this happen. Grethe, you know we can't.'

'I never thought I'd love any man again; but I love you, Harry Kerruish.'

Her lips brushed Harry's cheek, his brow, his closed eyelids, sought out his mouth and kissed it with a gentle, healing passion. He responded, hesitantly at first and then with the urgency of a love too long denied.

Slowly their bodies became one. And there, on the old rag-rug in front of the fire, they began to make slow and tender love.

Chapter 31

The little steam train rattled its way ever closer to Port Erin station.

In the last carriage sat Sergeant William Quine of the Catering Corps, kitbag on the seat next to him and a bulging suitcase at his feet. It was just as well there were no other passengers in the carriage – there was hardly enough room for himself and his luggage.

The sky was overcast, it was a typical March day. William checked his watch, though he had no need to. He knew the route by heart, could almost count the number of times the wheels would rattle before they slid alongside the platform.

He felt uneasy. It didn't feel like coming home, not really. Hadn't he and Grace decided that they would make their home on the mainland, not the Isle of Man? No, he reminded himself. *They* hadn't decided anything – it had been Grace who'd made her mind up that they both hated the Island. Now he was back for fourteen days' leave and he had a horrible sinking feeling that all was not well with the *Bradda Vista*.

Grace was standing on the platform, almost alone. She looked pretty and smart, as she always did – and wasn't that a new hat she'd bought herself to go with that cherry-red costume? His heart sank at the thought of her spending all his money; and then he felt guilty. She was his wife, after all. And she didn't look any more comfortable than he felt, shifting from one foot to the other, fiddling with the buttons on her gloves.

With a final exhalation of steam, the engine jolted to a halt and carriage doors began opening. William stepped out into a hissing white cloud and there she was, a few yards further on down the platform.

'Hello, Grace.' He covered his embarrassment by hoisting the kitbag onto his shoulder and picking up the suitcase, its lumpy contents bulging the canvas sides.

'Don't I get a kiss?'

''Course you do.' He dotted the briefest of pecks on her cheek.

Grace started talking nineteen to the dozen, as if she didn't want him to get a word in edgeways. William knew her well enough to be sure it was a bad sign.

'You all right then, Grace?' he hazarded. 'And the hotel?'

'Yes, yes, of course, everything's fine – why shouldn't everything be fine?'

He shrugged, mystified at her extreme reaction to a perfectly innocent question.

'No reason. I just wondered how you'd been getting on. How's Cora?' he added.

'I told you, everything's absolutely fine and you're not to worry. You're looking fatter, William.'

'Am I?' He glanced down at himself. 'I hadn't noticed.'

'Yes, you're all puffy-faced and pasty looking. You're obviously not eating the right things. You're not filling up on doughnuts, are you? I read somewhere that soldiers are always eating doughnuts, and you know what fresh yeast does to your stomach . . .'

'Hold on, Grace,' he cut in. 'Slow down a bit, you're losing me. Just give me a chance to get my breath back, will you?'

He stopped on the station forecourt and put down his suitcase, taking a moment to breathe in the cold, salty air and gaze across the bay to the headland beyond. Now *this* was home.

Yet people changed, things changed – and so had Port Erin.

'Those women over there – they're not locals, are they?' Grace sniffed.

'Internees. I try to keep my distance, but it's impossible. You daren't say a word you know, in case they hear.'

'Surely they can't all be bad.'

'I wouldn't trust any of them.' Not like Cora, she muttered under her breath.

'What did you say?'

'Oh, nothing. Nothing important. Now, let's get back to the *Bradda Vista*. It's been so long and there's a lot of things to tell you about.'

'What sort of things?'

He fixed her with one of his 'looks' – the looks that Grace dreaded. William always seemed to extract the truth from her, whether it was the price she'd paid for a pair of shoes or the fact that she'd burned his dinner.

'Nothing special, just *things*. Now, let's get on. Thomas wants to show you his leeks, God knows why.'

She walked off ahead, towards the promenade, and William knew he would have to be content with that, at least for the time being. Not that he would be content with it for long. He meant to get to the bottom of whatever had been going on.

'Come *on*, William.'

This time she just plain annoyed him, with her chivvying and her fussing.

'Give it a rest, Grace. I've been away for months, being shot at halfway to bloody Cairo. A man needs time to settle.'

She looked wounded, then resentful, her blue eyes hardening until they looked like a doll's glass eyes. For a moment he felt guilty; he hadn't meant to upset her.

'I only wanted to welcome you home properly.'

'Yes, yes, I know,' he sighed, and he quickened his pace to catch up with her.

As they walked through Port Erin towards the *Bradda Vista*, William noticed the butcher's shop, still well stocked with meat despite the war. It was obvious that things weren't as bad here as they were on the mainland. So why did Grace look so edgy?

That same afternoon, Grethe Herzheim was helping out at the camp nursery. She hadn't really wanted to: it only reminded her of the distance that separated her from Emil. But at least it took her mind off some of her other preoccupations. Like Harry Kerruish . . .

One bonus of helping at the nursery was enjoying the looks of outrage she got when she arrived with Sarah Rosenberg. She knew what they were thinking: Jews and prostitutes? They'll corrupt our precious German babies!

Grethe had just finished changing a little boy's nappy when Sarah came across and nudged her arm.

'I think you should go outside before someone notices,' she said.

'Go outside? Why?' Grethe looked up, and saw what Sarah was looking at. 'Oh.'

'Go on,' said Sarah. 'I won't tell.'

Grethe looked through the window. Harry Kerruish was waiting outside the hut, the collar of his overcoat turned up against the gale. Her heart sank. This was the moment she had dreaded, doing everything she could to avoid their paths crossing; afraid that her resolve might weaken.

'I could ignore him, pretend I haven't seen him.'

'Don't be a fool. He's been there ages. Do you want him to get into trouble? Go out and talk to him, sort things out. But be quick.'

Grethe steeled herself for what she knew must come. She walked across the hut and went outside, closing the door behind her so that no one would hear what she had to say.

'Harry?'

He looked up.

'Grethe. I was hopin' we could talk.'

'You know it's not safe to be seen together like this.'

'You never minded before.'

That was true, thought Grethe. But before, things had been different.

'Look, Harry, I . . .'

He touched her hand, but she couldn't bear it and drew away.

'Why have you been avoidin' me, gel?'

'I haven't . . . not exactly . . .' Her voice tailed off.

'It's what happened at the cottage, isn't it?'

Grethe couldn't find the words to answer him. If she spoke she was terribly afraid she would get it all wrong. She'd already made up her mind what should be done, but it hurt so much.

She nodded, dumbly.

'What have I done, gel? Is it about the boy?'

'No, no, of course not.'

'Then why? I thought we . . .' He couldn't say it. He tried again. 'You made me happy, Grethe. I thought it made you happy too.'

She raised her eyes until they were looking into his. His gaze was calm, steady, but sad and questioning.

'I'm not worth it, Harry.'

'What are you talkin' about?'

She raised her voice a little, determined that he must understand.

'I'm not worth it. You're a good man, an honest man. And what am I?'

'You're the woman I love.'

Please, no, she begged silently, don't say these things, Harry, don't make me go back on the promise I've made myself. Not when it was so very hard to make. I have to be strong.

'Hear me out, Harry. I'm a prostitute, a brass, a tart – there's no two ways of looking at it.'

'That don't matter to me.'

Her eyes flashed danger, the anger that came from too much love.

'Well, it should. You've no idea, have you? No idea of the things I've done. All the men I've been with and never even known their names?'

Harry was shocked; not by Grethe's life, but by the force of her rejection. Pain ripped at his heart as she tried to tear a gulf between them. He couldn't lose her now; not now.

'I knew that from the start, gel. If I gave a damn, do you think we'd have come this far?'

'Too far, Harry. Too far. It's my fault, I was lonely. But now it has to stop.'

'Grethe, gel, I don't understand any of this.'

'I'm stopping it now, Harry, don't you see why? If they catch us it's you who'll suffer, not me. Prison doesn't frighten me any more. But if it happened to you . . .' She saw Harry open his mouth to protest. 'Don't tell me you don't care, because you have no idea what it's like, really you don't.'

Harry felt angry frustration searing the pit of his stomach. He clenched his hand into a fist and punched the wall of the hut.

'You don't know what you're saying.'

She turned away, afraid of the emotions she might betray if she looked him in the face.

'I do, Harry.'

Harry gazed at her in utter despair, utter bewilderment. Why was she doing this? Why was she breaking down the one good thing that this savage, bloody war had brought into their lives? Defying her refusal to look at him, he took her hand in his. He felt it tremble.

'This isn't easy for me, gel. I'm not used to fancy words, but – I love you. I love you, Grethe.'

There was what seemed like an endless silence, broken only by the sound of the distant sea. Grethe's reply was scarcely louder than a whisper.

'Yes, I know.'

'I thought you loved me too.'

She looked up at him, her eyes brim-full of tears.

432

'Of course I love you,' she said softly. 'That's why I shouldn't see you again.'

Adrian Newell glanced at the address old Mrs Perks had scrawled on the back of a cigarette packet. Number seven, Roache Mansions, Streatham.

He walked down the bomb-damaged High Street and took a right turning, then a left. Goodrich Street was respectable-looking, not the sort of place you'd expect a prostitute to live. He wondered what he'd expected to find.

Four small boys were playing cops and robbers in the street. They looked up, curious, as he passed.

'Sixpence ter clean yer shoes, mister?' asked one hopeful entrepreneur. Newell shook his head.

'Not today, thank you.'

Another boy, a little older, piped up.

'Ain't no good askin' 'im, 'e's just a vicar, 'e ain't got no money.'

'P'raps ole Mr Wilks 'as snuffed it,' cut in his friend helpfully.

Newell took the cigarette packet out of his pocket.

'Can you tell me where this place is?' he asked.

The oldest boy shrugged.

'Can't read, mister.'

Newell felt more shocked than he ought to be.

'Roache Mansions,' he said. 'Number seven.'

The boy wiped his nose on his bare arm.

'Cost yer,' he said hopefully.

'In that case, I'm sure I can find it on my own,' replied Newell with a half-smile.

'Big 'ouse at the end on the left,' piped up the smallest boy.

'Thank you.' Newell took four pennies out of his pocket and handed them out.

'Fanks, mister. Sure yer don't want yer shoes polishin'?'

'Not today.'

He walked on up the street, following the curve until he

came to the big house at the end. It was a purpose-built block of flats in forbidding red brick, respectable if a little shabby. Heart in mouth, Newell walked up to the front door.

It was open. He walked in, almost colliding with a girl in a short skirt and a tight silk blouse. To his discomfort she winked at him.

'Hello, Vicar, don't see many of your sort round 'ere.'

He swallowed, his mouth suddenly dry.

'Number seven,' he said. He wondered if he had made a mistake in coming here. 'Could you tell me where I could find number seven?'

'First floor, second on the right, dearie.' She blew him a kiss as she left. 'Tell Claire from me, she's a lucky girl.'

He climbed the well-scrubbed stairs to the first floor. It was very quiet and there was no one about. A couple of times he thought about turning tail, but he sought out the door of number seven, and rang the bell.

A woman's voice, somewhere within, called out.

''Ang on, I'm not ready.'

He waited, listening to the crash of the wardrobe door, then footsteps on linoleum. It seemed to go on for ever. Then the door opened suddenly, taking him by surprise.

'Oh, I . . . er . . .'

The face was young and friendly, pretty too in an ordinary sort of way. Curled brown hair framed small features and a large mouth, very red and shiny with lipstick.

'Hello.' She looked at him curiously. A parson! Ah well, you got all sorts in this line of work. 'Sorry, Reverend, I thought you were my friend Jane. Did you want somethin'?'

'Are you Miss Claire Hodges?'

'Recommended, was I?'

'No, that is, yes . . . not in that way.' He eased his dog collar away from his constricted throat with his forefinger. 'I'm the chaplain at Rushen interment camp.'

Claire's face registered alarm.

434

'Grethe – it's not Grethe, is it? She's not ill or in trouble or somethin'?'

'No, no, nothing's wrong. Could you spare a few minutes?' Claire stood back, inviting him in.

'Sure I can, but why . . .?'

'I'd just like to have a chat with you about Emil Herzheim. I think you may be able to help.'

'It's no use running away, Mathilde.'

Mathilde stopped in her tracks, two steps short of the front door of Collinson's Cafe. She knew that voice and she didn't want to hear it. Slowly, very slowly, she turned round.

Olga Wissel was standing right in front of her, chin thrust out aggressively.

'You're a hard woman to find,' she remarked. There was a smile on her lips, but the look in her eyes was cold and hard.

Mathilde felt cold fingers running up and down her spine.

'I don't know what you mean.'

'Come on, Mathilde, you know you've been avoiding me. All I want is a cosy little chat. Let's go and sit over here; we don't want anyone listening, do we?'

Olga's grip on her shoulder made it quite clear that Mathilde had no choice in the matter. They walked around to the side of the cafe and sat down on a bench overlooking the sea.

'Right, Mathilde, it's time we talked straight. You know what they're saying about you in the camp?'

Mathilde knew, but she couldn't voice it. It was almost as if saying it out loud would make it real and true and dangerous. She looked down at her feet, hugging her coat around her shoulders.

'Then perhaps I'd better tell you. They're saying you let us down, Mathilde.'

'But I . . .'

'They're saying you let Marianne von Strondheim down, and the others. Why didn't the Jewish bitch pick you out when she identified them, that's what they're all saying. How is it that they're in prison and you're not?'

'I . . . don't know.' Mathilde's heart was thumping like a steam-hammer.

'Some of them are even saying you're a traitor.'

Mathilde looked up sharply, her eyes staring in a pale face. 'No, no, I'm not!'

'Well, that's what they're saying. Now, I'm not saying I believe them, or go along with the things they say we ought to do to punish you, but you've got to prove yourself if you want to be accepted again in this camp.

'Marianne and Inge and Frieda have gone. There's no one to protect you if you set yourself against us. Remember that.'

Olga got up.

'Just remember what I said. Either you're with us or against us, there are no half-measures. Understand?'

Mathilde nodded, struck too dumb to answer any other way. She understood all right. What she didn't understand was how on earth she was ever going to be free.

Dinner plates clattered and banged in the kitchen of the *Bradda Vista*. Pots and pans rattled, sandwich tins clashing together like cymbals as Grace rummaged on the top shelf of the pantry for exactly the right serving dish.

There were three people sitting at the kitchen table: William, Thomas and Cora. None of them looked as if they wanted to be there.

'Is everything all right?' Cora called out.

'Yes, of course everything's all right,' snapped Grace, dropping a large enamel roasting tin on her foot with a clatter and a curse. 'Why shouldn't it be?'

Cora exchanged glances with William. He offered up a silent prayer for patience. How often had he heard that phrase? Why shouldn't things be all right? Oh, no reason really – except that Grace had seized control of the *Bradda Vista* and everything was at sixes and sevens. He wiped a weary hand over his brow.

'Bit more ale, Grandad?' he enquired, indicating the large white pitcher in the centre of the table.

'Aye, why not?' Thomas accepted a second half-pint of beer with gratitude. He needed something to soothe his jangling nerves.

'Sure you don't need a hand, Grace?' ventured Cora.

'I can manage quite well, thank you,' replied Grace, stalking back into the kitchen with a white oval plate. She wrinkled her nose at the sight of the jug of beer. 'I do wish you wouldn't drink that stuff at the table, it smells like a public bar in here.' She set the plate down next to the cooker and took the oven gloves from a hook on the wall.

'It smells nice,' commented Cora. It did, too, much to everyone's relief. Grace might not be a *cordon bleu* cook, but she'd learned enough in her married life to roast a decent joint of meat. 'What is it?'

'Roast rabbit. I got the recipe out of *Good Housekeeping*. It's very economical,' she added, fixing William with a meaningful look. 'So you see, I do have *some* idea of how to run this place.'

'I'm not saying you don't,' replied William, with his fingers crossed under the table. 'What I'm saying is . . . look, never mind all that just now.' He raised his glass. 'This is supposed to be a happy occasion. To all of us. To the Quines.'

'And the Popes,' added Grace over her shoulder as she bent down to take the rabbit out of the oven. That was one of the problems with Grace, thought William. She'd never thought that his family was up to the standard of hers, even though her dad was little more than a glorified clerk in a wages office.

The rabbit was an appetising shade of golden brown, sizzling in its own juices.

'Smells good,' William conceded.

'Yes, well, I'm not totally helpless.' Grace served up the rabbit. 'Now, William, why don't you tell us all what you've been up to?'

'Oh, you know,' he ventured. Should he give them the sanitised version, or the plain truth?

'Is it really bad over there – on the mainland?' cut in Cora.

William took a drink of beer. He decided to be honest.

'Yes,' he said. 'You should see the mess Jerry's made of the London docks.'

Grace glared at him across the table as she shovelled rabbit and mashed potatoes onto his plate.

'Careless talk,' she reminded him.

'There's only us here, who's going to listen?'

Grace glanced up at the ceiling.

'You never know when *they're* listening,' she replied. She took off her apron and sat down at the table. 'How is it – in Banbury?' Her eyes searched his face anxiously.

'I don't know. Soon as we disembarked and got our fourteen days' leave, I came straight up here.'

'I've had no word from Mum and Dad lately.'

'Well, you know how it is, with the wartime post.' His eyes met hers. 'You rowed with them, didn't you?'

Grace took a sudden interest in boning a leg of rabbit.

'I may have done.'

'And that's why you left to come back here?' It was all falling into place now.

'What if I did? I'm here now.' This time her eyes issued a challenge. 'And that's what you always wanted, isn't it?'

William didn't have a chance to reply, as Thomas chose that precise moment to knock over the ale-jug. Grace sprang to her feet, beer dripping from the cloth into her lap.

'Oh, Grandad, how could you be so clumsy!'

'Sorry, gel, I mustn't've been lookin'.'

'Let me wipe it up,' volunteered Cora, dabbing at the table-top with a napkin.

This time Grace didn't protest, merely glaring at everyone as she got a tea-towel and started mopping the front of her dress.

'Everything's ruined,' she sniffed.

438

'Of course it isn't.' Cora rescued the dinner plates, the rabbit and a bowl of turnips, and whipped off the wet cloth. Running the cold tap, she filled a metal pail and dropped it in. 'There, a bit of a soak and it will be fine. Now, do you still keep the tablecloths in the same place . . .?'

William watched Cora bustling about with a mixture of regret and admiration. He'd often underestimated his sister and he felt bad about what he'd done, dumping the *Bradda Vista* on her just to follow one of Grace's whims.

'Now, let's sit down and start again, shall we?' Cora's stern gaze almost forbade Grace to have a tantrum. She sat down, tucking her legs under the table like a sulky child.

Cora fetched the rabbit back from the warm oven and they began eating again.

'Not bad, Grace gel, not bad,' conceded Thomas.

'Very nice,' nodded Cora.

'Bit salty,' commented William; Cora could have walloped him. She gave him a glare and he added, 'Tasty, mind. Very tasty.'

'You haven't told us about your posting, William,' began Grace.

'There's not much to tell. Most of the time it's boring, then it's all hell let loose. You know, baking bread one minute and the next, you're manning the guns. Anyhow, let's not go on about me. There's something I wanted to talk to you about.'

'Me?' asked Grace, her eyes round with anticipation. She looked very childlike at times, thought William, and that thought clutched at his heart; a silent grief for the child which had brought them together and then driven them apart.

'All of us. The family.' William put his knife and fork carefully together on his plate and dabbed his mouth. 'It's about this place.'

'I'm doing what I can,' butted in Grace defensively.

'But the fact remains, you're not very good at running a guesthouse, are you?' replied William.

'I'm learning the ropes,' sniffed Grace. She looked not just angry, but upset. Cora sensed how much it meant to her to impress William, and William could be thoroughly insensitive when the mood took him.

'That's not fair,' Cora found herself saying. 'Grace has been thrown in at the deep end.'

She wondered why she found herself defending her. After all, it was Grace who'd insisted on taking over, Grace who'd managed to annoy everyone from Dame Joanna to the mildest of internees.

'Anyhow,' William put up his hands to stop the argument before it started, 'things aren't going too well, are they? I took a look at the books. We were just about breaking even with Cora at the helm but lately – well, as far as I can see it's all going to pot. It's chaos.'

Grace was white-faced, but William kept on talking regardless. For the first time in ages, Cora felt grudgingly sorry for her sister-in-law.

'Now, Grace, we did the dirty on poor Cora last year, dumping the *Bradda Vista* on her like that.'

'It's all right,' broke in Cora, but William shook his head.

'No, you were fighting mad, and quite right too. We wanted out and I knew you'd take on the old place, if only for Mum and Dad's sake. That was wrong of me.'

'What I always thought,' said Thomas, slowly and reflectively, 'was that it weren't quite fair of your Ma and Pa, not leavin' nothin' to Cora in their wills.'

'Exactly,' nodded William. Grace looked suspicious, panicky even. Cora just shook her head.

'They knew I didn't want the place. You were always the one who wanted to learn the business. And I got Mum's bits of jewellery, and the good china . . .'

'It wasn't fair,' insisted William. 'You deserved a share of this place, and you deserve it even more now.'

'What!' exclaimed Grace, dropping her fork onto her plate with a clatter.

'I'm not sure what you mean,' said Cora.

440

'I mean, I want you to come into business with me. I want to offer you an equal partnership in the *Bradda Vista*.'

'No!' squealed Grace, the last vestiges of colour draining from her face. 'You can't do this!'

'No, really, William, it isn't necessary . . .' protested Cora.

'I *want* to do this. I'm not here to look after the old place, and you've done a first-rate job. It's only right and proper.' He glanced across at Grace. 'And heaven knows, Grace needs someone to keep an eye on her . . .'

'How could you!' cried Grace, getting to her feet with a look of absolute horror. 'How could you, after all I'm doing to put this place back on its feet . . .'

'It's all right, Grace.' Cora took hold of Grace's wrist and pulled her gently back down onto her chair. 'I'm not going to accept.'

'What?' It was William's turn to look shocked and appalled.

'I *can't* accept. It's kind of you, and I'm flattered, but I just took over to . . . well, you know, do my duty. I've done my best and it's over now. Behind me. It's time I moved on.'

'But, Cora gel!' exclaimed Thomas. 'You've been doin' a ter'ble good job of it. It'd give you a bit of security . . .'

'Come on, sis, see sense,' urged William.

'No, Grandad. No, William. I've said my piece.'

She glanced at Grace and saw that she looked positively smug.

'I know why she's not interested,' she chimed in. 'She's got herself that good-looking young vet, haven't you, Cora? Proposed, has he?'

'What?' William's eyebrows shot up to his hairline. Cora was full of surprises tonight. 'You've got a man?'

He wondered why the idea seemed so peculiar. She wasn't the worst-looking woman in the world, after all. She just hadn't seemed the type somehow.

'No,' replied Cora simply. She got up from the table, folding her napkin and laying it neatly on the tablecloth next to her plate. 'As a matter of fact I don't particularly want to *get* anyone, or anything. There are things I want to do. Things I didn't even know I *could* do until I took on this place. I've learned a lot this last year.'

'She's talking rubbish,' scoffed Grace. 'She's just going to go back to that shop of hers.'

Cora ignored her sister-in-law's rudeness. What did it matter anyway?

'This is the first time I've been really free,' she said. 'And I'm beginning to like it. I honestly think I can make something of myself if I try. But I don't expect you to understand . . .'

'And I don't,' said William gloomily. 'How can anyone talk about being free in the middle of a war?'

'I'm sorry, William,' said Cora, smiling at his schoolboy oafishness. He and Grace made a fine pair. 'But I'm just finding out what it's like to be me, and I'm not giving that up for anything. Not even the *Bradda Vista*.'

Chapter 32

'I can still hardly believe it – that soon we will all be together.'

Reuben bounced his baby daughter on his knee, listening to her delighted gurgles. No one could be a prouder father than Reuben Kotkin.

'Believe it, *bubeleh*, believe it. They have promised a married camp very soon. We will be a proper family!'

He laughed and Rachel laughed too. That was the thing about hope, it was infectious. There were other happy faces here too, other couples who had come gladly to the monthly meeting, knowing that they would soon be able to live together with their children. And faces, too, that were not so happy – for not every married couple was to be reunited.

'They say it's very big, the hotel we will be living in. It even has its own farm, for fresh milk every day.'

'That will be good for Esther,' agreed Reuben. 'But I wish she could be free – I wish we all could.'

'If we could find some work to do, they might let us go. They let Isaac go.'

'Isaac is a lucky man.' Reuben squeezed Rachel's hand. 'But I am luckier.'

'Will you miss it, your camp in Douglas?'

Reuben chuckled.

'Hutchinson? When I can be with my own sweet wife and daughter? Of course not, but I'll miss the good friends I made there.' He sighed. 'I'll miss Sachs.'

'This Sachs – he has no wife?'

'He has no one, so he must stay behind in Hutchinson

when we go to the married camp.'

'But he has volunteered to be a soldier, no?'

'Poor Sachs, he was so sure they would let him join the Pioneer Corps – then they tell him he has something wrong with his heart.' Reuben shook his head. 'Sachs was the one who kept me sane and made me laugh when I was sad. And now he is sad.'

'And you can do nothing?'

'Not unless . . .' A thought crossed Reuben's mind. Something that Sachs had mentioned on more than one occasion. 'Sachs is lonely. He talks all the time about how it would be if he had a girl. Just to write to . . .' He smiled. 'If they liked each other enough, they could always "discover" they were cousins, and then they would even be allowed to meet.'

'A girl? Who?'

'You have friends don't you? Unmarried friends?'

Now it was Rachel who was laughing.

'You don't mean you want me to play the matchmaker!'

'Why not? The *shadchen* is a fine Jewish tradition. And you must know someone.'

'No, no, I couldn't.'

'He is a *very* handsome young fellow. Not rich, *nebech*, but handsome, and with more brains in his head than any man has a right to. Can't you think of anyone?'

'Well, maybe – maybe there is someone I might ask. But if she says no—'

'Yes, yes, of course – just try, that's all I ask.'

'I could ask Sarah.'

'Sarah?'

'You know, Sarah Rosenberg, we were in the prison together. She pulled Elsa Nadel out of the sea.'

Reuben returned her gaze quizzically.

'You never told me anything about pulling people out of the sea.'

'Oh, it was so sad.' Rachel leaned across the table. 'Sarah

found Elsa walking out into the sea, trying to drown herself.'

Rachel shook her head. 'And to think poor Sarah has had so much trouble herself . . .'

Reuben was aghast.

'Why should Elsa want to kill herself?'

'Because of her brother – Max. They were twins, very close.'

'He died?'

'She had a letter saying he was on the *Arandora Star*, missing, presumed dead.'

'Poor *mensch*.'

'They told her he wasn't even supposed to be on the ship, but he must have swapped papers with someone. They never found his body. And Elsa never told a soul.'

'Did you say Max?' Something stirred at the back of Reuben's mind.

'Yes, why?'

'Oh, no reason.' He shook Esther's homemade wooden rattle and the child reached out delightedly for it. 'You wouldn't know what this Max . . . well, you wouldn't know anything about him, I suppose?'

'Nothing – except that he was an artist.'

'An artist. *Gotenyu*!'

'A painter. The Nazis threw him out of Germany for being "decadent".' She studied the changing expressions on Reuben's face. 'Are you all right, Reuben? Is something the matter?'

Her voice jolted Reuben out of his train of thought.

'No, nothing's the matter, I'm fine. But this Max . . .'

'I don't understand why you're so fascinated by him.'

'We have a man at Hutchinson, a talented artist, but the poor man took a knock on the head and he's half out of his wits. He was on the *Arandora Star* – a fisherman pulled him out of the sea.'

'But I still don't see . . .'

'On his papers it says he's a clerk called Ernst Müller; but ever since he's arrived he's been insisting that his real name is Max.'

'Cora! I was afraid you wouldn't come.'

James stood up, very tall and straight in his uniform. As Cora walked across the hotel dining room she saw the admiring glances he was drawing from other women. Quite right too: James McArthur was a good-looking man and a real catch. For someone.

'Of course I wanted to come. You're leaving for your regiment tomorrow.'

'That's why,' he coughed to clear his throat. 'That's why we really had to meet.' He pushed in her chair for her then sat down opposite, glancing around. The tablecloths looked grubby, and the little stage where the palm court trio had played lay deserted and dusty. 'This place isn't what it was before the war, is it?'

Cora fiddled with her menu.

'Everything's changed – so have we.'

'You really think so?'

Her hazel eyes met his and the shiver of love passed between them, so delicate and so fragile that it was almost painful.

'You know we have.'

An ancient waiter in shiny black trousers brought bowls of tepid Brown Windsor soup, and they ate slowly and warily, to the shrill accompaniment of spoons clinking against china.

'I'm sorry,' said Cora, out of the blue. James looked up.

'Sorry for what?'

'You asked me a question, and I haven't given you an answer.' She wondered whether James's heart was thumping as hard as hers was, making her light-headed, edgy.

'It's probably wrong of me to put pressure on you, only . . .'

'No.' She reached out and touched his hand, her fingers cool against his overheated skin. 'You're right to make me come to a decision. Neither of us knows when you'll be back.'

446

'Or if I'll be back.'

'Don't talk like that, of course you will. It's not as if you're fighting in the front line . . .' Her voice tailed off, her eyes drawn by his; her heart torn by a desperate desire to kiss him. 'I want to tell you something, James. I think it's time. I want to tell you that I love you.'

There was a catch in her throat as she spoke the words.

'Oh, Cora . . .' She saw a strange brightness in his eyes, wondered if he could feel it too.

'Do you still love me, James?'

'More than I ever knew. I should have asked you to marry me three years ago, the very first time I saw you.'

He took her hand and kissed it. She had never really seen beyond the wall of his self-assurance before, beyond the protective veil which kept him at one remove from the rest of the world. She did not pull her hand away. She wanted so much to let it linger.

'I can't marry you, James.'

He looked as though he had been struck by a thunderbolt.

'But, Cora, you just said . . .'

'I said that I love you. That's true, I love you very much. But I can't marry you.'

'Why, Cora?'

'Because this is the wrong time, the wrong place. We're in the middle of a war.'

'Lots of people get married in wartime.'

'And lots of people end up hating each other. Look at William and Grace.'

'That's different. They . . .'

'But I still can't marry you. It wouldn't be right.' She searched desperately for the words to express what she felt; the longing, the need. 'You've just joined the RAVC – why did you do it?'

'Because I want to . . . No. Because I have to do my duty.'

'So do I, James. Grace is running the *Bradda Vista* now, it's

447

not my concern any more. And I can't just sit around letting other people fight this war for me. Fenella's right. The time comes when you just have to get out and do something useful.'

'Cora . . .' he cut in, but she shook her head, speaking to him softly, praying he would understand.

'There's more to it than that,' she explained. 'I've changed – grown up. I can't go back to being just a shop-girl. I know now I can do more. There are so many things I can do with my life.'

She looked into James's face. It seemed sad and yet, in part, relieved. Her hand touched his, and their fingers entwined.

'You don't really want to get married right now, do you? You just want to have someone at home who loves you and who'll wait for you.'

James's eyes met hers.

'And will you? Will you wait for me?'

'I don't know.' There was an empty feeling in the pit of her stomach. She pushed her soup bowl away. 'I can't imagine not loving you, but this war keeps changing everything – things, places, people. The war could go on for years, and I want us to be free to go wherever it takes us.'

'So where do we go from here?' James's expressionless tone covered the hurt he felt. It wasn't so much the hurt of not winning, the sting of rejection; it was the ache of losing the one person in the world he had ever truly learned to love. It had taken his disastrous experience with Elsa Nadel to make him realise just how much Cora meant to him. 'What will you do?'

'Go into the Forces probably – maybe the WRENs or the WAAFs. I'm young and fit, there's work for me to do.' She looked across at him, loving him with her entire being, wanting him with a great surge of sensual warmth; wondering where she had found the courage to do this to him and to herself.

'And when the war's over?'

She twisted her napkin between her fingers.

'Who knows? Perhaps I'll see the world . . .'

'And us? What about us?'

'That depends on whether we both still feel the same way. Maybe I'll have found someone else by then. Maybe you will too . . .'

'Maybe. But I doubt it.'

They looked at each other, each contemplating the impossibility of loving someone else. It was James who broke the silence.

'I wish there was some way . . . of showing you that I love you. Marrying you would prove that, you see.'

Cora smiled at him; a secret, radiant smile he had not glimpsed before. She looked beautiful in that plain grey dress, he thought. On anyone else it would look drab, but she transformed it with her smile.

'We don't have to be married to show that we love each other.'

He looked back at her in surprise. Surely he'd misunderstood her.

'I don't know what's going to happen tomorrow, James, or the day after. But there's tonight.'

'Cora . . . what are you saying?'

'It's a long way back from Douglas to Port Erin. It's late and it's pouring with rain. Do you think the hotel manager would be able to find us a room for the night?'

William Quine stood in front of the wardrobe mirror, doing up the top button of his greatcoat. Grace was scrunched up in an unhappy bundle on the end of the bed, her knees drawn up to her chin.

Satisfied at last with his appearance, William turned round to face his wife. His buttons fairly gleamed, his three stripes neatly stitched to his coat sleeve.

'Will I do, then?'

'I don't see why you have to take so much trouble. It's only a uniform.'

'It's the King's uniform. While I wear it I'll take a pride in it.'

'Pride!' sneered Grace. 'All you do is run the cookhouse.'

William's expression darkened to an angry scowl, and he took his wife by the shoulders.

'I'm a soldier now, like it or not. I'm a soldier, I'm paid to kill people.' He saw her shocked face and let go of her. 'It's a war, Grace, not a game. The sooner we both realise that the better it's going to be for us.'

'You're leaving me,' said Grace, in a tiny, childlike voice. In the past he might have put his arm round her and comforted her, but now he rounded on her.

'Yes, I'm leaving you. I'm going back to my unit and I'm going to do my duty. You could do worse than do yours.'

'I'm doing my best,' she protested, uncurling her legs and standing up. She looked small and insubstantial next to her thick-set husband. 'I'm learning the business, what more do you want from me?'

'I want you to face up to the truth.'

He sat down on the end of the bed and sat her down beside him. It was like lecturing a child, but then who was he to cast the first stone? He hadn't exactly been behaving in a mature way either.

'Look at me, Grace.'

She raised sullen eyes to his.

'What?'

'We've been running away, do you know that? Running away from what happened here.'

'I don't want to talk about it.'

'No, you never do, do you? But we had a baby here, Grace, we had a son.'

'He's dead and gone,' she said flatly. 'I want to forget.'

'I thought I did too, but I was wrong. Not talking about Billy doesn't make you forget. It just makes the pain eat away at you until it makes you sick inside. And I *want* to remember him. So should you.'

'What's the good of that?'

He wanted to take her and shake her up.

'Stop feeling sorry for yourself and pull yourself together. Stop being a moody little bitch and sort yourself out.'

She glared at him, the look of a wounded animal behind the surly scowl.

'I should have known you wouldn't understand. You don't give a damn about me, do you?'

'Oh yes I do,' he replied. 'And that's why I'm telling you to get off your backside and make a go of this place. You haven't got Cora to pick up the pieces now. And you won't have me, either, not till this lot's over.

'So you'd better make the best of a bad job, hadn't you?'

Sarah Rosenberg thought long and hard before going to see Mathilde at the *Erindale*. She'd told herself a dozen times to keep away, to mind her own business and just be grateful; but the questions kept coming back to torment her.

She *had* to know.

An apathetic woman with a child on her hip grunted a greeting as she opened the front door of the guesthouse.

'Ja?'

'Mathilde. I want to see Mathilde.'

The woman looked mildly surprised, as if no one, positively no one, ever wanted to see Mathilde. Especially not some skinny Jewish woman in a threadbare skirt and darned jumper.

'Top floor, last room on the left.' She turned and walked away, leaving Sarah on her own in the hallway. She closed the door and began climbing the stairs.

They seemed to go on for ever, and with each step Sarah had the impression that she was moving deeper into a world she would rather not have anything to do with. Everyone

451

knew that most of the women living here were hard-line Nazis – some of them the wives of high-ranking German officials – and since the business with Marianne von Strondheim the atmosphere had become increasingly tense.

She was lucky. It was a dry day and most of the women were out at their classes or doing paid work. She made it to the top of the last flight of stairs and was faced by a single, peeling door at the far end of the corridor.

She knocked. There was a long silence, then:

'Who is it?'

'It's Sarah Rosenberg.'

'Go away, leave me alone.'

'I'm not going anywhere, Mathilde. If you don't let me in I'll stay out here until somebody comes to throw me out.'

The sound of hurrying feet was followed by the long, metallic scrape of a bolt being drawn back. The door opened and Mathilde bundled her inside, closing the door firmly behind her.

'What do you think you're doing, coming here?'

Mathilde's words were abrupt, aggressive even, but Sarah could tell that it wasn't anger that made her talk that way, it was fear. There were dark circles under her eyes and she was cadaverously thin.

'You don't look well,' commented Sarah.

'What's it to you?'

'Look, Mathilde, I have to talk to you, that's all.'

'I've got nothing to say.'

'Just tell me what's going on, and I'll leave.'

Mathilde sank wearily onto a rickety chair. Sarah took a look around the room, noticing how dank and depressing it was, with its sloping ceiling and its rusty iron bedstead. It stank of damp, and there was black mould all round the window. This must be the most horrible room in the whole house.

'What do you want to know?'

'I'd have thought that was obvious. I want to know why you helped me that day.'

'I . . . didn't help you, you must have been mistaken. I slipped.'

'You helped me, Mathilde. You told me to push you, and you would fall.'

Mathilde gazed out of the window.

'I can't talk about these things, especially not with you. It's not safe.'

'All I want is to understand. You saved my life, for goodness' sake. I just want to know why.'

Mathilde's face looked white and old as she replied:

'What do I look like?'

Taken aback, Sarah answered:

'I don't know . . . tired, ill . . .'

'Would you say I was a typical German?'

What kind of question was that? wondered Sarah. She looked at Mathilde's blonde hair, pale skin, dark blue eyes.

'Yes, of course.'

'You wouldn't say I looked Jewish?' She turned abruptly to look at Sarah. 'Well?'

'No.'

The penny dropped with lightning suddenness.

'You're telling me you're Jewish?' Sarah could hardly get her mind round the idea. 'You can't be!'

'Let me tell you a story,' said Mathilde, folding her bony hands in her lap. 'A story about three little girls with a German father and a Jewish mother. Two of the little girls were dark-haired, Jewish-looking, like their mother. But the third . . .'

'The third was blonde with blue eyes?' ventured Sarah.

Mathilde nodded.

'We were brought up as good little Jewish girls . . . It was a good life, Pappi had a job in a bank and we had pretty clothes, lots of toys. Then, one day everything changed. Hitler came to power and we had to move from our lovely house. Then Mutti and my sisters disappeared. Pappi said they'd gone away to protect Pappi and me, I couldn't understand why. I never saw them again. I heard a rumour later, that they had been taken to a camp . . .'

Sarah shivered, remembering her own experiences at Buchenwald; telling herself that in spite of it all, she was one of the lucky ones.

'Then Pappi told me that I wasn't a little Jewish girl any more, I was a little German girl. A good little blue-eyed Mädchen who hated Jews and spat at them in the street.

'I couldn't understand at first. But I grew up quickly, I had to. I saw what it means to be a Jew, and I knew I didn't want to be Jewish, not ever again.' She laughed bitterly. 'I thought if I was a good German, not a dirty Jew, people would like me and accept me. But now everyone hates me . . .'

Sarah stared at her, not quite able to believe what she had just heard.

'I had no idea,' she said slowly.

'You weren't supposed to. And if you breathe a word of what I've told you, I swear I'll kill you.'

Sarah extended a hand.

'I could help you.'

'To be a Jew?'

'If that's what you want.'

'Get out.' Mathilde was shaking, her eyes wide with fear. 'I was a fool to help you that day. I should have let them kill you. They'll kill me too if they find out . . .'

'You don't have to do this to yourself. Let me help you.'

'I don't want your help, I don't need it. You've got what you came for. Now get out and please, please, never come back here again.'

Once outside the door, Sarah hesitated. How could she go? How could she leave Mathilde like this? She could hear her muffled sobs through the door; longed to go to her and tell her that if they stuck together they would be all right. But she didn't even know if that was true.

And all at once, Sarah realised that, for all the terrible things that happened to her, none had been as bad as what

454

was happening to Mathilde. Time had healed her wounded mind and body.

But for some people, it seemed, the pain would never end.

Chapter 33

Farmer Idris Jones hauled another piece of timber out of the cart and handed it to Emil.

'Hold that still now, you hear?'

Emil held the wood gingerly across the gap at the bottom of the gate. Farmer Jones had a tendency to swing his hammer with more enthusiasm than accuracy, and Emil had a bruised thumb to prove it.

''Course, if you'd told me about this hole sooner, them sheep never would've got out,' commented the farmer gruffly, as he hammered the wood into place with six-inch nails.

'No, Mr Jones. Sorry, Mr Jones.'

Patch the sheepdog snuffled interestedly around Emil's muddy feet, but he didn't bend to pet her wet black muzzle. He knew he'd get a cuff round the ear if he didn't keep his mind on the job. He thought about his Ma. She'd said he could have a dog one day. He wished he was back home, with her and Auntie Claire.

The sound of a car engine made Farmer Jones look up. A very ancient, very muddy Ford was bouncing and bumping its way up the lane.

'*Diw*,' he cursed softly under his breath, wiping his hands on the seat of his pants. 'It's Parson Llewellyn again.'

Emil brightened visibly.

'Will 'e 'ave a letter from me Ma, then?'

Farmer Jones threw him a look.

'Show some respect, boy. Tuck your shirt-tails in, and wipe that muck off your face.'

He trudged out into the lane and watched the Ford judder to a halt. Sure enough, Llewellyn was at the wheel, but there were two other people inside – another, younger man and a woman.

Lord bless us and save us, thought Idris Jones as he watched not one parson but two climb out of the car. The younger man opened the rear door and out slid the woman. Such a woman as Idris Jones had never seen in his life before – all shiny hair and lipstick, and hardly a stitch of decent clothing on her, with her tight skirt and high-heeled shoes.

Emil stood in the gateway and stared, open-mouthed. At first he couldn't believe it. Auntie Claire was standing in the lane, ankle-deep in mud in her best shoes.

'Auntie Claire!' he gasped. And Claire's red mouth blossomed into a broad grin of pleasure as she held out her arms to hug him.

'Emil Herzheim, what you bin up to – rollin' in mud?'

Llewellyn stepped forward and nodded his greeting to Farmer Jones.

'Morning, Idris. This is Reverend Newell and Miss Hodges. She's a . . . er . . . friend of Emil's mother.'

'Mornin', Reverend.' With difficulty, Farmer Jones averted his gaze from Claire Hodges's long, slim legs and fixed his eyes on the young vicar. 'I'm Chapel myself. Come far, have you?'

'From London.' Newell looked at Emil and Claire and knew that he'd been right to take the risk; right to ask her to come to the court with him and speak up for Grethe Herzheim. 'We've got a court order.'

'What's that?' piped up Emil, bright as a button.

Claire squatted down so that her face was on a level with Emil's.

'It's a special piece of paper,' she explained. 'It means we can take you to your Ma on the Isle of Man.'

It was a chilly April morning, windy and bright; but inside the hut it was a friendly jumble of warmth and noise. The camp nursery had become a popular place for mothers and their children to meet.

Sarah Rosenberg sat cross-legged on the floor, showing little Esther Kotkin how to play with a set of painted wooden bricks. Esther sat up on her chubby little bottom, banging them together and giggling with delight.

'Rachel, she is a heart-stealer, this little *bubeleh*!'

Rachel laughed, her heart full of love and pride for her daughter.

'Reuben says she takes after her mother.'

'And so she does. She'll be a beauty when she grows up.'

Rachel got down onto the floor and hoisted Esther onto her lap.

'Of course, she is getting much too fat.' She stroked the baby's plump leg affectionately. 'It is the terrible food they give us now – hardly anything but bread and slops.'

Esther sneezed and her mother wiped her runny nose.

Sarah clucked sympathetically. She knew how hard it was at the *Bradda Vista* since Grace Quine had taken over.

'She needs vegetables and fruit, that's why she gets these colds. You must tell the house representative.'

Rachel shook her head.

'It will be better when we go to the new camp. And I don't want to cause trouble, not now when we're going to be a family . . .'

Sarah nodded. She could understand that. Why, hadn't she caused enough trouble of her own, what with all that business about Marianne von Strondheim? She tried to shut the bad things out of her mind, and by and large managed it, but the one thing she couldn't forget was the look on Mathilde's face.

'You're right,' she said, looking up. 'Nothing is more important than that.'

Dropping her wooden brick, Esther reached out to Sarah for a knitted bunny rabbit one of her dozens of doting 'aunties' had made for her. Joining in Esther's smiles and laughter, Sarah played peep-bo with the rabbit. Rachel watched with pleasure. They'd come a long way since their first meeting in Holloway, when Rachel had been scarcely more than a terrified child and Sarah had suspected everyone, everything.

'I'll miss you,' she said, 'when we are in the married camp.'

'I'll get permission to come and visit you.' She looked down. 'I'll miss you too.'

'Perhaps they will release you soon?'

'Perhaps. I hope they will. But I am not a "priority", as they say. And there are some who have me marked down as a trouble-maker.'

'Have you thought about what Reuben said?'

'About . . . ?'

'About his friend Sachs. He is lonely too.'

Sarah wagged her finger reprovingly.

'What is this – you are a matchmaker now?'

'Do it for me, Sarah, just write to him. You don't have to meet him if you don't want.' She reached into her dress pocket for the pencil-sketch which Ernst Müller had made of Sachs. 'Look, he is quite handsome.'

She held it out and Sarah took it dismissively. She sniffed.

'I've seen better.' Which she had. But as she looked down at the sketch she saw an honest face, a friendly face with large, dark eyes which wouldn't let her go. 'He looks like some spoilt college boy. I suppose he's rich?'

'He has nothing, not a penny. His parents are dead, he is just a poor writer who lost everything when he escaped from Belgium. He's lucky to be alive.'

'Oh.' That changed things somehow, made the young man with the dark eyes and the stubborn chin seem more approachable. 'But why should he want to write to me?'

'He doesn't know he does yet. Reuben thought it would be a nice surprise.'

'Don't you ever stop interfering in other people's lives, Rachel Kotkin?'

'I think you'd like each other. I'm certain you would.'

'No, no, I couldn't do it. I don't want to. I don't need a man and he doesn't need me.'

Rachel sighed.

'Well, I asked. I will tell Reuben that I asked but you did not want to. I understand.'

She reached out to take the sketch back, but Sarah held on to it at the last moment.

'I'll keep this,' she said.

'But you said . . .'

'If I'm going to write to my long-lost cousin, I think I ought to know what he looks like.'

Evie Bannister welcomed her unexpected visitor with open arms.

'Cora, dear, what a lovely surprise. Do come in. Mind the paint, it's still a bit wet.'

'You've been busy,' commented Cora as she edged in past the freshly painted door of the shop and walked through to the sitting room at the back.

'It may be wartime, Cora, but I don't believe in letting my standards slip. George got the paint for me, it's a lovely bright colour, isn't it? I may not have much stock worth selling, but the customers do like to see a nice tidy shop.'

As Evie put the kettle on, Cora took off her hat and coat.

'It's about the *Bradda Vista*,' she began.

Evie nodded her greying locks, spooning tea into the big brown pot. She liked her tea good and strong, but one per person and *none* for the pot, that was what Lord Wilton said.

'I must say, I was surprised to hear you'd handed it over to Grace. Not that it's any of my business,' she added. She opened a drawer and took out two shiny cake forks. 'You'll take a slice of ginger parkin?'

'Yes, that would be lovely.' She settled herself down in one of Evie's comfy chairs. 'This is just like when I used to work here and we took our morning coffee together.'

461

'Yes, isn't it just, dear? I do miss you, you know. And the customers still haven't got used to Daphne. It takes a long time to turn a silly sixteen-year-old into a proper sales lady.'

Cora smiled.

'I was a silly sixteen-year-old too – do you remember?'

'You may have been sixteen,' replied Evie. 'But silly? Never. That's why I always hoped you'd take on the shop when I retire.'

'That's what I always dreamed of doing,' admitted Cora. 'But everything's turned out so different.'

'That's war for you. If it hadn't been for the first one, Bessie Teare and I would probably be grandmothers by now.' Evie gave Cora a long, hard look as she set the teapot on the table. 'I must say, I always thought you and James McArthur might . . . well, you know . . . I thought he might have popped the question. But now he's gone . . .'

'I'm sure he'll be back when all of this is over,' cut in Cora. It was so hard to think about James, about the one blissful night they had spent together before he left for England. A night when she had come so very close to changing her mind. 'And . . . so will I.'

'How do you mean, dear?' Evie sat down opposite. 'You aren't going anywhere, are you?'

'As a matter of fact I am. I've decided to join up.'

Evie looked as shocked as if Cora had said she was going to be a nun.

'I can't believe it.'

'There's nothing here for me now,' pointed out Cora. 'The guesthouse is Grace's responsibility – I'm just in the way.'

'Don't be silly, you kept that place from going under. And if you leave that girl to her own devices, it'll go under yet,' she added.

'The *Bradda Vista* belongs to William and Grace, not me. And I can't just stay here where it's cosy and safe, when so many people are out there doing their bit. There's Fenella, and Bessie's niece and nephew . . .'

'You can do your bit here,' replied Evie. 'Daphne's hopeless, and anyway, she keeps saying she wants to go off and be a Land Girl. Now, I couldn't take you on full-time just yet, but in time . . .'

'I couldn't,' protested Cora. Yes you could, whispered a voice inside her head. It would be easy. Turn round and walk right back into your old life, comfortable and well worn like a pair of old slippers.

'If it's this new law they've passed in London,' commented Evie, 'I shouldn't worry about it if I were you. The Keys will never agree to conscription for Manxwomen.'

'No. No, I expect you're right . . .'

'So what do you say? Will you come back to the shop?'

Easier than easy, whispered the small voice. You can do your bit right here, do your bit of war-work, keep well away from the bombs and the danger. Say yes.

But the word stuck in her throat.

'It's so kind of you,' said Cora. 'And I'm going to miss you terribly. But really, Evie, I just came to say goodbye – and to ask if you'd take care of Bonzo for me until I come home again.'

Grethe felt angry and excited. She'd read and re-read the telegram from Claire, again and again. What was going on?

She was standing near to the perimeter fence of the camp, gazing out along the empty road beyond. The gates were closed, the guards' khaki uniforms giving off steam in the hot sunshine that followed the sudden April downpour.

Grethe hardly noticed the weather. She was straining her eyes, scanning the far horizon for the first glimpse of the bus that would bring Claire with the other visitors to Rushen Camp.

In her mind, she ran over what Claire had said: 'Coming to visit you Wednesday, tell you what it's all about when I see you.'

'What it's all about . . . ?' Grethe burned to know. She *had*

463

to know. Claire had said that she knew where Emil was, that Adrian Newell had been in touch with her, but she hadn't given Emil's address. Why, why? She thrust her hand into her pocket, twisting the handkerchief between her fingers.

Claire was coming to see her, coming all the way from London especially to see her. It was going to be a strange reunion. She had changed, she knew that; would Claire have changed too? And most of all, would she really, truly, have news of Emil?

The rain began falling again, at first softly, then in great rods which sparkled like glass as they speared the empty road. Sunshine flooded the sky, from underneath low, fluffy clouds. And then Grethe saw it.

The vehicle was moving slowly along the road; at first just a speck, then a dot, then a dark shape which resolved itself gradually into the form of a bus. Grethe tapped her foot, impatient, anxious.

The bus drew up on the other side of the double row of barbed wire.

'Everybody off. This is as far as we go.'

The door opened and the first figure got down; an old lady with a shopping basket and an umbrella. Then a couple of middle-aged men in raincoats, three or four little girls and – much to Grethe's surprise – Adrian Newell. He was smiling as he walked towards the gates and handed over his identity card. Smiling at Grethe.

Who was that behind him – was it Claire? No, not Claire, just some girl who looked a bit like her. Disappointment felt like a stone in her stomach. Maybe she hadn't come after all. Maybe she'd been refused a pass. Then another figure got down from the bus, a jaunty figure in a rust-coloured coat and a hat with a feather.

'Claire. Claire!'

Grethe wanted to run right out through the gates but a guard barred her way.

'Sorry, miss, you just keep right back there, all right?'

'Claire!' she called, and Claire turned towards her, waved and smiled.

'Be right with you, kid,' she called back. 'I got somethin' for you.'

And she reached out her hand to someone who was still on the bus.

'Come on, don't be scared. Don't want the bus to go right back with you on it, do you?'

Grethe was shaking, she didn't know why. Yes she did, it was because of a thought which had entered her mind like a lightning bolt and which she didn't want to surface into consciousness.

The small boy got slowly and tentatively off the bus, gas-mask case slung over the shoulder of his sleeveless green pullover. His shorts skimmed a grazed and scabby knee, and his blond hair looked as though it had been cut with garden shears. But there was no mistaking him, though he must have grown a good inch or two since Grethe had last seen him.

'Emil! Emil!' she gasped, her voice no louder than a shocked gasp. So this was why Claire had been so mysterious, refusing to tell her what was going on.

Emil stood very still for a few seconds, his hand clasped tightly in Claire's, his blue eyes wide and staring blankly. For a horrible moment, Grethe wondered if perhaps he didn't even recognise her. Had she changed so much? Was he trying to punish her for leaving him like that? She wanted to call out to him again, but her heart was in her mouth, her throat parched dry.

Disengaging his hand from Claire's, he took a step forward, then another. Then broke into a run, hurtling through the open gates towards his mother's waiting arms.

'Ma, Ma, Ma,' he gasped as she held him close. 'They took me an' put me in this place. Then Auntie Claire and the vicar come an' fetched me back . . .'

'I'm sorry, I'm so sorry.' She wept silently as she kissed his scruffy blond head. 'They won't take you away from me again, I swear they won't.'

It was almost three o'clock in the morning when Grace was awakened by a ferocious hammering on her bedroom door. She groaned, rolled over, tried to drift off back to sleep; but the hammering just went on.

'Grace, Grace, come quick, come quick!'

With the utmost reluctance Grace sat up and swung her legs out of bed, muttering curses as she dragged herself to the door and switched on the light.

'What is it *now*?' she scowled as she opened the door. Frau Kessler was standing outside, her face as white as a sheet. 'Well? This had better be important.'

'It is Esther, Frau Quine. The little one is very sick . . .'

Something froze in Grace's blood, but she shook away the thought.

'She's probably just teething or something. You woke me up to tell me that?'

'No, no, please, Grace, it is very serious. Little Esther . . . she is burning hot . . .'

'All right, all right, I'm coming.' Grace grabbed her dressing-gown. 'Has somebody called Dr Jefferson?'

'Miss Cora is on the telephone now,' nodded Frau Kessler. 'Hurry, please.'

Cora again, thought Grace grimly. If she was such a bloody saint, why couldn't she sort this out on her own and let Grace get her sleep? It wasn't as if Cora had anything else to do.

She clumped down the stairs to the first floor. Long before she reached Rachel's room she heard the commotion coming from inside. People were talking all at once, somebody was crying, and over the top of it all came the sound of Rachel's voice, high-pitched and hysterical:

'Esther, my darling baby . . . no, no, no!'

Irritation welled up inside Grace. These foreign women had no self-restraint, and it was bound to be nothing. Shoving

466

her way past Grethe, Nadia and Frau Feldmann, she stormed into the room.

'What is the meaning . . . ?' She stood frozen in the doorway, horror chilling the blood in her veins. 'Oh my dear God.'

Four years were stripped away in an instant. All at once she was the young, helpless mother with her dying child in her arms. Dying because of what she had done and what she had not known how to do . . .

Rachel was huddled on the floor, sobbing, her face bloated with anguish, tears dripping in a wet veil from eyes, nose, mouth. All dignity gone. Her round, dark eyes were staring fixedly at Elsa, who was cradling the naked, beetroot-red body of her child.

Grief and fear caught in Grace's throat.

'What is going on? What is wrong with her?'

As she spoke, Esther became totally rigid in Elsa's arms, the tiny limbs twitching, the eyes rolling back in her head so that only the whites were visible. She shook violently, all consciousness gone from her tiny, helpless body.

'*Gevalt!*' screeched Rachel. 'My baby, my Esther, she is dying.'

'No,' said Elsa. 'I've seen this before, it's a convulsion. The baby has a fever. We must get her temperature down. Get a bowl of tepid water, lots of it. Towels, flannels, anything we can sponge her down with.'

There was frantic activity in the room, people running about. Frau Kessler arrived with an enamel bowl full of water, then Nadia with a bucket and two face-flannels.

Grace watched in utter horror, reliving every moment of her own child's death, convinced in her heart that history was repeating itself. Her Billy had died in here. Died in her arms . . .

Elsa laid Esther on the floor, on a towel. Her body was rag-limp now, arms and legs dangling like dead weights. Elsa began sponging the tepid water over the fragile, burning-hot skin.

'Frau Kessler, help me, would you? That's right, more water. I think she's beginning to cool down a little . . .'

All activity was centred on the tiny, naked body on the sodden towel. Grace turned to look at Rachel Kotkin. Everyone seemed to have forgotten about the mother, crouched in a crumpled, sobbing heap; alone and terrified.

All at once, their eyes met and Grace felt the full force of Rachel's grief. She was afraid. Afraid of allowing herself to feel like this again. And why should she feel for this foreign woman, this enemy with whom she shared nothing but hatred?

Slowly she walked across the room, knelt down beside Rachel; took her in her arms and began rocking her.

'My baby, my baby,' wept Rachel, her head on Grace's shoulder.

'Everything's all right, Rachel,' she whispered. 'Everything's going to be all right now.' Please God, pleaded Grace in the darkness of her thoughts. Please God, don't let this child die.

Chapter 34

Reuben stood beside his daughter's cot at Noble's Hospital.

'Rachel, oh Rachel, when they came to the camp to fetch me here, I thought we must lose her.'

Rachel Kotkin, still in her dressing-gown, sat looking at her sleeping baby. She reached up and took Reuben's hand in hers. It felt ice-cold.

'The doctors say Esther will be all right. It is just a fever. But they must watch her for a while, in case the convulsions come again.' She squeezed Reuben's hand. 'Stop pacing up and down and sit here with me.'

'I'm sorry, *bubeleh.*' He sat down beside her and put his arm round her shoulders. 'I was so afraid, all the way here from the camp I was asking the guards: "My wife, she is well?", "my daughter, she is very sick?", over and over again. I think I was half-crazy.'

'And I thought I was so strong,' said Rachel. 'Then Esther got sick and I just screamed and wept, until Elsa came . . . and then Grace Quine . . .'

'God be praised; but – Grace Quine?'

Rachel nodded.

'After all the bad things she has done to the house, the things she has said about us, I could not understand it. But suddenly she was kind to me.'

'How long must you and Esther stay in the hospital?'

'A few days, no more.'

Reuben took Rachel's hand to his lips and kissed it.

'I have news. The Commandant spoke to all the married men yesterday morning.'

Rachel looked into his eyes, drinking in his words.

'News – about the new camp?'

He nodded.

'You must go back to Port Erin, but only to collect your things. At the weekend they are transferring the married couples to Port St Mary.

'We are never going to be apart again.'

No one had slept very much at the *Bradda Vista*. As dawn crept up over the hills, Grace Quine sat in the kitchen, her hands wrapped round a tin mug of cocoa.

Cora hesitated before coming into the kitchen, closing the door very softly behind her.

'You'll catch cold,' she said, 'without your dressing-gown on.'

Grace shook her head.

'I'm fine, I don't feel cold.'

Cora couldn't help noticing how red and puffy Grace's eyes were. She must have been crying for hours.

'I could cook us some breakfast, if you like.'

'Not for me, I'm not very hungry. Perhaps later.'

Cora half filled a pan with milk and water, and lit the gas underneath it.

'Are you all right, Grace?'

'Yes. Yes, of course. Is there any news about the baby?'

'I rang the hospital just now. The Sister said Esther is going to be fine. It was just a high temperature.'

Grace seemed to deflate like a burst balloon, relief taking the last bit of strength from her. Guilt stabbed at Cora as she saw how worn-out Grace looked. She was only a kid really, but there were fine lines around her swollen eyes and her lips looked cracked and sore. Perhaps she'd been wrong about Grace after all.

'I think we should talk,' said Cora, pulling out a chair and sitting opposite Grace. 'I saw you – with Rachel. I saw what you did, you were wonderful. But I thought . . .'

'I know what you thought.' Grace's eyes were moist, the whites very pink from crying. 'And I know what everyone else thinks. You all think I killed my baby.'

'No. No, I never believed that.' It was hard to know exactly what she had believed, only that she'd never liked Grace and she'd been glad to have a reason. 'But you've always seemed . . . I don't know . . . so cold.'

'Do you know what it was like when Billy died? Do you?' Grace's eyes seemed to trace invisible patterns in the old pine table-top as she spoke. 'No, of course you don't, how could you?

'I didn't want Billy when he was born, but I suppose you worked that out yourself. I hated him, that was why God took him from me.'

Cora reached out, then drew back, afraid to touch Grace. 'You know that isn't true.'

'I hated him, and I hated William for getting me in the family way and ruining my life. But you can't hate your own child for long, can you? Billy was my whole life, the only thing I really cared about in this godforsaken place.'

She lit a cigarette from the crumpled pack and dragged on it nervously.

'I was going out that night, whether William liked it or not. I told him so. We had a big row. I decided to take a bath – do you remember?'

Cora nodded. The events of that night could never fade. She wondered how vividly they must be pictured in Grace's thoughts. Discomfited, she got up and turned off the gas under the milk.

'Look, Grace, you don't have to tell me this . . .'

'Yes I do. I want you to know what really happened, not what vicious old women whispered in corners.' She stubbed out the half-finished cigarette in her saucer and lit another. 'I ran it really hot, the way I liked it. I was only out of the bathroom for a minute, I swear I was. How was I to know Billy would fall in and scald himself all over like that? I thought he was with his Daddy.' Her words ended in a dry sob. 'You have to believe me. Why wouldn't they believe me?'

'I do believe you,' Cora heard herself say. 'And so did the inquest.'

'But you didn't believe me then, did you? Nor did William, damn him. You all thought I'd killed my Billy. You thought I just wanted rid of him, didn't you?'

Cora tentatively laid her hand on Grace's shoulder. It was easier to stand behind her, not to have to look her in the face.

'Nobody thought that of you. It was just that . . . you never cried, see, not once. Not a single tear, not even when they buried him. It seemed like you just didn't care.'

'Cry?' Grace took a deep breath and the shaking stopped. 'What's the use of crying? My baby's rotting in the ground, crying won't bring him back.'

'No.' Cora went through the motions of making herself a milky cup of coffee. She didn't really want it any more. 'You're sure you won't have a warm drink?' She sat down at the table. 'You and William never thought about trying for another baby?'

'I can't have any more babies. Something went wrong when I was having Billy – something tore inside me and they had to take it all away. So I really have been punished, haven't I? Then, when I saw Rachel's baby . . . it brought it all back, like it happened yesterday.'

'I . . . I'm sorry. I never knew.' Cora swallowed a sip of coffee. It tasted bitter. 'I really am sorry, but I don't suppose that's much comfort, is it?'

'As a matter of fact I think I owe you an apology,' said Grace, out of the blue. 'I've been a real cow to you ever since I came back here.'

'Let's just say it's water under the bridge.'

'You made a good job of running this place, Cora, and I've made a mess of it so far. You were right. But you've never interfered – you've just let me get on with it and find my way. I should thank you for that.'

'There's no need.'

Grace wiped her eyes and tucked her handkerchief into the sleeve of her nightdress.

'We never loved each other, you know, your brother and me.'

'Oh, I'm sure he loves you. William just isn't very good at showing his feelings.'

'No, it's all right, you don't have to try and make me feel better. I don't even know if we'll last this war out. But I will,' she said, looking up. 'I will, and so will this place. I have to make a go of it now, you understand don't you?'

'I understand,' said Cora. And for the first time, she really did.

The first thing Reuben noticed when he arrived back at Hutchinson Camp was the little gaggle of men standing outside House forty-one.

'Kotkin, *vi geyts bei dir*? How is the little one?'

'Your wife and child, all goes well?'

'How is Rachel, and the *bubeleh*?'

Reuben held up his hands, smiling at their concern. He would miss them, all of them. They had become his friends.

'They are well, both of them. And now they are taking us to the married camp.'

As he walked up the front steps and headed for the room he shared with Sachs, Reuben wondered how his friend would take the news of his departure. Sachs hadn't been his irreverent self lately. And then there was Ernst Müller – or was he really Max Nadel? Would the Commandant forget all about him when Reuben was not there any more to plead his case?

'Sachs,' he called out as he reached the top of the stairs. 'Sachs, are you there?'

'Come in, Kotkin *mensch*, but carefully!'

Reuben pushed open the door and stuck his head into the room. A jumble of boxes and open suitcases lay all over the floor, and Sachs was on his knees in the middle of a mess of books and clothes.

'Sachs, you *shlock*! What are you doing?'

'I am looking for something.' Sachs looked up, his face flushed with effort. 'How goes it, Kotkin? The baby . . . ?'

'She is well now. It was a fever, the doctors say she will be fine.'

'Praise God.' Sachs turned to a heap of old books and began rummaging again. 'Ach, here it is! I knew it was here.'

'What is it?'

'My book of Aesop's Fables. I knew it must be here somewhere. Do you not think it would make a fine gift? I have so little to give . . .'

'Steady, Sachs, you've lost me.' Reuben perched on the edge of the rickety iron bedstead.

'Now, Fischbein and Gold have both lent me jackets, which do you think I should wear?' Sachs held up two jackets, one black and shiny, the other brown and threadbare.

'What for – a jumble sale?'

'For my photograph! Captain Hollingsworth has a camera and he says he will take a picture of me so I can send it with my letter.'

Reuben thought he might, just *might* be beginning to understand. He smiled to himself. He was glad to see Sachs brightening up again; hadn't the man become his best friend in the whole world? He hesitated before announcing:

'I've come to collect my things. They're moving me to the married camp this afternoon.'

At this news Sachs's face fell a little.

'I knew it must be soon,' he nodded. Then he winked. 'If the next child is a boy, name him after me.'

Reuben laughed.

'And risk him growing up like you, *boychik*?'

'What better way for a boy to grow up!'

'You seem a good deal happier,' remarked Reuben.

Sachs beamed, reached into his trouser pocket and waved a piece of paper, covered with line after line of tiny, neat handwriting. Attached to it was a small photograph of a young woman with a thin face and dark hair, wound into a full, soft knot at the nape of her neck.

'I have had a letter.' He lowered his voice and tapped the side of his nose. 'From my *cousin*.'

'Oh yes?'

'Strange that, Kotkin. I never even knew I *had* a cousin, and certainly not one in Port Erin.' He gave Reuben a sideways look. 'Who would have thought you were such a devious man, Reuben Kotkin?'

Reuben chuckled.

'Every bachelor in this camp has "discovered" a cousin or a niece in the women's camp. Rachel and I thought, why should Sachs be any different?'

Sachs flopped onto the bed next to Reuben; lying on his back, he gazed up at the dingy yellow-brown ceiling.

'You're a good man, Reuben Kotkin, but don't tell anyone I said so.'

'Will you meet her, this cousin of yours?'

'God willing. If the captain's photograph doesn't make me look like Nosferatu. And if the Commandant believes our story.'

'He will, Sachs. You could charm the birds off the trees with your stories.'

Thank God for Rachel, thought Reuben. He had been dreading saying goodbye to Sachs, but now that the moment had come, he knew he was leaving his young friend with a heart full of hope.

'Will you do one thing for me, Sachs?'

'Ask it only.'

'Ernst Müller. You will see that he is well – that he is looked after?'

Puzzled, Sachs nodded.

'Of course.'

Sachs held out his hand.

'Shalom, Kotkin. We will meet up again – when we are released.'

Reuben nodded.

'Rachel will cook you *kishke* and *latkes*.' He grinned. 'And I shall make you a suit of clothes for your wedding.'

Grethe and Emil were playing Ludo in the common room when a car drew up outside the *Bradda Vista*.

'It is Rachel!' exclaimed Maria Bertorelli, dropping her crochet to push back the curtain and take a good look at the chaplain's car.

'Is Esther with her?' asked Grethe.

They had all been so frightened that night, every mother in the house understanding how it must feel to come so close to losing a child. For Grethe it had been especially poignant. She looked across at her son and knew she would willingly die rather than have anything bad happen to him ever again. Adrian Newell and Claire had taken such a chance, going down to Wales and bringing Emil back to her. She wondered how she could ever find a way to thank them.

'She is getting out of the car . . . she has the baby . . . oh, she so beautiful.'

'Your go, Ma.' Emil nudged Grethe's arm.

She threw a four, then Emil threw two sixes in a row and fairly scampered round the board, taking three of her counters. Normally he would have been delighted, but today he looked thoughtful, his lower lip jutting out with the effort of concentration.

'Ma . . .'

'What?'

'Are Rachel and Esther comin' back to live 'ere?'

'No, they're going to the family camp in Port St Mary, with Reuben. We're going there too, soon.'

'Oh.' Emil thought a bit more, rolling the die in the palm of his hand.

'Will there be other kids there, then?'

'Lots.'

'An' dads?'

'Y-eees. Why?'

'Ma . . . when you go to the family camp, does that mean they give you a new dad?'

Grethe ruffled Emil's tousled head, her heart going out to him. What would things have been like if Emil's dad hadn't been a vicious pimp who'd turned his back on them both before the kid was even born?

'No, *liebchen*.'

'Why haven't I got a dad?'

She couldn't face the innocent, searching eyes, or the barrage of questions which would follow, as they always did. It would be even worse when he got a bit older and started asking what a whore was, because that was what all the other kids were calling his mother.

'Come on,' she said. 'We'll finish the game later. Let's go and see Rachel and the baby.'

All was upheaval at the *Bradda Vista*. Boxes, bags, prams and brown paper bundles lay heaped on the landings, and Rachel had to pick her way carefully up the stairs to her room.

Elsa Nadel was helping Frau Kessler to tie string round a bundle of cashmere sweaters.

'That's right, put your finger there, hold it tight.'

'*Verdammte* thing, it keeps slipping.'

'Give it to me, there! That's it. Now how about you, Immi? Do you need someone to take care of little Leo while you pack his suitcase?'

Rachel smiled at the sight of Elsa, brave Elsa who had dragged herself back from the brink of despair. Then she thought of the man who might or might not be Max, and wondered what she should say. Would it be too much for Elsa

477

to bear, if it all turned out to be some sort of misunderstanding?

'Hello, Elsa.'

Elsa turned round and smiled. She looked older than she had looked a year ago, when she, Rachel and Grethe had first met in Holloway Prison. There were a few flecks of grey in her short brown hair, a few small lines on the flawless complexion.

'Rachel – and Esther! How is she?' She waded through the mess of boxes and bags, to fuss over the baby.

'She is well now, thank you for everything you did.'

'It was nothing, just my job.'

'Not just when Esther was so sick. What you did for me in Holloway, too. I don't know what I'd have done without you and Grethe.'

Esther smiled and giggled, and grabbed hold of Elsa's finger.

'You see, she likes you,' said Rachel. 'She'll miss you – and so will I.'

'You're going to the camp today?'

'Tomorrow, then Grethe and Emil will come a little later. Reuben is already there. I can't believe we're going to be together again.'

'You shouldn't be in an internment camp at all, they should release you. They will soon.'

'If God is willing. But all I really care about is being together.' Rachel reached into the pocket of her cardigan and took out a tiny paper packet. 'I want you to have this.'

Elsa took it, surprised.

'What?'

'Go on, unwrap it.'

She unfolded it carefully. Inside lay a fine silver chain.

'Rachel, I can't take this – it's your necklace.' She held it out, trying to give it back. 'It's all you have . . .'

Rachel shook her head and folded Elsa's fingers over it.

'It is nothing. Gold and silver are nothing, I have my husband and my child. I want you to have it, Elsa, to remember us by. I wish I could give you more, but this is all I have.'

It was two days later that Elsa received a summons to Mrs Pantin's office.

She arrived to find not only Mrs Pantin there, but Adrian Newell too. He looked sympathetic, Mrs Pantin apprehensive.

'Come in, my dear,' said Mrs Pantin. 'And take a seat.'

'Has something happened? Have I done something I shouldn't?' Thoughts flashed into Elsa's mind – memories of that terrible day when she had made up her mind to end it all. 'I'm much better now,' she added. 'I've started organising classes again . . . you're not going to send me away to Ballamona?'

'No, no, nothing like that,' the chaplain assured her. 'We just want to talk to you, and show you some pictures.'

'Photographs,' explained Mrs Pantin. Opening the side drawer of her desk, she took out a small brown envelope and eased out half a dozen snapshots. Slowly she laid them face-down on the desk.

'What is this for?'

'Turn them over and look at them, please. Then tell me if you know any of these men.'

Puzzled, Elsa looked at the first of the photos: it was a head and shoulders portrait of a middle-aged man with dark hair and a flat nose. She shook her head.

'No. No, I've never seen him before.'

'And this one?'

'No.'

She turned over the third and then the fourth. Mrs Pantin watched her expression. It showed not the faintest glimmer of recognition. It was the fifth photograph which made her gasp.

'Fräulein Nadel – you recognise this man?'

Elsa stared down at the photograph in her trembling fingers. It showed a man in his late thirties, with a face which had once been handsome in a rough-hewn sort of way. But

479

the hair had been hacked and shaved almost to the skull, and a huge, bone-deep scar ran down the left side of the face, from hairline to throat. The grey eyes seemed vacant, only half-comprehending . . .

'No.' She shook her head vigorously. 'No, no, no.'

'Tell us, Elsa. Do you recognise him?' asked Mrs Pantin gently. But all the gentleness in the world couldn't soften the blow.

'It can't be. It can't be him.'

'Can't be who, Elsa?'

'Not Max. Max is dead.' She looked up, fixing Mrs Pantin with anxious grey eyes. 'You've found his body, haven't you? You've found Max's body . . .'

'No.' Adrian Newell got up from his seat and crouched down on his haunches, taking Elsa's hands in his. 'No, we haven't found his body, Elsa, but we think we've found your brother.

'He's alive, Elsa. Max is alive.'

Chapter 35

Right, thought Grace to herself. If it has to happen, it might as well be now.

She contemplated the wreck of the frying pan, lying steaming in the sink, and knew that things had to change. Nadia was willing enough, but if this went on much longer they'd have gastric ulcers or a riot, or both.

Grandad Quine took out his false teeth, gave them a good suck and pushed them back into his gums. He burped queasily.

'My gough, gel, them fritters was a bit rough.'

'Yes,' sighed Grace. 'I shall have to do something about this.' She bent down and scooped up Archie, who gave a startled wheeze as she hoisted him onto her shoulder. 'And we'll have to get some proper fish-heads for you, won't we, boy?'

She tickled him under the chin and – much to his own surprise – Archie began to purr. Thomas looked on, baffled. It wasn't like Grace to get soft over animals. It was hard enough getting her to be pleasant to people.

'You all right, gel?'

'Yes, I'm fine, Thomas. Never better. Did I tell you I'd had a letter from William? He's in Africa, so we'll all have to knuckle down and get things done, won't we? Can't have this place falling about our ears.'

Thomas blinked.

'You're right there, gel. Couldn't make us a cup o' tay, could you?' he hazarded. That was the acid test of Grace's temper.

'Of course I can. I'll do it as soon as I've had a word with Mrs Bertorelli.'

Thomas's expression hovered somewhere between hope, terror and expectation.

'Maria Bertorelli?' He had distinctly mixed feelings about Mrs Bertorelli. She might be after his body, but she made the best cakes and pies he'd ever eaten in his entire life.

'Don't repeat everything I say, Thomas,' replied Grace cheerfully. 'People will think you're a parrot.'

Taking off her apron, she headed out into the hallway. Grethe was there, talking to one of the Czech girls. Thomas watched through the open door. Everyone knew what Grace thought of Grethe Herzheim, but here she was patting Grethe's boy on the head and passing the time of day, as civil as you please! If that wasn't a turn-up for the book, he didn't know what was.

May sunshine filtered into the hallway through the taped-up windows, making patterns on the carpet and illuminating little swirling clouds of bright dust.

'Ah, Grethe,' said Grace breezily. 'I understand you're leaving us soon.'

'I . . . yes,' said Grethe, momentarily lost for a witty riposte. She would have been tempted to say 'good riddance', only Grace looked almost genuinely interested.

'Well, I hope you'll be happier there. And your boy,' she added, giving Emil another pat on the head. He pulled a face and stuck his tongue out, but Grace seemed not to have noticed. 'Must be off, there's the domestic rotas to sort out.'

She found Maria Bertorelli sitting in the common room, unravelling a pair of old socks.

'Signora Bertorelli . . .'

At first Maria pretended not to have heard, but Grace wasn't so easily put off.

'Signora Bertorelli, please . . . I wanted to apologise.'

Maria's eyes snapped up.

'What you say?'

'I wanted to say, I'm very sorry for the way I've been treating you. It was . . .' she swallowed hard. This didn't come easily to her. 'It was wrong of me.'

A slow smile spread across Maria Bertorelli's face, but she suppressed it.

'Okay, you say sorry.' She shrugged and went on unravelling the sock. 'You want something else, yes?'

'I was hoping you might agree to become our cook again. You'd be paid of course,' added Grace. She would have offered Mrs Bertorelli a pay rise too if she'd been allowed to, but camp rates of pay were strictly enforced.

Mrs Bertorelli began winding the speckled green wool into an irregular, wiry ball.

'I busy, very busy,' she sniffed.

Grace knew that she wasn't. In fact, everyone knew how bored Maria had been since she had been forced to give up the cooking. She had knitted, unravelled and re-knitted that pair of socks at least a dozen times.

'I'm very sorry, Signora . . . Maria,' said Grace. 'Won't you reconsider?'

'Why should I? You make it very clear I not wanted.'

'Yes I know.' Grace took a deep breath. Humble pie took some swallowing – a bit like Nadia's cooking. She thought of the fritters and went on. 'I was wrong. Please say you'll think about it. You see, I really can't manage without you.'

The chaplain's car took Elsa all the way from Rushen Camp to Hutchinson, stopping just outside the camp gates.

The last time she had been in Douglas it had been just before Christmas, and she remembered buying all those tiny presents for the women at Port Erin. She remembered her anger and her pain too.

How things had changed since then. James McArthur had left the Island, Cora was telling everyone that she was leaving, and so many of the others had gone now too: either released to do war work, or transferred to the new camp in Port St Mary.

'I'll come in with you,' said Adrian Newell, parking the car and handing his documents to the guard on the gate.

'This is where they are keeping my brother?' She looked around her as they walked into the camp, at the men walking and talking; at the green square in the centre of block after block of Victorian boarding houses.

'*If* he's your brother. We can't be absolutely sure,' pointed out the chaplain. 'And if it is . . .'

'I know.' Her mouth was dry, her palms sweating. It was a bright and breezy May day, but Elsa felt hot and light-headed. 'He'll have changed.'

'I fear so.'

They walked together through the square, watched by curious faces for whom the sight of a woman – and a tolerably good-looking one at that – was still something of a rarity.

A young officer was waiting for them at the Commandant's office; a captain in his mid-twenties, one-armed, his empty sleeve neatly pinned to his side.

'Miss Nadel.'

Elsa nodded. She couldn't take her eyes off the young soldier's mutilated arm. Would Max be like that? What was wrong with him that they hadn't told her about? Would she even know him when she saw him?

They shook hands.

'Captain Hollingsworth. I've known Ernst – I mean Max – since he arrived in the camp. It was his paintings which first made me notice him. He paints the most exquisite landscapes.'

Elsa nodded.

'He is very talented. Please . . . please may I see him?'

Captain Hollingsworth nodded.

'Of course. But you must understand, he is not as you would remember him. He has been through a very great ordeal, as I'm sure the doctors have told you. Really he shouldn't be here at all.'

484

'How . . . how is he?'

'The head injuries were severe; we don't know quite how badly his brain has been damaged, but his memories are almost all gone. That is why it has taken us so long to establish his real identity.'

'Yes, yes, I understand. But I *have* to see him. Don't try to protect me, he's my brother.'

'Come with me. He's painting outside, in the garden.'

Elsa followed Captain Hollingsworth through the house to the little enclosed garden at the back.

'You're sure?'

'Of course.'

Her stomach was in knots. What if it wasn't him? What if . . . ? But what ifs were pointless. She had to know.

The captain opened the door to the garden and she saw him; a frail, wasted figure in a suit two sizes too big for him, sitting on a folding chair with an easel set up in front of him.

His cropped hair and shaven chin made him almost unrecognisable from the wild-haired, bearded, Bohemian figure Elsa had known back in Germany. But she had only to look at the brush, moving confidently across the paper, to know that it was Max.

'M-max.' His name came out as a whisper. He did not turn round, but just went on painting, with a savage intensity. It was clear that nothing existed beyond the picture: sweeping brush-strokes and blocks of vibrant colour. She walked down the back steps into the garden and spoke again, this time raising her voice. 'Max, it's me.'

He turned round, brush in hand, and she saw his face for the first time. It was horribly scarred, the deep indentation on the left side distorting its whole shape, dragging down the corner of eye and mouth so that he was left with a monstrous, lopsided expression.

There was no understanding in his eyes; no love; only a searching, questioning fear. He took a step away from her.

'N-no. Not her, she's gone.'

'Max, it's me. Elsa. Don't you remember?'

It was like talking to a frightened child.

'Elsa?' The word sounded in his brain. He thought somewhere, very far away, he heard an echo. 'Elsa. Who is Elsa? Elsa is gone.'

'Elsa, your sister, your twin sister,' said Captain Hollingsworth. He turned to Elsa. 'This is your brother?'

She nodded, tears springing to her eyes. She had thought she was ready for this, but nothing could have prepared her for the sight of her own brother's fear.

'Don't be afraid, Max. Don't be afraid.'

She reached out to him, and this time he did not shy away. He looked into her eyes, questioning, searching for the answer.

'The lady in my dream. You're the lady in my dream.' His eyes opened wonderingly as he gazed into hers, a flood of confused emotions and fragmented memories crashing in on him.

He knew her face, he had seen it every night in his dreams, painted it into the fabric of every picture. And now it was here, right in front of him. He knew nothing about it except that he had loved this face, and loved it still.

'Elsa?'

'That's right, Elsa. I'm your sister.'

'I don't remember.' He put his hand up to his head. 'I can't remember, I wish I could.'

'You will remember. Just give it time. I'll help you remember.'

Gently she put her arm round him and drew him close. She was weeping, and it was more than Max could bear.

'Don't cry, Elsa, don't cry,' he whispered. 'Everything's all right now.'

She remembered all the times she had comforted Max when they were children together, in Germany. All the times she had been the strong one. Now she felt weak, she needed his strength, but he was like a child again in her arms.

'Everything's all right,' she echoed, and hugged him to her.

Sadness was all around her, but her heart was filled with joy.

Cora sat in Dr Jefferson's waiting room, listening to the ticking of the grandfather clock in the hallway.

Bessie Teare sat opposite, her shopping in a basket by her side.

'Are you ill, dear?' she asked, peering at her over the top of her horn-rimmed spectacles.

Cora smiled and shook her head.

'I hope not. I'm here for my medical.'

'Medical?'

'For the Forces. I've decided to join up.'

Bessie tut-tutted gently.

'Ah yes, Evie Bannister told me. I was so surprised to hear you were thinking of leaving us.'

'It's my duty.'

Bessie shook her head resignedly.

'I think you're very brave. My niece is a nurse in London, you know, and I worry about her all the time. And then there's her brother, he's a navigator . . .'

'I'm hoping to join the WRENs. If they'll have me. If not, I'll go wherever I'm sent. I want to do my bit.'

At that moment, Dr Jefferson's housekeeper put her head round the door of the waiting room.

'Next, please.'

Bessie got up, picking up her heavy shopping bag.

'I know you do, dear. But let's hope this wretched war is over soon, then you won't have to.'

But I want to, thought Cora, and she was filled with a strange, foolish excitement. It makes no sense at all, but this is what I want to do.

Harry Kerruish felt as nervous as a sixteen-year-old schoolboy.

As he came out of church he fiddled with his tie, uncomfortable with the formality of it. Juan was at his side, babbling on about something and nothing, but all Harry could think about was Grethe. Would he see her? Would she be there, as she had promised in her note?

'What do you think then, Uncle Harry?'

'What?' He shook Grethe out of his thoughts for a moment and stared at Juan. 'What was that you were sayin', boy?'

'About them British Fascists, the ones they've locked up over Peel way. What do you think about it all?'

'What is there to think?'

Harry scanned the horizon for a sign of Grethe, but he could not see her.

'Old Chalse is sayin' they're spies, the lot of 'em. They signal to German U-boats by switchin' the lights on an' off . . .'

'What's that, boy – stop your bletherin', will you? There's somethin' I have to do.'

'Grace is expecting us for our dinner.'

'Well you go on ahead. I have to see somebody first.'

'Can't I come too?'

'I said, go on without me. Tell her I won't be long.'

He watched Juan loping off in the direction of the *Bradda Vista* with a mixture of relief and apprehension. It wouldn't do for anyone to know exactly where he was going or who he was hoping to see.

'Mornin', Parson.' He nodded to Adrian Newell as he headed off towards the harbour.

'Good morning, Mr Kerruish. Nice to see you in church.'

Harry felt a twinge of guilt as he jammed his hat back on his head and beat a hasty retreat. The occasions he attended church or chapel were few and far between, and he had to admit that this particular visit had just been an excuse to come to Port Erin. It had been far too long since he had seen Grethe Herzheim.

He caught sight of his reflection in a cottage window as he passed, and wondered what she could possibly see in him. He was nothing to write home about: just a middle-aged fisherman with flecks of grey in his beard and holes in his pockets. He looked all wrong in a suit.

There were few people around on this May Sunday morning, and as he reached the quayside he saw that the row of huts was deserted. He walked more quickly and unlocked the door of his hut, went inside and left the door ajar to let some fresh air in. It smelt fusty inside, the pile of damp nets reeking of rotting seaweed.

He cleared a space and moved some crab pots and a bucket of tar onto the floor. Then he sat down on the wooden bench seat. He glanced at his watch. Gone half-past and she wasn't here yet. Maybe she wasn't coming after all, maybe she'd changed her mind again, and didn't want to see him. Perhaps he should head off towards the *Bradda Vista*. For something to do, he picked up a net and started to mend it.

Footsteps and voices outside made him stiffen and look up. There were two voices: a woman's and a child's. The woman's voice he knew better than any other voice in the world. Letting go of the net, he got to his feet and smoothed down his crumpled suit, adjusting the knot on his one good tie.

Grethe and Emil walked along the quayside towards the huts.

'Where are we goin', Ma?'

'To meet a friend.'

'Why do we have to pretend we're just goin' for a walk?'

'Because . . . just because.' She stopped and, bending down, took Emil by the shoulders. 'It's very important that you don't tell, you do understand, don't you?'

'Is it a secret, Ma?'

'That's right, it's a secret. You can keep a secret, can't you?'

''Course I can,' replied Emil indignantly. 'I don't peach.'

'No, no, of course you don't. Come on, we're late already.'

She took Emil's hand – much to his dismay – and led him towards Harry's hut.

'Is this where your friend lives?'

'No, he lives at Port St Mary, where we're going to live.

This is just where he keeps his boat.'

The door was slightly ajar. Grethe reached out and knocked softly.

'Harry – Harry, are you there?'

The door opened inwards, letting light into the small room. Harry Kerruish stepped forward into the light.

'It's good to see you, gel,' he said. He wanted to hold her in his arms, but there was someone with her. A child. A boy, perhaps six or seven years old, and the living spit of his mother.

Harry's eyes met Emil's and the two studied each other for a few moments. Grethe nudged Emil forward.

'Say hello to Mr Kerruish, Emil.'

'Hello.'

Harry took Emil's proffered hand and shook it, man-to-man.

'Pleased to meet you, Emil.' He smiled at Grethe. 'He's a fine boy, gel. A credit to you.'

'My Ma likes you,' said Emil.

'Well I like her too, boy.'

Emil paused.

'Are you goin' to be my new dad when we go to Port St Mary?'

'Emil, don't say things like that!' snapped Grethe. 'Harry, I'm sorry, he doesn't know what he's saying. You know what kids are like.'

'Sometimes kids talk sense,' replied Harry softly.

Panicky feelings were welling up inside Grethe. Feelings that were too much to cope with. She'd felt like this only once before, when she was seventeen, and that had been a terrible mistake. Ever since then she'd sworn to herself that she wouldn't let love make a victim of her again. She changed the subject.

'I had to see you, Harry. I wanted to tell you that Emil and me, we're off to the new married camp next week.'

Harry beamed with delight.

'To Port St Mary, gel? That's wonderful.'

'Even so . . . it's best we don't see each other any more. I don't want to get you into trouble.'

Harry took hold of her fluttering hands and held them still.

'Calm down an' look at me, gel.'

'I'm looking.'

Her blue eyes seemed to be pleading with him, don't do this to me. I can't help myself, I'm hopelessly in love with you and I need you to be strong.

'Now listen, Grethe gel. There's been words spoken between us, I won't repeat them in front of the boy, it's not proper – but you know the promise I've made to you.'

'You don't have to promise me anything, Harry.'

'I don't *have* to do anything. I *want* to. Now, it seems to me there's little enough love in this world. I won't hold you to any promise, but mine holds good for as long as you want me.'

Grethe returned his gaze, steady and calm; and loved him more than she could have believed possible.

'You know I do, Harry, but . . .' She glanced down at Emil. 'It's not that easy.'

'Hush.' Right and proper it might not be, not in front of the boy, but at this moment Harry didn't care. He kissed her.

'Harry!'

'Grethe, when all this is over . . . would you think about marryin' an old fisherman?'

She stared at him, drawing away, totally shocked by his words – the words she had not even dared to dream.

'Oh, Harry, you know it would be impossible. They'd never let us.'

'Nothin's impossible, gel,'

'They'd punish us – they'd send me back to Germany and put you in prison.'

Harry shook his head. He'd long since made up his mind what mattered to him, and what mattered more than anything else was the love he felt for this woman. The love which, he prayed, she felt for him.

'The boy needs a father and I . . . I need you, Grethe. If you tell me to walk away and leave you be, I swear I will. But if you want me I'll make it happen.

'I love you too much to let anythin' come between us.'

Chapter 36

The married camp at the Ballaqueeney Hotel was paradise for Reuben and Rachel Kotkin. Or it would have been, if it hadn't been behind barbed wire.

Rachel sat by the window in the great dining hall and looked out at the sea.

'This is the most beautiful place I've ever seen,' she sighed. 'But I'd be happy if I never saw it again.'

Reuben stopped spooning puréed carrot into Esther's mouth and wiped a smear of food off his shirt. Parenthood was a messier business than he'd bargained for. He loved it.

'We'll be out soon,' he said.

'It's all right, you don't have to try and make me feel better. I have you, that's what matters.'

'You are right,' said Reuben, gazing round the dining hall. It was vast, one side kosher and the other liberal, to accommodate the dietary requirements of the internees and their children.

There had been a few disputes at the camp – it was inevitable in a place with hundreds of internees unwillingly crammed together. But somehow the children had brought people together, made them think less about the present and more about the future.

What's more, they were the lucky ones. Not every couple had been allowed to come to the married camp. There were plenty of husbands, wives, lovers and children still kept apart in different camps. Yes, thought Reuben. All in all they had been incredibly lucky. Lucky to get out of Germany, lucky to get out of Holland, luckier still to have each other.

'That Herzheim woman's looking very pleased with herself,' sniffed a middle-aged theatre director's wife at the other end of the table. 'I don't see what she's got to be pleased with, a woman with her reputation.'

Rachel glanced across the dining room. Grethe was laughing and joking as she took her turn at waiting on table, and it warmed Rachel's heart to see her looking so happy.

'Grethe is a good woman,' she declared, much to the surprise of the director's wife. 'Honest and kind.'

'I don't see how you can say a thing like that. Everyone knows how she earns her living – and I certainly wouldn't eat anything she had touched!'

'She has been a very good friend to me,' replied Rachel firmly. 'I'm glad to see her happy.'

She hugged the secret of Grethe's happiness to herself, knowing that she was only one to whom Grethe had entrusted her secret. Rachel hadn't even dared tell Reuben, not because he would disapprove, but because the fewer people knew about Grethe and Harry, the less the chance that they would be found out and punished. It seemed very hard to Rachel, that two people could be punished for loving each other.

'Rachel, *mamenyu*,' began Reuben, passing his empty plate down to the end of the table and lifting Esther onto his lap.

'Mmm?'

'When I told you we might be released soon, there was something I did not tell you.'

Rachel stopped to look at him, a glass of water halfway to her lips.

'Reuben, something bad has happened?'

He shook his head, smiled.

'No, nothing like that, nothing bad. Something good. The Commandant has had a letter from your cousin Isaac.'

'From Isaac! He is well?'

'Very well. He flourishes.'

'Why did you keep this letter from me? Why did he write to

494

the Commandant and not to me?'

'Because he wanted to ask something – on our behalf. The farmer he works for has a friend, a very rich friend.'

'*Nu?*'

'A friend who owns a clothing factory in Bradford. Before the war they made suits and dresses; now they make surgical gowns for hospitals.'

Rachel set her glass down, slowly and deliberately.

'This man – he would offer you work?'

Reuben nodded.

'He is a Jew too, a Pole. He escaped in nineteen-thirty-seven, came to England and began his business all over again, from nothing. It is not really a tailor's job, but I have the skills. If I am willing, he will write to the Tribunal on my behalf . . .'

Rachel's voice quavered slightly as she voiced the question she feared to ask:

'And Esther and me?'

'You would come with me. Oh, Rachel, you do not think I would leave you, not after all that has happened?'

He drew her close to him, slipping his arm about her waist.

'Nothing is certain. This may not happen. But wherever we go, *bubeleh*, we will go there together.'

The monthly meetings between husbands and wives, sweethearts and cousins, were noticeably depleted since the opening of the family camp in Port St Mary.

But the reunions were still tearful and touching, the dance-hall at Derby Castle echoing to the sounds of laughter as couples fell into each other's arms, remembering again how good it was just to be together, to be alive.

Sachs clutched the photograph as he was ushered into the hall by a soldier with a fixed bayonet. It was an incongruous touch of menace in an atmosphere of joyful informality.

'She here then, is she?' demanded the corporal, sneaking a Spam sandwich from the plate by the door.

Sachs glanced down at the photograph of his 'cousin' Sarah, then scanned the room.

'I . . . er, can't see her yet,' he replied lamely.

'What's up mate, don't yer recognise yer own cousin?' sniggered the corporal, evidently wise to the deception.

'I haven't seen her since I was six years old,' replied Sachs. That at least shut the corporal up.

'If she don't show, we'll 'ave to take yer straight back,' said the corporal. That was the last thing he wanted; guarding the monthly meetings was a real doss, and there was grub to scoff if you were discreet about it.

'She will, I'm sure she will.' I hope, thought Sachs. He was still surprised that Sarah Rosenberg had agreed to meet him, more surprised still that their respective commandants had gone along with the little white lie. 'There she is!'

There was no mistaking the long, thin face or the sweep of black hair, secured in a loose knot. She was better-looking than in her photograph, thought Sachs – not beautiful or pretty, but striking. Even in that drab brown skirt and ancient jumper she drew the eye. Before they'd exchanged a word he'd decided she was the best-looking woman in the room.

'*Cousin*!' She greeted him with an ironic smile. He wondered, momentarily terrified, if they ought to embrace for form's sake, but she took the decision for him, planting a chaste peck on his cheek. 'How many years has it been since I saw you?'

'Years and years. At Uncle Chaim's birthday party.' He winked. 'You probably don't remember.'

They walked to a far corner of the hall and sat down on either side of a wobbly card table. A Red Cross lady was going round with a massive teapot and they accepted two cups of stewed tea.

'I can't think why I'm doing this,' said Sarah, fiddling with her cup.

'Because I'm the most handsome man you've ever had the good fortune to meet?'

'And the most modest?'

'Certainly.'

'Don't flatter yourself, Mr Sachs.'

'Sachs, please. We're cousins after all.'

Sarah looked across at Sachs. He was impossible, an empty-headed joker. *This* was impossible, a huge mistake.

'I wouldn't have come at all if it hadn't been for Rachel Kotkin,' she told him.

'Ah, Rachel. A lady of impeccable taste.'

'That's what I thought,' replied Sarah darkly. 'Now I'm not so sure.'

Sachs wondered why he was behaving like a court jester. He'd rehearsed what he was going to say enough times to be word-perfect. He was going to be serious, intellectual, sensible like in his letters. Only now that he was sitting opposite Sarah, he couldn't think of a single sensible thing to say. She must think he was completely brainless. Women usually did.

'I brought you something,' said Sachs, reaching under his chair for the brown-paper packet he'd brought with him.

'What is it? Is it a book?'

'Open it and see.'

'I only read serious political works and a little philosophy.'

'You can always give it me back if you don't like it.'

She unwrapped the paper and found Sachs's leather-bound copy of Aesop's Fables, his prized possession.

'I haven't read this since I was eight,' declared Sarah.

Sachs's face fell.

'You hate it, don't you?'

'I didn't say that.'

He reached out.

'It's all right, I'll take it back.'

'No.' Her fingers curled round it. It felt nice in her hand. The picture on the cover was pretty. 'It's a lovely book.'

'You really think so?'

'I don't say what I don't think.'

'It's my favourite.'

'I can imagine.' She treated him to an ironic smile. Sachs

497

was the little boy who'd never quite grown up. Whatever had Rachel been thinking of? He was entirely unsuitable for her.

She liked him already.

It was all-change at the *Bradda Vista*, with comings and goings and no two days the same. Grace Quine came into the kitchen and dropped a basket of ironing onto the table.

'I won't have it you know!'

'Won't have what?' enquired Thomas, chewing on the stem of his pipe.

'Now they say they're going to take away all my internees, and replace them with bombed-out families from Liverpool.'

'I thought that was what you wanted, gel,' mused Thomas. 'Evacuees an' that.' Women remained a mystery to him.

'Yes, well, so it was – but that was before. I'm just getting used to this lot. What am I going to do if they release Mrs Bertorelli and there's nobody to do the cooking and cleaning?'

'You'll manage, gel, you'll manage,' replied Thomas serenely. He'd seen a new side of Grace, these last couple of weeks.

'Yes,' she sighed, flopping down onto a kitchen chair. 'Yes, I daresay you're right. But they're from the slums! They'll be dirty, and they'll wet the bed, and we'll all catch ringworm from them . . .'

'I s'pose you could always write to William,' pointed out Thomas. 'Tell him you can't cope . . .'

He knew that would do the trick.

'Of course I can cope! Don't you go telling William I can't.'

''Course not, gel. If you're sure . . .'

'Sure? Of course I'm sure.'

'Then there's Cora. She's not goin' till tomorrow. You could ask her for a bit of advice . . .'

Grace's hackles fairly bristled.

'I don't need anyone's advice. I'll manage on my own. But who do they think they are, expecting me to take all these people at a moment's notice . . . ?'

Thomas chuckled as he watched her bustling around. He'd seen all this before.

He could tell things were going to be just fine.

Elsa Nadel arrived at Hutchinson Camp with one suitcase and a bundle of books, all that she had arrived with, save for the small gifts she had received from Grethe, Rachel and Cora Quine.

Max was waiting for her at the Commandant's office. Someone had given him a better-fitting suit and a shirt; someone else had donated shoes and a hat. A small cardboard suitcase lay across his lap, a few pictures tied into a bundle by his side.

Before she entered the room, Captain Hollingsworth drew her on one side.

'You're happy about this, Fräulein Nadel?'

'Happier than you would understand.' She extended her hand. 'Thank you. Thank you for what you've done.'

He shrugged.

'Max is ill. He should never have been brought here. And he has a great talent, it's wasted here. You too, you should use your professional skills.'

Elsa walked through into the room and Max looked up at her. This time his eyes registered pleasure, recognition.

'Elsa, you've come.'

'Didn't I promise I would?'

'Are we going somewhere? Where are we going?'

She knelt down beside him, taking his hands in hers.

'We're going to a beautiful house in the country. On the mainland.' She didn't say the word 'sanatorium', because she didn't want to spoil the pleasure of the moment. Working as a pharmacist at the small country hospital would suit her very well, and provide the money to pay for Max's convalescence.

'We'll be together?'

'Of course we will. Just like we used to be.'

'I can't quite remember all of it. I wish I could.'

'I told you, I'll help you remember.'

'Will they let me paint?'

'All day long, if you want to. It will be wonderful.' For both of us, she thought to herself. The day the release papers had come through, she had sat down and cried for a whole hour, for the sheer relief of it all.

She got to her feet.

'Time to go now, Max. The chaplain's waiting to drive us to the boat.'

Max stood up. He was stronger since Elsa had come back; even the frayed threads of his memory were beginning to disentangle themselves, little by little. Happier too. A big yellow sun had switched itself on inside his head, and he found himself wanting to sing. He picked up his suitcase and Captain Hollingsworth took charge of the bundle of paintings.

'Where is Reuben?' asked Max suddenly.

'Reuben is in the married camp now. With his wife and baby.'

'Oh yes. I forgot.' Max passed his hand over his brow, readjusting the flickering memory so that it came back into focus. 'I wanted to thank him.'

'He knows.'

'Come on, Max,' said Elsa, taking his hand and guiding him towards the door. 'They're waiting for us outside. It's time to say goodbye.'

Cora had come a long way in one short year. So had the *Bradda Vista*.

As she watched George carrying her trunk out to the van, she remembered how angry she had been when Grace and William had gone off to Banbury, leaving her to manage this place all on her own. Angry and afraid, so sure that she would never cope.

Such good friends she'd made in that year: Elsa, and Rachel, and Grethe. And now they were all gone and she was going too. Going into the unknown, to welcome whatever tomorrow might have in store for her.

'You're almost ready, then?' Grace walked across the room and joined Cora at the window.

'As ready as I'll ever be.'

'Thomas isn't going to the boat with you?'

'We've said our goodbyes. I think it's best if I just go. He seemed upset.'

'He's worried for you.' Grace paused, then added: 'We all are.'

'I'll be fine. And so will you.'

'You really think so?'

Cora glanced around the common room. It was clean, tidy, immaculately dusted.

'All you ever needed to do was believe you could do it.'

She put on her white gloves and picked up her small suitcase.

'I'd better go – George gets so impatient, and I don't want to miss the early sailing. I have to be in Portsmouth by tomorrow teatime. The Navy won't wait!'

'Take care.' On impulse, Grace gave her a hug and kissed her on the cheek. It was an awkward, fumbling sort of hug; but it was a start. Coming from Grace Quine it was a revelation.

'And you. And make sure Evie takes good care of Bonzo. Do you think Harry is coping with Fergus?'

Grace laughed.

'Your Uncle Harry dotes on that dog. It thinks it's died and gone to doggy heaven.'

'Well . . . best go. I'll be seeing you.'

Cora turned and walked quickly down the front steps of the *Bradda Vista*, afraid to turn back in case she changed her mind. She wondered if it had felt this difficult for James when he left the Island behind.

Bradda Head rose up against a pale blue sky, the bay curving round in a generous sweep and the sea breaking gently against the rocks. It was a perfect day.

501

On the beach, children were playing – a group of evacuees who'd just come over from the mainland. There would be more soon – some of them at the *Bradda Vista*. So Port Erin was getting its evacuees after all.

Everything changes, thought Cora. And I've changed too. Who knows how much more it will have changed when all this is over and I come home again?

More Enchanting Fiction from Headline

Janet MacLeod Trotter

Shortlisted for *The Sunday Times* Young Writer of the
Year Award

THE
DARKENING SKIES

A MOVING SAGA OF THE NORTH EAST IN WARTIME

Though by nature an optimist, when Sara Pallister arrives in the
mining town of Whitton Grange she cannot help but be
appalled by the welcome she receives. Her father having died
leaving their farm bankrupt, Weardale-born Sara is now the
poor cousin, reluctantly taken into the household of her
officious, narrow-minded Uncle Alfred whose wife Ida does
little but spoil their unbearable seven-year-old, agree with her
opinionated husband and attend endless W.I. socials.

Determined to make Sara pay her way, Uncle Alfred hires her
out to work in Dolly Sergeant's grocer's shop where she meets
funny, bashful Raymond Kirkup and his warm-hearted aunt,
Louie. And it is through Raymond that Sara encounters the
family that is to change her life: the Dimarcos, exotic, extrovert
and Italian, the owners of Whitton Grange's popular ice-cream
parlour. Even as the shadows of the Second World War grow
more menacing and hostility increases towards the foreign
Dimarcos, Sara finds herself irresistibly drawn to leather-
jacketed, motorbike-riding Joe Dimarco . . .

Praise for Janet MacLeod Trotter's writing: 'Full of warmth and
courage' *Sunderland Echo*; 'Wonderful . . . if you don't mind
losing sleep as you read by torchlight into the night, do get this
book' *The Miscarriage Association Newsletter*; 'Truly a novel for
saga lovers, weaving together the lives of many characters with
compassion and affection' *Northern Echo*; 'You'll believe you are
there!' Denise Robertson

FICTION / SAGA 0 7472 4359 X

Wendy Robertson

Under a Brighter Sky

An impassioned story of love, repression and freedom

When Greg McNaughton first meets the lively Shona Farrell, lovely in spite of her dusty pit clothes, he knows he should forget her. For she belongs to the staunchly Irish Catholic community regarded with fear and suspicion by his own outwardly severe Protestant family. And her fiery-tempered brother Tommo makes it plain that Greg is not welcome in their home, throwing him out into the cold, County Durham night in a fit of temper.

But Greg can't get Shona out of his mind. And Shona is fascinated by the stranger and his perplexing family; in particular she wants to find out what happened to his wife, the shadowy mother of his little daughter Lauretta. When Greg suddenly leaves for Manchester after the brutal murder of the good-hearted local prostitute, Shona won't believe he's the killer. And so she follows him to the teeming city, determined to unravel the mysteries of the past and live under brighter skies . . .

'Good story, good background, good characters, another winner from Wendy' *Northern Echo*

'Carefully crafted novel . . . spirited, widely different and colourful characters' *Sunderland Echo*

FICTION / SAGA 0 7472 4410 3

A selection of bestsellers from Headline

LAND OF YOUR POSSESSION	Wendy Robertson	£5.99	☐
TRADERS	Andrew MacAllen	£5.99	☐
SEASONS OF HER LIFE	Fern Michaels	£5.99	☐
CHILD OF SHADOWS	Elizabeth Walker	£5.99	☐
A RAGE TO LIVE	Roberta Latow	£5.99	☐
GOING TOO FAR	Catherine Alliott	£5.99	☐
HANNAH OF HOPE STREET	Dee Williams	£4.99	☐
THE WILLOW GIRLS	Pamela Evans	£5.99	☐
MORE THAN RICHES	Josephine Cox	£5.99	☐
FOR MY DAUGHTERS	Barbara Delinsky	£4.99	☐
BLISS	Claudia Crawford	£5.99	☐
PLEASANT VICES	Laura Daniels	£5.99	☐
QUEENIE	Harry Cole	£5.99	☐

All Headline books are available at your local bookshop or newsagent, or can be ordered direct from the publisher. Just tick the titles you want and fill in the form below. Prices and availability subject to change without notice.

Headline Book Publishing, Cash Sales Department, Bookpoint, 39 Milton Park, Abingdon, OXON, OX14 4TD, UK. If you have a credit card you may order by telephone – 01235 400400.

Please enclose a cheque or postal order made payable to Bookpoint Ltd to the value of the cover price and allow the following for postage and packing:

UK & BFPO: £1.00 for the first book, 50p for the second book and 30p for each additional book ordered up to a maximum charge of £3.00.
OVERSEAS & EIRE: £2.00 for the first book, £1.00 for the second book and 50p for each additional book.

Name ....

Address ....

....

....

If you would prefer to pay by credit card, please complete:
Please debit my Visa/Access/Diner's Card/American Express (delete as applicable) card no:

Signature .... Expiry Date ....